First Printing, May 2013

ISBN 978-1-291-3590-91

Visit the website for location guides, merchandise and news…
www.darkship.co.uk

Like it, love it or just have comments…
https://www.facebook.com/darkship.book

Dark Ship

Dedicated to my beautiful Jen.

Chapter 1

The Wave

The Atlantic Ocean in March is often an inviting playground for sailors looking for peace and solitude; out of season, empty and with terrific sunsets, it tempts yacht owners with a pre-season treat. However the further out to sea, the swell renders this a less than desirable option, to the demise of many a small vessel. Freak waves often break out at sea, accumulating thousands of tonnes of water and sometimes creating walls a hundred metres tall.

To Elizabeth Thompson it was ideal. Her father, a multi-millionaire oil tycoon, lent their family yacht, *The Royal Wave* to her childhood friend James Arrowsmith, who had recently completed his Sea Captaincy award, to the delight of Elizabeth and their four friends.

This was their first night away in the yacht; something that James had aspired to do since the family first purchased it, while he and Elizabeth were in their early teens.

The conditions were perfect; daylight had faded, the sea was calm and the vessel bobbed up and down on the mild swell that lapped gently at the brilliant white hull. The cabin lights projected a subtle, shimmering glow onto the black water outside.

Inside James held out a bottle of champagne to his friends, topping each of the awaiting glasses to the brim. They raised their glasses to one another and chinked a toast.

James stood firm, Elizabeth on his left arm, grinning up towards him with pride. He was a tall, well groomed young gentleman with dry, gelled hair and dark stubble. He cleared his throat and incorporated it into an over exaggerated cough.

'I would also like to make a toast to…', he looked around at each of them; his gaze stopping at the girl stood next to him, '…Elizabeth's father who rather stupidly leant me his pride and joy!'

The group cheered and promptly emptied their glasses.

He turned to Elizabeth as the rest of the group began to dance on the plush, cream carpet.

'Can you believe that your father let me take you out on this thing?'

'You had just better return it in one piece or else, Captain Arrowsmith', she said with a grin and a slur.

James half smiled, 'I'd say you had better take the same care with that necklace. And in any case, it isn't me you ought to be worried about', he said through pinched lips and nodded towards the rest of the group.

He pulled her close and wrapped his arms tightly around her.

'That thing looks beautiful on you, you know', he gestured down towards her Cartier necklace with a smile.

Elizabeth looked down and ran her fingers over the diamonds.

'It should be', she whispered, 'it is nearly...'

'One hundred and fifty thousand pounds worth...' he interjected, 'how many times have you told me that?'

'I know, I'm sorry, I just can't believe that father actually bought it. It all seems too perfect, this necklace, us being here on *The Wave*... me, with you'.

James tightened his grip around her and pulled her close towards his chest.

'Aw, get a room!' a slurred voice shouted from the living room.

James rolled his eyes and smiled then returned his gaze to Elizabeth.

'Do you think we should kick them overboard? Make them walk the plank?' he spoke with a stereotypical Cornish-pirate accent.

'And how would we explain that one to father? Your son decided to swim home because he was jealous that it wasn't him who father let captain *The Wave*?'

James looked toward her brother, slightly overweight and in his late teens, drinking from a bottle of Cognac.

'Do you think he is still annoyed?' James asked with concern.

'Oh yes', she replied confidently, 'I think he will always be bothered by it. He is young and reckless. Father wouldn't let him drive the Jag let alone pilot the Wave', she sniggered.

'Come on, let's get back to the party before they wreck the place', James suggested as he pulled her hand.

As they entered the lounge she felt her brother's eyes following them. She glanced to him and gave him a token smile. He nodded in recognition and bent down to an inset wine cooler set against the oak panelling. He opened the door and produced a bottle of champagne and stood up holding his prize aloft.

'Who's for a glass of fizz?' he offered unwrapping the gold foil from the neck.

'I don't think father agreed to us drinking his Dom Perignon when he loaned us the boat, Robert'.

'For your information, my dear sister, I bought the champagne myself', he smirked.

The two girls seated on the white leather sofa stood up and held out their glasses as Robert began to untwist the wire.

'With father's money no doubt', Elizabeth dug.

'Alright siblings', James interjected, 'let's calm down and stop the bickering before it all gets out of hand'.

Robert winked at his sister as he massaged the cork from the bottle. She retaliated by sticking out her tongue.

'Vince, put something else on will you?' James shouted to a short, Oxbridge teen who was furiously fiddling with an MP3 player.

'Yeah, got something now', he replied as he thumbed the controls.

After a short silence Queen's "Another One Bites the Dust" blasted through the surround-sound system in the cabin, causing Robert to instinctively robot dance, holding aloft the half opened bottle.

'Very nice Bob', James applauded as he glided across the carpet.

Suddenly the cork popped from the bottle, ricocheting from the low wood panelled ceiling just above James' head. Foam erupted from the bottle and cascaded onto the carpet.

'Shit!' Robert screamed as he rushed past Elizabeth into the galley.

James clapped his hands with laughter at the rebellious man; suddenly domesticated and eagerly returning with a handful of tea towels and dropping to his knees, desperately dabbing at the sticky puddle that had formed in the centre of the room.

The group regained control from the episode and began to systematically dance to Vince's unusual choice in music as he struggled to roll a cigarette.

'Can you believe that these are *our* friends?' Elizabeth whispered into James' ear as she stood on her tip toes.

As James joined the delegated dance floor, he noticed Elizabeth walking towards the stairway leading to the master bedroom. He looked at Robert, who had become the centre of attention with his attempts at breakdancing, then looked back with intrigue at Elizabeth, who had disappeared into the darkness of the stairwell. He crept backwards slowly so as not to arouse suspicion from the group. When far enough away he turned around and strode up the steps two at a time. As he reached the wooden door of the bedroom he peered through the gap into the darkness, the cabin windows being the only source of light.

The sound of the rest of the group began to fade as he ventured into the dark room, feeling for the light switch on the wall to his right.

'Hello?' he whispered.

He felt in his pocket for his key ring torch. The small LED lit an area around him. He walked forward carefully with his left hand outstretched, feeling his way in the pitch black room. This was Elizabeth's room into which he had never ventured prior to this moment, albeit once during the tour around the boat by her father a few hours prior to their departure. It was up to him, being Captain, to take charge of the gas and electricity duties. The isolator, on this model of boat, was in the master bedroom behind a small panel inset into the wall. He couldn't remember the layout of the room, far less the layout of the boat itself.

God help me if the electricity or gas does fail, he thought. No one in the group took any notice of how the yacht worked during the two hour health and safety briefing that Elizabeth's father inflicted upon them.

'Hello, is there anybody there?' he whispered in a ghostly voice.

No reply.

He crept further into the darkness. As he moved the torch light flickered as his thumb struggled to hold down the tiny sprung button.

The thuds of the bass, mixed with the sounds of their friends' feet on the hollow floor beneath him, engulfed the dark cabin. James switched on the small, insignificant torch a second time. He reached a wall with his left hand and turned around to see Elizabeth's naked shoulder and outline of her bra strap in the dimness of the glow.

'Shhhh', she slurred, inadvertently spitting in his eye. Giggling to herself she reached towards him to wipe his face with her wrist.

'I am sorry about that James'.

'Are you…'

'Naked?' she finished his question, 'Sort of', she teased, 'but not quite'.

She held his hand and brought him closer to her. The torch went out again.

'Leave it', she whispered to him.

Although he couldn't see her, he could sense her close to him, her breath on his neck, the warmth of her body radiating in front of him.

He moved forwards slightly and found her lips with his. Since he was a young boy he had always imagined being with her and his thoughts, however overconfident, concluded that she had persuaded her father to let them sail *The Wave* specifically for this reason.

James moved closer to her and kissed her deeply, her hands wrapped around his neck stroking his hair. He pushed his hands from her shoulders down her back until he felt her bra strap under his fingers.

He fumbled with it for a few moments to no avail and to her amusement.

'So complicated!' she taunted.

'Shhh', he spat as he continued his attack on the impossible strap.

She laughed again as he lunged with desperation until at last he managed to unclip it. Sighing with relief he slowly released it from her shoulders until it hit the soft carpet.

They kissed again as she began to pull his shirt up from his waist.

The vessel listed to the left.

James stopped and pulled away from her. The listing became a little stronger.

As Elizabeth tried to keep her balance she tripped, pulling James over onto the bed with her. As he tried to get his bearings in the darkness, they slid off the side of the bed and onto the floor. The noise of which, followed by their laughter, didn't go unnoticed by the rest of the group who acknowledged their fumbling with wails of laughter and whistles.

Suddenly the vessel listed again to starboard and Robert lost his balance, knocking a bottle of rum from the table that smashed onto the carpet.

'Shit! What the hell is going on?' James shouted as he stood up reaching for the light switch.

Elizabeth picked herself up and reached across the bed, feeling for her top that she had discarded earlier. She looked out of the porthole at the waves lapping at the hull.

'It's got rough out there suddenly', she gestured.

'I'm going to go and see what's happening', James said with a sense of comforting leadership.

He emerged from the stairwell to find Robert picking himself up from the floor amongst the shards of broken glass.

The two girls looked at each other worriedly for reassurance.

'Don't worry guys', James offered calmly, 'I'm sure it's a brief storm or something, it'll pass by…'

He looked out of the galley window. In the distance he could make out the tiny light from the Seven Stones Reef Lighthouse blinking in the distance. The waves began to die down and the boat relaxed once again. The group looked at each other nervously.

'Blimey Jim', Vince piped up, 'you managed to part the waves then?'

One by one the group began to laugh, breaking the tension. Elizabeth stood at the stairwell and began to giggle in relief.

James brushed his black hair from his head and stretched out his arms as his adrenalin levels normalised. Elizabeth walked to the champagne bottle on the polished mahogany table in the centre of the lounge area and picked it up, pouring it into one of the empty glasses and then holding it into the air for a toast.

'Here's to parting the waves!' she shouted.

The group burst into laughter and held up whatever drinks they could find for the toast. James grinned and raised his eyebrows to her as he began to collect the shards of glass from the weave of the carpet.

Vince moved to the main cabin to change the music. He turned the click wheel of the MP3 player to select another track as the rest of the group began to dance around the cabin once again.

Suddenly the lights and the music went off, plunging them into darkness.

The group went silent. After the initial shock, Rachel - the youngest of the group - screamed instinctively, creating an unsettling tension.

'What's happening James?' Elizabeth asked in a quiet, trembling voice.

James looked around the dark cabin trying to focus his eyes. He searched his pockets for his key ring torch but remembered he had dropped it when he was in the bedroom.

'Robert?' he called out.

'Yeah?' a slightly nervous voice replied.

'Did the power trip out?'

'How the hell should I know?' Robert replied, annoyed that he couldn't answer a question like that. How would he know? The lights and music had both gone off simultaneously, what are the tell-tale signs of a power cut on a boat?

'Did anything… go pop, over there?' James enquired.

'Be careful of the glass everyone', Elizabeth advised as she sensed people moving around the pitch-black cabin.

As the vessel rotated slightly on the swell of the ocean, the moonlight found its way through the skylights, casting a subtle blue glow inside.

'Nothing went pop, no.' Robert replied after a brief recollection.

James looked into the moon-lit cabin.

'What the hell caused that then?'

'Could it be the fuses?' Elizabeth offered.

James scratched his head, trying to remember what her father had told him to do after a power surge or blow out, his memory numbed by the alcohol he had consumed.

As the group began to calm down, a tremendous, terrifying thud came from above them.

'Jesus! What the hell was that?' Robert shouted in fear.

The girls began to panic, moving around the cabin defensively, looking up at the ceiling.

'James, what's happening?' Elizabeth asked, paralysed by her fear.

'I don't know', he replied desperately racking his brains for a suitable answer, be it the right one or a suitably calming one. He knew he had to dispel the brewing fear that was developing within the group.

It came to him.

'I know what it bloody well is! Robert, it's the boom, I never battened it down, and I bet it's been thrown over with the swell and its hit the power cable on the outside of the bridge!'

Perfect. Not only was it a distinct possibility but it had certainly extinguished the fear that was beginning to spread uncontrollably. The sighs that came from the darkness of the cabin confirmed to him that the situation had been tamed.

'Robert, we're going on the roof mate, come on, we've got to batten that boom down and reconnect the power'.

Robert looked at James in the dim light with a disapproving look.

James felt his way into the galley to the stern for the key hook next to the main double doors of the cabin. He knew they were there - they also unlocked the drinks cabinet.

Twirling them around his forefinger and jingling them in the air he waited for the reluctant Robert to accompany him.

'Come on Bobby, it's not rocket science! We'll be up there and back in before you know it'.

Robert frowned. Bobby? He hadn't been called that for over a decade. James knew that this would wind him up and spur him to spring into life. It worked.

'Okay, I'm coming', he replied reluctantly, taking the bait and making his way to the cabin entrance, his shoes cracking on the broken glass as he walked past his sister.

'I'd say there's a fair bit of cleaning to do in here too', Elizabeth joked, in a semi-serious manner, again to the relief of her frightened girlfriends.

James reached for the bolt at the top of the main doors and slid it open. The same loud thud came from above them again. Then a succession of similar smaller thuds followed.

'Christ, that's footsteps!' Claire shrieked.

Whimpering noises came from the darkness of the lounge as the thuds became more prominent and closer.

'God, James!' Elizabeth shouted, grabbing his shoulder and squeezing it.

'Seagulls?' he offered, looking around for agreement.

He tried hard not to sound frightened himself and his attempt at raising moral fell on deaf ears as the group stared at the ceiling. One by one they began to instinctively crouch on the floor of the cabin.

James ran through a variety of emotions and eventually stood up straight.

'What are we doing? There is bound to be a perfectly adequate explanation to this!'

'Shhh, get down James!' Elizabeth ordered under her breath as she tugged at his trouser leg.

James picked up on the trembles in her voice.

'Look, we are in the middle of the sea for God's sake!' he shouted, looking around at the pale blue highlighted faces.

'You coming or not Robert?'

Robert nodded in compliance and stood up slowly, constantly staring at the ceiling.

Softer thuds sounded above them and eventually stopped at the stern.

James took a deep breath and unlatched the remaining bolt from the cabin doors. He placed the key in the lock and turned it. The lock slid open, amplified by the tense silence.

He took another deep breath and pushed the doors open. Elizabeth ran to the other end of the cabin, past Robert and into the huddle of girls who held each other closely. Vince stood nearby, still holding his MP3 player.

'Vince, get down!' Rachel demanded.

The panic stricken teenager remained frozen with fear, unable to speak.

The sounds of the waves breaking in the distance, combined with the lapping of the water around the stern, filled the cabin and created an ambience that seemed to calm them a little, providing temporary respite from the stress of the unknown.

James made his way outside followed by a cautious Robert.

'Hey, grab the torch from the kitchen shelf will you?' he asked him.

Robert's eyes had adjusted to the darkness and he reached for the torch with ease and passed it to him. James clicked it on. Nothing.

'What the…?' he asked in confusion, bashing the rubber torch against the door frame, attempting to shock it into life.

He dropped it on the floor and impatiently strode outside.

As he stood on the stern deck in the clear night air, he breathed the intoxicating sharp cold air and exhaled plumes of light blue steam.

'It's a beautiful night Bob!' he said as he looked around the cloudless sky. He looked back at his companion.

'See', he started, with relief that he tried to disguise as conviction, 'nothing out here!'

He stepped onto the seating on the bridge to look on top of the cabin roof.

Robert watched nervously, not convinced by the statement, as his friend stood on tip toes to reach up to the roof.

The yacht rotated naturally again in the swell of the ocean, blotting what light there was from the cabin, again plunging the group into darkness.

James climbed up the chrome ladder to the roof of the bridge.

'Yeah I actually do think it was the boom!'

Robert rubbed his arms to warm himself.

Another loud thud emanated from the cabin roof.

'Jim?' Robert whispered to the roof.

The girls watched Robert's moonlit silhouette.

'Jim!' he persisted.

No answer.

'Jim, this isn't funny!'

Silence.

'Don't make me come up and get you, you arsehole!'

Robert looked up at the roof. There were no sounds and no movement except for the swell of the ocean, lapping at the stern.

'Jim!' he tried again, this time louder and with an unintended sense of panic, his voice breaking slightly.

'You bastard…'

The girls watched Robert climb the ladder to the top of the roof. In the distance they picked out Robert's voice calling out once again, quickly followed by another loud thud.

Rachel screamed.

The yacht was plunged once again into a deep silence and numbing darkness.

Tense moments past as the girls remained crouched on the floor of the cabin, frozen with fear, unable to speak.

Another thud broke the silence, this time from inside the galley – only a few metres in front of them.

'Oh my God, oh my God, oh my God, oh my God!' Rachel began to chant hysterically.

Elizabeth watched the galley, her teary eyes wide open, her breath rapid, her heart pounding in her chest.

She sensed a motion in front of them.

'Who's there? James? Is that you? What do you want?' She screamed.

'James?' she desperately called out, 'Is that you?'

Clear footsteps started to make their way towards them slowly.

Elizabeth stood up unexpectedly, shocking both her friends and herself. Panic had given her a sense of self-preservation which frightened the others even more.

'Come on then you bastard! What do you want? Huh? Do you w-w-want me? DO YOU?'

The footsteps stopped.

'Coward!' she screamed at the top of her broken voice, her reddened eyes streaming.

The yacht bobbed up and down softy on the mild swell of the ocean.

The noise of the lapping waves only broken by a short and terrifying scream.

Then silence enveloped the night and the yacht lay steady as a rock.

The waves died down and the cold night became still once again.

Chapter 2

<u>The Meeting</u>

The Sikorsky S61 helicopter rumbled through the air, two thousand feet above the crashing waves of the early winter morning ocean of Cornwall's South coast. It was a cloudless morning and Simon Jenkins could clearly see the light beams from the Portland Bill lighthouse below him.

He looked at his watch; 5:30am, they should be in Plymouth for 6:00am which would leave him… he searched the inside pocket of his overcoat and pulled out a folded printout of an email… half an hour before his meeting. He folded up the sheet and put it back in his pocket.

He looked out of the window again and reflected on his unusual invitation with a self-satisfied smile. He reached forward for his disposable coffee, took a sip and returned it to the vibrating plastic tray - more to replace the cup in its original place on the table than to take a drink as the vibrations in the helicopter had moved it a clear six inches from the cup holder, rendering it dangerously close to the bevelled edge of the surface.

The speaker in the cabin crackled to life: 'We're starting our descent now, and should touch down in approximately ten minutes'.

Simon checked his watch again; the helicopter was travelling far faster than he had imagined. He didn't know that much about helicopters; he was a Revenue and Customs Agent. He had travelled in helicopters hundreds of times before, but had no idea how they worked. It wasn't in his remit to know such things.

The Sikorsky thundered overhead of the fishing boats arriving at Cowes and started to descend into Portsea. He finished his coffee and started patting down his pockets and searching the seats nearby for his belongings. A sudden shock of nerves overwhelmed him. He wasn't one for worrying; in fact he had always remained calm on operations and during interrogations - but this was different. Usually he had an idea or prior knowledge of a situation but not this time. Part of him wondered if he were in some kind of trouble.

The helicopter's wheels eventually touched down on the tarmac inside the Naval Base. After two or three bounces in the light wind, the turbines started to drone down and the propellers began to slow. Simon unbuckled his harness and stood up, straightening his coat as he did so. Had he remembered he would have taken it off prior to take-off; not only had he irreparably creased the back, but he sensed the dampness of sweat patches under his arms. After a quick private curse he picked up his briefcase and made his way to the exit, stooping awkwardly for the low ceiling.

As he began to descend the metal steps of the helicopter's exit, his eyes squinted at the bright headlights of a black Land Rover parked close by. Holding his arm above his forehead - to shield his eyes from the beams - he made out a naval officer in a rain coat standing next to it. The officer started walking towards him.

Simon walked down the steps, still shielding his eyes from the unreasonably bright lights.

'Mr Jenkins?' the officer asked with formality.

Simon recoiled.

'Y-yes?' he stammered, questioning the question.

'Ah splendid, here, let me take that for you sir', the officer said as he took his briefcase from him. Simon was stunned, and probably came across so. Was this man expecting another Mr Jenkins? Should he make sure that he was the right Mr Jenkins and there wasn't a Captain Jenkins still on board the helicopter?

'Please get in, the heater is still on so it should be nice and toasty', the officer chirped, pointing towards the passenger door for Simon to get in as he loaded the briefcase into the back seat.

He opened the door with an expression of disbelief. The officer shut the back door, skipped to the driver's side and climbed in.

The vehicle was immaculate unlike the vehicles of the Revenue and Customs or Coastguards of Cornwall. This vehicle was definitely confined to tarmac and probably had never seen life outside of the base. It certainly hadn't seen any dirt. There was an overwhelming smell of "new car" and the leather seats crackled as Simon moved about on them.

'Did you have a good journey Mr Jenkins?' the officer asked politely as he started the muted engine to pull away from the helipad.

This was a tactic employed by taxi drivers to make polite conversation in order to get a tip. Should he tip? He had just landed in another world; he was not expecting to be treated with such importance.

'Yes, yes it was fine thanks', he responded. It wasn't fine. It was rough, loud and it was still too early to be awake. The coffee was tasteless and he was sweating from the heat of the airless cabin.

As the officer drove the Land Rover around the warren of small tarmac roads of the base, he picked out points of interest lit by the powerful headlights. It felt more like a guided tour.

'How far is it?' Simon asked, not sure where he was going.

'Oh, not too far, just behind the building in front of us now in fact', the officer replied with a "customer care" voice.

The Land Rover pulled up outside a huge sandstone building that had the appearance of Trafalgar era architecture. He considered asking about it but the officer was already busying himself getting Simon's briefcase from the back seat and returning it to him. Simon pretended to be looking in his inside pocket for something, just to see if the officer would open the door for him. He did.

'Here you go, sir. I will be here to pick you up and take you back to the helicopter after your meeting'.

He gave a "have a nice day" smile and returned to the vehicle, pulling it away and leaving him standing in front of an ornate sandstone staircase leading to a double breasted glass entrance. He began to ascend the steps, adjusting his coat once again on the way up. As he approached the glass doors, he caught sight of his reflection and began to furiously smooth his hair.

Upon entering the building he was presented with a vast, cavernous reception area with high-gloss marble flooring.

The noise of heels began to echo around the painting adorned walls. He adjusted his coat once more and made another attempt to straighten his hair; futile - he was as he felt; a sweaty mess. He couldn't blame the cabin heat or the warmth from the inside of the Land Rover - this was nerves. He could feel beads of perspiration forming on his forehead.

The heels were getting closer. He turned in their direction and saw a very smart, petite lady of about fifty years approaching.

'Mr Jenkins?' she asked with an educated voice.

'Simon, please', he replied. Why did he say that? What happens to a man when a well presented lady speaks to him? She had only asked him his name.

'The Vice Admiral will see you in a few moments, if you would like to follow me…'

She started to ascend a red carpeted staircase to the side of the reception area. He followed obediently. The stairs spiralled anticlockwise to an ornate landing; the walls were covered in maritime and naval oil paintings, framed by large and heavy decorated gold frames. The lady opened the glass doors off to the right and held one open for him.

Simon strolled through.

'Can I take your coat?' the lady asked.

He smiled and began to unbutton his coat but remembered the possibility of the sweat patches. She stood waiting, her arm out to receive it. Reluctantly he took it off and handed it to her.

'Would you like coffee? Or tea?'

'Coffee, white with one sugar, thank you' he replied.

He picked up his briefcase and made his way to an array of antique wooden chairs adjacent to two huge oak doors complimented by black iron studs.

After a short while, the lady returned with a cup of coffee on a saucer with a small biscuit balancing on the side.

'Please make yourself comfortable, Mr Wilkinson will be available to see you shortly'.

She handed him the cup and saucer and returned to her modest oak desk where she sat bolt upright, and began to touch type, gazing into her monitor.

Simon realised he was staring. He turned to face the bay window and reclined in in his chair.

After what seemed an eternity of staring out of the window onto the rooftops of the barracks, Simon heard the heels approach him once again.

He turned in his seat to face the lady.

'Mr Wilkinson will see you now, Mr Jenkins', she said in the most polite tone of voice.

Simon swallowed; his nerves began to burn his stomach. He also realised that there was no time left to psyche himself for the meeting. Why did he just stare out of the window for all that time and not rehearse his conversation. How could he? He had no idea why he had been called.

'Th-thanks', he stuttered unavoidably.

He stood up, picked up his briefcase, and walked towards the oak doors as confidently as he could. The lady waited at them and pushed one open, trailing a hand inside, inviting him to enter.

Simon nodded a thank-you and smiled. As he entered the lady closed the door behind him; the heels faded into the distance outside.

The office was vast. Wood panels made up the first eight feet of wall, which led to scarlet painted plaster walls and a highly decorated bevelled cornice. Huge portraits hung out from the walls; Drake, Raleigh, Nelson and behind a huge polished walnut desk - a painting of Sir Cloudesly Shovell; Rear Admiral and Captain of the ill-fated Association that struck Scillies Western rocks in 1707. Simon's maritime history was his forte. To the left of the room was a large bay window that overlooked the edge of the base and then the sea. Standing proudly in front of it was a brass telescope, obviously of some naval significance.

'Mr Jenkins, I assume', a deep, south-western voice bellowed from behind him. Simon turned on the spot. With his marvel at the décor, he hadn't noticed the Vice Admiral sitting at the desk. He snapped his mouth shut and walked at quick pace towards him with his right hand extended.

'Yes, sir, it is an honour to meet you'.

Wilkinson stood up and moved around to the front of the desk to greet Simon.

The two men shook hands. Wilkinson was a large man with a rugby player stature. His face was clean shaven, bearing a scar that ran the length of his chiseled cheek bone – a memento of his infamous tour of duty aboard the British fleet in both the Falklands and the Gulf. He was wearing a dark blue suit with gold Navy buttons running down the front. Simon stared at the large array of multicoloured ribbons and gold ropes that adorned his vast chest.

'Please take a seat', he boomed.

Simon sat like an obedient puppy, placing his briefcase beside him on the floor.

'I trust your helicopter journey was hell!?'

Simon had no idea how to answer. Should he tell the truth? This was the Vice Admiral. He was transported by a Navy helicopter; he couldn't tell the truth could he?

'The coffee could've been better', he said diplomatically, cocking an awkward half-smile.

Wilkinson laughed, 'Yes the Royal Navy has a lot to learn about coffee unfortunately, I must apologise'.

Damn, that didn't require an apology; it was supposed to be a humorous statement, him not mentioning the rough helicopter ride. Hang on, he thought, get it together, and just relax.

'I'm not going to beat about the bush, Mr Jenkins…' Wilkinson began sternly, sitting himself down on his leather throne, 'have you caught the news this morning at all? Radio? Local television?'

Simon shook his head; he had woken up, showered, threw on his clothes and left for the Heliport.

'I didn't catch it this morning, no sir'.

Wilkinson leaned forward to his desk to reach his cup from the saucer.

'At approximately two o'clock this morning, *HMS Clyde*, returning from a six week training mission in the Arctic with the Endurance…' Wilkinson pointed a finger at a photograph on his desk of the HMS Endurance with her crew lining its decks, '…spotted a blip somewhere approximately three hundred and twenty five miles south west-west off of Lands End'. He sipped his coffee and returned the cup to the saucer.

Simon watched his every move intently.

'They reported the blip to us directly, following a protocol placement, of course'.

Simon nodded in agreement. He hadn't a clue what the protocol was but the Vice Admiral of the Fleet was the instigator of protocols.

'And subsequently we gave the order to investigate. At around four o'clock they made contact and reported back to us that they had found another…' he held up both his hands and made speech mark signs in the air '"drifter"'.

'Now, I know what you are about to ask Mr Jenkins; you are about to ask, why wasn't the Coastguard made aware of this, correct?' He sat back waiting for a response, although it was evidentially a rhetorical question. Simon nodded again in agreement.

'I'll warn you, Mr Jenkins…' Wilkinson started, '…what I am about to tell you, is highly secretive and has not been released outside of the Royal Navy here in Portsmouth for the past sixteen years'.

Simon looked into Wilkinson's eyes, 'Yes sir', he nodded in agreement, acknowledging the severity of the conversation.

Wilkinson lifted himself from his chair and walked towards the giant bay window. His highly polished regulation shoes tapped his every step on the parquet flooring.

'On the sixth of February, Nineteen Ninety Two, in the early hours of the morning, a fishing trawler reported to the Coastguard off South West Cornwall that they had picked up a drifting yacht, eighty seven miles from the coast of St Agnes, Isles of Scilly'.

Wilkinson held his hands behind his back and straightened his posture as he stared out across the edge of the complex. The sun was rising and cast a warm orange glow into the room.

'They boarded it', he continued, 'And do you know what they found Mr Jenkins?'

'No sir?' Simon stared at Wilkinson's back.

'Nothing!' Wilkinson bellowed.

There was a short silence as if he had wanted to emphasise the significance of the last point.

'They found nothing at all: no people, no food, no water, no maps, and no trace of anyone being on that boat whatsoever'.

He slowly walked back to his desk, his hands clasped tightly behind his back and his head tilted upwards.

'The yacht must have broken its anchor, we thought, and that is the report we filed in the interim. The trawler, *The Blue Dragon*, towed it back to Penzance Harbour where we were notified by the Coastguard. And eventually the call came in that a group of dignitaries had gone missing at sea'.

Simon looked perplexed. He tried not to seem confused but the flow of information wasn't quick enough and he wanted the point to come prior to the history. It was enduring enough to try and take all of the information in and he desperately wanted to write it all down. That was how he worked – he wrote everything down, to ingest at his leisure later. But in doing so he risked coming across as an amateur. He concentrated all of his energy on taking in what Wilkinson was detailing to him.

'Are you with me so far Mr Jenkins?' Wilkinson gestured with an open hand.

'Y-yes sir, yes, of course'.

Wilkinson paced back towards the bay window. Simon couldn't resist it any longer; he took the opportunity to take a notepad and pen from his briefcase and began furiously regurgitating the information relayed so far. Wilkinson took a deep breath and continued.

'We made the decision there and then to keep this under wraps. We contacted the Coastguard and put them under duress not to disclose any information to the police and especially not the press'.

Simon paused and looked up at the Vice Admiral, questioningly.

'We then persuaded the yacht hire companies to deny all knowledge of anyone having been on the vessel until such a time that we could release full details'.

Simon frowned.

'But, why didn't you contact the police, surely it is their jurisdiction and requirement to investigate?' he enquired.

'Usually yes, but if we had released this information it would have been picked up by the press which would have made National, maybe International news. It was Nineteen Ninety Two for goodness sake!' Wilkinson snapped.

'We were at war in the Gulf; we had little or no resources left. If the police had been informed they would have searched for naval resources which we just didn't have. We had barely enough vessels patrolling our own seas let alone any spare for a major investigation'.

Simon looked visibly astonished. Wilkinson's expression morphed into an agreeable smile.

'Okay Simon, I understand that this is a shock, and you are probably wondering what you are doing here, right?'

Simon nodded.

'During the few weeks that followed the initial discovery we gave the Coastguard an official jurisdiction, sanctioned by myself in Her Majesties name, to answer to ourselves only and we created a special department whose sole responsibility was to investigate. This allowed us to work simultaneously alongside our naval presence in the Gulf'.

Wilkinson watched Simon furiously scribbling every word on his pad and smiled.

'About two months later, another yacht was found floating off the coast of Cork. It was exactly the same find as the first one; nobody on board, no maps, no prints, nothing!'

'We now realised that we had a pattern and that this was not just a single occurrence'.

Simon stopped writing and looked up from his pad.

'Forgive my asking sir, but was this hushed up also?'

'Yes!' Wilkinson answered sternly.

'We had our own legitimate investigation under way. We couldn't expose that this was the second occurrence, and we couldn't afford any more resources as with before. Not only were we at war but our fleet was under attack, we were losing both vessels and men and in order to retain a good public eye we had to retain our valiant image and not that we were covering up local tragedies. It was too late. We had left ourselves in a position that only we could sort out. It was for us to investigate - and solve it we tried'.

'For how long?' Simon asked.

A few moments passed giving Simon a chance to update his notes. A tense silence ensued.

Wilkinson slowly turned his head to face him.

'It is still going on', he sighed.

'You mean, today's find is linked?' Simon asked in an uncontrollably high pitched voice.

'Yes, sixteen years later, Mr Jenkins, which is why you are here'.

He sat down, slowly, illustrating a historic back injury.

'Would you like another coffee Mr Jenkins?'

'Please', Simon replied.

Wilkinson leant over to a silver box on his desk, flicked a catch and opened it. He fished around for a few seconds and pulled out a large cigar.

'Do you…?' he asked.

'Erm, no, thank you'.

Wilkinson lit a large cannonball shaped lighter, put the cigar to his lips and pressed a button on a large aluminium box, illuminating a red light. He lit the cigar and puffed on it until it glowed.

The smart lady opened the doors and walked into the room with a tray of mugs, a sugar bowl and some biscuits. She laid them on the desk in front of them. Wilkinson sat back and exhaled a plume of blue grey smoke into the air.

'Thank you Charlotte', he said as she began her journey back to her desk.

Wilkinson reached for his cup and dragged it closer to him. Simon stared at him, a frown rippling over his forehead. Why was he so calm and collected? What he was saying was of such magnitude that it smacked of piracy and was unbelievable in every sense of the word.

'This isn't only the third occurrence Mr Jenkins', he said; reading Simon's intrigue.

'Since June the third, Nineteen Ninety Two, and before last night's findings, we have…' he paused.

Simon held his breath in anticipation as he sipped his coffee.

'…one hundred and eighty two recorded occurrences of this nature'.

Simon coughed, inadvertently spitting coffee over his notepad.

'How many?' he asked rhetorically as he retrieved a handkerchief from his trouser pocket.

Wilkinson looked at Simon as he dabbed at his notepad and his trousers.

'Altogether; one hundred and eighty five. Do you need a hand with that Mr Jenkins?'

'No, no thank you, I am sorry about that sir, I didn't mean to…'

'Don't apologise Mr Jenkins, don't apologise. I am surprised you took the news so well. It can't be easy to take on board what I am telling you'.

He sucked hard on the cigar; the embers crackling on the tip.

'So, why are you here?' Wilkinson pre-empted the big question while exhaling another cloud of smoke.

Simon smiled awkwardly.

'You are here because I need your help'.

Simon looked up from his notepad.

'My help?' he asked innocently.

'Yes. You see, this brings me back to my original point. This morning the *Blue Dragon* brought into Penzance Harbour another luxury yacht; *The Royal Wave*'.

He leaned back to reach for a newspaper. He folded it in half and tossed it to Simon who caught it between his elbows; one hand holding his coffee, the other his pen.

'Penzance Harbour was relatively quiet at three o'clock this morning with the exception of a few fishermen, the dock crew and a Mr Brown of the Cornish Guardian.'

Simon opened the newspaper to read the headlines:

"DEATH YACHT FOUND DRIFTING OFF COAST"

'Mr Brown was sent to the harbour to photograph a two hundred and twenty five pound Cod that was reputedly caught off the western coast and to interview the fisherman responsible'.

Wilkinson sucked at the cigar until the embers glowed and exhaled another plume of smoke, saturating the atmosphere above them.

'This second rate reporter spotted *The Royal Wave* being towed into dock and ambled over to take a look. After all, being a local lad he'll have a keen interest in boats, right?'

Simon nodded.

'So he took a closer look and started taking a few personal photographs, the Wave being quite an affluent vessel. As he zoomed in he spotted a hand print on the bow. On closer inspection he noticed it was stained with blood. Instinctively, he took more pictures and reported it back to his paper. For a local paper that reports on oversized cod, a story like this would be a real stir'.

'And now the story has leaked, right?' Simon stated, now grasping the situation.

'Spread like wild fire. It has even been received by the BBC!'

Wilkinson sat back in his chair and stared at the ceiling, blowing smoke every now and again from the corner of his mouth.

'And now you need someone to…'

'Bingo!' Wilkinson interrupted, sitting up to face Simon, 'We need an investigation sanctioned by, but separate to, the Royal Navy. Outside help one might say'.

'But, why me?' Simon asked, presumptuous in his question.

'Several reasons Mr Jenkins. Firstly; because you have a history in the Royal Navy; because you were trained as a naval officer. Because you are an ambassador for the Revenue and Customs department and are highly knowledgeable in the area of piracy and smuggling'.

'Piracy and smuggling?' he asked, again in an overly high pitched voice.

'Potentially I think we can assume that is the case, yes'.

Wilkinson stood up out of his chair once again and moved towards him, perching his vast body on the edge of the desk in front of him.

'And secondly, Mr Jenkins, because you have a relationship with a man who I want you to team up with; a man who has a history in the smuggling game and who has a very…' he paused to choose his words appropriately '…healthy obsession with, as he calls it, the "Dark Ship"'.

'Mike?' Simon responded abruptly, 'Mike Williams?'

'Yes. The hundred or so photographs that he submitted over the past ten years were kept on record. They nearly cost him his career but we kept them all the same'.

Simon was staggered. These photographs were taken over a period of about fifteen years. Mike was a fine, reputable coast guard and once happened upon a dark grey vessel in thick fog whilst stationed on the Seven Stones Lightship, during a routine maintenance period. The photographs were non-conclusive of anything with the exception that there was an unexplainable dark presence on the image. No one had batted an eyelid at his photographs before. For years Mike submitted reports and files to the Coastguards to send to the Royal Navy - following the correct procedures - but to no avail. Then in the summer of Nineteen Ninety Nine he was called from the Vice Admiralty in Portsmouth with the order to stop sending the files and that any further communication on the subject would result in his decommission. After a few months Mike had spotted a clear shape of an unidentified vessel from the powerful telescope in his own living room, which he again photographed and submitted with the intention that it was a significant and important find and as such he was willing to sacrifice his career. A few days later a letter came through the post which officially dismissed both his claims and his contract as Chief Coastguard of the West Coast of England.

He was then professionally advised that any further unofficial activity of this nature would lose him both his job and his pension.

Mike continued on a nonprofessional level; it became his hobby. He purchased an observatory grade telescope and became obsessed with the "dark ship" that had cost him his command. To this day he was frowned upon by the Royal Navy for the unlawful use of both his capacity and his resources, and looked down upon by his fellow colleagues.

So why, Simon thought, would the Vice Admiralty who was responsible for Mike's demotion, want him back as a co-leader of a newly formed department in search of what Wilkinson was insinuating that Mike had possibly found all those years ago? It didn't make sense. It seemed that this was immaterial at this point and that Vice Admiral Wilkinson had made his decision, despite what had happened in the past. Both he and Wilkinson knew that Mike would jump at the chance to become involved.

Wilkinson stood up from the desk.

'I am sure you will be pleased to learn that I am now going to come to the point. I want the two of you to head up and lead a department that hasn't seen the light of day since the late nineteenth century. Over the past few months we have been recruiting various men from the Navy and training them. This latest spate of...' Wilkinson stumbled for a word to describe the situation '...this latest find, has coincided with the launch of, Her Majesties Preventive Service'.

Simon shook his head in disbelief. This was deep; if the Vice Admiral was suggesting that a new department was to be created to combat piracy then it would suggest by its very title that there was an element of large scale smuggling involved. Therefore this would have to be known to the public and to the Nation. Was he really serious?

A few hours passed by. Simon looked at his watch; eleven o'clock. A thick layer of smoke hung in the air below the ceiling, casting bright rays of light into the room.

Wilkinson pulled out another file.

'I need you to sign this one also Mr Jenkins'.

Simon clicked his pen again, leaned over the stack of papers and folders on his lap and signed his signature on the form that the Vice Admiral had his hand on.

He picked up the paper and tore a carbon copy from the bottom.

'This one', he started, as he handed Simon the copy, 'is your weapon licenses for yourself and Mr Williams'.

Wilkinson had told Simon that they would be armed. Even though he had known for the past three hours that he would be a dedicated commander of the newly formed and armed Preventive Service, the details remained overwhelming. On one hand he was excited and couldn't wait to get started but on the other he was petrified about the scale of the operation. He wouldn't necessarily be hailed a local hero as Wilkinson had previously suggested; a lot of the locals, especially around the coastal villages, depended upon illicit trading as part of their income and throughout the centuries have come to look upon it as part of their livelihood. Certainly in the past, the Preventive Service had dealings with the smugglers themselves to supplement their low wages.

What Wilkinson was launching them into was a dangerous entanglement between doing the right thing and the consequential disruption and destruction of those they were protecting.

'I think that about does it Mr Jenkins', Wilkinson passed over another paper for him to sign. This one allowed him jurisdiction over local law enforcement. As he signed it he clenched his teeth together. This was deeper than he could have imagined and far more so than Wilkinson was leading him to believe.

Wilkinson stepped back and extended his right arm to bid the shocked Simon farewell.

He stumbled with his papers and files, pushed them onto the desk and held out his hot, sweaty hand to accept the handshake.

'Good luck Simon, and if there is anything I can do for you please let me know'.

'Thank you sir'.

Simon opened his briefcase and shoveled the files and papers inside. He tried to fasten the clip but it had over reached its capacity. He gave the Vice Admiral a smile and a nod, which was received and returned and headed off towards the doors.

'Don't forget, Mr Jenkins…' Wilkinson boomed '…I want regular updates as we discussed'.

Simon turned and nodded as he opened the heavy wooden doors.

When the door closed behind him, the pressure in Simon's head pulsated with every heartbeat.

The smart lady offered him his coat. He dropped his briefcase at his feet to receive it.

As he slipped it on, Wilkinson's secretary looked at her clipboard.

'Right Mr Jenkins, I hope your meeting went well'.

She didn't know the half of it, he thought.

'There is a car waiting for you outside to take you to the helipad. Mr Wilkinson is keen that you and Mr…' she looked closely at her notes on the clip board, '…Williams, report to the Nelson Building in Penzance as soon as you can, to meet the rest of your team and collect your equipment. Your vehicles will be waiting for you at Penzance Police Station'.

My God, he thought, this was already in motion. He and Mike were the last two pieces in this departmental jigsaw. It was happening around him, it was happening now and it was happening at a tremendous pace.

He nodded in agreement, buttoned the top two buttons of his coat and picked up his briefcase. The crisp morning air hit him as he descended the stone steps from the entrance; the muffled thumps from the helicopter's rotor in the distance filling the air of the busy base. He paused before he got to the last step, to reflect on the past few life changing hours, looking up at the windows of the offices where he had been only moments ago. As he looked into the pink morning sky he sensed the presence of someone nearby; the officer who had picked him up from the helipad earlier waited patiently a few feet in front of him.

Chapter 3

<u>The Call</u>

"OUT OF OUR HANDS, PREVENTIVE SERVICE CREATED FROM HIGHER AUTHORITY. NXT TARGET – EMPRESS APROX 1730 HRS 45N 36W. SAFE CODE 12,17,69,23 NO TRACE THIS TIME"

A manicured thumb moved over the "send" button and pressed it.

"MESSAGE SENT"

The ocean pounded the cliffs blowing sea spray into the crisp, fresh sky. At the top of the cliffs, across the sun bleached sea grass fields, a white washed stone cottage stood proudly, nestled within the indigenous foliage inherent of the coastal plains. The crumbling boulder walls reflected years of neglect as Mother Nature had begun to replace the ancient grouting with thick intrusive vines. The cracked, peeling window frames showed decades of various colours blistered by the sun and scraped away by the shore breeze.

The front room window overlooked and reflected the cliff top and the ocean beyond. In the bay of the window stood a large and complicated telescope, adapted to look out on a horizontal plain. The living room of the cottage bore a resemblance to a squat; remnants of the previous night and the night before takeaway cartons littered a large low-level oak coffee table. A Canon camera with various filters and attachments lay on a season's worth of *Coast Magazine* stacked neatly on the threadbare carpet.

Ring Ring....

A computer in the corner of the room played a slideshow of random photographs as it sat idle on a makeshift trestle and drift wood desk. On the wall above and at a precarious angle, a pin board hung delicately under the weight of overflowing photographs and that spread onto the wall and beyond.

Ring Ring....

The corridor leading from the living room was dim, the walls plastered with pictures of ships, galleons, yachts, sailors and boatmen; an entire life history in pictures.

Ring Ring....

Inside the bedroom a body lay in foetal position deep below a heavy tog duvet.

Ring Ring....

On a small bedside table with a wealth of coffee mugs, a small mobile phone flashed and vibrated closer to the edge of the surface with every ring.

Ring Ring....

A hairy, solid arm slid out of the side of the duvet and grappled at the phone, took hold of it and retracted into the warm dark confines.

'Hello?' a grumbling deep southern voice answered.

'Mike, it's Simon, I need to talk to you urgently…' the voice crackled.

'Simon?' Mike's unshaven face pushed above the duvet and rested on the wooden headboard.

'You will never guess where I am?'

'You're right', Mike replied, semi-consciously running a hand through his unkempt hair.

'Portsmouth!'

'Fabulous!' Mike said with extreme disinterest and sarcasm.

'I should be with you in an hour or so, get some clothes on and be ready for me okay?'

'Okay'.

Tiredness overcame confusion as Mike thumbed the "cancel call" button and slid down underneath the duvet.

Simon boarded the helicopter, turning to wave to the driver of the Land Rover and rushed to the same seat he arrived on. He sat down as the powerful engines started up, vibrating everything not battened down in the cabin. A thick cloud of smoke found its way inside the cabin just before the external door closed. Normally this would have been a source of annoyance to him but his mind was preoccupied with the bombshell that had been dropped onto him.

Like an overexcited school child he began to extract the various files and folders from his briefcase, laying them out over the drop-down plastic table.

The helicopter ascended into the air and immediately started forward.

From his office window, Wilkinson watched the Sikorsky fly low over the base and out of his view. He returned to his desk with a confident smile.

Beep Beep – Beep Beep

An oil stained, boiler suited arm picked up the phone that vibrated on the dark metal surface. A greasy thumb pressed the "view" button. After a few moments the thumb began to flick from one button to another and a message began to manifest on the tiny screen:

CONFIRMED. KEEP THESE BASTARDS AWAY. WILL LET U KNOW WHEN DONE!

The thumb pressed the "send" button:

"MESSAGE SENT"

Ring ring

Mike reached for the phone on the pillow and answered it immediately.

'Yes!' he shouted.

'It's me, Simon, are you awake? I am in my car on my way to your house. I will be there in ten!'

Mike switched the phone off and sat bolt upright. He swung his legs out of the duvet and sat up on the edge of the bed. After rubbing his hands through his hair for a few moments, he stood up to reach his dressing gown from the back of the door; he slipped an arm through it and made his way down the dim corridor towards the living room.

After slipping his other arm into his robe he tied the belt and reached for the remote to the television, routinely flicking it on. It was the conclusion of an episode of Antiques Roadshow.

"…I don't think we are in any doubt that we won't be seeing one of those again in a hurry…"

Mike flicked on the kettle on the end of the bar of the kitchenette and reached for the coffee jar. On auto-pilot he scooped two mounds of coffee from it and flicked them into a nearby mug.

"So that's it and from all of us here at Chatsworth House in Derbyshire… Goodbye."

The distinctive music began and developed into a monotonous murmur in the background.

Impatiently he switched the kettle off prior to it boiling and poured the water, stirring it with a spoon he snapped from the kitchen surface.

Taking a sip of the lukewarm coffee, Mike shuffled back into the living room just as the news was starting. Casually looking at his watch he realised that in any moment Simon would turn up and he was still in his bathrobe.

Slamming the coffee on the sideboard, he ran through to the bedroom.

"Good afternoon, I am standing on the harbour side at Penzance where earlier this morning fishermen from this trawler behind me, the *Blue Dragon*, towed in to the harbour a twenty four metre luxury yacht called *The Royal Wave*, which allegedly showed signs of an ominous nature. I have with me Mr Ian Brown from the Cornwall Guardian who saw the yacht earlier today. Good Afternoon Mr Brown.

Hello.

Could you explain what you found this morning?

Yes, I was standing here admiring the yacht and as I looked at her impressive stern I noticed there was a handprint which looked like it had been smeared on in oil. I thought it was strange, as the vessel was so clean, that someone had left such an obvious mark on it. As I looked closer, I realised it looked like blood…"

The television droned as Mike came rushing back into the living room half dressed in his coastguard uniform. He looked at his watch.

'Shit!' he exclaimed as he grappled with the television remote turning it off.

Simon's beaten Land Rover hugged the edges of the narrow coastal roads, cutting the corners and spraying clouds of loose gravel into the air. As he approached the cottage gates he pulled on the handbrake and steered into the entrance, sliding the back of the vehicle over the wet tarmac and into the driveway. He pulled on the brakes as he neared the front door, burying the tyres deep into the pebbles.

Mike rushed past the kitchen window as a scattering of pebbles and dirt hit the porch.

'Jesus!' he exclaimed as he picked up his keys and wallet from the coffee table. He unbolted the front door and stepped out to a very excited looking Simon, beckoning him from behind the steering wheel.

'What's going on Simon?' he shouted over the roar of the engine.

'Just get in for God's sake!' Simon shouted back.

Mike shut the door behind him and locked it.

Simon crunched the gears into reverse and pushed his foot flat to the accelerator. The passenger door swung open; Mike just managing to hold onto it to pull it shut before they neared the narrow gateposts. Simon swung the steering wheel round and crunched into first, propelling forwards, spinning the rear wheels on the wet road.

'There had better be a damn good reason why I am sitting here now doing…' Mike leaned over to look at the speedometer '…sixty five miles an hour down my country road, when I should be, by all rights, in bed, asleep'.

They screamed down the road, clipping the curb as Simon mauled the vehicle around the tight corners.

Mike didn't take his eyes off him, as he held onto the seatbelt for stability.

'You gonna tell me what is going on then or what?' he asked impatiently.

'I, I don't really… I can't think of what to say…' Simon stuttered, desperately trying hard to find the words to explain the events prior to his arrival.

As the Land Rover screeched around the corners Mike's temper began to rise.

'Simon! For God's sake slow down and tell me what the hell is going on!'

Simon, realising that he had virtually kidnapped Mike, also realised that he needed to inform him of the situation well before they arrived in Penzance. He spotted a lay-by ahead and made a direct line for it, unnerving the tired and bewildered Mike who grabbed at the dashboard with both hands. Simon directed the vehicle into it and pulled on the handbrake, bringing around the back end so that it stopped dead, parallel to the road.

Simon shuffled round in his seat to face his irritated passenger who was looking back at him under his brow.

'I think now is the time to find the right words to tell me…' Mike paused, '…WHAT IN GOD'S NAME IS GOING ON!!!' he shouted.

Simon smiled, 'Ok Mike, I really don't know how to tell you this but… you know I told you before I was in Portsmouth?'

Mike nodded silently.

'Okay, well… you aren't going to believe this'.

'Try me, please try me!'

'I was… with Vice Admiral Wilkinson!'

'Wilkinson?' Mike hesitated, 'Are we in trouble?'

'Ha!' Simon inadvertently laughed out loud, 'quite the opposite my friend'. He composed himself and looked into the air to find the right way to deliver the news.

'Okay Mike, did you catch the news this morning?' he started almost replicating Wilkinson's introduction.

Mike shook his head.

'Ok, I'm gonna tell you straight'.

'Thank God!'

'Wilkinson has formed a new department within the Navy, superseding law enforcement authority, to investigate a recent spate of piracy and to emplace coastal patrols around the South West, ultimately to dissolve the smuggling trade and to bring the perpetrators to justice'.

Simon regurgitated key notes from the files he had read through on the helicopter, but couldn't believe what he had just landed on Mike.

Mike looked stunned and gestured for elaboration.

'He wants us to head it up, to lead it, to manage a team of… Preventive Servicemen'.

Simon leaned over the back of his seat to reach for his briefcase. He flicked the catch and prised it open with his fingers to extract a folder.

'Take a look at this Mike, we really don't have much time, I'm sorry'.

Simon dropped the manila file onto Mikes lap, snapping him out of his daze. He looked down at it and opened it, fanning the pages inside. As Simon started the engine, he glanced at his colleague who was running his thumb over the embossed admiralty letter head of a page he had extracted.

'It's genuine Mike'.

Mike looked back at him with an expression of disbelief.

The Land Rover spun from the lay-by and rejoined the road leaving a stale blue trail of exhaust fumes behind.

The large, silver Mercedes pulled through the gates of the Portway Marina and onto the gravelled carpark. Trevor Burke looked out of the side window in the rear of the car, repositioning himself on the black leather seat to get a better vantage point of the luxury vessels moored in front of them.

'Well, my little brother, you've deserved this', he said to the man sitting next to him, furiously tapping away on his Blackberry.

'If it wasn't for you, that job would never have worked out the way I planned. For that I cannot thank you enough'.

Martin looked back at his proud, older brother and smiled in response. Sliding the stylus back into the Blackberry, he lifted himself up from the crackling leather seat to holster it and adjust his jacket.

'Thanks Trev, it was a bit of a long shot but we got there. I'm just glad that we pulled it off', he said, slapping his hand down on his brother's knee.

The Mercedes coasted into a reserved parking space. A large Asian bodyguard opened the passenger door and climbed out, patting down his long black coat to remove the creases.

He opened the back door and moved swiftly to the other side.

Almost simultaneously the two brothers climbed out of the car, both adjusting their collars and sunglasses.

Trevor trotted over to his younger brother and put his arm around his shoulder and the two men, closely followed by the bodyguard, walked towards the floating harbour underneath a large metal sign: "Welcome to Portway Marina, Falmouth – Chartered Luxury Yachts".

As the three men paced across the floating harbour, an expectant man in a dark blue suit waited at the end next to an eighty five foot luxury catamaran; the white finish of which was creating a blinding reflection from the midday sun.

As they approached, the suited man extended his hand to receive his clients.

'Mr Burke it is indeed a pleasure to see you again sir', the man said excitedly in a pseudo-French accent.

Trevor took off his sunglasses to admire the vessels splendour.

'You are kidding right?' Martin asked his brother with a toothy grin.

'Everything is in order Mr Burke', the man said proudly, 'the merchandise has been transferred into the safe, as you requested, there is champagne on ice inside and here are the keys'.

'And…' the man leaned over to Trevor's ear; 'the girls are also inside waiting'. He looked over to Martin and winked.

Trevor stepped back and held out his left hand to lead Martin onto the deck.

'Seriously? Are you serious?' Martin asked in awe of the magnificent vessel.

'I told you, brother, this is an important time for the business. What better way to transport the diamonds to our beloved father?'

Martin turned to face his brother and shook his head.

Trevor turned to the patient Frenchman.

'Thanks Jean-Claude, you are my saviour!'

He pushed a folded fifty pound note into his upper jacket pocket.

'It is my pleasure as always Mr Burke', he replied pushing the note deeper into the pocket to conceal it.

Trevor hopped onto the deck and waved at Jean-Claude who returned it. The bodyguard acknowledged the departing wave with a subtle nod.

Jean-Claude watched Trevor as he made his way towards the central cabin kissing his fingers and affectionately patting the vessels name plate *The Empress*, mounted above the main doors, as he entered. He turned around to walk back to the sales chalet and pulled out a phone from his pocket. He pressed a short dial and held it to his ear, stopping momentarily to look back at the yacht.

'They are leaving now'.

The Land Rover slowed down as it approached the town centre of Penzance.

Mike had calmed and was reading the notes that Simon had taken during his meeting earlier.

'This is unbelievable', he started, 'after all those years of sightings and my decommission; the ridicule from my own department.'

'I know Mike, but look on the bright side'.

'What bright side?'

There wasn't a bright side- Simon had just backed himself into a corner.

Mike collected his thoughts. This was exactly the break he was looking for, but on a tremendous scale. He continued to pull out papers from the folder and came across a sheet entitled "Weapon Licensing Certificate".

'What the hell is this?'

Simon smiled nervously; he could tell that his colleague was as bewildered as he was only a few hours previously but he also sensed the excitement. Mike wasn't one for the run-of-the-mill jobs that he had been demoted to doing.

Nelson Building, formerly the Market Hall, stood impressively atop Penzance town centre. The large dome reflected the town's history amongst the flanking modern architecture.

As they approached the vast limestone building, Simon's foot began to tap infuriatingly on the clutch. A guard stepped close to them from his post at the main entrance near the statue of Sir Humphrey Davy.

'Calm down', Mike whispered. Simon rolled down his window to talk to the guard.

He hesitated.

'Erm, H…M, P, S?' he asked, intending to inform them but resulting in a question. The guard looked blankly at Simon who stared back with anticipation. A few moments past before Mike pulled out a sheet of A4 from the manila folder. He leaned over Simon and passed it to the guard.

The guard read the first few lines.

'Ah, sorry sir, you are expected inside'.

The guard stepped back, to allow the Land Rover to park on the kerb side. Mike nudged Simon to put the vehicle into gear and they coasted up onto the pavement.

'You are going to have to get it together Si, if we are going to do this', Mike suggested.

Of course he was, but that was easy for him to say. It had only been an hour since he himself was sitting in disbelief.

As they entered the large decorative and cavernous foyer of the impressive Nelson Building, a young lady walked across the marble floor to greet them.

'Déjà vu', Simon muttered under his breath.

Mike stepped forward to greet the lady.

'Mike Williams', he said, shaking the young lady's hand, 'and this is Simon Jenkins'.

Mike had instinctively taken lead which came as a huge relief to Simon as he wasn't a born leader and needed a route to follow, especially taking into account the scale of what lay ahead.

'Pleased to meet you both', she said with a very heavy Cornish accent.

'We won't keep you too long. You need to go along the corridor…' she started to point out the route, '…actually, I will take you myself, it is like a rabbit warren down here'.

She walked along the marble surface which became Victorian tiles as they veered off into one of the many narrow corridors. Her footsteps echoed around them as the two men followed closely.

Eventually they arrived at a large armoured door marked "Quartermaster".

'Here you will collect your uniforms and your weapons', she paused and looked at the two men awkwardly, 'you did know you were being fitted out with weaponry didn't you?' she asked politely.

'Yes, of course. We have the papers right here', Simon replied, taking out a handful of documents to show her.

'Ah, that's good. You wouldn't believe the amount of dumbstruck men that I have delivered here lately for weapon detail. You can give those papers to Sergeant Lawton inside, thank you'.

She knocked on the door, turned around and walked back down the corridor.

'Come in!' a military worn voice barked from behind the metal door.

Mike twisted the iron handle, pushed at the gloss-painted frame and the two men entered the prison-like room, like two schoolboys entering a Headmaster's office.

After a few hours the two men arrived back at the reception, both of them holding blue, plastic fishing crates piled high with overcoats, site jackets, boxes of ammunition, more paperwork and a Blackberry balanced precariously on top.

'Ah, good you are back', the young lady said, leaving her desk and walking towards them.

'I have been asked to escort you to the carpark. We have had your vehicle delivered. If I can ask you to sign here…' she said holding a pink warrant form towards the men.

Mike put his crate down and pulled a pen from his jacket pocket.

'Just sign here', she pointed at a dotted line, 'this is for your vehicle outside'.

Simon stooped to look through the small windows in the entrance door.

'And if you could just sign this one to relinquish your old vehicle, which I believe belongs to the Revenue and Customs department?' she asked handing a yellow slip to Simon.

Simon dropped his crate and took the pen from Mike to sign the vehicle over.

'Thank you gentlemen; here are your keys'.

'Our number and the number of the department is programmed in your new phones, so if you have any questions, which I am sure you will have…' she smiled at Simon who responded with a flirtatious wink, '…please call'.

'Will do, thanks', Simon answered; his eyes following the young receptionist back to her desk.

The two men picked up their crates and walked towards the main entrance doors.

As they walked down the steps, in front of them sat a brand new, dark blue Land Rover Freelander, bearing the livery of the HMPS in luminous orange, vividly reflecting the afternoon sunlight.

'You are joking?' Simon said with his mouth wide open.

'Apparently not', Mike responded.

The two walked around the glossy vehicle. Mike pressed the remote on his key and unlocked it. He dropped his crate and opened the rear door. The "new" smell engulfed them. The two men peered inside like curious boys.

As they loaded their crates inside Mike stood back and noticed the blue emergency light on the roof and smiled.

'This is ridiculous. I swear I am still asleep'.

They opened the doors and climbed inside. Simon looked at the battered, dented Revenue and Customs Land Rover he had parked awkwardly on the kerb. It was missing a tail light and the rear window bore a crack down the right side. A dent and part of a hawthorn bush adorned the nearside wing and corrosion had begun to devour the front bulbar. It was a wreck. Had he known he was returning it he would have perhaps given it a clean. This was probably going to result in a bill or an angry phone call from R&C headquarters at the least.

'It's a fair swap don't you think?'

'Where shall we take her?' Simon asked as Mike busied himself ingesting the information in the file again.

'I want to take a look at that yacht. Let's get down to the harbour'.

'You are taking this rather well Mike, if you don't mind me saying'.

Mike paused and pouted his lips.

'I think that if I stop and think, this will become incredibly overwhelming. I am trying to just let it take me, if that makes sense'.

Simon nodded and started the muffled engine. He grinned as he applied the accelerator.

'The harbour is about two hundred yards away Mike…'

Mike looked up from the file, 'And?'

Inspector Burnside looked pensively down at the gleaming, white yacht from the stone harbour wall. The forensic team, dressed in white nylon suits, made their way from the moorings at the foot of the harbour and up the stone steps to where Burnside waited tapping his foot in anticipation. The head investigator shook his head disappointingly to the young inspector as he past him.

Burnside was fresh into his career and was appointed this investigation by his DCI. Desperate to make an impression he had ensured that every available resource was available for the case which was creating more publicity with every minute. He watched the forensic team shake their heads to one another as they packed away their equipment into containers at the back of the harbour wall then returned his gaze to the Wave.

'Why aren't you giving anything up you bitch?' he mumbled to the vessel beneath him.

The harbour was littered with police officers interviewing dock workers, fishermen, ferry passengers and yacht owners. Blue striped tape fluttered in the breeze as it weaved around the dock posts like bunting at a sea shanty festival.

Burnside reached into his long coat pocket and retrieved a vibrating phone.

'Burnside', he answered.

He looked into the sky as he ingested the phone call.

'Yes, yes I am here now', he responded. 'Who? Of course sir, yes, I will make myself available of course'.

As the Freelander turned the corner into the harbour, Burnside clocked it.

'They are here now by the looks of it sir', he said as his eyes followed the dark blue vehicle coast along the harbour cobbles towards him.

'Yes sir, their jurisdiction, yes sir', he repeated and closed the phone, returning it to his jacket pocket, eyes still focused on the approaching vehicle.

The Scillonian III, passenger ferry, had recently arrived back from the Isle of Scilly and the harbour was almost impenetrable with weary looking passengers; the Scillonian being renowned for its rough passage between the islands and the mainland.

Mike and Simon walked over towards the inspector, having to physically move people out of the way to get to him. The police had started to disperse the crowd, who had heard about the incident from news reports on the radio. A small cluster of passengers had assembled near *The Wave* to take photographs, which in turn attracted more attention, creating a dense crowd that the police were trying to manage.

Mike and Simon produced their new warrants from their pockets, simultaneously presenting them to the awaiting inspector.

'Mike Williams, and this is Simon Jenkins, we are from the…'

'HMPS', Burnside interjected, 'yes, I just got off the phone from the DCI. He said you guys would turn up at some point'.

Burnside looked particularly unimpressed. This was his crime scene and his patch; he didn't like the idea of handing it over to a third party.

Mike and Simon looked at each other.

'What do we know then, Mr….?' Mike fished for a name.

'Burnside, Inspector Burnside', he looked back towards the yacht and frowned.

'Forensics have been on board and been over every square inch but found nothing, not a damn thing!'

Simon raised an eyebrow, recalling the information Wilkinson had given him earlier. He squatted at the edge of the harbour above the yacht.

'The sample we collected from the hand print was blood - no doubt about that, but how it got there or from whom - we have no idea', Burnside spoke in a downbeat manner.

Mike looked at the yacht and rubbed his unshaven chin. Simon stood up and made his way towards the steps down to the mooring.

'Are we okay to go onboard now?' Simon asked.

'Be my guest', Burnside answered, 'but you won't find anything'.

Simon walked down the stone steps, onto the ramp and stepped on board the waxed, oak decking.

'Has anyone reported missing persons with regard to this boat?' Mike asked the inspector who was looking out of the corner of his eye at the agent, clambering around on the decks of *The Wave*.

'Erm, yes they have', he answered, flicking through the pages of his notepad.

After a few moments he fingered a page.

'Mr Thompson saw the news report this morning and called his local police station who contacted us. Apparently, his daughter and five teenagers took *The Wave* out from a marina in Plymouth early yesterday morning. They were celebrating her twenty first, apparently'.

Mike looked at the floor in remorse and then back to the yacht.

'Teenagers?' he asked rhetorically, 'Ah, that's terrible. Thanks Inspector'.

He walked quickly towards the harbour steps and down onto the deck of the yacht.

As he made his way inside he marvelled at the interior.

'Like new isn't she?' Simon pre-empted Mike's thoughts.

The two men walked around the beige carpeted cabin.

The interior was immaculate. The cabin windows were unusually clean, the carpet was bright cream and, with the exception of traces of dusting powder from the forensic team, the surfaces were spotless.

Mike paused as Simon continued to open cupboards and cabinets.

'A group of teenagers?' Mike pondered out loud.

Simon looked up from a concealed wine cooler set into the oak panelling in the lounge area.

'How old is this boat Si?'

Simon sat back on his heels, 'Err, about six years old?' he guessed, looking around at the fixtures and fittings.

'That's about what I thought more or less'.

He turned to look through the rear doors at the aft deck.

'There's a bit of corrosion around the railings and the mast outside; yet the interior looks about a week old. What time was the yacht found by the trawler?'

'About two this morning', Simon recalled from his meeting with Wilkinson.

'Two this morning', Mike retorted, his mind furiously working on a line of thought.

'Who has had access to the yacht since it was brought into the harbour?'

Simon flicked through his notepad, the answer being amongst the reams of pages he had written. Eventually his finger traced a section of the scrawl.

'Nobody was allowed on board', he read, 'the harbour master was alerted and then the press arrived'.

'This doesn't make sense. What would you do on your first night at sea with your mates?'

Simon looked at Mike strangely, 'Probably party?' he offered.

'Exactly!' Mike snapped, 'who wouldn't? You are with your mates, miles away from anybody. You are a teenager…'

'She was in her early twenties I think'.

Mike rolled his eyes, 'Well, early twenties, what difference does it make? You are on the first night of your birthday celebration and you would have an all-out party, right?'

'What are you getting at Mike?'

'What evidence of a party do you see in here?'

Simon looked around at the immaculate interior and shrugged.

'None, I guess'.

'That's my point', he concluded as he paced into the affluent lounge. He bent down to one of the units on the floor and pushed at the bottom infill panel flush to the carpet.

'Ha!' he exclaimed excitedly.

Simon bent down to see what he had found.

Mike pointed at the carpet under the unit – it was a distinctively darker colour than that outside of it.

'It's been cleaned Si, someone has cleaned it'.

Simon rubbed at the carpet divide.

'Bloody hell, I think you are right. It even feels different'.

'We aren't looking for evidence of someone being here. Whoever was here has cleaned this thing intensely. We are going to have to look deeper than the surface!'

Mike stood up and walked back to the galley and out through the stern doors onto the aft deck.

'Inspector Burnside!' he shouted.

Simon pulled out a pen and began to document their find. Neither of them were detectives and they lacked the skills of one, yet the fact that this simple find had been overlooked by a team of trained forensics began to worry him. Why hadn't the police sent a more experienced team to investigate, especially as this thing had reached mass media?

The inspector arrived inside the galley.

'Have you found anything?' he asked, with a shimmer of panic in his voice; worried that he had missed the obvious and thus damaging his prospects. This was his first case and he couldn't afford to mess it up, although it had occurred to him as being odd that he was entrusted with something as grand a scale as this and with national coverage.

'No, but I think I know why…'

Mike turned left at the galley entrance and made his way up the exterior ladder to the bridge.

'Have your boys been over this thing then?' Mike shouted behind him.

Burnside stepped back outside and looked up towards him, 'Yeah, yeah they finished as you arrived'.

Mike positioned himself at the controls in front of the Captain's chair. The keys were still in the ignition.

'Have you started her up?'

Burnside shrugged and shook his head, 'No, not that I am aware of'.

Mike switched the ignition switches, put the vessel into neutral and turned the key.

Nothing happened.

Simon and Burnside looked up the steps towards him.

'No power!' Mike informed them, 'this vessel has lost its power'.

He climbed out of the chair and walked to one of the many light switches on a panel mounted on the wall. He pressed the brass switch; nothing.

'Even the leisure battery is dead', he exclaimed, 'leisure batteries have about forty eight hours of continual use without charge and this boat was drifting for about an hour and it has only been about sixteen hours since it was picked up'.

'Meaning…?' Simon asked.

Mike drummed his fingers on the bar surface as his thoughts churned in his mind.

'She was found at… when was it, two thirty?'

'Yeah, two or two thirty', Simon replied pointing at a page of notes.

'Let's say two thirty, to give the benefit of the doubt. If this boat was found at two thirty that means that whoever did whatever at about one to one thirty. It would take a crew of six, or so, about an hour to clean a cabin to this standard taking us back to twelve thirty'.

'Mr Williams…' Burnside started impatiently.

'How long do you think it would take a group of teenagers to get to sleep? Bearing in mind that it has to be a deep enough sleep not to hear someone board your yacht? Maybe half an hour at the very least? That takes us to twelve o' clock; Midnight!'

Simon nodded slowly as his colleague's theory began to make sense.

'This boat set sail yesterday morning right?' he directed to the inspector who nodded.

'So what group of teenagers do you know who would go to bed at midnight on the first night of a trip in a luxury yacht that they would've been likely to have been planning for months?'

Burnside, realising the point, begrudgingly began to write in his own notepad and then stopped mid-sentence, looking up questioningly.

'So what has the lack of power got to do with it?' he asked.

Mike rolled his eyes.

'What better way to attack someone? If you plunge the yacht into darkness you evoke fear, which in turn lowers an individual's defences. If you cut the power to the engines you eliminate any possibilities of escape'.

Mike looked positively victorious. Not only had he potentially solved the mystery of the floating vessel but more importantly he had outwitted the police inspector.

'How?' asked Simon, 'how do you cut the power to a yacht without anyone noticing, Mike?'

Mike looked at him out of the corner of his eye and felt Burnside's gaze burning through the side of his head. There was a pause as Mike bit at his lip.

'I have no idea', he admitted, 'but I would like to know if the other hundred-odd drifters were in the same condition as this one, when they were brought in'.

'The harbour master's remit involves the recording of every vessel to enter the harbour walls. I bet he will be able to help you', Burnside jumped in with a smile.

'Thank you Inspector Burnside', Mike said genuinely, albeit with a hint of harmless patronising.

The inspector's mobile phone rang; he excused himself and made his way back up the stone steps to the harbour to take the call.

Simon walked over to Mike.

'What about the crew Mike? Where are they? I am assuming you are assuming they are…'

Mike looked at him, his eyes falling to the ground.

'I don't know, Si'.

'What now?'

Mike looked at him thoughtfully, his mind unwinding the complex weave of questions yet to answer.

'What time is it?'

Chapter 4

The Attack

The Empress skipped across the tops of the waves, the bright, white keels slicing the peaks as she passed through; her sails bulbous in the wind flow.

The weather was perfect and the sun a bright, white haloed circle against the dark blue evening sky. Small, grey woolly clouds dotted the reddening horizon and the wind just enough to push her effortlessly along her trajectory. The new engines of the catamaran purred from the twin hulls, giving her the extra stability on the spring swell.

Trevor looked up from the polished wooden wheel, his sunglasses reflecting the brilliant flash from the setting sun. This was the life he and his younger brother had worked all those tiresome nights meticulously planning, spent all those days watching and researching and why he had recently overcome treatment for a stomach ulcer. It had finally paid off. They had lifted more than enough to enable them both to retire.

He smiled as he heard the combination of his brother's laughter and the giggles of the girls that he was entertaining inside. He grinned, held the wheel and flicked at the switch marked "Auto" on the beige leather console. He lowered himself from the command seat and checked the sails. After double checking the coordinates: 45N 36W, he peered at the radar in its brass mounting. He pushed his arm out to raise his sleeve and looked at the double face of his de LaCour watch: 17:21; they were making excellent time. Content, he casually strode into the central cabin to find Martin sitting, legs astride flanked by the two women in matching bikinis. Trevor winked at his brother and moved towards the galley where a silver champagne stand stood in the corner.

'Well, ladies and gentlemen, it looks like we may be in for a perfect sunset!' he announced as he pulled at the bottle inside the bucket of ice.

'Bugger, we're running low on the old champers…' he mumbled intentionally loudly.

'Hey, we're thirsty over here!' Martin shouted waving an empty flute in the air.

His brother raised his eyebrows at the outburst and retrieved a cube of ice from the bucket. He moved into the galley and tossed the cube at his companions as he opened a large, freestanding fridge to select another bottle.

'We should be nearing Cork in about three hours at present speed', he announced as he stripped the foil from the top of the bottle and began to untwist the wire.

'I took the liberty to book us into the Capella Castlemartyr for nine, so that gives us…' he paused and looked at the two ladies, flirtatiously smiling back at him, '…some time to kill'. The champagne cork popped unexpectedly spraying the sticky wine over the white carpet and wooden panels of the cabin.

Trevor sucked at the end of the bottle and placed it on the breakfast bar, reaching in the above unit for a serviette. He wrapped the neck and poured four glasses.

'There you are girls, there's plenty more of that', he boasted, returning to the galley to rinse his hands.

'Here's to the business', Martin toasted.

Trevor jogged back into the lounge and plucked a flute from the glass table.

'To you my young brother, who, without your help we wouldn't be here now, en-route to fathers pad complete with rocks and in such luxury!' He turned to the large Chubb safe built into one of the ground units beneath a large Bang and Olufsen sound system mounted on the wall and raised his glass towards it, 'I think we may have secured our retirement this time Martin'.

'I'm hungry', one of the girls suddenly piped, rubbing at her stomach.

'I'll get some nibbles', Martin offered, prizing himself from the leather sofa. Trevor plunged himself into his brother's place.

As Martin walked towards the galley, the boat started to roll slightly.

'Whoa!' he said as he reached for the fridge, 'think it's gone to my head, this stuff'.

Trevor looked out of the skylight at the horizon, 'Doesn't seem like a storm?'

Martin stood at the fridge gathering a selection of cheeses on a large wooden platter. The boat rolled again, this time pitching further causing the empty bottle to slide off the glass table, taking the empty flutes with it onto the carpet with a loud clatter.

The two girls retreated into foetal positions on the sofa, clutching their ankles. They both looked around them as the ornaments on the shelves began to move.

Trevor sat up, alert as the boat listed once again, this time crashing down onto the waves.

'What the hell is going on Trev?' Martin asked through gritted teeth in an effort to hide his fear. 'You know I can't flippin' well swim!'

'Nothing, everyone be calm, it's probably the swell from a passing tanker or something'.

He stood up and awkwardly shuffled, crab like, to the bridge, spreading his weight over his stance to counter balance the now violent movement of the yacht.

'I'm going to be sick!' one of the girls shouted after him.

As he positioned himself at the controls the cabin lights went out, the music station silenced and the engine began to drone down.

Although it was dusk outside, the cabin went dark causing one of the girls to scream.

'Calm down for God's sake!' Trevor shouted as he looked down at the floor from where the droning sound of the propeller shaft slowed to a silence.

He ran past his petrified brother to the bridge and looked into the black screen of the radar and futilely tapped at the LCD membrane.

'Damn!' he cursed under his breath.

Martin watched his brother through the dim evening light, furiously flicking at switches and repeatedly turning the ignition key. He looked towards the girls, who were visibly shaken.

'Ha, what's he done? Probably hasn't put his pound in the meter!' he offered as a token gesture to no avail.

Martin moved from the galley precariously towards his brother who continued cursing as he turned the ignition key.

'What is it Trev? What's going on?' he asked as he arrived, clinging to the chrome rail as the yacht rolled powerless against the waves.

'No idea, no idea at all, we just lost power', he said as he pushed at a different set of switches.

Suddenly a loud metallic thud came from the upper deck above them.

'What the hell was that?' Martin said crouching on the floor with his hands above his head as if protecting himself from a falling object.

Trevor reached under the wheel unit and pulled out a Maglite. He pointed it towards the roof hatch and pressed the rubber button on the side. Nothing.

'Trev, what is happening?' Martin trembled. The girls, witnessing the gradual break down of their male companions, started to become uncontrollable.

Another thud followed, then another; both of which were evidentially footsteps.

As the two men looked above them at the ceiling, tracing the sounds towards to the rear, two louder thuds occurred behind them, outside on the aft deck.

The two men spun round.

'Mart', Trevor whispered, 'get my briefcase'.

'What the hell do you want your briefcase for now?' Martin spat back.

'Just reach it for me will you, it's there!' he pointed to the case next to the bar close to Martins foot, 'my gun is in it!'

Martin, realising his brother's intention, slowly crept backwards towards the case.

There was a terrifying silence and the vessel stopped listing.

The thuds outside had stopped.

Martin grabbed the case and slid it along the laminate flooring towards his brother.

Trevor clutched at the case and frantically flicked the catches open, smiling with relief when his hand found the automatic inside.

Sweat dripped down Martin's forehead as he watched his brother pull the gun from the case and point it towards the cabin entrance. He pulled back the chamber and released it with a loud click.

A few tense moments passed as the nervous Trevor aimed the shaking gun at the double glass doors.

'Maybe I should just shoot through the doors', he whispered.

Then panic set in; what the hell was going on? Who are they? What do they want? His thoughts began to overwhelm him and he started to shake all over.

'Do you think it's the police? Or maybe the Coastguard?' Martin whispered to his nervous brother.

'No way. They would have announced themselves'.

Martin watched the doors in anticipation . The girls huddled together on the seat at the other end of the cabin, clutching at each other's arms.

Suddenly the entrance doors flung open, taking both men backwards in surprise. Trevor fell and fired off two rounds towards the huge, dark figure that emerged. Both rounds pinged off the bulkhead near the doors, spraying plastic shards into the galley. The figure strode over and grabbed him around the throat. Martin was paralysed by anxiety. He watched his brother's body being dragged silently through the doors of the galley and onto the outer deck. The second figure strode towards him. He spotted the automatic next to drops of blood where his brother had fallen. He moved towards the weapon but the second intruder got there first. He hurled himself towards the gun but was overpowered by a blow to the head.

The girls watched helplessly, their eyes wide open, unable to move or make a sound as the second figure lashed out with a metal object, catching Martin's head for the second time.

Martin fell to the floor. The second man dragged Martin's body outside as the first figure made his way back inside, heading towards the girls. As he got closer to them one of the girls fainted, falling to the floor amongst the broken glass.

The huge figure stood in the darkness in front of her and raised a large blade that twinkled in the darkness. The girl's eyes widened as she shrieked, a long drawn out, terrifying scream.

The catamaran bobbed up and down on the heavy waves and returned to silence once again.

Simon walked back from the Harbour Master's Office, across the cobbles of the causeway and towards his colleague who stood, sucking his teeth looking across the bow of *The Wave* below him.

'This is quite interesting Mike; apparently, the Navy sanctioned the use of several marinas in the South West for storage of these drifters', he stated as he stepped over the rusty chain of the harbour boundary.

'What for?' Mike said, continuing his impenetrable stare.

'Well', Simon began, after a long drawn out breath, 'I guess, because of the amount of vessels that were recovered, they dispersed them amongst the other yachts in various marinas so as to avoid suspicion. The harbour master recorded every vessel that was brought into the harbour in order to charge docking fees to the respective owners; it's an age old practice apparently'.

'You have the records?' Mike asked.

'Yeah, I have them here, well; photocopies'. He opened a folder and started to extract the pages.

'Excellent', Mike said in monotone, his teeth gnawing at his forefinger. A frown broke his concentration as he turned to look up at his partner.

'Strange Wilkinson didn't divulge this to you initially… but I guess there was a lot to take in, right?'

Simon nodded and returned to his stack of papers, 'What next then?'

'What time is it?' Mike asked.

'Just after…half past six'.

'I think we should visit one of these marinas. Which one is closest?'

Simon fanned through the papers, searching the letterheads and logos for an address.

'There's one in Falmouth, one in Portsmouth, Liverpool, Anglesea… ah, there's one here; on the Lizard'.

Mike clicked his fingers agreeably and stood up to face him.

The Land Rover began to reverse the length of the harbour, weaving backwards through the sea of tourists and dockyard crew.

'If these vessels have been stripped of their cargo', Mike started as he navigated out of the back window, 'then surely they will have established a smuggling network'.

'That is, if all of these attacks were orchestrated and carried out by the same people', Simon added.

Mike flung the Land Rover round the corner and into the road, much to the annoyance of the on-coming cars. He put it into first and overly applied the acceleration, spinning the rear wheels on the wet tarmac of the road.

'Sorry about that', Mike said grinning towards Simon who was gripping the grab rails on the ceiling.

'Yes, you are right about that, but nevertheless, there must be a system in place to get the loot from the main ship to the shore and into hiding'.

Simon nodded, nervously watching the road ahead of them.

Mike started to drift into thought and inadvertently ran through a red light at a crossing.

'Jeeesus!' Simon exclaimed, 'watch out will you!'

Mike blinked to reality, 'Blimey, didn't see that'.

He applied the foot brake and changed down a gear, much to the relief of his nervous companion.

'There must be a safe house, or collective of safe houses put in place to hold this stuff, if this has been going on for the last sixteen years or so, that is a tremendous amount of cargo to hide aboard a ship! You would need a tanker!'

Simon looked back at him. It was a good point, the involvement was potentially huge. A successful find would likely render them very unpopular as with the case with the nineteenth century Preventive Service where people relied heavily on the illicit trade of rum, silks, tobacco and other goods seized from merchant ships. Although times had dramatically changed and modern day life was not comparable, the locals who depend upon fishing and tourism wouldn't generally turn away a healthy sum for the looking after and storing of illegal goods. When trade dies down in the winter months it makes a nice side earner for the coastal inhabitants.

Simon scoured his notepad once again to find the address of the marina and punched the postcode into the satellite navigation device mounted on the dashboard.

Mike smiled. He wouldn't have thought about that, he would have driven close to the Lizard Peninsular, stopped and asked for directions. Simon was far more practical than he could ever have hoped to be, which was why they always worked together so well in the past. Mike was recognised for his "getting the job done" as was detailed on the commissioners report following his foiling of a large scale smuggling operation in Bristol eight years previous that led to his promotion to Chief Coastguard of Devon and Cornwall, just prior to his dismissal for wasting Naval and Coastguard resources in searching for the "dark ship".

The Land Rover pulled into the entrance of Fowey Harbour; an idyllic marina and home to a plethora of luxury yachts and cruisers with a backdrop of affluent apartments clad in dark timber flanking the shore line. Mike recognised Fowey for boasting over a million tonnes of exported cargo every year and being one of Cornwall's busiest harbours; as such a perfect location to start the investigation, although being almost impossible to record all of the vessels that pass through. Mike nodded as they passed by the rows of sparkling hulls and tall masts; it would have been child's play to hide a dozen yachts here, he thought.

'You could have painted them bright pink and you would still have difficulty finding them', he inadvertently said aloud.

As they neared the reception building Simon ran his finger over the names on his list.

'This is going to be a big job Mike', he sighed.

Mike ignored him and scanned for a parking space, eventually pulling into a disabled parking bay adjacent to the reception building.

Before he got out he reached to his hip and pulled an automatic from its holster.

'Mike!' Simon shouted under his breath, 'what the hell do you think you are doing?'

He reached across, opened the glove compartment and slid the weapon inside.

'It occurred to me that the last thing we want to be flashing around is these'.

Simon followed suit, somewhat relieved.

Inside the reception building a man in a smart shirt sat casually behind a desk watching a small LCD television. He saw the two men enter and sprang to his feet, fumbling for the remote to switch it off.

'Good…' he looked at his watch, '…evening gentlemen, and what can we do for you today?' he asked in text book salesman style.

Mike and Simon simultaneously produced their identification.

'Agents Williams and Jenkins, we represent Her Majesty's Preventive Service'.

The man squinted and looked back at them, confused.

'You are who?'

'We are a department formed to patrol the coasts of South West England to prevent the smuggling and piracy that has been hitting our waters lately, endorsed by Her Majesties Government', Mike retorted.

'I see, and what can I do for you?' the man asked slowly and suspiciously.

Mike walked over to the viewing window overlooking the marina and stared out at the vessels moored in front of them.

'We have a list of boats, some of which will have been brought here over the past few years'.

Simon produced the lists and placed it onto the counter. The man perched a pair of pretentious reading glasses on his nose and held the lists in front of him.

'If these yachts were here Mr… Jenkins, they will be in this record book', he pointed towards a large black book on his desk, 'however there is not a cat in hells chance that you or anyone else bar the police will be looking at it!' he said, folding his arms.

'Look', Mike started, 'we have authority above the police and if you don't let us see the book we can have you arrested for…' Mike paused. He had no idea what they could arrest him for. Maybe they had started too quickly. Only twelve hours ago he was asleep in bed, with no idea of what lay ahead. He wasn't even sure if they *could* make arrests.

'With what exactly, Mr Williams?' the man asked.

Simon stepped forward seeing the dead end.

'We are looking for about one hundred and eighty yachts that could have been involved in acts of piracy. Did you see the news earlier Mr...?'

The man looked at Simon curiously. Of course he had seen the news - the same news flash had preceded every scrolling headline of "News 24" since lunchtime.

'Cox, and yes I did see the news', the man answered unnerved.

'Mr Cox, some of the vessels from this list could have endured the same fate as *The Royal Wave* and it is our job to investigate it. We have been sanctioned by Vice Admiral Wilkinson for this and I doubt that he, nor the police, who are assisting our enquiries, would take it very well if you, Mr Cox, were holding up our investigations'.

Mike rolled his eyes. Again, Simon had won with the softly-softly approach. His forte was brute force; that was the guaranteed method, albeit usually leading to legal issues but it saved a tremendous amount of time in the past. Be that as it may, Simon was making headway so he wandered outside to the harbour.

After a few moments Simon joined him.

'Right, he is cross referencing our lists with his book. He has it backed up on his computer and he's printing us off a matching list now'.

'I don't understand how you manage to get through to guys like that'.

'It's my natural charm', Simon grinned as he lit a cigarette.

"EMPRESS CLEAN AND DRIFTING. CONTACT UR MAN @DZ. WILL BE READY OFF COAST FOR 0100 HRS. TXT WHEN AREA SAFE"

The manicured thumb pressed delete and the message disappeared.

Cox emerged from the reception of the marina holding a handful of papers.

'Here are the records matching your criteria', he said proudly, 'and if there's anything else I can do for you gentlemen please don't hesitate to contact me', he concluded fanning out a deck of business cards. Simon took one and acknowledged him with a nod.

As they began to walk away from the reception building Simon started to thumb through the papers. He could feel Mike's gaze.

'What?' he asked questioning Mike's stare.

'What the hell did you say to him?'

'Nothing much', he played.

'Come on, one moment he was refusing to tell us his name and the next he is kissing your arse!'

'I just have a way with people, you know, it's my natural charm'.

They walked along the floating walkway between the scores of luxury yachts that bobbed in time to the gentle stir of the evening tide. Simon rifled through the papers to find the closest match.

'Ah, T16', he said pointing to one of the entries on the list, '*The Sorcerer*, she's up here I think'.

They turned off the main walkway onto a rabbit warren of smaller trails, each leading to its own vessel.

'T2, T4, just up here… here she is T16, *The Sorcerer*'.

They both stared up in awe at the huge Codecasa Motor Yacht, gleaming white in the ultra violet of the fading evening light.

'Blimey', Mike exclaimed, 'she's a beauty!'

'She sure is', Simon agreed, flicking through the data sheet, 'built in 2005, fifty one metres long, bought for twenty five million Euros. She was purchased in June last year'.

The two looked at the mighty vessel for a few moments until Mike exhaled a long drawn out sigh.

'You know, it occurred to me as we were walking down here, just how serious this is'.

Simon turned towards him.

'How do you mean?'

Mike chewed at his thumb nail.

'Look at this thing Simon. These things are not just owned by any Tom, Dick or Harry; they are owned by celebrities, dignitaries… royalty even. God knows who'.

Simon puffed out his cheeks and nodded. The gravitas of the case hadn't had time to settle on him either.

'And God knows where they are now'.

Silence ensued as if the two were marking their respect. Mike turned back to him.

'You did bring keys didn't you?'

Simon put the notes under his arm and put both hands in his pockets bringing out an entwined handful of keys, labelled with the mooring numbers.

'Ta-dah!'

'I didn't doubt it for a second', Mike stated. *He* would have forgotten the keys without a doubt. His faith in Simon's ability to read his mind and remember what he would have forgotten was justified time and time again. Simon searched through the keys and picked out a black metallic shark shaped fob with the inscription "Sorcerer" etched into it with a sticky label reading "T16" wrapped around the ring.

Mike pulled a torch from his pocket and clicked it on as they made their way up the boarding ramp. The two men stepped precariously onto the oak stern deck and Mike shone the torch beam through the glass doors and into the cabin, highlighting details of the fixtures within.

'I still cannot believe that the Navy could cover up the disappearance of a yacht like this', Simon said, shaking his head at the notes from the folder.

'Pass me the keys'.

Simon gave Mike the keys and he pushed them into the brass lock in the middle of the doors.

'What about the alarm?' Simon suggested.

Mike gave him an arrogant smile and pushed the door open. Nothing.

'If that alarm had gone off...' Simon started.

'What alarm? I bet you ten quid that she has no power!'

The two ventured inside the darkness of the cabin. Mike shone the powerful torch beam around.

It was immaculate as Mike had expected; the interior was of showroom quality, albeit for some natural dust that had gathered and the occasional cobweb in the corners of some of the cabin windows. He approached the stairs to the upper deck leading to the bridge and began to ascend them. Once inside the vast bridge he seated himself at the leather Captain's chair and adjusted it to his height. He placed the key into the ignition and turned it. Nothing happened. Downstairs, Simon flicked at a light switch and almost simultaneously the two men concluded: 'No power!'

Mike clattered back down the steps into the galley.

'How many vessels are on that list?' he asked, knowing that Simon would have tallied it up in anticipation of such a question.

'One hundred and fifty one', he answered firmly.

'Spread over how many marinas?'

Simon looked back over his notes, 'Twenty five, spread all over the country and one in Ireland'.

Mike looked at him, with an authoritative expression.

'Right, I want teams of two to go to every location and I want them to enter every boat. I want photos of every vessel, every interior, the carpet lines, and reports on the power...'

He paused to take a breath.

'And I want it done as soon as possible!'

'I'll get on the blower then', Simon said obediently, clicking his pen closed. He had no problem with Mike assuming authority; it wasn't his idealism anyway and Mike had the arrogance and level of aggression that his position warranted.

He stepped out on the deck and pulled out his phone to speak to Nelson; their first contact since they had left earlier that morning.

'Sylvia, hi, it's Simon Jenkins…' Simon spoke into his Blackberry.

Mike pushed at the bottom panel of one of the units in the galley confirming his thoughts; the carpet under the unit was again darker than that outside, as it was on *the Royal Wave*. Mike sucked at his teeth. How could the attackers cut the power? How do you remotely cut power to a yacht without being seen? What is it that cuts the power? The questions circled in his mind as Simon stepped back into the cabin.

'Ok, I have dispatched sixteen groups of two to visit the marinas on the list the harbour master gave to me. One lucky couple will be going to… Ireland!' he said in a game show host style.

Mike smiled, 'Let's move on to the next one Si', he said standing up from the floor.

Simon's smile faded and he sighed. It had been a long day and he was hoping that this would have been a good enough confirmation of his suspicions to leave and go home.

He looked at the list and ran his finger over the next closest match.

'V23', he said, in an overly exhausted manner in a hope that Mike would pick up on the hint.

'Right', Mike started as he made his way outside.

Cox's complexion was pale as he paced up and down behind the reception desk, holding the telephone between his shoulder and his right cheek, fidgeting with the coiled telephone wire with his left hand.

'…But what could I do? They were officers of Revenue & Customs, Preventive Service or something, they said…'

His bottom lip began to twitch as he listened.

'I will tell them I am locking up, ok, I will get rid of them… no they haven't asked any questions really… well nothing that would… no, I haven't said nothing incriminating I swear it!'

He took hold of the receiver and held it away from his ear looking into the mouth piece; the recipient had put the phone down. He placed the phone into the cradle and looked through the blinds of the window into the marina. He could just make out the two agents approaching another vessel. He grabbed his coat from the hat stand in the corner of the office and clumsily dashed outside.

As they walked towards the next boat Simon noticed that Mike had obviously latched onto another chain of thought because of the way he tapped his forehead with his pen; a classic and amusing illustration of his concentration.

'One thing that has occurred to me is; if these yachts are being looted, where is the loot being off loaded to, and by whom? There must be a huge smuggling operation being led by someone and others turned a blind eye. Something of this scale can't be swept under the carpet. Not for sixteen years!'

Simon looked at him as he searched in his pocket for the next set of keys.

They stopped in front of a smallish boat with a tarnished black canvas hood. The hull bore a complex pattern of scratches, dents and algae.

'Are you sure?' Mike asked.

'V23, that is what it says here, and these are the keys', Simon confirmed.

As they moved towards the stern Simon read from his notes.

'Err, a Nineteen Eighty Two Sea Ray Three Fifty Express at thirty five metres. She's been here since Nineteen Ninety Four… as you can tell', he said looking at her solemn contrasting appearance.

Mike stepped onto the rear deck and moved towards the entrance. Simon passed him the key and he unlocked the doors, pushing hard to open them due to the corrosion from the long spell in the marina. He shone the torch beam inside. It was extremely dusty but under that the cabin was, again, immaculate. Almost instinctively now, Mike made his way to the upstairs bridge. Simon looked around at the interior, pushing with his foot at the lower unit panels; exposing the carpet underneath. The white leather seats of the bridge looked like they had never been used. If Mike was right, whoever cleaned up after them made a superb job. He perched upon the seat, which crackled beneath him, and switched the ignition to the "on" position. He climbed down the stairs, flicking at a light switch on his way down.

'Not a sausage!' he exclaimed.

As he walked into the cabin his footsteps made a hollow thump on the floor.

They both looked down at the carpet. Mike bent down and wiped the dust from a metallic catch.

'Engine access?' Mike sounded surprised, 'if this is the entrance to the engine then there is absolutely no way that someone could cut the power from the outside, right?' he looked up at Simon standing above him.

He pulled at the catch and the panel opened with a corrosive screech then shone his torch inside.

'Well…' Simon pointed at a translucent plastic tube, 'that is the fuel line there, doesn't look like it's been cut, there's diesel still inside it, look'.

Mike shone the beam around the components. Sure enough the yellowing fuel line had the distinctive red diesel inside it. He shone the beam towards the engine itself.

'It looks ok, no sign of a burn out'.

He leant right over into the compartment to the manual ignition.

As he grappled with it he stopped and levered his way back out again.

'If the engine cut off, then maybe it isn't to do with the engine after all', he suggested. He stood up and made his way to the fuse box on the wall of the galley. He opened it up as Simon watched curiously and pulled at a fuse labelled "ENGINE". The fuse came away from its housing and he held it in front of the torch light towards Simon.

'Fuse has blown!' he concluded. Returning to the fuse box he pulled all of the remaining fuses from the housing and examined each one individually in front of the torch beam.

'Every one of them has blown'.

Simon went over to the fuse box and rubbed at the wall above it.

'That's odd, there's no sign of a burnout, are you sure they have all gone?'

Mike tapped at his head with his pen again, this time more vigorously.

'Very interesting', he said quietly with a half-smile.

'Excuse me!' Cox's voice sounded from outside the yacht.

'Ah, Mr Cox…' Simon began as he made his way to the stern doors.

'I'm afraid, gentlemen, I am locking the marina now and I must ask you both to leave'.

'Okay Mr Cox, we're done here now anyway', Simon replied, relieved at the inevitable escape for the night.

As the two men left the boat, Cox held out his hand to receive the keys. Simon delved into his pockets and dropped the huge pile into the nervous man's hands.

'Thank you for your time and help Mr Cox', Simon said to his saviour from something that could quite easily have taken all night.

Cox hurriedly stepped on board to lock the boat's doors.

Mike and Simon strode off along the bobbing walkway towards the carpark.

'What was with him?' Simon asked whilst wiping the sweat from his hand onto his jacket.

'Strange that he didn't mention closing up before', Mike said, looking behind him at the anxious Cox, running to and from the yachts checking the doors.

'If I were feeling impulsive I would say that he was frightened'.

'Yeah, I wonder if he got a warning or something?'

'Are we going to call it a day?' Simon asked hopefully.

Mike stared straight ahead for a few moments until they reached their vehicle. He pressed the remote and the repeaters flashed as it unlocked.

As they both got in, Simon could tell that Mike was preoccupied. Not daring to ask in fear of not going home that night, he looked at him enticingly.

Mike turned to him.

'I've had a thought', he said excitedly.

'Oh?' Simon replied uncomfortably.

'How do you fancy going to the pub?'

'Music to my ears!' Simon said, exhaling in relief.

They both put their seatbelts on and Mike started the engine. As they pulled out of the carpark and onto the road Simon tapped at the passenger side window, 'There's a pub just down there on the right Mike'.

Mike continued to drive down the road in the opposite direction.

'Do you know of a better one?' he persisted.

'The Ship'.

'The Ship? Where?'

'Mousehole', Mike stated, while still staring at the dark road ahead of them.

'Mousehole?' Simon questioned, 'that's got to be nearly an hour away!'

'I am thinking that we can look over every single yacht on our list but what we really need to find out is who is behind the smuggling operation. We know the trend of these yachts and it is baffling me to say the least. What we don't yet know is where whatever was stolen is or was being held'.

Simon slid down his seat and put his head in his hands.

'We get to the bottom of who is heading up that and we break into who is providing the loot'.

'Hang on Mike, are you sure that's such a good idea?' Simon asked, wide awake with concern.

'I have a feeling that if anyone were to know anything about anyone, Black would! You know his connections to the Game'.

The Game, as Mike referred to it with affection, is a maritime term for smuggling, stemming from hundreds of years of illicit goods and contraband trafficking past the watchful eyes of the Preventive servicemen. From the beaches to the safe houses; this was a highly dangerous but essential system that was endured. They were hailed as brave heroes and due to the nature of the business and the risks and strategies involved (the fact that they could be shot and killed on sight by any Preventive man not on the smuggling payroll) they referred to it as "The Game".

As the Land Rover made its way towards Mousehole, the two agents discussed their strategy. Simon furiously scribbled away in his notepad to take in all of the finer details. Although his experience of interrogations was not in question – his strategising was.

'How do you know that he will tell you a thing Mike? Didn't you betray him? I know that you had personal connections to that place but do you think you can just march in there and demand information?'

Mike was dead pan, 'No, but if I play it right, I have a wild card up my sleeve. If it works we will emerge with what we want to know, or at the least; everything *he* knows'.

'How?' Simon asked.

Chapter 5

<u>The Ship Inn</u>

The sun had long since set and had melted into the horizon saturating the sky with a burnt umber gradient. A bitter cold breeze blew into Mousehole cove from the open sea beyond its defensive harbour, creating a symphony from the masts of the moored up boats. The roads were wet with sea spray and Mike turned on the wipers of the Land Rover as he negotiated the tight roads leading to the picturesque harbour.

'What time is it Si?'

'About midnight', Simon said looking at his watch from the light of the passing streetlights.

'Good, so any tourists that *were* there will be long gone by now'.

'And if they aren't?' Simon quickly interjected.

Mike smiled, 'They'll be gone, don't worry. Black will have kicked them out bang on eleven'.

'We can't just barge in there and find ourselves confronted by twenty American tourists in shorts and t-shirts', Simon played with Mike. He knew that wasn't going to happen; it wasn't even tourist season, he was just fishing, but Mike wasn't going to bite.

Mike trickled the Land Rover down the steep coastal road into the small fishing village; a road that he had driven a thousand times previously.

'Did you know that it is one of the smallest active fishing harbours in Britain?' Mike regaled as they neared the brow overlooking the framed postcard view of the village below.

Simon looked at him awkwardly, 'Yes, I have been here before you know'.

'Yes, but did you know that fact?'

Simon shook his head, 'Well, no, but...'

'Ah, you see, little known facts such as the Ship being an early sixteenth Century inn where Sir Walter Raleigh smoked his first pipe tobacco?'

'No, I didn't'.

Mike looked over towards his bemused companion and smirked. His childhood had revolved around Mousehole and he felt a sense of pride as they neared it.

As the Land Rover pulled into the harbor, Mike slowed down and gazed out of the side window at the granite building facing the harbour with a large metallic gold sign "The Ship Inn"; the exterior lanterns of which illuminated the shallow waters below it.

'The Ship. If anyone knows anything, I'd bet my pension Bill Black will'.

They trickled down the paving to the adjacent carpark near the harbour wall and pulled into a vacant space.

Mike reached across into the glove compartment, pulled out his weapon and slid it into his hip holster.

Simon looked under his brow at the weapon being hidden under the navy overcoat.

'You expecting trouble Mike?' he asked with a slight nervous undertone.

'Honestly, Si, I have no idea…'

He looked over his shoulder at the glistening lights of the pub.

'It's been a long time since I last walked through that door… a lot has happened since'.

The pair walked towards the pub, the reflective strip of their HMPS uniforms highlighted by the string of lights attached to the railings of the harbour.

As they approached, Mike stopped and looked at his partner.

'Right, remember…'

'…Don't worry Mike, I know what to do', Simon interrupted in an attempt to reassure him.

'Good luck!' he said raising his eyebrows.

Mike wrenched the corroded iron handle clockwise and pushed the door open with a piercing squeal.

As they walked through the porchway towards the inner door to the main bar area, the stench of stale cigarette and cigar smoke combined with the odour of spilled beer hit them; although compensated for the undertone of sweat emanating from the twenty or so fishermen, fresh from their shift, standing at the bar. Mike peered from the inner doorway at the photography on the walls; local heroes, fishing boats and famous wrecks supported by model ships in yellowing plastic cases. Pewter tankards hung awkwardly from the ceiling beams along with various fishing paraphernalia and netting.

As they stepped forward from the safety of the porch and into the bar area, the ambient mumble from the cliental feathered out to a silence. A large bare patch of ground opened up before them as the mesmerised fishermen looked at the two agents, dressed in their blue and florescent orange jackets stepping precariously towards the bar.

Through the parting crowd of dubious onlookers Mike made eye contact with the landlord.

Black was a colossal individual with a long entangled and neglected grey beard; his head bald and sporting various scars illuminated from the strong spot lights above the bar. His vast arms lay flat, palms down, on the beer sodden bar, like giant stabilisers. His blackened eyes were small slits beneath the years of wrinkles which began to widen as Mike moved closer to him. With every step Black's expression mutated from jovial grin into a wrinkled leathery frown.

An overwhelming sense of nostalgia rushed over Mike as he picked out the familiar faces from the crowd. Desperate to nod, smile and gesture to his past acquaintances he knew that he couldn't show remorse for his betrayal nor could he show signs of weakness. He had to remain strong.

Relaxing slightly, he quickened his pace the last few steps to the foot of the oak bar and Black stood up to his full height behind it.

An awkward silence ensued as the two men ingested each other's appearance.

Simon fidgeted nervously with the Velcro pads of his jacket pocket.

'Hello William', Mike broke the silence with a slightly cracked voice.

Black looked around at the surrounding fishermen, who in turn looked back at him with equal perplexity.

Mike put his hand in his jacket pocket, causing unintentional concern from the crowd who moved defensively backwards. Black remained silent and visibly dumbstruck; his darkened eyes bulging, taking in the unexpected confrontation.

'I need to ask you a few questions…' he fished out his identification card and laid it onto the bar.

Black's eyes darted down and back up again; quickly acknowledging the identification card. His tanned skin began to deepen into a grey mulberry colour and his forearms began to shake.

'Is there anywhere we can go to talk William?' Mike pursued seeing the building rage in front of him.

Black opened his mouth beneath the grey overgrown moustache and inhaled a long, deep rattling breath through his crooked tobacco stained teeth.

'You have got a lot of nerve showing up here!' he exhaled in a deep gravely Cornish crackle. He picked up the identification card and closed, it 'and maybe you will be thinking twice about where you drink in the future you faithless, fucking degenerate!'

On the last words he threw the identification card at Mike's face. The wallet dropped to the sticky floor boards and Mike calmly stooped to collect it.

Black's rage had reached boiling point and he gritted his tarnished teeth.

'Get rid of him!' he roared.

The mob shuffled towards them, drawing an assortment of blades and knives.

Mike and Simon responded by drawing their Automatics from their hip holsters. They had both had weapons training prior to their surprising new roles; Simon in particular had used his weapon in self-defence on numerous occasions on drug smuggling operations, but this seemed somewhat grittier and he had never been in this kind of situation. If Mike hadn't brought his weapon from the Land Rover he wouldn't have thought about bringing his.

They held a defensive stance in front of the grumbling nervous crowd in a second tense silence.

Mike moved his aim towards Black as two men holding archaic revolvers made their way in front of the crowd.

'Steady Simon, take it easy', Mike whispered, assessing the situation and his colleague's undoubted disposition.

He made his way forward a few steps until the barrel of his automatic met with the purple leathery skin of Black's forehead.

'As I was saying Bill', Mike caught his breath, 'I need to ask you a few questions'.

Black stepped backwards, leaving a large indentation from the barrel in the centre of his forehead. He looked out of the corner of his squinted eyes and nodded to the restless crowd, who responded by lowering their weapons and retreating from the bar.

The pressure behind Black's eyes began to disperse, his temper began to calm and he slowly returned to his natural blemished tan. Without taking his eyes from his adversary, he pushed his hand below the bar and retrieved a bottle of rum and with his other he pinched two yellowing crystal tumblers from inside a nest of pint mugs on a shelf above him. He turned and reached behind the till, retrieving a balsa box of cigars and shuffled his vast body along the floorboards to the edge of the bar; the reverberation from his footsteps clinking the glasses stacked precariously on the shelving.

'Tom!' Black shouted, 'lock us in will yer, we don't want any more uninvited guests in 'ere tonight'.

A small stocky man in yellow, canvas fishing trousers walked purposefully to the porchway and slid a huge, metal bolt across the main door. He closed the inner door behind him and flicked a switch that shut off the external lights.

The agents holstered their weapons and moved together. Mike leaned towards Simon and mumbled under his breath, 'Stick around and watch your back, I'll be a while… and don't forget…' he added with a wink.

He started after Black who was making his way towards the stairs marked "Private", that someone has humorously suffixed with an 's'.

A tall, scruffy man in blue, waterproof trousers walked towards the back of the pub, cautiously, watching as Black disappeared into the smoky hallway. He stopped at a well-used metal payphone and picked up the receiver.

The phone was answered and he slipped in a coin.

'It's me', the fisherman spoke quietly into the abused mouthpiece.

'Bill's just gone into the back room with some official looking guy, could be Customs…'

As they walked towards the stairs, Black looked back at Mike who had clocked the box of cigars he was carrying.

'I got a receipt for these you know', he said followed by a long drawn out cackle. Mike cocked a half-smile; Black's humour is what kept their spirits up during the long nights at sea. As he reached the staircase, he stopped; the pictures on the walls overwhelming him with dusty memories. The Ship had been a base for him since he was twelve; his parents having been killed at sea in a ferry accident and orphaning him to the local fishing community, who brought up the young and impressionable boy. The pub, in turn, became a home for years after. Mike had worked behind the bar at thirteen and by his fifteenth birthday was living and working under Black.

As Black precariously ascended the steep, groaning stairway, clutching his rum and cigars, Mike followed; his eyes flicking from left to right at the plethora of framed photographs. He stopped at one and turned to face it. Black sensed this and turned around to find him staring at a picture of himself aged around eighteen along with Black's crew aboard "The Osprey".

'You can cut down a five hundred year old oak tree, chop it up and burn it', Black began, 'but its roots will always remain firmly where it once stood'.

Mike looked up at him with a questioning look.

'You have sold yourself out, laddy; become what we despised and what we worked all those years against, but your roots will always remain here...' he paused, 'here in Cornwall, in smuggling'.

Mike looked back at the picture as Black continued his ascent.

There was nothing that he could say; he knew only too well that he had "sold out" as Black firmly referred to it. An overwhelming sensation of remorse shrouded him as he watched Black's bulk arrive at the top of the stairs. It could have been so easy to have given everything up and return to what he had once had a passion for but times had changed; he couldn't justify grand piracy and potential murder as he couldn't ignore it. He screwed his eyes up and continued up the hazy stairs, two at a time.

At the top was the house office with a desk and two chesterfield armchairs that formed the bow and stern of Mike's ship when he played as a child. Black was an exceptional father figure to him and would play with him for hours, relentlessly using what precious little time he had left in his day for him. Nostalgia once again reared its ugly enticing head.

Black was seated behind the desk. He had opened the rum and was in the process of pouring two glasses, one of which he pushed along the heavily used mahogany desk towards Mike.

'Bill, I need to know...'

'Michael, do you know what was the first thing I felt when you walked through those doors?' Black interjected.

Mike chewed his cheek pensively.

'Disappointment. Not anger, but disappointment'.

Black's tongue protruded from his purple lips and ran along the ridge of his moustache.

'And do you know what the first thought that occurred to me when you approached the bar? What would your father make of you, standing there all prim and proper in your flashy uniform'.

Mike looked down at the floor. The same thought had occurred to him the very second he had enrolled as a Customs Officer trainee.

'Do you think he would be proud of you?'

He straightened himself and looked into Black's darkened eyes.

'Bill, I need you to…'

'And another thought I had was; what makes you think I am gonna tell you a damn thing boy?' Black interrupted again.

Mike stared at him. He was grinning under the cloaking moustache and was already pouring his second glass of rum. Mike took a deep over-accentuated breath.

'Let me make this clear Black!' Mike even surprised himself in the tone that he had mustered, 'we have enough evidence to put you away for a very long time'.

Black shrugged, 'And what evidence is that then matey?'

'We have been hatching a case against you for months and with one phone call I could confirm a detail that would send you down for a minimum of, say, twenty five years?'

Black's beard widened revealing a toothy grin and he chuckled a tarry laugh.

'What case?'

'The Cuban Cigar scam of Nineteen Ninety Seven'

Black stopped and gave an unintentional, yet unavoidable look of concern.

'You have nothing on me, that was over ten years ago… they'd have caught me long ago if that was the case. And besides, you know you have nothing on me and who are ya gonna call? Eh?'

Satisfied with this, Black wrenched his feet upon the desk and crackled another laugh as he picked a cigar from the wooden box. He sniffed at it and wedged it in his mouth, striking a match on the wall behind him. He lit the cigar and flicked the spent match at Mike.

Mike calmly wiped at the spot on his jacket where the match had hit, and returned his focus to him.

'Black, this is your one and only chance of staying out of prison', he said calmly as he pulled out the large, heavy chair and sat to face him, pushing his large, boat sized boots to one side.

'Tell me who is behind the recent spates of piracy on the shipping lanes! At the very least I need the main contact for the shoreline'.

Mike fixed his gaze as his interviewee shuffled uneasily in his seat. He knew that by mentioning the shoreline Black would suspect a far deeper investigation. Shoreline contacts were the quintessential aspect of any smuggling operation and paramount to the successful link between pirate and consumer.

'What makes you think that, even if I did know anything, I would tell the likes of you?'

He moved his feet from the desk, leaned forward and blew a billow of smoke into Mike's face.

'Do you have any idea where you are?' Black asked, 'You don't just walk into *my* pub and start issuing idle threats at me, my boy!'

Mike stood up from the chair and walked across the room. He took his mobile phone from his jacket and faced an array of old photographs adhered to the wall with yellowing sticky tape and pins. It was time for the wild card.

'What if I were to say the name Alan Whitaker?' Mike prompted still facing the wall. He didn't need to look at Black's expression to know that name will have wounded his confidence.

Black shuffled again, his eyes fixed on the back of Mike's head.

After a few seconds of thought Black lowered his gaze.

'A name that, I doubt, you have any connections to whatsoever, certainly not by "Alan"'.

Mike turned around safe in the knowledge he had struck the right chord, that Alan Whitaker, Director of HM Customs in London would be the man who would have killed to put the likes of Black away, in his "Cleansing of the Coast" operation that earned him his position.

Black looked nervous, his eyes had widened and he was chewing his bottom lip.

'What if…' Mike started again, 'I had the evidence against you that Whitaker needed to close the case and put you away for what would probably equate to…' he paused, '…the rest of your life?'

Black nodded, knowing the possibility of this being the truth. The grapevine had warned him of the arrests that had been made in and around the Caribbean only a few months previously.

Mike began to push a number into the phone. Black stared at it.

'What are you doing Mike?' he asked with a subtle tremble to his voice.

'What I need from you, William, is for you to nod if you are going to help me or shake your head if you are not'.

Black kept his eyes on the phone. Mike pressed the "speakerphone" button and the phone crackled to life with the ringing tone. On every note, Black's right eye twitched, reverberating his cheek.

Mike's confidence began to rise, extinguishing his anxiety.

Ring Ring.

Ring Ring.

'Whitaker', the recipient's London accent crackled the phone to life.

Black froze.

'Alan, its Mike Williams, how are you?'

'Mike!' an excited voice responded, 'so good to hear from you again. When are you coming to London again, I owe you dinner…'

A noticeable bead of sweat ran the length of Blacks brow, down onto his cheekbone and finally settling on the fringe of his beard.

'Yes, soon Alan, thanks. I was just touching base on the…'

'Cuban Cigar Scam!' the voice interjected, 'yes I was going to email you about that. Can you confirm that Black was involved yet? We only need evidence of him being out of the country at that time, that's all we need to nail the lid on the bastard, Mike'.

Mike looked towards Black for a long tense moment; inviting him to answer.

Black crushed the cigar between his thick fingers and remained transfixed with the phone call. The hot embers landed on the thick grey-ginger hairs of his forearm. Without a flinch he slowly nodded.

Smiling, Mike turned on the spot and walked to the other end of the room.

'Yes, that was what I was ringing you about, I am sorry to tell you Alan that Black was in Cornwall during that time. I have evidence supporting it unfortunately'.

'Ah shit', the voice crackled, 'ah well, you win some, you lose some eh Mike, that's the nature of the business I guess'.

'I guess so. I have to go Alan, I'll be in touch'.

'Okay Mike, thanks for the call'.

The phone went silent.

Mike slid the phone back into his pocket and walked over to the desk where a very sombre looking Black sat staring into his empty glass.

Outside the pub Simon lit another cigarette and closed his phone, smiling.

'Alright William', Mike started again, 'I need names, contacts, anything and everything you know, and I need it now'.

Black stood up and walked wearily towards a chest of drawers.

'You are one thoroughbred bastard!' he croaked under his breath, 'you have sunk low, Michael, you hit the bottom…'

'Just give me what I need and I will get out of here'.

'You want to watch your back my friend. It's not me you want to be afraid of'.

He wrenched at a large metal box from the bottom of the wooden drawers.

'You are going to be upsetting a whole host of people with your poking your nose where it doesn't belong'.

'I'm running out of time and patience Bill', Mike spat, 'it only takes one phone call remember'.

Black screwed up his leathery face and worked at the rusting padlock with an equally tatty key.

Outside, Simon dropped the cigarette onto the floor amongst an array of other spent butts and looked at his watch; it had been nearly an hour since the hoax call.

Mike clicked his pen shut and closed his notepad.

'I need the name of the instigator Bill; I know you know more about it than you are letting on. You have given me five names here, but none of them hold any real threat, not high enough up any food chain to orchestrate such a grand scale operation as this'.

Black knew what he wanted. He looked up at Mike and sighed.

'We don't know who it is. No one does. It is a contingency in case the operation was compromised…' he paused, 'like this'.

'But you can get me the name right?' Mike pushed. He had applied about as much pressure as he had dared like a snake charmer with an angry Python – it wouldn't have taken much to have pushed Black into killing him there and then.

'Yes', Black mumbled under his moustache. He looked at his watch, 'I will call him tonight to drop the name to me here, later'.

'Why can't he tell you over the phone?' Mike asked impatiently.

'He doesn't trust the phone. We all agreed that at the time'.

'Then I will wait until he gets here'.

'If he suspects anything he will run a mile and you will never find him. It will also sever me from any connections at the same time'.

Mike stared at Black intently.

'William', he spoke softly to the broken man, 'if you are bullshitting me, you will go down! Do you understand what I am telling you?'

'I have already agreed to help you haven't I, Coast guard, now go, and leave me be!'

Feeling a pinch of compassion for the crumbled smuggler, Mike started for the door to the stairs.

Black reached out and grabbed his shoulder, gripping him hard.

'I'm a fucking dead man you know, a dead man if anyone finds out!'

'Then pray that I won't tell anyone', Mike answered threateningly.

The sense of compassion overwhelmed him as he began to descend the stairs and he paused. He looked back at him and relaxed his composure, 'you'll be safe Bill, don't worry. You get me that name and I promise you will be safe'.

Under the watchful eyes of the now, very drunken mob, Mike made his way to the inner door, slid open the latch and opened it. He turned to catch Black's gaze as he retook his position behind the bar. The two men acknowledged one another before Mike disappeared into the porch, slamming the solid exterior door behind him. Black closed his eyes in relief and began scratching under the bar for another bottle of rum. He pulled out a fistful of bottles and slammed each one on the wet bar.

'C'mon lads, lock that blasted door Tom, and let's finish this rum for God's sakes'.

The two agents turned to hear the almighty cheer from inside the old inn and then continued across the harbour to the car park.

'How did it go?' asked the relieved Simon, putting out another cigarette on the cobbled harbour side road.

Mike started to unload his automatic. 'Good; the call actually worked, well done. Although I am not sure Whitaker is a Londoner but still'.

Simon looked at Mike's expression with a querying look.

'What, you didn't think it was going to?'

'I don't know Si, I knew it was his weakness but Black is a volatile man. He would have crawled across broken glass before going back to jail'.

He got into the vehicle and pushed the keys into the ignition.

'What next?' Simon asked, intrigued by the apparent success.

'Black buckled under the pressure and gave me these notes'.

Mike handed over the notepad to Simon, 'But he doesn't have the full list of contacts for each part of the scheme. He has a man who is going to drop it off to him tonight. I said we would pick it up first thing in the morning'.

'He admitted his part in this?' Simon asked excitedly.

'Indirectly'.

'What time do we come back tomorrow?'

'We're coming back in about two hours'.

Mike started the engine and switched on the lights, which illuminated the spray from the breaking waves on the outer rocks.

Black watched the Land Rover disappear from The Ship's bar window then down to the mobile phone buried in the palm of his giant hand.

As he left the window and re-adjusted the curtains a small, dark dinghy puttered through the narrow harbour entrance opposite the inn's frontage, and disappeared into the mass of fishing boats in the shallow moorings.

The Land Rover navigated its way around the hairpins of the coastal road. Mike looked dead ahead replaying the nights events in his mind.

'Jesus!' Simon exclaimed as he held up the notebook, 'I can't believe he has implicated John Moore'.

'I know', Mike said without a flinch.

'He has implicated him as point of contact for allowing contraband into Penzance. He is the harbour master I spoke to earlier, for God's sake!'

Mike glanced at Simon's astonishment.

'How long do you think this guy has been abusing his position of trust for? How many others like him do you think there are, Mike?'

Mike continued to concentrate on the dark roads. Simon's naivety illustrated his sheltered city life.

'I have absolutely no idea', he responded.

He pulled the Land Rover over into a lay-by and turned it around to face the way they had come and switched off the engine.

'I'm gonna get some kip. In two hours we're going back. I want to keep up the pressure on him'.

He slid down the seat and rested his head on the head rest. Simon, watching his every move, copied and put the notepad down. He opened his cigarettes and took out his lighter.

'Not in here!' Mike snapped with his eyes firmly shut.

Simon rolled his eyes and slid the cigarette back into the packet.

Mousehole Harbour was almost silent save for the dim rumblings of the ocean and the subtle jovial sounds emanating from The Ship.

A man in a dark wetsuit negotiated the wet stone steps of the harbour wall in front of the dimly lit inn. He stepped onto the road immediately in front of the wooden door, held his arm up in the air and gestured towards it. Five similarly dressed men joined him on the road, each one producing a small silenced automatic machine pistol from holsters strapped to their chests.

They moved closer to the door of the pub and took up strategic positions. One of the men moved towards the door and loaded his weapon.

Inside the pub, Black watched as a few of the men began to wrestle on the rug in front of the fireplace and, cracked his first smile since Williams had left, as they lost their balance and fell over an ornate brass table. Could he really give all this up? But was he prepared to sell them all out in order to keep it? The torturous thoughts soon turned his grin into a frown as another countless glass of rum passed underneath his obtrusive moustache. He was ashamed that he had been pressurised into breaking but he still had the choice of running.

He shook his head as the thoughts ran into suggestions of finding out where Mike was living. He couldn't risk killing a man who was investigating him; it would be like walking into a Police Station holding a blood stained knife.

Knock knock

The pub went silent.

Black re-adjusted his blurred vision with a succession of blinks and stared at the wooden door inside the porch way. The men at the bar shifted around nervously.

Knock knock knock

The tall, scruffy fisherman in the tan trousers barged forward through the crowd of nervous spectators towards the door.

'I'll get it', he confidently shouted.

Black looked suspiciously at the man, and darted his eyes toward the other men at the bar who looked back at him with equal confusion.

The scruffy fisherman peered through the spy-hole and began to unlock the door.

'WAIT!' Black shouted.

The pub door burst open and the fisherman's body burst backwards against the porch wall with a mist of red spray.

The publicans scattered and overturned the tables for cover.

Black shook violently as he reached behind the bar instinctively for two sawn off double barrelled shotguns. He pulled them into view, aimed them at the door and fired.

The first intruder through the door bore the full brunt of Black's shot and was flung backwards against the wall, clearing it of the picture frames as he fell.

In the small, white washed cottage across the road, John Hicks, a retired fisherman, sat bolt upright in bed.

'Margaret, did you hear that? It sounded like...'

His wife quickly interjected, 'A car back-firing? Go back to sleep John'.

John climbed out of bed and peered through the net curtains of the bedroom window just as the sound of Black's shotgun rang out a second time. As he squinted to pick out the detail he saw a flash from inside the doorway as the intruders grouped together to return fire.

'My God Marg, ring the police, get the police, it's bloody gunfire!'

The second intruder burst through and returned fire as Black reloaded his weapons. Black crouched behind the bar beneath the raining splinters of wood and glass.

The intruders had taken strategic positions behind walls and tables and were firing indiscriminately at Black's men, who were dropping with each burst of muffled fire.

Black opened a cupboard beneath the bar and pulled out a metal container. Bullets pinged all around him. He opened the box and emptied an assortment of revolvers onto the bar floor. He looked towards the far end of the bar and saw Tom taking refuge behind a brass table.

'Tom!' he shouted above the tremendous noise of smashing glass and thuds of rounds hitting the old stone walls.

'Tom!' he shouted again. Tom found Black's gaze. Black slid a couple of the antiquated revolvers across the debris covered floor towards him.

Tom retrieved them and gave a wave and a grin. They were always loaded and were kept under the bar from the days when Black and his men used them for scaremongering.

Tom cocked two of them, drew a deep breath and stood up from the brass table to return fire.

He fired the full six rounds of each pistol at the door; the shots rang out loud as splinters of the ancient wood scattered across the entrance way and out onto the street. The smoke from the gunfire had accumulated in the centre of the bar causing the intruders' confusion. A terrifying silence followed.

The intruders began to move in closer towards the bar; their footsteps highlighted by the crunch of broken glass beneath them. They each fired indiscriminate short bursts through the smoke, into the bar area. As they got closer Black made out one of the silhouettes. If he were to stay put much longer he knew he was a dead man. He crept to the end of the bar and raised his shotgun in preparation to make a run for it. As the intruders came into range he fired.

Two of the men fell to the floor clutching their shoulders as Black made a dash for the back room.

'It's Black, I'll take him', shouted one of the men.

'Yes sir!' replied the other, who stooped to help one of his wounded colleagues.

Black dashed through the upturned tables and chairs and found the doorway to the stairway.

As he ascended them, three at a time, the leader of the masked intruders got to the archway at the bottom. He loaded his weapon with a fresh clip, drew back the reloading mechanism and emptied the clip into the stairway corridor. The bullets ripped through the plasterwork and picture frames.

As the smoke cleared he began to ascend towards the office, reloading with a third clip.

Mike sprang up out of his seat of the Land Rover as two police cars raced around the coastal road in front of them with their sirens blaring. As he rubbed his eyes another followed, then a police van and an ambulance.

'Bloody hell!' he exclaimed as he turned to Simon, who was still asleep with his MP3 player blasting through his earphones. Mike yanked them out.

'What you do that for?' Simon shouted, startled.

Mike started the engine, 'Something's going on and I don't like it!'

He pressed a large orange switch on the roof near the sunroof controls and the vehicle's blue lights started trailing followed by a high pitched siren.

As he reached the top step, the intruder burst out a few more shots; Black returned fire, hitting the doorframe which collapsed. The intruder crouched down, covering himself from the heavy oak frame. He reloaded once again, sprang up and flung his weapon around the corner, spraying the room with rounds until the clip emptied. He waited a few seconds; made his way inside. Black was sitting back in his armchair covered in blood, his feet on the desk in front of him. He had been hit several times in the chest.

Satisfied, the masked man turned to leave the room as the sirens began to penetrate the ringing in his ears. Pushing on the wall, he propelled himself down the stairwell.

'Let's finish up', he shouted to the other men who had become aware of the approaching sirens.

'Take them to the boat and start the engine', he pointed at the two injured men on the floor.

The masked intruder made his way to the bar, grabbed a surviving bottle of vodka from the shelf and smashed the neck on the bar's bevelled edge. He reached into his pocket, pulled out a lighter, ignited it and dropped it onto the soaking floor which flared up instantly.

The fire began to engulf the lounge as the last man ran out of the smouldering doorway. He stopped and turned to see one of his colleagues slumped against the back wall of the porch where Black's first shot threw him. As he crouched down to pull him away from the threatening flames, he heard the sound of the dinghy motor from the harbour, coupled with the unmistakable sounds of the approaching sirens. He turned back to the burning wooden door and jumped outside onto the road as two police cars screeched around the corner towards the harbour wall. John Hicks watched from his window as the man jumped down the harbour steps and into the darkness of the moorings.

Mike crunched the Land Rover into second gear to slow it down as he approached the harbour town, which was completely saturated by police and flashing lights, strobing the frontages of the harbour side houses. As he trickled the vehicle further down the road he watched the crowd, who had accumulated, being kept at bay by police officers. In front of them; the burning pub they were in not an hour ago.

'Shit!' Mike shouted furiously, 'call this in Si and let them know we are here. They should know already with the police being here but call it anyway'.

Mike pulled the vehicle up alongside an ambulance and snapped on the handbrake.

Si picked up the CB from the dashboard and turned to Mike, the glow from the fire illuminating their faces.

'I doubt he would have coughed up, to be honest Mike. I reckon he would have run anyway'.

'I guess it doesn't matter now', Mike replied through clenched teeth as he climbed out of the vehicle.

The locals had, by this point, started to put the fire out, and had it well under control by the time the Firemen had arrived and unloaded their hoses, attaching them to the mains water supply valve located at the harbour steps.

Mike and Simon strolled over to a better vantage point. Over to his left Mike noticed a frightened looking lady in her dressing gown and her husband talking to a cliché of a police inspector.

As the two marched over they pulled out their identity cards. They knew that, due to the authority and jurisdiction that the Admiralty had granted them, the police would have to inform them of any evidence collected at the scene. Useful, as neither of them had been forensically trained.

The tan, trench coat wearing police inspector turned towards Mike as he stepped close.

'HMPS. I saw you arrive'.

They presented their warrants.

'DCI Raymond, Devon and Cornwall Constabulary', the inspector introduced himself.

'Mike Williams', Mike returned, shaking the DCI's hand, 'and this is Simon Jenkins'.

'I have to be honest, I don't like this at all', Raymond said with distaste, 'I don't like this sudden divulgence of information to a department that was created on the same day that something like this happens. If you excuse the pun, I think it's a bit fishy!'

Mike looked at the smouldering remnants of his former childhood home.

'To be honest Raymond, I don't particularly care, just give me what you've got and we'll be out of your way'.

Raymond clenched his teeth. He knew that due to the circumstances surrounding this situation the HMPS would be directly involved and that he was under authority to aid them in their enquiries.

'Yes, I did see an email to the effect, this afternoon. I didn't much care for that either'.

Sighing, he relinquished his notepad.

'This is Mr and Mrs Hicks. John Hicks, here, witnessed pretty much everything outside of the pub. He and his wife also saw…' Raymond looked at the old couple, shivering in their nightwear, 'four or five was it…?'

'About four men ran from the pub door just before the police arrived, jumped down the harbour steps just here...' Hicks pointed a pale, elderly finger towards the harbour wall, 'and they sped off in a small motor boat. They were wearing frog man suits, like what divers wear. Rubber suits. Black, they were'.

'Thanks Mr Hicks, Mrs Hicks, why don't you get yourselves a cup of tea and we will be in touch a little later on'. Raymond closed his notebook and turned to Mike. A WPC took the elderly couple aside and back towards their cottage. The agents and the DCI walked towards the pub, through the waterlogged road from the extinguishing efforts of both the locals and the fire brigade.

'They had machine guns too!' Hicks shouted behind.

'Thank you Mr Hicks', Raymond shouted after them in a condescending voice.

Mike looked to Simon out of the corner of his eye.

'It's all in the report', Raymond concluded with a half-smile, noticing Mike's bemusement.

As they reached the entrance a uniformed officer walked out of the charred doorway.

Details of the remains of the interior were being infrequently lit by beams from the flashlights of the investigating officers inside.

'There are a lot of bodies inside sir', the officer started to the DCI.

Mike barged forward.

'You talk to me from now on!' Mike said, arrogantly.

Simon looked at him with concern.

The young officer looked back at his DCI in query, who nodded in agreement.

'Yes, that's right. You have to talk to Her Majesties... what was it again?' Raymond played.

'What have you got constable?' Mike asked the confused officer.

The officer turned, sceptically towards Mike and Simon as Raymond backed off a few steps.

'We have found a lot of local types in there sir', he pointed behind him, 'but we have also found another body; a man in a wetsuit'.

Mike snatched the flashlight from the officer and shone it behind him at the body propped up on the floor near the smouldering remains of the doorway.

'What the hell?' Mike mumbled under his breath. Simon joined him as he scanned the flashlight over the body.

'Has this guy been processed?' he asked the young officer.

'Yes sir, we quickly photographed and detailed the scene in case the place collapsed, which it may yet do'.

Mike carefully lifted the balaclava from the dead man's head, revealing his charred face.

'Jesus Christ!' Mike muttered to Simon who looked back at him with a questioning look.

He shone the beam over the body again, illuminating a machine pistol. He trailed the beam across the floor as hundreds of small cartridge cases twinkled back at him. The two agents stood up and Mike gave the flashlight back to the officer.

'What is it Mike?' asked Simon.

Mike spun round to Raymond and the young officer.

'I want every single detail of this scene collected, every piece of evidence catalogued and I want forensics in here immediately! And I want that man there identified!' Mike barked, pointing to the body of the man in the wetsuit.

'And you report to me directly, you got that Inspector?'

He stormed off towards the Land Rover. Simon gave Raymond a contact card and followed like an obedient dog. Raymond looked at the card and ran his thumb over the embossed admiralty seal.

'We know how to do our job coast guard!' Raymond mumbled under his breath.

Mike stopped and turned around to face the inspector.

'And NO press statement Raymond! I am serious! I don't want anyone knowing anything about the nature of this investigation!'

'Oh, and what shall I say happened then? The pub just burst into flames? Candle caught the curtains?'

Mike spun around once again, 'I don't care what you say Raymond, but if one word of this gets out...'

Raymond watched the two men walk to the flashing blue lights of the Land Rover and shook his head in disbelief before making his way back inside the charcoaled shell of the pub.

Mike hesitated before opening the car door.

'What's going on?' Simon asked as he climbed inside.

He started the engine and continued to stare forward as he drove the Land Rover clear of the harbour wall.

'I'm sure I know that man!' Mike said, with a sickly feeling in his throat.

'Get someone from Nelson to get down here as soon as they can will you?'

Simon leaned forward to pick up his mobile phone from the dashboard.

As he was doing so he looked at Mike's sombre expression, 'What's spooked you Mike?'

'Make sure our team collects every scrap of information available, and get someone to interview that man, Hicks again. I don't want to overlook anything that Raymond and his team may have missed'.

As Simon began to dial the numbers on his phone he turned to Mike, 'Who was he?'

'If I'm right...' Mike paused. He looked out of the side window at the coastal lights of Penzance in the distance.

'If that man is, who I think he is...' he paused again, 'it doesn't make any sense'.

Mike's thoughts were conflicting and fighting his concentration.

'What was his name?' another long pause.

Simon watched, frustrated by the lack of an answer.

'Greene!' Mike suddenly shouted 'Jonathan Greene! That was his name.'

He looked relieved but his expression immediately turned sour.

'Who was he?' Simon asked, trying to crowbar the information out of his confused companion.

'Who was he?' Mike repeated.

'He was...' another drawn out pause.

'He was a Royal Marine Commando'.

Simon sat back, frowning in confusion 'A Marine? Are you sure?'

Mike stared through the windscreen wipers as the Land Rover whipped up the coastal road.

Simon held the phone, his thumb hovering over the "call" button.

The obvious question to ask was what the Royal Marines were doing tearing up a local pub. Evidently this was the question that was bugging Mike. A shoot out with the Royal Marines didn't make sense. What threat would warrant the use of such a resource? And why would they purposefully evade the police. And more importantly who would have sanctioned it?

Simon pressed the "call" button and it was answered instantly.

Simon's voice faded into obscurity as Mike rubbed his eyes. He pushed his head back to the headrest and wiped the sweat from his brow with his sleeve.

After dropping Simon off at his seafront house in Newlyn, Mike drove on into the town and pulled up outside the local Spar shop, bumping the vehicle onto the high kerb off the road.

He got out, flicked the remote locking and walked through the sliding glass doors of the shop.

After filling a basket of French lager, bread, milk and a pizza he stepped up to the till where a young girl sat filing her nails and chewing a mouthful of gum.

She acknowledged her customer with a "how may I help you smile" and began to swipe the products over the infra-red scanner and pushing them down the other side. Mike noticed her yawn as she picked up the large box of lager bottles.

'Do you know the time at all?' he asked.

'Ten past one', she replied in monotone signalling the end of the conversation.

He opened his wallet and laid it on the conveyor belt near the metal security tag remover.

'I wouldn't put that there if I were you Mister', she advised awkwardly.

'Oh, sorry', he said genuinely, pushing the wallet down the escalator next to his goods.

'Not if you value your credit cards that is', she added.

Mike smiled and nodded, not really grasping her point.

'Fifteen pounds thirty one please', she demanded, as she looked up at him.

Mike began to count out his money onto the metal counter.

She looked at his wallet; still dangerously close to the security device.

'Probably too late now anyway, you wouldn't believe how many people do that you know, I bet the banks have a headache having to replace all the cards that thing destroys'.

Mike poured the mixture of coins and notes into her hand and she began to count it back to herself.

'Should be exact', he said, collecting his wallet.

'Thanks', she replied, as she opened the till drawer to deposit the money.

'If you do have problems using it…'

'What did you say?' Mike asked with a startled realisation as to what the girl was telling him.

'I said - if you do have problems…'

'No, no, not that bit, the bit about wiping my card? How does it do that?'

She looked at him blankly.

'Do I look like a scientist Mister?' she asked through a mouth of gum. 'It's got something to do with this security device remover here', she pointed to the metal box near the conveyor belt, 'if you put your credit card, watch, phone or anything electrical on this thing, it will pretty much knacker it!' she said proudly tapping it with her long red finger nails.

Mike looked at the unit closely and read the label;

"WARNING: THIS DEVICE CONTAINS AN ELECTROMAGNET WHICH CAN DAMAGE CREDIT CARDS, MOBILE PHONES AND OTHER ELECTRONIC DEVICES!"

He stood up and put his hand to his mouth.

'Oh my God!' he said under his breath, still staring at the unit.

The young girl looked at him with disgust.

'Are you drunk?' she asked, 'cus if you are I have to get security to…'

Mike gathered his shopping and left the store.

He emerged from the mini-mart with a victorious smile, pulled out his keys and pressed the remote button, opening up the Land Rover. He swung his shopping onto the passenger seat and started the engine. With a look combining excitement with intrigue he slammed the vehicle into first gear and sped off through the town.

Chapter 6
<u>The Theory</u>

The side hatch on the bridge of the forty nine metre deep-sea fishing trawler *Kingfisher II* slid open with an abrasive crunch as a wave collapsed on the bow deck, pushing a fountain of fine spray over the weathered face of James Morgan as he peered out to survey the netting as it hauled in on the giant winches.

He smiled, and rubbed his jet black beard free of the salty spray, at the size of the bulbous net. Although the crew were experienced with the adverse conditions that deep-sea fishing presented, they were clinging tight to the railings as the giant *Kingfisher II* cut through the steep troughs against the constant barrage of dark Atlantic waves.

Morgan looked forward into the grey curtain of vertical rain and further out at the violent watery terrain ahead of them. He shook his head and leaned out further to see the lower deck where a well-built man in yellow waterproofs stood, desperately trying to draw on a pipe while hanging on tightly to the starboard chain railings.

'Sebastian!' Morgan shouted down to him, 'haul in nets five and six, we're gonna make for home! Tell the lads to pack up and stow!'

The grey haired officer signalled a salute and made his way precariously along the slippery metallic deck against another aggressive pitch.

Morgan pulled hard on the rusting iron handle and slid the hatch shut, blowing on his blue-grey digits protruding from the frayed fingerless holes of his gloves. He instinctively checked the instrument panel and glanced at the radar, brushing the sea spray from it with the palm of his hand; it was all clear. He grappled at a large tartan thermos as it slid towards the edge of the instrument unit and twisted the top open. As he began to pour some of the tepid remains into the plastic cup, a small *beep* sounded from the radar. He placed the thermos at his feet and put his hand in his pocket to retrieve a hipflask.

Beep

Morgan blinked and wiped the sea spray that had collected in his thick stubborn eyebrows with the sleeve of his overcoat and stared back at the radar. The white scan line revolved the empty, dark green screen then highlighted a tiny white dot with another *beep*. Morgan stood up straight and looked through the wiper blades of the bridge windows.

'What the hell is that?' he asked himself as he reached for a pair of binoculars from a hook on the wall behind him. He opened the hatch again and stuck his head outside, put the binoculars to his eyes and looked hard in the direction of the radar blip, but it was as futile as he had expected through the opaque mist.

He returned to the radar and made a note of the coordinates on a small pad next to the pane and leaned his head out of the hatch once again.

'Seb!' he shouted over the deafening noise of the winch engine that was currently hauling the final netting on board.

'Seb!'

'SEB!'

The grey haired fisherman looked around and spotted Morgan beckoning him towards the bridge.

Morgan slid shut the hatch and sat back on the well-used leather chair in front of the wheel rubbing at the growth of dark hair on his chin.

The bridge door opened and Sebastian stepped inside, shutting the door after him.

'What's that skip?'

Morgan stood up and moved towards the radar and pointed.

Beep....beep

'Who's that? Who the hell is out there in this stuff?' Sebastian asked, standing back in amazement.

'I have no idea but they are bloody close!'

'This is our bloody patch, I cannot believe that someone would be so...' Sebastian started.

Beep...beep-beep-beep

The two men looked at the radar again.

'Jesus!' Morgan exclaimed, 'we are right on top of them!'

As the two men looked out of the rain-beaten main window of the bridge, they made out a small white yacht blinking amongst the vast dark waves. At the bow of the ship the crew had also spotted the craft and had begun to make preparations to stop the machinery.

'All stop!' Morgan shouted as he slammed the gear controls into reverse.

Sebastian punched a large metal switch on the wall behind them sounding the ship's horns.

Morgan struggled against the waves and pushed the wheel hard to starboard. The engines roared below the decks as the prop shafts plunged into reverse.

Morgan sneered at the craft and reached up to the control panel above his head, he pulled a large black lever and the ship's sirens blared into the darkness of the night.

'Why isn't she putting out?' Morgan fumed.

'We're gonna hit her! I'm gonna drop anchor!' Sebastian shouted as he raced to the exit.

The trawler sliced through the waves only a few hundred yards from the lifeless catamaran, being relentlessly thrown into their path.

Morgan watched Sebastian run across the dangerously slippy decks to the bow. He jumped over the winch and threw himself at the anchor controls, pulling back on the release lever. The anchors on both sides dropped simultaneously and disappeared below the surface. The chains spun the winch reels until they stopped as the anchors hit the sea bed and began to drag. Morgan watched nervously as the catamaran dropped into the slip stream. Suddenly there was a violent jolt as the anchors found a ledge pushing the front of the ship forwards into the waves. Her crew clung for their lives to the bow railings as the stern crashed back down onto the surface.

Morgan ran out of the bridge onto the upper deck and slid down the metal ladder. He crashed through the men and clung to the railings to look at the vessel immediately at her bow. With a furious rage building inside him he leaned over to the catamaran bobbing below them, 'You stupid bastards!'

Sebastian looked at the floating vessel and put his hand on the captain's shoulder to attract his attention, 'I think she's a drifter, Skip'.

Morgan looked deep into her dark lifeless cabin windows.

'My God, you are right…' he turned to Sebastian, 'get me the Coastguard!'

The rain had calmed and had reverted to an annoying drizzle that pattered at the windows of Mike's cottage. A laptop was the sole illumination, glowing at the side of the room displaying a web browser page; "Electro Magnetic Pulse; from Wikipedia, the free encyclopedia". The desk and keyboard were littered with notes and print outs mixed lazily with mini French beer bottles and discarded crown caps. Mike's jacket slumped over the desk chair and a slice of pizza sat on a plate, balancing precariously on the edge of a stack of books.

Ring Ring…

Inside the bedroom, Mike stirred from beneath the bed clothes.

Ring Ring…

He moaned in response.

Ring Ring…

As he pushed his head through the duvet he looked at the red display on the alarm clock.

'Four thirty?' he grumbled.

Ring Ring…

'Oh for the love of…'

He reached for the phone from the bedside table and pressed at the answer button.

'Yes, what? It's four thirty!'

Mike's eyes started to open wide.

'The harbour? I will be there in ten minutes!'

He slapped the phone down and darted out of bed towards the wicker chair in the corner of his room where his discarded clothes lay in a pile.

As he rushed past the laptop he stepped back and peeled the last slice of the pizza from the plate, stuffing the corner into his mouth as he collected his notes from the chaos of the desk.

The Land Rover screeched around the narrow streets and through the opening onto the cobbles of the harbour wall. The flashing blue lights reflected in the damp, mossy walls.

As Mike pulled the vehicle to a stop; adjacent to the lighthouse at the end of the harbour, he saw the familiar markings of the Coastguard vessel bobbing on the shallows. As he walked towards the boat he heard a voice call out.

'Mr Williams?'

Looking into the darkness of the harbour he noticed a familiar face, standing on the foredeck of the tiny boat, dressed in orange.

'Mike!' The figure shouted above the drone of the vessels twin engines.

Mike stepped onto the boat and shielded his eyes from the driving rain to see the figure who was calling him; a stocky man, clean shaven and of similar age.

'Nathan!'

'Hello Mike, we're in a bit of a rush, get yourself battened down…'

Mike nodded and manoeuvred himself into the small cabin as the twin engines roared into life, propelling the bow into the air.

Nathan shut the door behind them and strapped himself into a seat next to his former colleague.

'I didn't make the connection of Mr Williams, Mike!' Nathan shouted above the deafening hum.

'I didn't recognise your voice on the phone', Mike responded as loud as he could muster after his sleepless night.

The boat skimmed the swelling, dark waves and negotiated the troughs as it disappeared from view.

Nathan looked at Mike with concern; he was starting to become anxious and his colour had faded to a pale grey. He stretched his hands out to steady himself on the metal arm rests in an attempt to level himself as the boat skipped from peak to peak.

Nathan moved over towards him; 'You ok Mike?' he shouted.

Mike looked back at him and nodded.

He sat back and couldn't help but smile that Michael Williams was suffering from apparent sea sickness; it was as ridiculous as an airline pilot who was scared of flying.

'We're nearly there!' the pilot shouted.

Mike moved as close to the windscreen as his harness allowed. The pilot switched on the vast spotlights on the roof, projecting a beam deep into the mist, faintly picking out a fishing vessel in the distance.

'There they are now Mike', Nathan shouted to him as he pointed in front of them.

'They found the drifter about an hour or so ago and apparently they have tethered themselves to it to prevent it being swept out. The current is quite vicious out here tonight'.

Mike nodded again fighting the nauseous urge to disgrace himself in front of his fellow coast guards, 'you don't say', he mustered.

The boat drew close to the rusting, metal hull of the trawler and slowed to a stop as Mike unbuckled his harness and began to pull himself out of the small bucket seat.

'Nathan, throw 'em a line!' ordered the pilot.

Nathan opened the rear doors of the powerboat and reached for a coiled rope at the back of the cabin. He stepped out, clinging to the rails of the roof and threw the line to one of the crew of the *Kingfisher II*, who pulled it tight through a guide ring mounted on the decking.

The pilot released the controls, keeping the engine in neutral and stepped out of the back door. He climbed onto the cabin roof and onto the front of the powerboat with another coiled rope. Mike watched him jump from the deck to the stern of the drifting catamaran. He tied the rope off onto the rear railings and pulled the boats together.

Once tethered he gave Mike a signal to come aboard.

Mike left his seat and steadied himself. Although the journey was over, he could still feel the motion sickness in the pit of his stomach with every movement.

He climbed onto the roof and pulled himself up and over the cabin onto the front deck. Once there he composed himself, aware of the crew of the *Kingfisher II* watching his every move from above them, and casually stepped onto the stern deck of the drifter.

'Empress', the pilot shouted into his ear as he pointed towards the name plate above the cabin doors.

Morgan and his crew watched from the bow deck as Mike fished in his pocket for his flashlight. He aimed the powerful beam through the rear glass doors into the cabin, illuminating the plush cream interior.

'Has anyone boarded her at all?' he shouted up at the fishermen through the sound clash of rain and waves.

Morgan stepped forward and leaned over the guard rail.

'Aye, one of me crew jumped aboard her to tether her to us'.

'Has anyone been inside her?'

'No, just aboard her decking, where you are now'.

Mike signalled a wave of gratitude and moved towards the cabin doors. He rotated the brass handle and pushed on them, opening them wide. He shone the beam inside and grinned.

'Thought so', he said to himself through a smile.

The whole cabin was, as he had expected, immaculate. He reached into his pocket and pulled out his digital camera which he began to use, documenting every detail, the carpet, the surfaces, the windows; everything.

Outside, the fishermen amused themselves at the flashes which emitted from every window of the cabin.

After a few moments Mike emerged, putting the camera back in his pocket and shut the doors behind him.

'Where are you headed now Captain….?' he shouted up at the crew, baiting for a name.

'Morgan!'

'Morgan. Morgan?' Mike asked, 'Captain Morgan?'

'I know, unfortunate isn't it?' Morgan replied.

Mike thought about the implications and shook his head, dismissing the coincidental irony.

'Not really. Where you headed Captain?'

'Newlyn'.

Mike smiled, 'Do you think you could do me a favour Captain Morgan?'

'Of course'.

'I need you to tow this vessel back to Newlyn for me'.

'It would be our pleasure sir!' Morgan shouted down to him.

'Thank you Captain… just one more thing'.

'Aye?'

'How long do you think it would take a boat like this to drift to the deep seas from a safe shipping route?'

After a few moments deliberating with his crew Morgan shouted back to him.

'Probably about four hours in this weather; best guess'.

Mike waved at Morgan and stepped from the *Empress* back onto the powerboat. The pilot untethered the two vessels and coiled the rope before regaining his position at the helm.

'Nathan, that was a good call my friend', Mike shouted as the boat's mighty engines kicked in, propelling them at high speed away from the scene, leaving a vast white swell.

Message Received.

"THEY'VE FOUND THE EMPRESS ALREADY! IS IT CLEAN?"

Reply.

"CLEANED! DON'T LOSE UR NERVE!"

Send.

Mike waved at the powerboat as it turned around in Penzance Harbour. He opened the door of the Land Rover and pressed a speed dial on his phone as the powerboat roared towards the harbour entrance and back out to sea, aggravating the moored boats in its wake. The phone was answered.

'Hello?'

'Simon, it's Mike'.

'Mike, what's up, you ok?'

'We have picked up another drifter; *The Empress*'.

'When?'

'Just got back from her, she is being towed into Newlyn by a trawler. I need to catch up with you; I think I may be onto something'.

'Great, meet me at the office in an hour, we need to fill in a lot of paperwork from last night'.

Mike sighed, 'Did the lab results come back about that body?'

'Yes, they are there waiting for us'.

The blue and white chequered Garda car trickled through the gates of the Crosshaven Boatyard. Inside, Richards and Harding, the two Preventive agents assigned the Ireland investigation, sat in the back seat behind two Garda officers, watching the luxury yachts and cruisers as they passed by.

'How long will you be wanting us for Mr Richards?' the tall ginger haired officer in the passenger seat enquired.

'We shouldn't be longer than a couple of hours', Richards replied, looking out of the back window.

'We could have a snooze John', the officer joked with the driver who smiled in response.

Richards rolled his eyes; another halfhearted attempt at evoking a response. The Garda's feelings were as personal as they were subtle and what the majority of law enforcement authorities in the UK felt; a waste of resources. Two officers of the Garda being assigned such a menial task as to escort two agents from a department that had only been in existence, officially, for a couple of months, was not how the police forces nor the public had expected their taxes to have been spent.

As they pulled into the carpark, a tall and well-dressed man emerged from the reception building and watched the car as it parked on the gravel surface.

Richards and Harding walked to the reception area. Harding held out his identification card to the expectant man standing at the doorway.

'Hello Mr…?' Harding waited for the man's name.

'Oakley, John Oakley'.

'Mr Oakley, we are from Her Majesties Preventive Service based in Cornwall'.

Oakley looked at the officers blankly, partly because he hadn't heard of them but mainly because he wondered why they were there. The HMPS uniform was designed specifically similar to that of a Coastguard uniform for instant recognition.

'Can we ask you a few questions?'

'Of course, please come inside', Oakley held open the door and the two agents entered the sandstone building.

Oakley whipped past them and made his way behind the reception desk.

'Now, what can I do for you, gents?' he asked in a very southern Irish accent that Harding found a little difficult to understand, causing him to pause and mentally translate prior to his response.

'We are here to take a look at a number of yachts on this list'.

Harding produced a folded A4 paper from his jacket pocket and handed it to Oakley.

'These yachts, we believe, may have connections to the recent spate of piracy that you may have…'

'That thing on the news?' Oakley interrupted.

'Yes. We need to take a quick look at these vessels and take a few pictures if that's possible Mr Oakley'.

Oakley shrugged and nodded in compliance. He turned to a large, metal cabinet behind him and opened it, revealing a selection of keys on brightly coloured plastic fobs.

He looked back at the list and checked the names on it to the names on the fobs, picking sets out as he found them.

Harding turned around to look at the yacht sale adverts on the walls and spotted a scruffy bearded man in a black polo neck and waders standing at the doorway. The man acknowledged him with a subtle nod. Harding nodded and turned back to face the reception where Oakley was placing the keys he had gathered from the cabinet in a row on the desk.

'I think this is your lot', he said proudly spreading the keys out for the agents.

'Thank you Mr Oakley, we will try and be as quick as we possibly can', Richards said, gathering up the keys and filling his jacket pocket.

Oakley picked up the list that Harding had given to him and studied it. Suddenly his eyes widened.

'Wait a minute'.

The agents paused and looked at the intrigued man.

'These yachts on this list of yours, I thought I recognised them'.

The two agents looked at each other.

'What is it?' Richards enquired.

Oakley stared at the list and then began to franticly flip the pages of a large, leather bound log book on the edge of the reception desk. As the agents looked on, he began to tap away on his computer.

'Mr Oakley?'

Oakley turned to the two agents.

'It's just that… it's probably a coincidence but, well since I… The previous owner, Mr Franklin, died three years ago and because he had no family and I was a part shareholder in the boatyard, he left this place to me. After the initial shock, which took a few months to get used to I can tell you, I began to computerise the records in this log book, creating a database - you know; digital bookings and such'.

Richards nodded in acknowledgement and to spur the story; conscious that their plane was leaving in three hours, and the longer they left the Garda in the car, the more abuse they would suffer on their way back to the airport; if they were still there.

'So, I subcategorised the vessels into three groups: privately owned, charter and hire. I only created the third category initially because of this yacht *Nevacanezzer*'.

He pointed at the vessel on Richards' list and then rotated the log book to face him, running his finger up and down the list under the page header "Hire".

'They're the yachts on your list!' Oakley said excitedly.

Richards and Harding looked closely, comparing the list and the log book.

'What is "Hire" exactly, Mr Oakley?' Richards asked.

'Basically, they are vessels that are neither privately owned nor available for charter; they are only available to hire by persons with sea captaincy certification.

We don't usually have a lot of these you see; very expensive and insurance is sky high so we make our money from chartering them with an on-board captain.'

Richards looked at Oakley blankly.

'So why would *our* vessels be hire only? And why are they the only ones available for hire?'

'I've no idea', Oakley confessed, anticlimactically.

'Thanks Mr Oakley, we'll go and take our photos and be out of your way as soon as we can'.

Richards and Harding gestured to Oakley as they started to head for the doorway.

Oakley thought for a brief moment and then shouted after them.

'Wait!'

The two agents sighed and turned to face him and the scruffy man at the doorway adjusted his vantage point.

'I don't know if this is any help either, but… a few years ago, when Franklin was in charge of the place, we had a phone call from a man asking about a yacht. He asked us if it had been hired to his brother a week previously, as he and his fiancé had gone missing, and he was told that he was hiring one of our boats that weekend to take his fiancé out for a couple of weeks sightseeing'.

Harding steadied himself on a shelf full of tourism literature in anticipation of another long winded story.

'And…' Oakley continued, 'Franklin told the gentleman that the yacht hadn't been hired and that he had no record of his brother ever having hired the boat'.

Richards; having recalled the Navy cover up sanctioned by the Vice Admiral in the briefing, nodded, 'Go on Mr Oakley'.

'Now, we were told to do so by the Navy to try and disguise a possible public fear, it was the time of the Gulf War and we were paid a lot of money to do so, partly to cover mooring fees but mainly to keep our mouths shut!'

Suddenly the scruffy man in the overalls at the doorway interjected, 'Mr Oakley, I think that these gentlemen have work to do, maybe you should let them get on with their jobs?'

Oakley stared at him with intent.

'How dare you talk to me like that Tom O'Sullivan!' he shouted at the man. 'Now GET OUT!'

The scruffy man pushed himself from the door frame and slowly made his way into the carpark.

'I'm sorry about him', Oakley apologised, 'a legacy from my predecessor's days'.

'Please continue, Mr Oakley', Richards looked into Oakley's eyes.

'Well, it's just that not only are all of your yachts on this list, marked in the log book with an asterisk by Mr Franklin, for anyone ringing up with an enquiry about missing persons in connection with these vessels. But it always struck me as odd that the sanctioning figure behind this was…' Oakley opened the log book to the back page where a frayed yellowing printout of a contract lay entitled: "Contract of acknowledgement for Official Secrets Act".

Oakley pointed at the bottom at the counter signature.

Richards and Harding looked closely.

'Jesus!' Harding exclaimed.

Richards looked at Oakley with a look of concern.

'Are you absolutely sure; certain that this is true?' he asked.

'Positive', Oakley replied, 'I thought nothing of it when myself and Franklin signed the thing but when I came to shift it all to the database I suddenly realised how odd it was that he had signed it himself and not through a representative'.

'Shit!' Richards exclaimed with a sickened look.

They backed off from the reception a few steps.

'Thank you Mr Oakley. Do you think you could continue to keep this to yourself for a while longer?'

'It's been fifteen years or more', Oakley shrugged.

The two agents made their way outside.

'We'll just be an hour or so ok?'

Oakley waved as he looked back at the contract.

Harding looked dazed.

'Let's take these photos and get back to headquarters', Richardson suggested as they gathered pace.

'I'm gonna call Williams', Harding with a hint of excitement.

Richardson looked at him and stopped in his tracks.

'No, don't. I am worried about this. If it *is* true and we uncover something then… well, it is a dangerous situation for all of us. We have got to keep a tight a lid on this as possible'.

Harding pulled out his phone.

'I'll arrange him to meet us somewhere then?'

'Yes, don't disclose anything just arrange for us to meet him somewhere, tonight'.

Harding nodded and began to dial his phone.

The scruffy man stood at the edge of the harbour nearby, slowly sweeping at the decking.

Harding held the phone next to his ear as it rang.

'Have you completed the paperwork on the Ship yet Si?' Mike asked from behind a stack of folders and paperwork that had materialized on his desk overnight.

'No, not yet, haven't even begun that yet Mike'.

Mike's phone rang and vibrated under the pile. He pushed his hand deep beneath it, sending most of them to the floor as he found the vibrating phone.

'Mike Williams'.

'Mike, its Phil Harding'.

'Phil, how's Ireland?'

Simon smiled from across the desk.

'We have to meet, can we meet? Lunchtime maybe?'

'In Ireland?' Mike asked in shock.

'No, our flight is at about twelve so we'll be back at Lands End for about one-ish. How about the Benbow?'

'Sure, two in the Benbow?'

'Thanks Mike'.

'Is everything ok?' Mike asked, detecting Harding's tone.

'Yes, fine, see you then'.

The phone went dead.

Harding put the phone back in his pocket and pulled out his digital camera.

'Come on, let's get this done and go!'

Mike rested his phone on his chin as his thoughts taunted him and looked towards his colleague busy tapping at his laptop in front of him.

'Simon?'

Simon looked up at him, 'Yeah?'

Mike chewed the end of his pen, staring into space; Simon continued to type.

'Does… what's his name?...Farnday? Farahway?...'

'Faraday?' Simon suggested.

'Doctor Faraday! Does he still work in this building two days a week?'

'Yeah, he works here permanently now, he lives in Gweek, he moved there from London a few years ago, why?'

Mike picked up his phone and dialled for reception.

'I have a theory, I will let you know after I have spoken to Faraday, ah, reception, it's Mike Williams, can you put me through to Doctor Faraday please?'

He tapped his pen on his forehead as he waited.

'Can you make two o'clock in the Benbow Si? Phil wanted to meet there, I think he got a lead on something… ah Doctor Faraday… yes it's Mike Williams, hi…'

The conversation drifted as Simon continued to write up the reports from the previous day. His fingers flashed across the keyboard as the screen reflected lines of notes on the lenses of his glasses.

Mike put the phone down.

'Are you okay holding the fort for an hour or so? I'm going to see Faraday', Mike asked.

Simon nodded, 'Two at the Benbow right?'

'Yeah, I'll come and pick you up', he replied putting his jacket on, 'where is Faraday's office?'

With his phone to his ear, Tom waited at the floating harbour, watching intently as the two agents ran back and forth between the yachts. The phone was answered.

'It's me', Tom spoke quietly.

'Two of them… Preventive agents are here at the marina, asking questions and snooping around on the boats. And another thing; Oakley spilled his guts!'

Tom waited as the recipient spoke to him.

'How? And Oakley? You can trust me. I will make arrangements for that too'.

He closed the phone and put it into his coat pocket.

Mike made his way down the narrow, grey corridor at the lower levels of Nelson. Huge iron pipe work ran the length of the mundane gloss grey walls; interrupted occasionally by dark, wooden doors. Mike approached one of the doors labelled with a brass plate: "Dr D J Faraday MSc, BSc".

He knocked.

'Come on in', a warm, cockney voice invited.

Mike opened the door and entered the room. It was a large office adorned by leather-bound books stacked on shelves dominating the majority of wall space and an eclectic mix of ancient scientific equipment covered every horizontal surface. A tubby man sporting wiry grey hair, and awkwardly wearing a white lab coat, peered from behind a large, well-used reference book. His ornate, white moustache defied gravity as it projected from each of his rounded cheeks.

He pushed a pair of circular wire-frame glasses onto the bridge of his nose and focused on his visitor.

'Michael Williams!' he shouted.

He stood up, negotiating the obstacle course of equipment and text books to greet him.

'Donald, good to see you again', Mike said with a genuine smile.

'So how's my old student doing in his new position?' Faraday asked as he lowered himself into the chair behind the desk.

Mike smiled and sat down opposite, 'How's my principle lecturer?'

Faraday laughed and leaned forward.

'We have both come a long way since the Royal Naval College my friend'.

Mike nodded, 'And now you are one of the government's leading figures in Naval Research and Development; commissioned on many occasions to oversee projects by MI6 and outsourced to the FBI. Both a living legend and an enemy. Head hunted by Libyan terrorists in the late eighties for knowledge on nuclear powered engines specifically the Trident class Fusion generator'.

Faraday smiled with a questioning uneasiness.

'Where in Moses did you get that?'

Mike pushed a piece of paper from the top of a nearby stack of books on the desk between them.

Faraday picked it up and gave an embarrassed smile.

'Part of my own retirement speech, given to me by the boss to check over for accuracy'.

He replaced the paper and settled back in the chair.

'You are finally retiring?' Mike asked.

'Yes. Not quite yet, they want me for some other special task or the likes first – they make you work for your money here'.

Mike smiled at the reference to academia.

'And what the hell can I do for you Mr Williams?'

'You are probably aware…'

'That you have been drafted in on this Preventive Service caper? Yes I know all about that. We were briefed about that months ago Mike. I have to say, it is a bit odd; I don't mean to undermine you but this is a drastic course of action the VA has taken, don't you think?'

'I am as surprised as you Donald. What do you know about EMP?' he asked, quickly changing the subject.

Faraday's expression turned quickly sour.

'EMP?' he paused and looked out of the window pensively, 'do you still drink coffee?'

Mike nodded and extracted a handful of notes from his inside pocket as Faraday stood up from the desk and shuffled towards a large, old-fashioned black percolator resembling scientific apparatus more than a coffee maker.

'I am trying to find out if it is possible…' Mike looked at Faraday as he filled the machine with coffee grounds from an old metal canister.

'In theory…' Mike changed his tact; anticipating a reluctance to divulge his work, '…would it be possible to cut out electrical currents using an EMP generator?'

'Of course it is, EMP can cut electrical power instantaneously', Faraday replied as he nestled himself behind his desk.

'So, do you think you could, in theory, cut out an engine with some kind of pulse?'

The room quickly filled with the smell of fresh coffee. Faraday scratched his head as he considered his answer.

'Possibly, I think so, yes, as long as the engine was electrically ignited'.

Faraday blinked nervously as he watched Mike's thought processes.

'So, what would the maximum range of this pulse be?'

Faraday pushed himself from the desk and moved towards the percolator.

'Does it have a maximum range?'

No answer.

'Can it be projected? Don?' Mike persisted.

Faraday added milk to two cups he had produced from a nearby filing cabinet.

'Don, I need this information, I need to know how these yachts have been attacked and I think I may be on to something.'

Faraday forced a smile as he shared the contents of the glass jar between the cups.

'I understand Mike, really I do, but I am treading dangerous grounds here'.

'Don, I need your help. With your knowledge…'

'I could be jailed!' Faraday replied, '…at best!'

'People are dying!' Mike began to raise his voice.

Faraday switched off the percolator and returned with the two cups, setting one down in front of Mike.

'You know, in Nineteen Eighty One, I signed the Official Secrets Act, and I swore that I would never disclose information about anything at all contained within it and I have never broken that contract, not once…'

Mike sighed emphasising his disappointment.

'I didn't know who else to contact. I can feel that I may be on to something Don. I'm not asking you to jeopardise your safety or your job…'

'Please let me finish Michael… I *wasn't* prepared to break that contract…' he paused and clenched his teeth, 'but this is different!'

Mike looked up from his coffee at the grimace that had replaced the chubby smile on the professor's face.

'I understand what you are doing Mike and I understand your frustration. I know that you know that I know about this project and I also know something that you don't – and it is for this reason that I will tell you what you want to know. It is this reason that will put us both in a great deal of danger. To be honest, I didn't think it would take you long to contact me. I have sort of being expecting you'.

Mike looked at him with empathy.

'BUT!' Faraday said sternly; holding out his finger towards his student, 'you must promise that whatever I tell you now will remain inside these four walls!'

'I will need to disclose it to my partner but…'

Faraday sat back in his armchair and waved his hand in front of him.

'I mean within the management, the high authority! Don't go writing any reports about this'.

Mike sat forward and looked at Faraday's desperate expression.

'I promise, Don… who are you afraid of?'

'Not your concern Mike', he snapped, 'now, what do you want to know?'

Mike took a deep breath and looked at his notes.

'Don, to get to the point; is there such a thing as an EMP projector? Or a…'

'…Weapon?'

'Yes, this is what I thought you would be asking me. Clever little sod!'

Mike's facial expression emphasised enquiry.

'In Nineteen Ninety Five, I led a project to test out the forces of electromagnetism. We created a generator and placed it inside a concrete bunker. We installed a variety of electrical equipment at various ranges and we turned the thing on'.

Faraday sipped at his coffee as Mike concentrated on his every motion.

'The damn thing not only fried every bit of electrical equipment inside the test centre but also my watch that was in the glove box of my car in the carpark; a quarter of a mile away. In answer to your question Mike, yes; it has a very powerful range and yes…'

Faraday paused.

'…We have tested it for use as a non-lethal weapon'.

Mike felt the hairs on the back of his neck tingle.

'In the late nineties we were commissioned to research a method of non-lethal force for use in the war against terrorism and the war in Iraq. This was our response'.

'Was it ever manufactured?' Mike asked, struggling to ingest what he was hearing.

'No. It was too heavy; it couldn't be transported over land. It took an eighteen-wheeled low loader to transport the components alone. The electromagnetic coil weighed nearly a ton'.

Mike licked his lips to prepare for the burning question.

'Could it… be transported by water?'

'I don't see why not, as long as the buoyancy was counteracted, yes, in theory, but transporting it over land proved…'

'But what could protect the EMP generator from being fried after it was fired off?' he interjected impatiently.

'Lead!' Faraday answered as if back in the classroom.

'So an EMP generator, encased in lead could be protected?'

'Yes, but the transporter would fry!'

'Could you encase the necessary components of that transporter in lead?'

'On land? No!'

'On sea?' Mike asked, delivering the questions as fast as they were being returned like a verbal game of squash.

'Yes, again, it's all about the buoyancy on the water. In theory you can float anything on water no matter how heavy it is as long, as the buoyancy ratio is exactly right to the weight'.

'Although…' Faraday stopped. Mike held his breath in anticipation.

'Although what?'

'Although, if you were to transport it by sea you would need a fair-sized craft to do so, something more than a yacht or a fishing boat. You would need something… more hefty', he said illustrating with his hands.

There was a short silence between the two as Mike tried desperately to interpret what he was trying to make reference to.

Mike leaned forward, 'How big?'

Faraday also leaned forward with a look of intrigue into his own question.

'Big!' he announced disappointingly, 'and strong; the generator at its smallest would weigh more than a couple of tons. We tried it on several occasions in Dartmoor and it buckled the axel of the ATV. If it were a boat; you are talking, in order for the thing not to break the structure, a tanker or at the least an industrial trawler'.

It was as if the two were talking in code. Neither of them felt comfortable talking about their individual secrecy binding subjects; yet speaking in tongues like this was wasting time and shrouding the conversation with confusion.

'Okay, Don', Mike started, 'obviously you know about the case'.

Faraday nodded.

'Well, I am wildly stabbing the dark here but…'

Faraday smiled, readying himself for another question.

'…well, I am trying to work out how every yacht that has been attacked in the last fifteen years has had its power knocked out, at range, and without anyone noticing'.

Mike exhaled with relief that he had finally opened up to his point. He stood up and paced across the dusty vinyl flooring. Faraday's gaze locked on to him as he moved from left to right in front of him.

'I mean; how do you creep up on a yacht in daylight, knock out its power, kill the crew, rob it and clean it inside a couple of hours?'

He stopped pacing to look at Faraday's reaction. To his satisfaction and surprise, Faraday started to scratch his head in thought. Obviously what he had said wasn't as unrealistic as he had thought.

Faraday looked back at him calmly.

'Think about what you are saying. There are three things that you have asked. Number one: How do you creep up on a yacht? Number two: How do you knock out its power and number three: How do you kill and clean inside the established timescale?'

With a combination of intrigue and satisfaction, Mike sat down in anticipation of a solution.

'Number one: Yes an EMP would do the trick, but transporting it is your problem. With all that lead required for protection, added to the weight of the generator you would need something specialised. Number two: Is your answer to number one'.

Mike began to unravel the puzzle that Faraday had cryptically challenged him with. After a few moments thought, the answer was as obvious as it was farfetched.

'A submarine?' he asked awkwardly, expecting Faraday to break down in fits of laugher.

'Elementary!' he congratulated.

Mike sat back in the chair, tapping his foot on the floor.

'Number three is a mystery as I am not a homicidal janitor', Faraday answered with a welcomed laugh.

'I need to gather my thoughts', Mike said as he stood up out of the chair, drinking down the last dregs of coffee and returning his cup to the filing cabinet next to the percolator.

'Where are you going?'

Mike opened the door, 'To gather my thoughts! Thanks Don, you have no idea how much I appreciate this!'

Faraday broke a slanted smile and nodded.

'Mike, I have already told you far more than I would have liked to. I have crossed a threshold. Whatever you are doing, do it fast...'

Mike nodded and shut the wooden door behind him.

Faraday screwed up his eyes and pushed his head into his hands.

The two agents jogged along the floating harbour back to the Garda car waiting for them. Harding continued into the reception building and presented his contact card to Oakley.

'If you can think of anything else Mr Oakley, please get in touch with us', he said, catching his breath.

Oakley took the card and looked back at the agent.

'I will thanks'.

Harding smiled and dashed out of the door. Tom watched the agents climb into the waiting vehicle as he mended a loose railing on the dock side.

'Ah Jee, we gotta go now? We were just enjoying spending the day staring at the sea…'

The driver's dig fell onto deaf ears as he started the engine and pulled out of the marina gates. Tom pulled out his phone and pressed a speed dial number.

'It's Tom, they have just left'.

Oakley looked out of the doorway at the vehicle and saw the scruffy man speaking into his phone.

'O'Sullivan, get your lazy arse in here now!' he shouted aggressively.

Tom closed the phone and reached over for his tool box and dragged it closer to him. While he focused on the entrance, he trawled the box with his hand, eventually pulling out a large fillet knife from a leather sheath. He pushed it behind his back and made his way to the cabin.

As he approached the entrance, Oakley stood at the reception desk with his arms folded.

'I have just about had it up to here with you!' he started, shouting at the top of his voice like a furious parent to a disobedient child.

Tom slowly moved towards him, clutching the knife behind his back in a tight fist.

'How dare ye speak to me like that! You are nobody Tommy, you are lucky that I even let you clean the place!'

Oakley's fury had superseded his concentration as Tom moved to within a few inches of him, 'What the hell do you think you are doing you stupid eejit?'

Tom pulled the knife from behind his back and immediately plunged it into Oakley's stomach, the force of which pushed Oakley backwards into a water cooler, knocking it from its pedestal. Oakley stared in shock at his killer as the blood poured onto the wet floor.

'Ye got a big mouth Oakley', Tom whispered to him as he removed the blade. A fountain of blood erupted from the wound and Oakley moaned, steadying himself on the cooler plinth. Tom watched his victim slowly sliding on the wet vinyl and thrust the blade deep into his chest.

Oakley fell to the floor. His blood ran from his body and quickly covered the reception area. Tom, non-perplexed, backed off and made his way outside, leaving bloody footprints across the paving and onto the gravel.

Mike ran over to his desk where Simon remained, relentlessly typing the reports onto his laptop.

'Okay…' he started, breathlessly, '…I think I know what we are looking for'.

Simon looked up from his laptop with red eyes and placed his head on his hand to the ignorance of his excited partner.

'Do we have access to a database of private sales of Navy surplus hardware?' Mike asked, carefully avoiding the point for the time being.

Simon began to tap his mouse as he navigated through the Nelson intranet.

'In answer to your question, yes they do. The Navy has to publish these sales internally for stock checking. Why?'

Mike stuck a tablet of chewing gum into his mouth and began to chew manically.

'I am following a thought. Who can filter these for us?'

Simon squinted at the small text at the bottom of the screen.

'Mrs Jacobs is the owner of the document, Mrs Margaret Jacobs based in Portsmouth'.

Mike picked up a pen from his desk and scribbled the name onto the back of his hand. He picked up the desk phone and dialled.

'Hello, reception? It's Williams… Can you put me through to Margaret Jacobs please? …Portsmouth'.

He held the phone between his ear and his shoulder as he stretched his arms behind his back.

'I have reformed and worked up that list of Blacks by the way', Simon proudly stated.

'I now know where three of the people he implicated in connection with the smuggling ring are located. I reckon we should pay them a visit'.

Mike raised his eyebrows and nodded as the phone crackled to life.

'Ah, Hello Mrs Jacobs? It's Mike Williams at Nelson; I am wondering if you could filter the Private Sales lists for me please… from Nineteen Ninety to Nineteen Ninety Five… Yes that's great. No, all the stock please… Really? That many? I'm sorry about that…'

He pulled a face to Simon indicating the trouble he had seemingly caused the lady.

'Thank you Mrs Jacobs that is great… via email if you please? Lovely thanks, yes thank you… thanks… excellent… yes Mrs Jacobs thanks for your support, good bye Mrs Jacobs'.

Mike replaced the phone into its cradle and exhaled.

'My God she can talk!' he exclaimed. 'Right, what's on that list then?'

Chapter 7

<u>The Accident?</u>

Richards and Harding walked out of the Arrivals exit of the Lands End Aerodrome Terminal and headed, in silence, towards the carpark. Harding clicked the remote and opened the rear door; they removed their jackets and utilities and threw them in the back.

Inside, they both drew and fastened their seat belts without a sound. Richards turned to his colleague.

'Is what we have found as bad as we think? I mean - he signed it, so is that really as bad as we're making out?'

Harding looked at him.

'He paid them off. If the Navy wants something doing they don't have to pay to have it done, they order it done. He has, in effect, bought their silence. That is verging on blackmail my friend, and further more...' he paused, '...how suspicious is that?'

Richards turned the key in the ignition and started the engine, pulling the Land Rover out of the carpark and onto the main road.

'I'll call Williams and check he is still okay to meet'.

Harding pulled his phone from his pocket and pressed a quick dial.

'Hello, Mike'.

'Harding! How was Ireland?'

'Good, are we still okay to meet?'

'Shit, I forgot the time, yeah, we'll be there for half past!'

Harding shut the phone.

Mike closed the phone and returned it to his pocket.

'Come on Si, we're due at the Benbow in twenty minutes'.

Simon looked at his watch and saved his work. He pulled on his coat and realised his laptop screen was in full view of his colleague; he shut the lid quickly and switched off his desk lamp.

Mike saw Simon's desperation at keeping the screen contents from him but instantly dismissed it; it was always too easy to become paranoid in situations like this.

The Land Rover clung to the tight bends of the high edged rural roads, occasionally catching the bramble branches like a slalom skier clipping the gates to maintain his speed.

100

'We're making good time Rich, slow down a bit', Harding finally demanded after a few terrifying miles.

Richards sighed and pressed the brake as a token gesture before returning to the accelerator.

As the Land Rover turned off onto the main coastal road towards Penzance, Richards looked into his rear view mirror in time to see another four-by-four turning off behind.

'Damn', he exclaimed.

'What is it?' Richards enquired nervously, turning himself around in his seat to see out of the rear window.

'Ah, nothing; it's just that this guy has been behind us since we left the Aerodrome that's all…'

'You're getting paranoid, relax'.

After a few further miles, and as they could make out Penzance Harbour lights in the distance across the bay, the following vehicle began to accelerate.

'I swear this guy is following us!' Richards exclaimed, 'he is getting closer'.

Harding looked in the wing mirror and then over his right shoulder.

'He probably got the same flight we did and is going to Penzance, so what? There aren't that many ways back from the peninsular. Probably just a coincidence'.

Richards pushed harder against the accelerator pedal and the engine responded with a growl.

'For God's sake!' Harding shouted, 'get a grip. Pull over and let him past'.

'This guy is gaining on us! I'm doing seventy and he is gaining; you can't tell me he isn't following us'.

Harding looked around again as the pursuing vehicle began to flash its headlights.

'What the hell is he doing? Maybe he's trying to tell us something?' Harding rationalised.

'I have no idea but if it gets any closer…'

The two vehicles tore around the lanes, clipping the curbs and spraying turf and dirt over the tarmac and the tyres of the Land Rover squealed as it accelerated out of the tight bends. Eventually the trailing vehicle began to retreat into the distance.

'There you see, he's slowing, probably just kids', Harding tried semi-convincingly, 'now come on, slow it down…'

Richards eased off the accelerator and the Land Rover slowed to a nominal speed.

The two agents looked at each other simultaneously and began to laugh.

'We'll probably be early now', Harding joked, pulling a packet of cigarettes from his inside pocket.

Richards smiled and casually glanced at his wing mirror. The smile vanished.

'He's back!'

The four-by-four came upon them at tremendous speed like a sped up action sequence of a sixties film. Richards thrust his foot hard onto the accelerator once again and the Land Rover responded, then lunged forwards as the pursuing four-by-four shunted them from behind. The rear window imploded from the impact, showering the interior with fragments of glass.

'Shit! He's hit us!' Richards shouted in terror.

'Get us out of here!' Harding followed up, looking over his shoulder through the broken rear window at the bright headlights behind them.

They lunged forwards again as the vehicle rammed them a second time.

The two vehicles screeched around the bends scattering debris of reflector and shards of plastic bumper in their wake.

Their pursuer slowed a little then accelerated at the next straight, colliding with the rear of the Land Rover again, this time tearing the rear bumper and tail door from its housing.

Richards wrestled with the steering as his vehicle swerved across the roads, clipping the jagged rocks of the cliff face. His eyes widened with fear as he saw the "Hairpin" warning sign whip past them. As they approached the sharp bend, Richards pushed his foot hard on the brakes and pulled up the handbrake. The Land Rover screeched the length of the narrow lane towards the crash barrier. He gritted his teeth as he desperately willed the vehicle to stop, as the reflection of the harbour lights in the cold, dark water in front of them fast approached. After a few terrifying moments of uncertainty, the vehicle began to slow down. Richards turned the wheel to apply acceleration out of the corner but the pursuing vehicle rammed them a final time. The impact forced Richards' foot from the brake pedal and the Land Rover jolted violently.

As they hit the crash barrier, Harding began to open the passenger door but it was forced shut by the impact of the metal defences. The Land Rover tore through the barrier and crashed down the rocks, causing the front two wheels to buckle. As it careered over the final rounded outcrop, it hit a defensive sea wall which flipped them over and projected them into the sea. Debris from the wreckage showered into the air and rained onto the surrounding rocks.

The pursuing vehicle screeched to a halt and the driver's door opened. A well-built man in hi-vis orange trousers emerged and stood in front of the twisted front end of his vehicle. He walked towards the edge and peered over at the trail of wreckage below him. The rear of the Land Rover protruded from the ocean, being wedged between a shallow ledge and the outcrop.

The pursuer watched intently for any signs of life and was disturbed after a few minutes as a vehicle approached from behind him. He stepped back and swept the immediate debris over the edge with the side of his foot before returning to his vehicle and haring off.

Simon and Mike sat in the back room of the Admiral Benbow amidst the afternoon drinkers. There was a subtle murmur of chatter from the cliental and a cricket match re-run was being played on a flat panel screen above the bar, attracting feedback from a few men who were gathered around it.

Mike drank the dregs of his pint and placed it back on the mat.

'What time is it Si?'

Simon looked at his watch, 'Twenty to three'.

He looked towards the main door and then back to his colleague. Simon drank the rest of his pint and placed it onto the table.

'Let's get another drink and give them until three okay? Maybe they have been delayed'.

Ted Barlow's red Mercedes sped around the minor coastal road above Newlyn. He grinned as his new company car took to the sharp bends with ease. He hummed along to an uncomfortably loud Pavaroti CD and applied the accelerator with an impressed grin.

As he approached a hairpin ahead of him, he noticed the pieces of red reflector glistening in the sun light. His expression changed as he spotted four sets of tyre marks in front of him. Slowing down a little he sat upright, removed his sunglasses and turned down the volume of the stereo. He reduced his speed to a slow trickle and then noticed the plastic bumper, the rear door discarded at the side of the road and the unmistakable twinkles of broken glass. He pulled the Mercedes over to the edge of the road and switched on his hazard lights. As he walked across the road he spotted the opening in the twisted, metal crash barrier.

'Oh my God!' he gasped as he peered over the edge.

'I'll give them a ring', Simon suggested after seeing Mike's clear frustration.

He plucked his phone from his jacket pocket and dialled.

As he held it to his ear, he noticed a few of the locals staring back at them and gesturing to one another.

'It's going straight to answerphone Mike', he said, dialling another number, 'I'll try Richards'.

Mike looked at the cricket score on the television above the bar and then slowly down towards the unsettled crowd that had begun to gather underneath it, staring back at him.

'What the hell are they looking at?' Mike sneered.

Simon shook his head, 'Richards' is just ringing out too'.

'Are they laughing at us?'

Simon began to wonder if staying put was such a good idea considering Mike's obvious annoyance coupled with his alcoholic induced temperament.

'Come on, I'm going for a smoke. Come outside with me', Simon offered as he collected his belongings from the table.

Mike stood up and walked across the pub towards the exit, his gaze transfixed on the ring leader; a fat man, wearing a football shirt and holding a half empty pint glass, who nodded as Mike walked past him.

'That's it coast guard, keep on moving!' he mumbled to his colleagues.

As they walked out of the door, the crowd began to laugh out loud. Mike slammed the pub door shut as Simon lit up a cigarette and dialled their colleagues' phones once again.

'Bastards!' Mike growled, 'who do they think they are?'

'Relax Mike. Look, I am not getting any joy with Richards or Harding. Maybe they headed back to Nelson?'

Mike sucked his teeth and looked into the air.

'Take my gun', he said quietly.

'What?'

'Take my gun'.

'What for?'

'Because I am going in there to belt the fat bastard at the bar and I don't want to end up shooting him in his fat face!'

Simon pushed on Mike's shoulder, forcing him away from the entrance of the pub and directed him towards the carpark.

'You knew that we would be the least popular people in Cornwall by taking this on Mike. You know that news travels fast in these tight circles – you mustn't let it get to you!'

Mike's phone rang as they got to the Land Rover. He yanked it out of his pocket.

'What?' he shouted.

A few moments passed as Mike listened to the call.

'Are you sure? Oh my God… Who called it in? Is he there now? The police?'

He slammed the phone shut and took the keys from Simon's hand.

As Mike threw the Land Rover into reverse and then forwards out of the carpark into the narrow streets of Penzance, Simon looked at him, hoping that he would offer an explanation but not daring to ask.

'That was Nelson, they just had a call from the police'.

Mike's face reddened as he spoke and his manic driving illustrated his anger.

'Their Land Rover…'

Simon swallowed. He felt his body begin to numb.

'…They've been involved in… in an accident'.

'Where?'

'On the Newlyn to Mousehole Road'.

As they sped through the streets, Simon flicked on the blue lights and the siren to forewarn the other motorists. Mike hammered the Land Rover across the curbs and cut straight across the main roundabout.

As they left the cliff side houses of Newlyn, they both saw the blue-flashing lights of emergency services in the distance.

"JOB DONE. OAKLEY AND 2 AGENTS DEALT WITH. PASS MESSAGE TO W. I EXPECT PAYMENT TONIGHT"

Reply

"GOOD WORK. YOU WILL RECEIVE PAYMENT WHEN SHIPMENT ARRIVES TONIGHT @0100"

Send

As the Land Rover approached the scene of the crash, the blue-flashing lights picked out the thousands of twinkles of glass fragments on the road surface.

Mike opened the door, leaving the engine running and jogged towards one of the policemen at the scene, standing beside a weave of blue and white tape fluttering in the breeze.

'Where are they?' he demanded.

The policeman turned to face him and held out his hand, preventing him from entering the scene.

'Sir, you cannot go any further I'm afraid.'

'I am Mike Williams of the Preventive Service and I want to know what has happened to two of my men NOW!' he butted at the officer.

'It's okay we just found out', Simon calmly relayed to the officer, presenting him with his identification card.

The policeman studied the card and looked at the two men.

'You mean …no one told you?' he asked.

Simon and Mike looked at each other and shook their heads.

'Told us what?' Mike asked wearily.

The police officer produced a small, black notepad from his upper pocket and began to recite.

'They have been taken to the West Cornwall Hospital Accident and Emergency'.

There was an uneasy pause.

'On St Clare's Street... in Penz...'

'I know where it is!' Mike interjected impatiently.

The officer returned to his notebook.

'One was pronounced dead at the scene but there is one survivor'.

Mike's eyes widened.

'What happened?' he asked, calming down at the temporary respite that the news offered.

'It looks like an accident…' the officer looked down, over the cliff edge where teams of rescuers hung on ropes around the wreckage of the Land Rover.

'…but, I personally think there is more to it than that; we need to investigate further'.

Mike turned and walked towards their vehicle.

Simon gave the officer a contact card, 'When you find anything out, call - ok?'

As he pulled the Land Rover around in the narrow width of the coastal road, Mike gritted his teeth and shook his head.

'We both know that was no accident', he said under his breath.

'We can't jump to any conclusions Mike'.

As they pulled into the ambulance bay of the West Cornwall A&E Department, Mike noticed an ambulance off-loading a stretcher. The coat of the victim beared the familiar reflective orange strip. He pulled the Land Rover onto the central island of the Emergency drop off point and ran towards the clear vinyl doors. Completely oblivious to the people trying to stop him in his path, he followed the stretcher trolley.

He ran around a corner smashing into a trolley full of instruments, to the aggravation of a nurse who was pushing it. As he approached the reception area, he saw a group of policemen and made his way towards them.

'Where's he been taken?' he shouted, breathlessly.

The officers looked back at him with confused expressions.

'Are you Michael Williams?' a rich Scottish voice came from behind the reception desk.

Mike spun around on the spot and staggered towards the red-headed lady.

'Yes, w-why?'

'Oh my God, Doctor Christian!' she shouted towards a group of doctors hurrying along the corridor away from them.

A tall, unshaven doctor stopped, turned around and began to make his way back.

'What is it?'

'This is Michael Williams', she announced.

Mike looked between them both. They were discussing his name but he recognised neither of their faces. How had infamy found him in this hospital?

'Good Lord, what a coincidence!' exclaimed the surprised doctor in an Oxford tone.

He pushed at Mike's back to get him to walk with him.

'We have just brought in one of your colleagues seconds ago'.

'Where is he? Can I see him?'

'He's asking for you Michael!'

Mike looked awkwardly at the doctor, without an adequate or suitable response.

The two paced along the corridor towards the operating theatre and stopped as the doctor placed his hand on Mike's shoulder.

'He wants to speak to you Michael but I have to warn you, he is in a bad way…'

'Will he make it?' Mike croaked.

The doctor looked at the floor and shook his head.

'He has massive internal injuries; to be frank – I doubt he'll last the night, I really am sorry'.

Mike lost the fight against his tear ducts and gave in to the inevitable as a tear streamed down his right cheek.

He pushed past the doctor and through the doors of the operating theatre.

The surgeons began to ascend on him to usher him away but the doctor followed closely and gestured that he had given him the authority be there.

Mike approached the bed where Richards' crooked and blood-stained body lay. Wires and tubes seemed to be connected to every part of his torso and a ventilator pumped noisily next to him. The surgeons worked away around them, cutting what remained of his clothes away from him and applying further wires and tubes.

The sound of the heart rate monitor beeped unstably and the room smelled of a sour mix of sea water and antiseptic. As he got close to Richards' bruised head, the heart rate monitor began to beep more erratically. Mike tried to speak but his vocal chords denied him. He managed a smile which Richards' returned.

'You smashed up the Land Rover!' he softly spoke, 'What the hell happened?'

Richards started to stammer; the heart monitor beeped significantly faster, much to the concern of the nearby staff who began to rally around the equipment. One of the nurses entered the room with a crash trolley and proceeded to charge it in anticipation.

'We…we…w-we, were… rammed!' Richards exhaled a gurgled breath.

Mike looked at him closely. He had already concluded this after visiting the crash site but hearing it sickened him.

'Who was it?'

'I don't…know…'

Time was not on his side. He was visibly deteriorating after every breath.

'Whose name was on that contract? Whose signature?' Mike persisted, desperately trying to remain calm and collected.

The heart rate monitor raced and the beeps became irregular.

The doctors pushed Mike aside as they adjusted the drip and tore open Richards' shirt, revealing his bruised chest.

'Who was it?' Mike shouted above the chaos.

The beeps became less and less frequent as the doctors raced around shouting obscure medical terminology to one another. The nurse laid the static pads onto his chest and rubbed the paddles of the defibrillator together. Mike watched Richards' mouth with desperation for some sign of movement.

Suddenly he pulled his oxygen mask aside.

'W…w…wil...'

An alarm went off as the heart rate monitor flat lined. The room filled with doctors and nurses who displaced Mike back out of the operating theatre. He looked on in disbelief as the chaos of resuscitation unfolded before him. Doctor Christian applied the electric paddles.

'Clear!' he shouted as he shocked Richards' lame body.

Mike stood, statue like, and helplessly watched through a small viewing window.

After a few long minutes Christian pulled a white sheet over Richards' body and solemnly left the room. He stopped next to Mike and clutched his shoulder.

'I'm sorry Michael', he said softly, 'he had massive haemorrhaging in his chest, his head... there was nothing I could do'.

Mike left the Emergency ward entrance and stood outside. He felt the uncontrollable nausea build up inside him and quickly dashed towards a nearby flowerbed to vomit. The sky had started to dim as the evening sunset turned the deep-blue sky into a vibrant orange.

Simon stood nearby smoking a cigarette and was alerted by the sound of retching. He looked around and spotted Mike doubled up, clinging on to one of the entrance pillars.

'I'm sorry Mike', he offered, 'I spoke to the police and they reckon it was an accident'.

Mike blinked out of his trancelike stare and wiped his mouth with the back of his sleeve.

'Bullshit! Richards told me himself they were rammed off the road!'

Simon frowned and exhaled a plume of smoke into the breeze.

'What? Did he manage to…' Simon paused, aware of the insensitivity of his question.

'Tell us whose name was on the contract? No!'

There was an uncomfortable pause as Simon waited for an elaboration.

Mike looked into the air and inhaled.

'Not a clue!' he exhaled.

The two walked slowly to the abandoned Land Rover, its blue lights still strobing the front of the Accident and Emergency entrance.

Mike stared out of the window and then towards Simon, who concentrated on his driving.

Simon felt his stare and turned to look at him.

'I'm going for a drink!' Mike spat.

Simon shook his head, with an exaggerated expression.

'Don't you think you'd be better off spending the time sleeping?'

Mike ignored him.

As they approached the harbour at Penzance, Mike started to take his seat belt off.

'Anywhere here is fine'.

Simon knew that arguing with his partner was futile and reluctantly pulled up alongside the weighbridge office.

Simon held out his left hand.

'Gun!' he demanded.

With a manic smile, Mike pulled out the automatic from his hip holster and slapped it into Simon's hand.

'Do you want me to…'

Mike slammed the door shut and disappeared into the dusky night.

'…pick you up?' Simon finished the question to himself.

Mike walked intently along a narrow back street of the town. There were very few people around as it had started to spit with rain. As he passed the line of pubs and inns on his way, he heard the happy murmur coming from inside, the occasional cackle of laughter and the sounds of cutlery on dinner plates. He could have been doing that; eating at his favourite restaurant, had it not been the fact that he had been thrown into this mess. Although he had only been working on this project a short while - it had felt like years. He had already achieved hatred by the public and had watched one of his colleagues die under suspicious circumstances. Why did the police jump to the conclusion that it was an accident so quickly? Why did it suddenly feel like everyone was against them?

He approached the Benbow main entrance and pushed the large wooden door open. As he walked inside, he watched the people eating their pub meals; tucking into steaks and spiking chips as they drank their drinks and laughed with their friends. An overwhelming feeling of loneliness descended onto him. As he made his way to the bar, he noticed the same crowd of locals that had taunted him earlier. They hadn't noticed him enter and were engrossed in the local news bulletin on the television.

He took off his jacket, laid it onto the floor in front of the barstool and slapped the bar to attract the barman.

'What can I get you?'

Mike looked at the ales on tap and then shifted his gaze to the whiskey shelf.

'Give me a double Jamesons'.

'Ice with that?'

Mike shook his head and turned his gaze to the television.

'Put it on a tab', he demanded.

He was more than aware of his obnoxious attitude but was too tired to exercise politeness and in any case it made him feel at ease.

"The main headlines again; a Coastguard Land Rover has been found a few hours ago, in the coastal waters off Cliff Road, near Newlyn. It was thought that it had lost control on the notoriously hazardous bend that has claimed the lives of countless drivers, and had crashed through the barrier, down the rock face and into the sea. Both the driver and the passenger were pronounced dead at the scene. Police have not yet released a statement but an official has stated that this is being treated as an accident. We will bring you more on that story when reports come in… In other news, a sperm whale was sighted…"

The sound of the television faded out into the ambient murmur of the pub.

Mike shook his head, returned his gaze to his drink and threw the contents back into his mouth, pushing the empty glass across the bar for a refill.

Simon sat down at his desk and placed the Land Rover keys in his in-tray.

He opened his laptop and logged in. The email was still on his screen.

"Urgent message: Regular reports req'd by Wilkinson on Williams. Wilkinson eager to know how he is coping with strains of job. Email direct to Wilkinson. Anything you need, pls ask. Kind regards, David Simmons"

Simon scratched his head and hit the reply button. He hesitated - his fingers hovering above the keyboard. This wasn't an easy task; he was to report on his colleague- his friend. What was he supposed to detail? That he was at the pub right now getting hammered? That he insinuated he would use his firearm in aggression towards locals at a popular tourist bar?

He placed his head in his hands and rubbed at his eyes.

The pub had filled to near its capacity as the locals and a few taxi parties had begun to settle in for the evening. Mike downed the last dregs of his lager and moved onto the whiskey chaser.

The fat local, that had taunted him previously, spotted him through the crowd and informed his colleagues who began to laugh once again. Mike watched them; he squinted through irritated eyes of inebriation and fatigue and once again shook his head. He drank the double whiskey chaser down and pointed at the lager pump as he swallowed. The bar tender gave a look of concern and began to pull another pint of lager as Mike pushed himself from his stool, lost his balance and steadied himself on the bar surface. After finding his footing he headed in the direction of the toilets.

The fat man smiled as he watched Mike stumble through the toilet door.

"Mr Simmons, all is well with project. Would like to report recommendation of commendation for Williams' professionalism in case. Making headway in investigation. Liaising with police as per protocol. Following up smuggling system early tomorrow morning. Williams controlling emotions since death of Harding and Richards. Concerned that his focus on the project isn't without personal feelings. Will continue updates as and when.

Yours

Simon Jenkins"

Simon read the email back to himself. It was accurate in as far as the case was concerned and he knew instinctively that this would be more than satisfactory to Simmons and for his report to the Admiralty. But, his report on Williams couldn't have been further from the truth. It was true that Mike was exercising an extremely professional outlook to the case and that they were making progress but he had skated over the details that Mike was very much affected by the deaths of their colleagues. Mike was, as far as Simon was concerned, not in a fit mental state to be carrying out their duties, let alone a loaded weapon. However, who could blame him. He had been thrown into a world of chaos three days ago and already they had lost two men in which the police were seemingly dismissing as an accident. They knew that this was not the case which was causing immense distraction to them both. He couldn't tell Simmons the truth; any headway they were making was down to Mike. He was the instigator; Simon was simply doing the official "red tape". Between them they were a perfect blend. Mike's background provided an invaluable source of underworld knowledge and his own background enabled them to act with authority and within the confines of law protocol. By reporting that Mike was seemingly suffering from the mental strain was unfair on him this early into the project and also detrimental. If there was a chance that Mike could be removed from the project it would terminate any further progress.

As he sat reading the email back to himself, he wondered how Mike was doing. Perhaps he had gone home. Perhaps he ought to omit any reference to Mike's emotions altogether?

After a few moments thought he clicked the 'Send' button.

Mike looked at the tiled walls in front of him as he used the urinal. He tried to focus on the grouting but his vision was impaired and the concentration involved threw him off balance. He knew that he was drunk but he fought it hard, trying to remain in control but he also knew that there was another pint of lager waiting for him at the bar, which made him smile like a young boy on his birthday.

Suddenly the door swung open; the metal door handle hit the tiles causing one to split. Mike slowly looked to his left to see the fat man in front of the same group of locals from earlier. Knowing there was an inevitable situation ahead of him, he zipped up his trousers and began to wash his hands, trying as hard as he could to ignore them. Much to their amusement, the men watched the intoxicated agent fight for his balance, using his right hand to steady himself on the hand dryer, accidentally turning it on.

'So Coastguard man!' the fat man started, 'are you looking for trouble in here? Is that why you came back tonight?'

Mike laughed out loud; a long and drawn out exaggerated laugh.

'You think I'd waste my time looking for trouble with you?' he slurred.

Although he had shown strength in his character, he knew that he was in trouble and had he thought before he had spoken he probably could have talked his way out of the situation.

He had counted five men in all and they were grouped at the doorway, completely obscuring the door and blocking his exit. Granted they were probably as drunk as he was but they looked convincingly threatening. His mind began to go back to his fatally wounded colleague on the operating table and what his last words meant. What was he trying spell out to him? Suddenly, he snapped back into the moment.

'Look at him, he's arseholed!' one of the men pointed.

'I tell you what – you've got some face crawling into this bar! This is a bar for real men what make a livin', you got no place in here coast guard!' the fat man growled.

'Shut the door Chris', he shouted over his shoulder.

Chris stepped outside and shut the door behind him, leaning on it preventing anyone from entering.

Mike felt the situation worsen. As the men started to move towards him, he began to panic.

'Look, I've had a really really bad day guys, just let me past and I'll get out here', he tried to reason.

'Oh! Oh that's fine then, Coastguard man, you can go…'

They began to shuffle aside, providing a corridor to the door. Initially Mike felt an overwhelming relief but quickly re-assessed the situation. He realised that there was no way out of what was inevitably going to happen and that his only option was to try and escape. His mind began to wander once again to Richards' body; lying on the operating table, covered with tubes, wires and cables; the nurse unplugging the various machines nearby and the doctor squeezing his shoulder. His rage began to build inside him; he knew it wasn't an accident and as for the police… they should've known it was a suspicious crash – anybody could've seen that!

'Oh no, Coastguard man is about to unleash his fury!' one of the men shouted, pointing at Mike's clenched fists.

'I don't want any trouble...' Mike slurred.

'I don't give a shit', the fat man returned.

Mike gritted his teeth, put his right foot against the wall behind him, took a deep breath and pushed himself towards the group. He barged the fat man out of the way and pushed hard at the second, forcing the door open and knocking the fourth man and the watcher outside onto the floor of the lounge; much to the surprise of the people seated nearby. Mike began to pick himself up from the entanglement of bodies and the pub silenced. The remaining two men walked out of the toilets behind him and each pulled him back by his arms. The fat man picked himself up from the floor and approached the dazed agent.

'My turn', he growled as he bowled a fist at Mike's cheek. Mike blacked out and hit the floor like a sack of coal. As he lay defenceless on the floor, the group of men began to punch and kick him indiscriminately in his head and torso.

Mike gained consciousness and managed to curl up in a foetal position. After a short, uninterrupted time – a large man dressed in a dark suit pushed the men away, one by one, from Mike's battered semi-conscious body.

'What the hell you do that for Frank?' the fat man shouted, fists still clenched.

The doorman helped Mike to his feet and guided him out of the ruckus and into the safety of the bar area.

'Thank you', Mike whispered through his bruised mouth, in appreciation.

'Get your sorry arse out of this pub, coast guard! You weren't welcome the first time you came in and I'd advise you not to come back!'

Mike looked at him in disbelief. It quickly occurred to him that the only reason why he had been plucked from the fight was to preserve the customers and the pub's reputation.

He snatched his arm from the doorman's grasp and shuffled quickly towards the exit. The rest of them watched the blood-stained and dishevelled agent walk precariously to the exit.

Once outside, he felt at his ribs and the bruises that had been inflicted upon him, wincing at every touch. It was raining hard and the blood from his face washed down his uniform and onto the pavement in front of him reintroducing his nausea. It also occurred to him, as he walked along the dark wet street, that what had just happened to him could be a result of Black's death.

Word travels fast in these circles and it is a historic fact that the majority of the population of coastal towns in South West England were all connected in some way to the smuggling industry. If he was reported as being the last person seen leaving the Ship by any of Black's associates, the news will have travelled fast and the fact that he died soon after will have led to an unmistakable equation.

Wilkinson sat at his large ornate desk with a telephone receiver under his left ear.

'The order of twenty destroyers is the prime issue of the meeting Lord Chancellor and will be at the top of my agenda, don't you worry'.

As he wrote notes on his pad, his laptop sounded an alert. He moved his mouse and clicked the notification; bringing his email client in view on the screen.

Simon's email was highlighted. He selected it and read the contents of the first few lines, nodding and smiling as he scrolled through it.

Chapter 8

<u>The Investigation</u>

John Coates, a retired fisherman now bulb farmer in his early seventies, looked at his watch; 00:50. He walked to the other side of his kitchen and laid down an empty coffee mug on the work surface and assessed his appearance in a small wall mirror. He rubbed his grey, stubbly chin and then pulled down the half netting of the kitchen window to look out over the fields towards the dark, wet horizon. He pulled on his wax overcoat and collected his torch from a shelf next to an assortment of copper-based pots and pans. Although he had done this hundreds of times before, he felt nervous about tonight. Perhaps it was the media hype of *The Royal Wave*? Perhaps it was a sign that it was time to get out? Whatever it was, it was bugging him. After fastening the large brass buttons on the front of his coat, he switched on the exterior lights to the farm house. On his way to the door he snatched a piece of notepaper from the fruit bowl, read the number scrawled upon it and then slid it into his coat pocket. It was a policy that he should memorise the numbers given to him but his mind wasn't what it used to be so he had taken to writing the numbers down. As he headed out of the door he picked up his phone and his binoculars from the post table.

The rain outside was more of a heavy mist than a fall. He pulled up the collar of his coat and pulled the stable door shut behind him and made his way along the footpath through the fields. As he neared the hardy foliage at the edge of the cliff, he looked to his right at the tiny light of the Coastguard point in the distance. He put his hand into his pocket and found his cigarettes, picking one out with his mouth. He turned his back on the hut in the distance and flicked open a petrol lighter, igniting the damp cigarette and sending plumes of blue smoke into the mist. Carefully he manoeuvred to the very edge and pointed his compass out to sea. As the needle settled he aimed his binoculars in the given direction and looked hard through them.

A tiny rowing boat signalled flashes with a faint torch light through the mist.

It always brought a smile to his face, from as far back as his childhood; when the boats came ashore he and his father would negotiate the slippery rock face of the cliff to meet them – his father would rub his finger and thumb together: "Pay Day".

He pulled his MagLight from his pocket and flashed twice in response. This system of communication, simplified by the advent of the mobile phone, had been implemented for centuries; evading Coastguard vessels as well as both the Royal Navy and the German Fleet during wartime, thus enabling the smuggling industry to continue despite the interruption of conflict.

John pulled out the paper with the number, punched it into his phone and sent his preset text "CLEAR!"

By implementing an intricate network of signalling and text communications they were guaranteed never to be traced. It was a fool-proof method that had brought in millions of pounds of illicit goods from all over the world. No individual knew the whole consortium and if an individual was compromised then the circle would tighten and cut that member out - that was the agreement. Furthermore by being severed it also meant that he or she would be removed from the smuggling network permanently which led to an overwhelming professionalism by every unit involved.

After he had made doubly sure that the text message was sent, he walked back towards the farmhouse garage. He started the engine of the Suzuki Jimny and pulled out without headlights and slowly careered to the drop off point.

The cliff was lush with green grass and exotic foliage, which, by a gracious and unknown force, suddenly fell through the hillside to the sea below, making a huge bottle-shaped cavern in the cliff where the waves crashed in and around making it a perfect and unobvious landing spot.

John stopped the vehicle nearby and uncoupled a rope from a large iron ring set into a stone at the edge of the hole. Satisfied the rope was tight; he lit a cigarette and waited for the boat to arrive. After a few minutes the rope began to tug in his hand. As he looked below he could see the small boat illuminated by the moonlight. There was another tug, signalling him to pull up the contraband. He heaved it up the fifty metres to the top and lifted it over the rocky edge of the hole, setting it down on the grassy bank next to him. He threw the rope down again and waited for a secondary tug signalling further packages. If after three minutes the rope remained loose; he knew that the either the boat was in danger and had left the drop off point or there were no further packages. Sure enough; there was a second tug.

After a while he finally pulled up the last of the cases. There were around seven or eight tea chests full of "catch". It wasn't his remit in the operation to know the content of the packages, but simply to store them. He loaded the chests onto the back of his jeep and made his way stealthily back to the cottage. He casually looked in his rear view mirror at the boxes piled high in the rear of the vehicle. This was an unprecedented amount; occasionally there were three or four packages but never as many as this.

Simon looked at his watch; 9:30am. He hadn't seen or heard from Mike since he dropped him off at the docks the previous night. He scratched his chin, closed his laptop and walked out of the office, snatching his coat from the stand in the corner on his way out.

Once outside he dialled Mike's quick-dial number. As usual the phone rang numerous times but this time there was no answer. Suddenly his phone rang in his hand. He pressed the "accept" button and answered.

'Mike?' there was an awkward pause, 'ah, sorry Mrs Jacobs. It has? Excellent! I will call him now and tell him. Thank you Mrs Jacobs. Yes I have been trying to get in touch with him too. Have you emailed him? Thank you Mrs Jacobs'.

He closed the phone with a look of relief. Mrs Jacobs had been a secretary at Nelson House for twenty years and had made it her business to know everything about everybody, both within the organisation and outside to as much an extent as possible, making her a valuable, yet unorthodox asset. Simon flipped the phone open and tried Mike once again. This news would surely rouse him from whatever state he was in.

Mike's bedroom door was open, his jacket hung awkwardly from the door handle. The sunlight battled to penetrate the thick, orange woollen curtains creating a dark amber glow in the stuffy warm room. The pictures on the walls leading to the bedroom were hanging awkwardly and some of them lay on the floor.

Ring Ring…

The duvet moved slightly in response to the piercing shrill of the call.

Ring Ring…

Mike pulled the duvet down slightly.

Ring Ring…

He threw a bruised arm out of the bed and onto the bedside table to retrieve the phone - it wasn't there. Although Mike was extremely hung over, he knew he couldn't miss the call. He looked at the alarm clock: 09:58.

'Shit!' he shouted as he sprang out of bed to search for his phone amongst the piles of discarded clothes that cascaded from the bed into a pile on the floor.

Ring Ring…

'Alright alright give me a chance'.

He squeezed at his coat pockets.

Ring Ring…

He realised that the sound was closer and instinctively felt at his trouser pocket realising that he was still wearing his trousers from the night before. He felt inside and retrieved the vibrating phone.

'Yes yes yes', he answered breathlessly.

'Where the hell are you Mike?' an angry voice enquired.

Mike kneeled on the bed and ran a hand through his greasy hair.

'I'm…'

'In bed?'

'Yes', he sighed; it was futile to try and conceive an excuse.

'Well get your arse onto your computer now, Mrs Jacobs has been trying to phone you, she has emailed you something that you may find interesting'.

Mike's face lit up, instantly curing his sleep deprived eye lines.

'The private sales list?'

'Yes. I need you to work it up this morning. I am going to follow up a name on Black's list. I'm on my way now. I'll meet you later on'.

'Sure', Mike replied as he shuffled through the debris-strewn hallway towards his computer in the living room.

As the Land Rover ambled over the picturesque coastal roads, Simon's phone began to ring on the dashboard. He slowed down and pulled into a farm entrance.

'Simon Jenkins'.

'It's me, Simon', the voice on the other end responded.

Simon's face dropped – it was Wilkinson.

'Hello sir', he greeted with anticipation.

'How is our man this morning? Heard he got into a fight last night?'

Simon closed his eyes and screwed them up. He had never asked Mike how his night of consolation had gone and assumed that as he was at home and everything was ok.

'I see', Simon said sombrely.

'I read your report Simon, thank you. I am still eager as ever to catch up on how Mike is doing so if you would please keep up the frequent reports – I would be grateful'.

Simon frowned in confusion. Why was he reiterating this? It was agreed in principal at the initial meeting.

'Yes sir', he replied without sounding confused.

'What are you following up today then Mr Jenkins?'

Simon looked increasingly irritated. Why the unprecedented necessity for information? Why was Wilkinson pestering him suddenly? It seemed, he thought, as though Wilkinson was checking up on their movements, and even if he was – wouldn't a member of his staff do it for him? He bit his lip.

'I have yet to discuss with Mike, sir. I'll keep you informed'.

'I would appreciate that Mr Jenkins, goodbye'.

The phone went dead. Simon looked at the ear piece and closed the phone. It was strange that Wilkinson; a man of such noble status - Lord of The Fleet - was ringing him to find out how an infant project such as this was progressing. He opened a folder from the passenger seat and pulled out Black's list from a plastic wallet. There were three names and locations written in Mike's scrawl. With an unsettling feeling, he pulled the vehicle back onto the road.

The inkjet printer in Mike's living room churned away, feeding paper into the rear and delivering reams of reports onto the receiver tray as Mike stared at the bright screen, while sipping a cup of steaming black coffee. After a few moments the printer stopped and he leaned forward to collect the stack of papers.

He stood up from the leather recliner and moved towards his sofa, pushing a pile of newspapers and magazines onto the floor to make room for his exhausted and weak body. As he sifted through the first few legal notes on the usage and privacy statements of the reports he came to the first sheet:

"PRIVATE SALE OF: 175FT PATROL VESSEL "HMS ARCHANGEL"

Mike scanned the documents details aloud.

'Sold in Nineteen Eighty Six, Mr Jefferson, three hundred and sixty seven thousand pounds, to be converted into luxury cruiser, nope, not that one…'

For a few moments he scanned the key details and then placed it onto his coffee table, moving on to the next one: 'Private sale, eighty six feet torpedo runner? Who'd buy that one?'

The Land Rover roared over the top of one of the typical Cornish country lanes.

Simon slowed down as he approached a farm entrance and checked the Satellite Navigation System set into the dashboard. He looked back at the gate. A large "For Sale" sign stood awkwardly at an angle over the wall. It was a new sign but the farm appeared empty or more so - abandoned.

'Not going to get very far with this one', he shook his head, moving his index finger over the next location. It was twenty miles away. With a prolonged sigh he tossed the list onto the passenger seat and continued along the road. The realisation of his stress of both the phone call with Wilkinson and the concerns over the case had come to a head; he would normally have listed the locations in order of distance.

Eventually he arrived at the second location; another farm. Simon took off his sunglasses and looked at the old gate – a huge metal chain hung around it, shackling it to the gatepost and secured by a large industrial padlock. He kept the engine running and got out of the vehicle. As he rested his hands on the dry stone wall surrounding the farm, he noticed a large sign planted in front of the farmhouse; "SOLD".

'What the hell is going on?' he said to himself through gritted teeth.

This was ridiculous and surely more than just a coincidence. Maybe someone had leaked that Black had talked, causing mass panic. He got back into the Land Rover and looked at the list. The last one was virtually back where he had started. Cursing to himself and rolling his eyes, he turned the Land Rover around.

"COATES, WE NEED U FOR LAST DROP. U R ON BLACKS LIST SO BE VIGILANT"

Coates read the received message and sighed. He scratched his head and stared out of his front window at the cliff and sea line beyond. This was serious - if he was implicated by Black then this would jeopardise the whole project and all involved. Worse than that, he would be forced to leave the farm; his family home for generations.

Eventually Simon arrived only three miles from the first location on the list. Expecting to find an abandoned farmhouse or another "For Sale" sign, he trickled past the main entrance. To his surprise the gate was open. He reversed past the gate and pulled onto the track leading to the main house, noticing the Coastguard building on his left in the distance. This, he thought, was a no-goer; there is no way that someone would operate a smuggling operation within a couple of miles of the Coastguard watch. He continued past an array of ancient, derelict overgrown stone barns and pulled up adjacent to the front door of the farmhouse.

Coates, still in deep thought from the text message he had received, heard the engine outside the kitchen. He rushed to the window and peered through the yellowing, lace curtains.

Simon knocked on the flaking, wooden door of the cottage, causing several layers of the ancient, white paint to scatter into the breeze.

The door was promptly answered by Coates.

He looked at Simon through squinted, tired eyes.

'Who are you?' he scowled through a grimace.

'Mr John Coates?' Simon asked.

'Who's asking?'

'I'm with Her Majesties Preventive Service'.

Coates looked perplexed; yet his stomach burned with adrenalin. He looked at the uniform and coughed impulsively.

'I am conducting a local investigation into a spate of smuggling in the local area and I was wondering if you could help me with my enquiries?'

Coates looked him up and down. Simon fished in his pocket for his identity card and produced it in front of the stocky old man. Coates' expression altered. He recognised the uniforms and the Land Rover from the local news from Mousehole a few days earlier and had been half expecting an encounter long before the text message came through from his contact. He reluctantly opened the door to allow the agent to step inside.

Simon stepped into a stereotypical farmhouse kitchen with Range Cooker, jars of jam and chutneys and half a loaf of bread sticking end up on a chopping board next to a very large knife.

'Nice place. I love the old...'

'What do you want?' Coates interrupted with a snarl.

'I am conducting an investi...'

'You told me that already, how is it that I can help you?'

It was time to change his tactics.

'I need to look around your property Mr Coates'.

'Not a chance!' Coates snapped instantly.

'I can get a warrant', Simon tried.

'Get one!'

Simon sucked at his cheek and clamped it between his teeth. Coates raised his head into the air with a smug expression.

'Fine!' Simon said without sounding too perturbed, 'I have no choice but to name you as a potential suspect in the investigation. I have the power to do this Mr Coates, meaning that we can take you into custody while I get a team to search your property – does that sound ok to you?'

Simon turned to leave the house, pulling his mobile phone from his pocket. There is no way that he could do this, the police didn't have that authority. He was gambling on the situation and Coates could very easily call his bluff. He would then have no choice but to leave. Coates was on Black's list. Maybe he could use that as leverage?

'Okay, Mr?...' Coates waited for Simon to reply.

'Jenkins', he answered smiling to himself.

'Jenkins... Okay Mr Jenkins, you got me, please feel free to look around the place. I got nothing to hide though; you are wasting your time'.

Simon stepped back into the kitchen nodding in approval to Coates.

'Would you like a cup of tea?' Coates reluctantly asked, making his way to the stove, armed with a box of matches.

'Tea, thanks', he responded as he looked around the kitchen. Where did he start? He hadn't really prepared for this. If Mike were with him he would know exactly what to do and where to look. One thing that occurred to him was that if Coates was hiding anything then he was taking a chance that he wouldn't find it. Maybe he wasn't hiding anything? Maybe Black wrote his name to buy himself some time?

He moved into the living room, under the watchful eye of the owner as he dropped a couple of tea bags into an iron kettle.

'You will find what you are looking for just under the first chair', he chuckled.

Simon, not amused by the taunt, moved into the living room and started to knock on the walls and stamp on areas of the floorboards – listening for the traits of hollow stow areas. He lifted the chair that Coats had joked about and quickly returned it.

After a while, Coates came into the room with two mugs of tea. He looked up as he heard the floorboards creaking from the bedroom and smiled.

'Found anything yet Mr Jenkins?'

There was no reply. Simon walked down the stairs, defeated. He had been in every room in the house and found nothing. He accepted the tea from Coates who was smiling at him directly.

In the days when he worked in Dover docks, Simon had been able to find the false compartments in coaches and lorries, and the fake panels in cars with ease. It was a gift his father had passed down to him. He genuinely couldn't find anything about the house that pointed to smuggling. Usually smugglers had an unusual amount of keys on hooks for all the lockups and secret stowaways. Coates had none of the hallmarks of being a smuggler - he was either a smuggling expert or completely innocent.

Feeling defeated and slightly embarrassed he drank his tea, desperate to leave the old man alone. As he drank from the china cup he spotted the derelict barns from the living room window; the ones that he had passed on the driveway.

'What do you keep in those barns?' he asked as he drank the dregs of tea from the bottom of the cup.

'Nothing, they are... they are crumbling away, I don't know why.... why I haven't demolished them... you are wasting my time...' he stuttered as Simon began to make his way out of the kitchen door.

Coates placed the cups on the surface and followed him with pace.

Simon strode towards the crumbling white stone buildings with a look of excitement.

'Seriously, you don't want to go in there Mr Jenkins, they are very dangerous structures', Coates tried.

Simon reached the first one and began to enter the broken doorway with caution. Nettles and brambles enveloped the beamed structure and prevented him from getting into the opening. The roof had long since perished and a few of the ancient beams stuck out at precarious angles from the grassy floor. As he began to make his way inside, holding onto the brick doorway for stability, he spotted a dead seagull in a state of advanced decay.

'Oh for f.....' he started, backing away from the building and snagging his trousers on one of the brambles.

Coates stood a few yards behind him chuckling to himself.

Simon turned to face him, completely demoralised.

'I am sorry to have bothered you Mr Coates'.

'No bother at all Mr Jenkins, it's been quite entertaining if the truth be told'.

Simon walked back to his Land Rover, wiping his hands on his trousers.

Coates watched as he pulled out of the courtyard and back onto the track.

As he drove away towards the gate, he saw Coates watching him. Retracing the events; Coates had seemed a touch nervous about something towards the end. He pulled out his phone and pressed a short dial.

"HMPS AGENT BEEN AND GONE - HE WON'T RETURN. WE ARE BACK ON TRACK"

Coates pressed the "Send" button.

Mike sat staring at his computer screen, his hangover having long since subsided. He jerked at the mouse; clicking intermittently, rapidly sorting through web pages and tabbing from one page to another with the printer churning away next to him- reproducing page upon page of text and imagery.

Amidst the noise of relentless mouse clicking coupled with that of the ageing printer, his phone vibrated underneath a stack of papers. He pushed his hand underneath and retrieved it without taking his eyes from the screen.

'Yeah…' he answered vaguely, transfixed on the monitor.

'Mike, it's Simon, I need your help'.

'Go on…'

'Do you recognise the name John Coates?'

Mike's attention turned to the phone call, 'John Coates? That's one of the name's from Black's list isn't it?'

'Yes, I have just left his farmhouse. I didn't find anything but there is something about him that doesn't feel right, can you… can I come and pick you up? I want you to go back with me - maybe you can spot something I missed?'

'Yeah sure… that name sounds really familiar…' Mike sucked the end of his pen.

'I'm on my way now, will be with you in about ten minutes'.

The phone went dead and as the printer stopped printing Mike spun the chair around to see the new page. As his eyes scanned the information he began to smile.

'Got ya!' he said under his breath. He took the page, folded it and slipped it into his trouser pocket.

Mike spotted Simon driving towards the cottage and searched through the paper stack for other relevant information as he finished his coffee. Simon sounded the horn signifying his impatience. Mike raised the pace; sifting through the stacks of papers he had printed and the notes he had made, ultimately scooping the lot into a card folder. He grabbed his coat and his gun from the kitchen work surface and left.

'Hi', Mike greeted his partner.

Simon looked at him with a hint of spite.

'You have a good night last night?'

He reversed the Land Rover up the driveway and out onto the road.

'What's wrong?' Mike asked with curiosity.

'You - last night, getting into a fight? Like our reputation isn't tarnished enough? What if the press had gotten involved?'

Mike sat back with his head down, like a naughty school boy being told off by his father.

After a few uncomfortable silent moments, Simon realised that he had been taking out his frustration on him and had he actually got anywhere with the investigations at Coates' farmhouse his mood would have been more amicable.

'Did you find anything out this morning? Your email from Nelson?' Simon asked in a lighter tone.

'Yeah, I think I am on to something…'

Simon began to smile.

'Yeah?'

Mike turned in his seat.

'Okay, what about this? We are looking for a vessel that is oblivious to the eye right? Has only been seen a few times and at great distance, that can disappear - vanish?'

'Right?' Simon responded, preparing himself for a revelation.

'We are also looking for a vessel, possibly ex-navy or at the least sold by the Navy, privately…?

'Okay…' Simon responded again, his eyes on the road ahead.

'Well…' Mike produced the notes he had printed earlier from the folder, 'here is a list of vessels that have been sold privately in the last thirty years. It's a big list. It includes err…' he traced a few lines with his finger, 'six torpedo runners, seventeen dinghies, five patrol boats, a cruiser… err…here!' he stabbed at the paper with his index finger.

'What?' Simon enquired.

'A Nineteen Thirty Nine German U-Boat; U-239, captured in the Channel in June Nineteen Forty Three, used by the Royal Navy as a training vessel in the fifties, dry-docked until July Nineteen Seventy Nine and finally moored at Cardiff until it was sold to a Leon De LaCruz in August Nineteen Ninety One. A private sale of two hundred and sixty seven thousand, four hundred pounds'.

He thrust the paper including an image of the vessel towards Simons face.

'And?' he asked, glancing at it.

'And, it is a submarine! It disappears. They used to drop rubber bombs on it during training exercises in the fifties. I would say a submarine is the perfect transport for the EMP generator! It all makes sense'.

Mike appeared genuinely excited by his find. Simon looked at him tentatively but bit his lip.

'Are you saying that this De LaCruz character sold it to the pirates?'

'I don't know? Could be worth a visit…'

'Where does he live?'

'Gibraltar'.

Simon looked at Mike who in turn looked back at him.

'Okay, we are here!' Simon said, pulling the Land Rover through the gates of Coates' farm.

'Oh my God!' Mike exclaimed.

'What's that?'

'I knew I recognised the name!'

Mike's excitement over the U-Boat discovery suddenly dwindled and was replaced by intrigue; his eyes darted to every detail of the approaching farmhouse.

'You know this place?' Simon asked.

'Know it? Of course. Johnsea! This is Johnsea's house!'

'Johnsea?' Simon asked.

'Johnsea! John-C, John Coates!'

The Land Rover pulled up in exactly the same space as his prior visit.

Coates heard the vehicle arrive. Annoyed, he pulled down the net curtains and saw the Land Rover pulling into the gravelled courtyard once again. He growled under his breath and stomped towards the kitchen door.

'You been here before?' Simon asked as they made their way to the decrepit door.

'Been here? I used to work here!'

He knocked, causing more of the paintwork to flutter into the wind.

'This could be awkward', he said quietly.

The door was answered almost immediately by Coates.

'What do you want this ti…..' he paused as he registered Mike.

'Hello Johnsea', Mike calmly greeted the old man, whose wispy grey hair contrasted his deep red face.

'M…Michael?' Coates stuttered, squinting his eyes to focus upon the figure he last saw as a teenager. His red complexion began to fade and his grimace began to form an unavoidable smile. His heart strings began to pull as memories of happier times flitted in his mind.

As his concentration turned to Mike's uniform, his expression returned to a grimace. Remembering Black's warnings of long ago when Mike had turned against them.

He began to shut the door but Mike's foot pushed it back open.

'What are you doing here coast guard?' he stabbed at Mike.

Simon looked between them both as Mike hesitated to answer. He knew there was a past but he hadn't a clue what it entailed and it was better left that way as far as he was concerned.

Mike straightened up. It was hard for him also. His involvement with Black had started here at Coates' house. This farm was used for smuggling by generations of Coates' and it was no secret: the first recorded arrest for smuggling in Devon and Cornwall was at Coates' farm in Sixteen hundred and six.

'I am not going to beat about the bush, I am going to ask you straight and you are going to tell me the truth; yes or no!'

Coates looked at him with a stubborn grin and nodded slowly.

'Oh you think so do you? What have you become? Your father...'

'Are you connected in any way to the receiving of stolen and or smuggled goods right now?' Mike cut him off.

There was an uncomfortable silence.

Simon looked between the two men as the silence prevailed.

'NO! Now bugger off!' Coates butted at the two agents and began to close the wooden door again.

Mike pushed his foot into the gap and pushed it open with his fist.

'Then you won't mind if I take a look around then?' Mike snapped as he spun around and stormed off towards the broken white barn building adjacent to the house.

Simon paced after him.

'Mike, I have already checked this out. There is nothing in there except for a dead bird!'

Coates looked nervous. He moved into the kitchen, felt around under an array of dirty tea towels hanging up inside a cupboard, retrieved a large box and then made his way outside.

Mike approached the doorway of the derelict barn.

'You see, it is totally overgrown!' Simon said in anticipation of another embarrassing apology.

Mike looked back at him with a confident smile and began to negotiate the overgrown entrance. As he arrived at the centre of the structure, he paused and looked at Simon who watched with apprehension.

Mike stamped his feet; the noise echoed below him. Simon's jaw dropped open in awe.

He bent down and felt beneath the grass, eventually finding a rusty linked chain. He leaned back to take the strain and pulled hard. Simon watched with amazement as a large oak board slid back on a concrete runner exposing a dark bunker.

'Jesus Christ!' Simon exclaimed.

'Bomb shelter, built in the late thirties. I used to play in this thing'.

Mike stooped and lowered himself down into the shallow room. As Simon moved closer inside the derelict treasure trove, he found his partner standing on the top of one of around thirty tea chests in varying states of dust accumulation. As the two agents paused to ingest their find, Coates arrived at the crumbling entrance.

'Don't you move another inch you double crossing bastard!'

Mike and Simon simultaneously spun around to see Coates standing above training a revolver over them.

Simon, being behind Mike and out of the line of sight of the old man, slowly reached under his jacket to his hip holster and released the press stud from the pouch.

Sensing Simon's movements Mike began to lower his hands.

'Don't move coast guard!' Coates screamed.

'What are you going to do, John? Shoot us?' Mike asked, trying to diffuse the situation.

Coates raised the antique weapon and aimed it at Mike's head.

'I can't let you do this Michael', Coates began.

'You are an accessory to this operation John, you are not a murderer!'

Coates pulled back the hammer, rotating the chamber to the next round.

Simon placed his hand on the handle of his automatic and began to slowly extract it from the holster.

'Do you know what will happen to me if I let you take this stuff?'

'You will help us with our enquiries, John. Then you…'

Simon quickly whipped his gun from under his jacket and pointed it at the old man. Coates in turn moved his weapon towards Simon as Mike took the opportunity to draw his.

'Put it down Coates!' Mike yelled.

Coates became nervous and began to shake, shifting the revolver back and forth between the two armed agents.

'Come on John, lower your weapon', Mike tried again, 'don't make this any worse for yourself'.

Coates closed his eyes and reluctantly dropped the weapon into the long grass.

Simon clambered across the barbed undergrowth towards the defeated old man and retrieved the weapon.

Mike turned his attention back to the chests in the bunker.

'Is there anything you would like to admit to now John?' Mike asked as he pushed his fingers under lid of the closest chest.

The restrained old man shook his head slowly.

Mike lifted the balsa lid of the chest and pushed it from its housing.

As Simon looked over the concrete edge, Mike pushed his hands inside the straw packing and felt around inside, suddenly pausing with a smile.

He pulled out a red leather briefcase with a tag tied to the handle.

'What's this John?' he toyed with the rapidly degenerating farmer.

Simon kept his hand firmly squeezed on Coates' upper arm as he stretched to look at what Mike had found.

Mike flicked at the catches and opened the case revealing tightly packed gold bars.

'Holy mother of God!'

The two agents peered into the case. The gold bars gleamed back at them in the afternoon sunlight.

'Is that...?' Simon started.

Mike straightened out the tag and read out loud;

"PORTWAY MARINA, LUGGAGE OF: TREVOR BURKE, THE EMPRESS. SPECIAL NOTES: TO BE PLACED INSIDE CABIN SAFE PRIOR TO ARRIVAL"

'*The Empress!*' he shouted at Coates.

Coates looked back at him.

'I...I never knew what was in them, nor... nor where they came from...' he stuttered, 'I was only ever a keeper of this stuff. My job wasn't to ask questions...'

'Stolen stuff, John! This guy, Burke, was more than likely murdered for this stuff!'

He shut the case and spotted Simon out of the corner of his eye dumb-struck by the find.

He climbed out of the bunker and walked to within a few inches of his prisoner.

'You are under arrest John, for receiving and hoarding stolen and smuggled goods! Thanks for calling me on this Si! Take him back to Nelson and put him in one of the meeting rooms, I will call a van to retrieve this stuff. I will meet you back there'.

Simon nodded and pushed on Coates' arm, leading him back to the Land Rover; the gravitas of the whole project unfolding in his mind. He loaded the cuffed farmer into the back of the vehicle and made his way to the front, watching Mike wrestle with the chests. As he reversed the Land Rover the length of the track to the main road, a satisfied smile forced its way across his face with an overwhelming sense of relief.

Mike rubbed his stomach – he hadn't a clue what time it was but felt hunger pangs. Either that or it was from the beating he had received the previous night, he thought.

The sky had darkened to terracotta as the last of the tea chests was loaded into the warehouse of the Nelson building. One of the agents pulled at the chain from the roller shutters and began to lock the padlocks on the exterior. Mike fought a yawn as he walked inside to fill out the confiscation forms. He reflected the catch with a crooked smile, distorted by the swelling on his cheek, towards the receptionist.

'Good evening Mrs Jacobs'.

She looked at him with intrigue, 'Good evening Mr Williams'.

Mike had never really shown any emotion since his arrival. He wandered towards the meeting room where Coates was being held.

Nelson Building had been dramatically recycled over the years, starting life as a Civic Centre of Penzance when it opened in Eighteen Thirty Eight then becoming the Market Hall and finally serving the Royal Navy and the Government. As much as it was an ideal location for the newly formed Preventive Service, facilities were crude but adequate. Nelson House, as it was latterly named was adapted for use as covert headquarters for Naval Intelligence. Throughout the years of service within the Navy it had been developed into a warren of offices and lecture halls that provided the Preventive Service with a host of utilities at its disposal, namely the interrogation rooms. Although crude, they served their purpose and, for Mike, the bare unpainted walls and metal framed furniture portrayed exactly the level of intimidation that he needed.

He pushed open a metal door adjacent to the innocently labelled "Meeting Room One" and stepped into the darkness. DCI Raymond stood concentrating on his colleague, who was interviewing Coates in the adjoining room. Simon acknowledged Mike's arrival as the three men watched through the two-way glass viewing window.

Raymond turned to face Mike with an intentional pause.

'Congratulations Williams', he sneered, 'it seems like this Mickey Mouse department has actually gotten somewhere...'

Mike ignored the comment and continued to watch the interview. His trust in Raymond had diminished since the neglect of the investigation for the "accident" and resulting death of his colleagues. He pushed passed the inspector and sat on a plastic chair next to his partner.

'How's it going?'

Simon looked at him and shook his head.

'They're not asking the right questions Mike; Coates is just sitting out the obligatory three hours until he is released!'

Mike turned to Raymond.

'Why aren't *we* interviewing him?' he asked. He knew the reason – they didn't have the authority. Unreasonably they weren't given the power to interview within their remit, adding the uncomfortable mixture of the police into the pot.

'We have nothing we can pin on him; he will be out of here in two hours!'

'Nothing we can pin on him?' Mike asked rhetorically.

The interviewing police officer sat in front of Coates with a coffee and proceeded to ask, 'Who are you working for?' for the fourth time and for the fourth time Coates replied, 'I have no idea what you are talking about, I works for meself'.

The whole scenario appeared staged.

Coates knew as well as they did, that he would disappear when he was released to escape further enquiries and, more pressingly, for his own safety.

Simon looked at his watch – it had been nearly two hours since the police officer started the interview. Mike wiped a bead of sweat from his forehead and rubbed it between his thumb and forefinger. The heat of the room, combined with the level of frustration that both he and Simon were experiencing was aggravating.

Suddenly a knock came from the door, breaking the tension. Raymond answered it. A young lady wearing a Navy uniform marched inside holding a cellophane bag.

'I was processing the suspect's belongings, Mr Williams, and this phone made a noise like it had received a text message, I thought you should know'.

She held the bag with the phone in front of Mike's face.

Raymond moved towards the young agent with his hand out stretched, 'This is a private room, an interview is under way, you have no right…'

Mike pushed Raymond's hand out of the way, interrupting his obtrusion. With his tired eyes wide open, he took the bag and stared at the contents.

'Thank you, thank you very much'.

The young agent left the room and Raymond slammed the door behind her.

'That is evidence, Williams, you can't touch that', Raymond stated as Mike unsealed the clear bag. He emptied the phone into his hand and looked at it.

'So it's got my fingerprints on it. I dare say it's got Coates' prints on it too!'

He pressed the "View" button and the screen illuminated.

"DROP TONIGHT @ 0100. LOW TIDE"

Mike turned to face his partner with a toothy grin and held the phone up for him to read the message.

'What does it say?' Raymond demanded.

Mike stood up and bolted out of the door, pushing past the inspector on his way out.

The interview room door burst open and Mike marched towards the desk. He slapped his hands down on the melamine table top, knocking over a polystyrene cup and spilling the contents on Coates' trousers.

'Where is the low tide drop-area Coates?' he shouted at the old man's face.

The force of Mike's outburst had shocked Coates away from the safety of the futile police interrogation and back into the situation.

'Huh?' he mumbled, trying to work out what Mike had discovered and how he knew what to ask.

Mike pushed the phone screen forward displaying the message, towards Coates and repeated himself with more ferocity.

'Where is the drop-off zone at low tide Coates? We have your phone, we have the loot and we have got you by the balls! Don't make this any worse for yourself old man! Where is the…'

'He doesn't know what you are talking about', the interviewing officer said sarcastically.

Mike looked around at him with disdain.

Coates saw the weakness in the relationship with Mike and the officer and began to relax once again.

'I don't know what you are talking about…' he muttered as he wiped the coffee from his trousers.

Mike continued to stare at the officer.

'If he went to court for this, would we be able to freeze his assets to pay for the costs?'

'Of course, but…'

Mike looked back towards Coates.

'This is your very last chance John… if there is a drop-off tonight then where is it? Where is the low tide zone?'

There was a pause. Coates shuffled forward in his seat.

'I have no idea what you are…'

Mike retreated back from the desk and straightened down his jacket.

'Officer, I want you to freeze a fishing trawler moored in Newlyn Harbour called *The Mary Elizabeth* for public auction to raise the funds for Mr Coates' trial'.

The devastating blow that Mike had counted on, hit home.

'What? You-you can't, you can't, she is my only income; I don't even own the farm!' Coates grovelled.

Mike stood fast. He tried hard not to grin but it was difficult.

'Please, I am begging you…'

Mike stepped forwards with his arms folded.

'This is your last chance. Where is the drop-off zone at low tide, John?'

Coates shut his eyes.

Mike turned to the vacant officer, 'A pen, do you have a pen? And a piece of paper?'

Simon watched from the doorway. As harsh as Mike had been with the frail old man, he knew where to hit and how much strength was required. He smiled as Mike approached the doorway, and signalled with a thumb towards the viewing window.

'I want you to organise a team of agents for tonight and get them to this point', he said fingering to a location written on the notepaper.

Simon looked at it, squinting in the dim light.

'This is… right outside Coates' farmhouse!'

'Correct!' Mike confirmed, slapping Simon's shoulder as he left him standing at the doorway.

'I'll meet you there at midnight and I'll ring you with details in an hour', Mike said as he jogged down the echoing hallway.

Simon looked back at the notes.

'And bring Coates with you!' a faint voice followed.

The wind was sharp and strong and howled around the cliff faces of the small cove.

Although it was past midnight, the sky was petrol-coloured against the black clouds. There was little light pollution around these coasts; the closest source of amber from Penzance, providing an uninterrupted view of the stars.

Mike rubbed his upper arms as he looked hard into the horizon.

He turned to see the headlights of a Land Rover approaching him. He looked around the cliff edge and towards the tiny light of the Coastguard watch to his right.

The Land Rover pulled up next to him and Simon jumped out.

'Okay, I have got the RNLI to loan us three life boats. They are patrolling…' he began to unfold an OS map onto the bonnet. He switched on a small pocket torch and shone it from above his head, '…here, here and… here', he stabbed with his finger.

'I have got three agents stationed on the Seven Stones Light Ship, two on Bishops Rock, there are two dinghies patrolling the outer edge here', he pointed at the opposite side of the cove, 'and I have placed a couple of agents on this deep sea salvage vessel stationed…. here. Oh, and I got your old Coastguard patrol, the *Anglian Princess* sweeping these waters here. There is no way that anyone can slip in or out of this circle Mike'.

Mike looked at the areas Simon had pointed out.

'Unless they slip underneath them?' he suggested.

'It is a twenty-mile barricade Mike, we'll spot them easily – submarine or no submarine'.

Mike smirked.

'What is the time?'

Simon looked at his watch, 'Ten to one'.

'Right Coates, what do we do now?' he turned to the old man, shivering beneath a large dark jacket.

'Wait until you can see the boat, then send the text message to this number', he pulled out the note with the number from the previous nights drop, another reason that Coates was glad to have written it down rather than trying to memorise it.

'Then we wait for the torch signal, reply to that with this one and… that's it'.

'You had better be right about this John'.

'I am not about to give up me livelihood for anyone! To be honest, I had kind of lost me bottle anyway, the amount of loot they were pulling; it was getting beyond a joke'.

Mike put his digiscope to his right eye. The digital telescope that they had been provided with was new naval technology, surprising both Mike and Simon at the time of issue. Combining digital camera technology with a Karl-Zeis lens and SMS connectivity, it enabled multiple clear digital format images to be taken and sent to mobile devices or via the internet.

Or at least that is what the quartermaster had told them.

He scanned the horizon and spotted the *Seven Stones Lightship*.

'Nothing so far', he concluded.

Simon's phone began to ring.

'Yeah', he answered.

'Right, thanks', he snapped the phone shut, '*Anglian Princess* has just spotted a motorised dinghy approaching the shoreline'.

Mike held up the digiscope and scanned it across the dark waves, his thumb and finger working frantically at the zoom controls.

'I can't remember how to use this bloody thing', he mumbled.

Suddenly the device focused.

'Got him!'

Coates pre-empted the next question, 'Just type "CLEAR!" and send it to that number'.

Mike tapped at Coates' phone and double-checked the number from the scrap of paper. He pressed send and held his breath.

After a few moments a tiny light began to flash about half a mile from the beach.

'That's it, that's him', Mike whispered excitedly.

'Flash back at him twice', Coates whispered.

Mike flashed his torch twice as instructed and waited.

'Is that it?' he asked.

Coates nodded.

Mike turned to his colleague, 'Get the men ready and tell them not to act until I give the go ahead'.

Simon nodded and moved crab-like away amongst the dark shrubs of the cliff top.

Mike pulled a loud speaker close to him and switched it on, illuminating a small red LED.

He watched intently as the small black dinghy drifted closer to the beach. The tide was out but not too far and the waves pushed white foam along the stony beach.

'A perfect night for a drop', Coates whispered with a sense of nostalgia.

Mike stayed steady as a rock, constantly watching the dinghy as it drew close to the shore line.

Eventually after what seemed an eternity; the dinghy caught the waves and slid up the beach- the distinct noise of the rubber underside sliding along the sand. The dinghy held three or four medium sized wooden tea chests and as soon as the boat drew to a stop a figure stood up and began to lift one of the chests clear of the side of the boat and placed it carefully onto the beach.

As soon as the chest touched the sand Mike drew a long breath and stood up with the loudspeaker.

'Go Go Go!' he shouted, his voice echoing around the bowl of the cove.

Three large spotlights clanked to life with a tremendous metallic whir, illuminating the beach as if it were the morning sun and twelve fully armed agents stood from their positions in succession and aimed down on the figure.

'This is Her Majesties Preventive Service, you are surrounded. Stay exactly where you are and place your hands above your head!'

Mike's heart was pounding and stinging adrenaline pumped through his body.

Simon watched as the man in the boat raised his hands.

'Well done Mike. I will contact the offshore agents and the boats and get them to keep an eye out for the mother ship'.

'I'm going down there', Mike said, drawing his weapon and pulling the chamber back, 'get two agents to accompany me will you?'

Simon nodded and jogged off towards the armed men on the cliff edge.

Mike turned to Coates.

'Thank you John', he said with sincerity.

Coates looked back at him with a grimace, 'Despite me getting cold feet over this, I never thought I would sell out like you did Michael!'

Mike nodded, 'I understand'. It would have been easy for him to begin a moral issue of "doing the right thing" but there wasn't time. The two selected agents arrived clutching Heckler and Koch MP5 machine guns.

'Si, put Coates in the Land Rover, you two, come with me'.

Mike began to descend the steep, sandy banks of the cliff edge, placing one foot after another on the tufts of firm sea grass for stability. The two agents followed his route, occasionally slipping on the loose, sandy mounds.

As they stepped onto the beach they began to walk slowly towards the nervous looking male figure in the boat. When they got within a hundred feet of the dinghy Mike raised his gun and pointed it towards him.

'Stay where you are, don't move…'

With confidence, Mike quickened the pace. He couldn't wait to get hold of this man, to interrogate him, to find out who he was working for and to find out who the project leader was. The excitement was nearly overwhelming him as he and his two agents stomped the wet sand towards the dinghy.

The bright light of the explosion blinded the three agents as the deafening roar followed, echoing around the cove. It ripped apart the dinghy, the tea chests and the figure. The immense force threw Mike and the two agents backwards onto the sand amongst the shower of burning debris. The agents on the cliff line jolted as the small cloud of burning vapour rose from where the dinghy had come ashore.

Simon ran instinctively down the sandy bank of the cliff, jumping over the rocks and the hard, grassy tufts until he reached the beach.

'Mike!'

He ran towards the three men that lay among thousands of pieces of charred debris, some of which still burned in the sea breeze. He crouched down at Mike's tattered body.

'Mike, are you okay? Can you hear me? Mike?'

Mike began to cough into the sand. Simon slowly turned him over onto his back.

'Get me an ambulance!' he shouted up towards the cliff line of agents looking down at them.

He coughed again and opened his eyes, his face blackened and his nose streaming with blood.

'W-wh-what happened?' he asked in a dazed voice.

Mike sat in the back of the ambulance, a medic dabbing at his cheek bone which had caught a piece of shrapnel from the boat's engine. Simon stood nearby, talking into his phone.

'You need to spend a few hours in hospital so we can keep an eye on that cheek, I think it may be slightly fractured', the medic said softly.

Mike looked at his partner. A police helicopter buzzed in the background with a heavy searchlight pointing down towards the sea.

Simon closed his phone and walked towards the ambulance.

'I think someone is desperately trying hard to block our investigation', he said through a cigarette.

Mike looked down at the floor.

The medic stepped away to survey his other wounds.

'When you are ready Mr Williams we'll take you to the Emergency centre to check you out I think'.

'I'm fine!' Mike snapped, throwing off the blanket and standing to his feet with an awkward pose.

Simon nodded to the medic who in turn shrugged his shoulders and moved on to one of the other injured men.

'Is there anything left down there?' Mike croaked as he pulled on his tattered jacket.

'No, nothing. Nothing left of the chests either', Simon exhaled a puff of blue smoke.

'Someone knew we were close', Mike said as Simon lit another cigarette from the stub of the previous one.

'Yeah'.

'But who? How did they know?' he rubbed at his blackened eyes.

'The police inspector said that it was likely to be a bomb that was detonated remotely. In other words; not by the man in the boat'.

Mike looked intently at the horizon.

'Then who? And from where? Did our boats see anything?'

Simon exhaled another large plume of blue smoke into the night sky.

'No, nothing... I am beginning to think you are right about a submergible Mike. The police are all over the place now and the anti-terrorism unit have been called in response to the explosion. Protocol apparently. So - what next?'

Mike pushed his bruised hand into his trouser pocket and pulled out a crinkled paper, handing it to Simon who unfolded it, exposing the sales docket and buyer information for U-239.

'We go to Gibraltar'.

Chapter 9

The Culprit

The cumbersome 747 flew steadily over the tiny network of roads and the patchwork quilt of farmland. Simon looked out of the window as he drank from his plastic cup of Gin and Tonic.

Mike flicked through some papers, balancing them on the plastic fold-down tray in front of him.

It had been three weeks since the explosion on the beach and the extent of his injuries had forced him to a two week break in hospital. His cheekbone, as the medic had suspected, was fractured and without his knowing a piece of shrapnel had found its way into his upper right arm.

However tedious; the break had enabled him to catch up on some research and to ascertain exactly what had caused the explosion.

The police report detailed it as being a professional grade device with a ranged detonator, activated by SMS. The anti-terrorism bomb squad had combed the scene and found fragments of the device scattered over the beach describing it as an "incendiary device designed to destroy traces of evidence".

'The police have stated that they were now "intrigued" and wanting to become "more heavily involved with the project"', Mike read out loud from one of the press reports, 'it seems that we are in the limelight', he said turning his head to his colleague.

Mike scratched his head with the end of his pen. It was concerning him that someone was always one step ahead of them and seemed to know exactly what they were doing and where they were doing it. The other burning issue was the death of his two colleagues coupled with the death of Black and the owner of the marina in Cork right after Harding's and Richards' visit.

'What's on your mind Mike?' Simon asked having watched the expressions on his face change with the route of his thoughts.

'Do you get the feeling we are being… watched?' he replied quietly.

Simon sat back and stared out of the window again. He went cold and began to shift uncomfortably in his seat. Surely the reports that he had been submitting to the Admiralty couldn't be conducive to their apparent failures? Maybe they were intercepted and leaked? Perhaps he should tell Mike about the reports? If there is a leak from the "inside" then perhaps it would help them in their investigations? He sat and thought for a while; he needed to confer with Mike but he knew that this was a betrayal. Or was it? It was a protocol implemented in the very beginning by Wilkinson himself and someone was exploiting that protocol. Surely the fault couldn't lie with him?

Plagued by his thoughts, he drew the conclusion that it was time to clear his conscience. They were twenty thousand feet in the air, it's not like Mike could storm off or lash out at him.

He manoeuvred himself to face his partner.

'Mike?'

Mike looked up at him over the top of his reading glasses.

'Yeah?'

Simon paused, his mouth making the phonetic shapes but making no sounds. How on earth was he to start this confession?

'What?'

'Mike, I have something to tell you…'

Mike took off his glasses and placed them, folded onto the tray in front of him.

'What is it?' he asked concernedly.

Another pause.

'You know you asked how people know… no… you know you were wondering…'

Mike took a breath to combat his frustration.

'Mike, I have been reporting on you, on us, on our movements to the Admiralty since the project began!'

A thick silence ensued as Mike looked at him with curiosity - a dull look that Simon couldn't translate.

'What?' Mike broke the silence.

'It was part of my protocol from the beginning, something that Wilkinson asked me to do throughout our duration. I… I am sorry Mike'.

'Sorry?'

'I didn't mean to…'

'Didn't mean to…? Why are you telling me this? Are you supposed to be telling me this?'

Simon sat back, his expression of shame obvious.

'Why, Simon? What was he checking up on?'

Mike was a fair man and he trusted Simon implicitly. Their history was concrete, which is why Wilkinson had teamed them together.

'I honestly don't know Mike; the only thing I do know is that he wanted to know how you were getting on, how you were coping…'

Mike rubbed his chin. This had confirmed his suspicions about how their every move was compromised. But, was it really emanating from the inside? From Nelson? From Portsmouth?

'I'm going to the toilet', he said as he slipped out of his seat.

Simon sat back and cursed to himself. Had he ruined the future prospects of the project? Was it he who had compromised their movements? Possibly initially but he hadn't filed a report for about three weeks. His Inbox was full of emails from Wilkinson, his administrative department and Mrs Jacobs, all gunning for updates.

Mike walked past the rows of seats of sleeping travellers; some watching the in-flight film, others rocking to the sound of the music in their earphones.

Three rows behind them, two more HMPS Agents that were accompanying them to Gibraltar lay slumped in their chairs asleep. As he neared the rear of the plane he felt a tense feeling as if he had missed something. He stopped dead and turned slowly around; his eyes flicking over the main cabin to try and identify what had caught his attention. Shaking his head and putting it down as sleep deprivation, he turned around and continued up towards the toilet cabin.

Simon switched on his Blackberry and selected "Airplane Mode". There was a rapid succession of alert noises as his Inbox synchronised with the email server in Nelson, flooding it with emails; the subject headers ranging from "Report outstanding" to "Update required". He looked out of the window. What was he supposed to do? Continue protocol and update their movements at the expense of his loyalty? Or stop altogether and put a strain on his career?

Mike pressed the flush button and washed his hands in the compact sink. He unlocked the door and it slid open. As he walked out of the cubicle, one of the passengers collided with him. Their eyes caught one another. The man was about six feet tall and was dressed in scruffy jeans with a thick weave black pullover and was incredibly familiar. The two slowly and awkwardly slid past one another, their eyes locked.

Mike continued to his seat, occasionally looking over his shoulder. Who the hell was he? He had obviously recognised him, but how did they know each other? He sat back in his seat as his mind worked overtime to try and place a name or at least a location to the face.

Simon turned to him.

'Mike, I..'

'It's okay'.

'No, but I…'

'Shut up!'

Simon flung himself against his seat in protest at not being able to provide a defence for his actions, like a child throwing a tantrum after not getting an ice cream.

Mike's thoughts stirred but he couldn't break the recognition. After a few moments he sighed as he drew a blank. He looked behind him, towards the toilet cubicle but couldn't see him.

'What is it Mike?'

'I… I think I have just seen someone I recognise…'

'A friend?'

'No… it isn't a pleasant feeling to be honest'.

Dismissing it for the time being, Mike returned to the other pressing matter.

'Simon, when is the last time you made one of these reports?'

'I think it was about three weeks ago…'

Mike pondered for a moment. If there was even a slim chance that these reports were related to the project being compromised then he needed to combat the issue. Also, it was evident that Simon had had the same thought. Simon was a stickler for protocol, illustrated by his continuous promotion at Revenue and Customs. If he had stopped the reports and contravened the regulations then there was a reason. This brought about a temporary comfort.

'I don't want you to make any further reports, but I don't want you to stop reporting… if that makes sense? I want you to keep a regular report but I want you to fabricate it'.

Simon looked confused, 'Fabricate?'

'I just want you to make something up okay? Something that will keep them happy, something mundane. Something like we are wrapped up with making enquiries…?'

Simon nodded.

'Who knows we are on this flight?'

Simon pinched the top of his nose and screwed up his eyes, trying to trace the breadcrumb trail of communication.

'Mrs Jacobs. She is the one who booked our tickets'.

'And that is it? No one else?'

'No, but it has to be signed off so you can bet management know, and finance… and of course the team knows…'

'So everyone knows then, is what you are saying?'

The penny had dropped.

'Yeah…'

'Okay, so they know we're in the air. Send a report right now that we didn't make the flight. Our lead went dead and we are returning to Cornwall to follow investigations from home'.

Mike thought for a few moments - it wasn't going to wash; if Nelson found out they were on the flight and had reported to the contrary then they will know they had lied.

'Scrub that! Tell them our lead went dead but we found out after touching down in Gibraltar and we are going to get the next flight back… we cannot leave anything to chance and it is imperative that we cover ourselves. At least for now, until we have proof that they are responsible for our dead ends… or not'.

'I will have to order new tickets?'

'So order new tickets, we don't have to use them'.

It was a depressing situation that they were being monitored but it was, paradoxically, enlightening. If they had found the obstacle they could now make plans to bypass it.

'I am going to organise someone to meet us at the airport', Mike said as he fingered a page of his notebook, typing the contact into his Blackberry.

'But, we have a hire car booked'.

Simon knew that this was a stupid comment immediately after saying it. Of course, the hire car was also booked by the administration at Nelson with sign off by management and finance. If they were going to proceed with caution and beneath the radar from Nelson then they must appear to have not used the bookings, especially if they were supposed to be returning on the next available flight. Simon wasn't a natural born liar; he was a complier. It was going to take a bit of getting used to.

'I know someone who will help us, Mr Fredrico', Mike pointed out a name in his notebook.

'Fredrico?'

'He is an old friend… and coincidentally - Chief of Police in Gibraltar… I knew that would come in useful at some point'.

Mike keyed in the details into his Blackberry.

'Si, go and inform Robinson and MacLeod, tell them to refrain from reporting back to Nelson also. Don't tell them why, I don't want to freak them out, but it is important we don't send contradicting reports…'

The cabin speaker came to life and a stewardess gave the order for everyone to begin to make their way back to their seats as they were beginning their descent.

Mike knew that the man from earlier, whom he had recognised, would be returning to his seat, or already be there and now would be a good time to catch another glimpse of him to try and jar his memory.

After a few minutes scanning around the aisles behind them he spotted him on the port wing seat – asleep. He unbuckled his belt, left his seat and made his way quickly up the aisle, past the stewardess.

'Sir', she began, 'you must get back to your seat, we are starting our descent'.

'I just have to… I need the toilet, I won't be a second…' he hurried past the aggravated girl.

As he approached the sleeping man he reached up to the luggage compartment above him slipping his Blackberry from his pocket and activating the camera. He held it steady in the palm of his hand so not to attract attention whilst rummaging inside the compartment with the other. He pressed the camera button and dropped the Blackberry back into his pocket, shutting the compartment with his other hand. He turned around and casually made his way back to his seat.

The four agents left Airport Immigration and walked onto the hot concrete surface.

In front of them stood three armed policemen and a very well dressed man in a white linen suit and fedora.

'That's Fredrico', Mike explained.

'Michael!' Fredrico shouted across the concreted carpark with open arms.

Mike picked up his pace and formed an enthusiastic trot over to the Chief of Police who immediately embraced him.

'It is so good to see you again Michael'.

Fredrico was of Italian origin but had lived in countries all over the world, including England which is where Mike had first met up with him; coincidentally at The Ship in Mousehole. They both worked for a local tradesman as teenagers; running goods, legitimately to the best of their knowledge, from one harbour to another. He had also been an acquaintance of Black. Although his accent was distinctly Italian, it had undertones of Spanish. He was immaculately dressed in white and his moustache was groomed to perfection. As Simon watched him, he couldn't help but liken him to Poirot.

'It is good to see you too Fred', Mike said.

Fredrico clocked Simon and the other two Agents.

'Ah, let me introduce you to Simon Jenkins, my partner…'

They shook hands.

'…and my two agents, MacLeod and Robinson, and everyone, this is Fredrick Fredrico, Chief of Police here in Gibraltar', Mike said finishing the pleasantries.

They began to walk towards the white Mercedes flanked by two armed officers and Mike stopped to approach MacLeod. He was a giant of a man and sported an obtrusive military haircut. Mike did a double take and rolled his eyes, 'I want you two to collect a car from that hire company, under Fredrico's name and follow that man over there', Mike pointed into the distance near a taxi rank, 'I saw him on the plane and I am certain I have seen him before somewhere. I have emailed you an image of him and I want you to follow him and find out who the hell he is. But, don't report back to Nelson okay, and stay low'.

Mike pushed a hire warrant into MacLeod's hand.

'Yes sir, we'll stick with him and give you regular updates'.

'And buy a hat!' Mike added as he turned away.

The two agents hurried towards the hire car company building.

Mike rushed to catch up with Simon and Fredrico and his escort.

'So, Mike, you want to meet De LaCruz right?'

'Yes, if possible, do you know where we can meet?'

'I know everything Michael', Fredrico boasted, winking at Simon.

'As it happens he is doing a seminar at the Theatre Royal this evening. It is part of his three day show. I was there on opening night, very interesting; Smuggling and Piracy of the Eighteenth Century. I will get us tickets'.

'Thank you…'

'No problem Michael, it starts at eight, I will pick you up at six; we will eat at half past and be there in plenty of time for a drink – perfect!'

Simon smiled involuntarily. It would have been difficult not to warm to the man even if he didn't want to. He suddenly felt a sense of safety, a feeling that he had not felt since he left his position at Dover.

MacLeod entered the Ford Mondeo hire car and started the engine without taking his eyes off the man that Mike had pointed out. He pulled out of the forecourt of the Hire Company and began to follow a few cars behind the taxi that the man had hired.

'Rob, check the Sat Nav and find out where we are will you?'

Robinson, an ex-Royal Marine, found their location and placed the navigation system into the cradle on the dashboard.

'He could be heading anywhere', he said looking at the route.

'Where does this road lead?' MacLeod asked, transfixed on the taxi ahead of them.

Robinson pressed a button on the navigation system and zoomed out of the map.

'The other side of the Rock'.

The evening provided a spectacular sunset. Mike wandered down the steps of the Caleta Hotel to join his refreshed partner who was smoking a cigarette, admiring the sea view.

'Nice view', Mike started.

'Hmm'.

Mike looked at his sombre partner.

'You okay?'

'I am concerned Mike; I am bothered that Nelson could be working against us'.

'Why? They may not be, I am just being overly-cautious'.

'I know, but what if they are? Who do we turn to? We are on our own…'

'So?' Mike asked. Working on their own was a bonus to them; they would have no restrictions, no protocols to adhere to, and no regulatory updates.

'So? So?' Simon's voice began to get louder, 'so, not only have we stirred up a hornets' nest in the smuggling community, turned every coastal Cornishman against us but we have alienated ourselves from the people we work for! We don't trust the police and we have pirates trying to blow us up! The way I see it is we are on our own Mike!'

'If you are right then that strengthens the reason why we have to continue with the project. If we can't fall back then we don't have a choice. What if we do put an end to this and come out on top?'

Simon appeared slightly less miserable thanks to Mike's confidence.

'I suppose so', he grumbled reluctantly.

A large, silver limousine pulled into the forecourt of the Caleta next to them. The tinted driver's window opened to reveal an unshaven driver in an impecably pressed police uniform.

'Mr Fredrico sent me to pick you up', the driver spoke in a rough, flat East London accent.

Mike and Simon looked at each other and smiled. They had not expected a limousine and had even less expected an ex-pat to be driving one.

'And that, ladies and gentlemen is one reason why they were so rich!'

A wave of laughter followed a crackle of applause that erupted from the exceptionally well dressed audience and echoed around the Theatre Royal's spectacularly decorative period walls.

On the stage a gentleman in an immaculate tuxedo, strutted up and down in front of a table with a jug of water and a pile of books.

Simon and Mike sat uncomfortably amongst the affluent audience of "De LaCruz"; feeling a little underdressed in their formal trousers and shirts. Mike wasn't particularly bothered but it was a source of annoyance to Simon whose tailored Savile Row suit sat idle in his wardrobe back home.

'You have to admit it Michael, De LaCruz is marvellous isn't he?' Fredrico whispered into Mike's ear whilst clapping along with the audience to another well-presented point.

Mike nodded in response. His mind was plagued by what he was to do. He knew they had to meet with De LaCruz but how? What could they say to this admired local hero to create a relationship? They obviously had to remain under cover and thus he had to create an alter ego for them both. They weren't spies. They were a mishmash of Customs and Excise officers.

De LaCruz took a sip of water from the crystal glass and paused as the clapping simmered to a silence.

'In the eighteenth Century, the government created trade routes between many countries; safe passages to supply one country with another's product. These trade routes became a safe haven for smugglers. They could pick up Jamaican rum from Cornwall, sail it around to London, pick up some cotton, transport it to the Indies, drop off the cotton and sell the rum at a higher price than the original buying price when it first landed. No one would ever get in the way of a trade ship!'

Ring Ring.

Mike's mobile phone rang out from inside his trouser pocket. He fought to retrieve it before it rang again.

Ring Ring.

'Bugger!' Mike exhaled as he yanked the phone out of his pocket to answer. As politely as possible he side stepped along the narrow platform between the knees of the audience on his row and burst through the exit door at the back of the hall.

'Mike Williams', he answered breathlessly.

'Mike, it's MacLeod, we have established contact with the target'.

Mike's eyes lit up.

'Where are you?'

'We are about three hundred feet above the target now off Europa Road. There is a small group of them below us and…'

Mike looked at the phone.

'And?' he repeated.

'And… they are standing around a medium sized fishing boat full of…'

'Tea chests?'

'Correct, and I would bet my life they don't contain tea!'

'Shit, this is great! Stay hidden, but keep with them okay?'

This was a serious development. It was by pure coincidence that they were in Gibraltar at the same time that this was happening, but a welcome relief that something was actually going their way.

'Will do sir'.

'MacLeod, do you have your scope?'

'Yes sir'.

'Take photos, as close a range as possible - close on his face, the chests, everything you can … but don't…'

'…report to Nelson?'

He had pre-empted Mike's order, which was a heartwarming addition to the paranoia that surrounded them.

Mike closed the phone and punched the air. Loot in Gibraltar! Mike couldn't help but think that if they had followed procedure and reported that they had landed and stayed in Gibraltar then this may not have occurred. The fact that they hadn't reported their true location and had happened upon a drop off made him think that the scale of this project was larger than he had originally perceived and also that both of their suspicions had been verified.

He opened the double doors and made his way back into the theatre where De LaCruz's voice boomed through the sound system and around the curvaceous theatre.

'Because, when the monarchy was running low on funds they actually turned to the pirates and granted legalisation of their criminal ways, only they called it Privateering. Privateering?'

The audience began to laugh and the low rumble of discussions began to get louder.

'Privateering! Basically, we'll chop off your head, cut you open and burn your body but… we need the cash! That is what it boiled down to. A pirate or smuggler could sign up to become a Privateer who could then legally climb aboard a Spanish vessel, kill the crew, steel the loot AND the ship and bring it back to England! The ship was added to the vastly growing British fleet and the loot added to the wealth of the Monarchy and the Empire became bigger and bigger and greater and greater… Then after the war with the Spaniards, anyone caught "Privateering" would get their head chopped off again! Double standards! That's what I say!'

The audience exploded in laughter again and stood up to applaud De LaCruz. The noise was deafening and followed by whistles and hollers. Simon joined in although judging by his expression, Mike realised he had missed a vital element that made the final punch line so prolific.

In the foyer outside the theatre hall, Fredrico led the two agents to the central plaza where champagne was being served and through a dense wall of people queuing with copies of De LaCruz's book for signing.

'Mr De LaCruz!' Fredrico shouted over the crowd.

De LaCruz turned as he heard the familiar Italian tinge of the Police Chief.

'Wonderful show again Leon, my warm congratulations to you', he offered, shaking his hand vigorously and cupping it with the other.

De LaCruz was a very elegant man in every sense of the word and his persona emanated celebrity status.

'Thank you Fredrick, thank you… I am surprised to see you again so soon, you enjoyed my show so much eh?' he beamed, exposing his perfect teeth through an immaculately groomed dark moustache. His speech was accent-less denoting a very exclusive education.

'Well, it's the delivery Leon. I want you to meet two friends of mine'.

Mike and Simon stepped forward awkwardly on cue.

Mike extended his hand towards De LaCruz.

'Thomas Greene, pleased to meet you Mr De LaCruz'.

Simon looked nervous. Although Fredrico was in on the scam it felt wrong. He didn't lie; Mike knew that, yet he still had to pull off an authentic alter ego, as they had previously agreed, in order to retain their anonymity.

'Pleased to meet you Mr Greene, and you are?' De LaCruz turned to a pale faced Simon.

'S-Steele, James Steele', he stuttered.

Greene and Steele? Where did Mike get these names from for heaven's sake? Simon thought whilst grinning inanely. It sounded more like a seventies cop show than two business men.

'I will leave you to chat while I mingle then', Fredrico excused himself and pushed past them, sinking into the crowd.

'How do you know Fredrick then Mr Greene?' De LaCruz asked Mike.

'We have been friends for a very long time, similar interests one might say'.

'I see, and what may they be?'

Mike inhaled through his nose, a long drawn breath, in an attempt to create an atmosphere in the prevailing conversation.

'I think *we* could do some business Mr De LaCruz, I think you know what business I am referring to?'

De LaCruz squinted his eyes and a smirk settled to one side of his mouth.

'I don't have a great deal of time but I will hear you. Let us talk, come, walk with me'.

The three men moved into a far room and De LaCruz shut the door behind them, instantly drowning out the overwhelming noise from the crowd.

'Ah, that's better', De LaCruz sighed with an agreeable smile, 'so, what would you like to talk to me about gentlemen? I don't have long…' he looked at his watch, 'would you like a brandy?'

Mike glanced at Simon, his cheek twitching nervously.

'Theoretically, and correct me if I am speaking out of place, but I may have some… work for you?'

De LaCruz stopped pouring a brandy from the crystal decanter on the table.

'Work?' he repeated.

'A job', Mike tried. He needed to sound like he was still in the business without sounding too much like he was trying to sound like he was still in the business.

De LaCruz was playing with him, trying to get him to spell it out. Everyone knew that De LaCruz was a smuggler or at the very least, a retired smuggler. Fredrico knew only too well but De LaCruz romanticised it and turned it into an academic subject, a series of books and a career. Somehow this smoothed over the illegality of it all and gained him fame rather than notoriety.

'There is a yacht...' he paused. It dawned on him that he hadn't actually researched what the yacht was called. His pause had been noticed.

'Yacht?' De LaCruz questioned.

'The... *Golden Raj* leaving Portsmouth on Friday this week, a dignitary trip and as such fully loaded with...'

De LaCruz bit the bait.

'...With what? If I am interested in your proposition it had better be worth my interest'.

Mike paused. What would this fabricated yacht be fully loaded with? Drugs? Gold? Money? Bonds!

'Three million pounds worth of bonds, unsigned and untraceable...'

De LaCruz continued to pour the brandies.

'Bonds eh?'

Mike bit his lip, not knowing if he was interested, if he was insulted or even if he would try and report them to the police?

There was a tense pause as De LaCruz ingested what Mike was asking him. A smile began to emerge across his clean shaven face as he raised his glass into the air.

'Well, here's to bonds!'

Mike fought hard to keep his happiness at the bite from showing too prominently.

'How long are you two in Gibraltar?'

'As long as we need to be Mr De LaCruz', Mike answered.

De LaCruz smiled and produced a business card from his inside pocket.

'I have a little villa on the side of The Rock, come tomorrow for about seven, I will prepare some food and we can talk more about these...bonds'.

Mike took the card to read the address.

'I have a party to host gentlemen, so if you don't mind...'

'Not at all, thank you Mr De LaCruz'.

Mike glowed inside - they had befriended him. The next problem was that they had to link him to the purchase of the U-Boat without sounding too suspicious. It was still only a slim chance that the U-Boat was actually the vessel that the pirates were using.

De LaCruz left the room and closed the door behind him leaving the two agents alone.

'The *Golden Raj?*' Simon asked.

Mike looked at him, 'It was the first thing that came to me; there is a restaurant across the road from the hotel called the Raj of India'.

Simon rolled his eyes.

'You realise that he will check up on it, he'll check it out, and we now need to register a yacht in that name'.

Simon was right, he hadn't thought of that. If there was a chance that they were actually going to gain his trust and pull this whole thing off they had to make it bomb proof.

'Ah yes, perfect… I got him, I have got him!' MacLeod whispered to himself as he lay on his front at the top of the hill, above the small jetty where a gang of men stood around the unloaded tea chests; his digiscope protruding through the long sea grasses. He had managed to close in on the man from the plane that Mike had seen and began to focus on his face. He pushed a button on the small control panel on the side of the scope and recorded the images.

'Be quiet will ya?' Robinson whispered.

He looked around at the hills behind them to look for anyone approaching from the darkness.

Robinson felt at his gun for peace of mind and unfastened the holster catch.

'Jesus!' MacLeod exclaimed.

'What?'

'They just opened one of the chests… it's full of… it looks like bags of…'

'What?' Robinson repeated.

MacLeod paused and moved away from the edge, turning to face his colleague, visibly shaken by what he had seen.

Mike and Simon walked across the road towards the hotel and stopped at the foot of the entrance steps. Simon smoked the remains of his cigarette while Mike spoke on his phone.

'Thanks for that Fred, I really appreciate your help… we'll see you at breakfast'.

He shut the phone and sighed with relief.

'Fredrico is going to help us set it up! He has a yacht- well his brother in law has a yacht- moored at Brest, France, and he is going to have it re-branded and re-registered as… The Golden Raj!'

'Bloody hell', Simon exhaled, 'why is he being so generous? It isn't his remit to help us and it certainly isn't in his jurisdiction'.

'We go back a long time and he… he owes me a thing or two'.

MacLeod's rapid footsteps echoed against the walls of Buena Vista Road. Oblivious to the traffic in the small settlement; he ran in and out of the road avoiding the oncoming nightlife.

With his automatic in one hand, he reached into his coat pocket with the other, retrieving his phone.

Ring Ring.

Partly asleep, Mike slapped his hand onto his phone on the bedside table of his hotel room and brought it to his ear.

'Yeah?'

'It's MacLeod… we've been… rumbled…'

Mike sat bolt upright.

'What? Where are you?'

'Running… through the streets of…'

A crackle of gun fire and ricochets drowned out his voice.

'MacLeod, are you there?' Mike spoke into the mouth piece frantically.

'For God's sake help me Mike!'

Mike pushed himself out of his bed and began to put on his shirt from the floor, holding the phone between his cheek and his shoulder.

'Where are you?'

'…Flat Bastion Road… I think…'

Another crackle of gunfire followed by a close ricochet.

'I'm on my way, take cover somewhere', Mike shouted as he one-handedly struggled with his trousers.

'I will ring you when I am near!'

The phone went silent and Mike rushed around the room collecting his essentials. He slipped out the magazine from the automatic, checked its capacity, slid it back in and pulled back the hammer mechanism before slipping it back into his hip holster.

As he neared a junction, MacLeod darted into a back alley. His heart was pounding and his leg muscles burning. He pushed himself off an adjoining wall and jumped behind a skip for refuge. As he peered down the alley, he spotted a shadow projected from the street light from the main street; it was one of the pursuers who had stopped to look for him.

MacLeod drew out his digiscope and turned it on. As he looked into the screen to navigate the menu system another crackle of gunfire echoed down the alleyway. A bullet ricocheted above him, scattering wall debris onto the scope. Unsure if the gunfire was an attempt to flush him out or if they had spotted him – he stood up and continued to run. The dull thumps of silenced shot sounded close behind him followed by a succession of small explosions in the ancient brickwork around his head, showering him in rubble.

Mike crashed through the hotel entrance doors, jumped the stairs and ran to the hire car.

He slammed through the gears and threw the car out of the carpark. As he navigated the tiny streets he pushed MacLeod's quick dial.

MacLeod's phone rang out in his pocket. He tried desperately to silence it but the pursuing men had heard it echo out of the alley way and began to home in towards its origin.

MacLeod sprinted into the cover of darkness of a small yard and crouched in one of the corners to answer it.

'MacLeod!' he whispered.

'Where are you?' Mike shouted, wrestling for control over his vehicle as it swerved over the busy night roads.

MacLeod looked around and located a street sign.

'Governor Street, I am heading North'.

Mike looked at the Sat Nav.

'Got it! Be there in a few minutes!'

MacLeod concentrated on his situation. He would be better off in a crowded area but he was exhausted; it was thirty degrees and he could barely breathe.

'Where's Robinson?' Mike asked as he battled to hold the phone between his cheek and shoulder, spinning the steering wheel with the palm of his hand to navigate around the dense traffic.

There was a long pause.

MacLeod's pace slowed slightly as the gravity of the question hit him. He had been concentrating for so long on evading his pursuers that he had momentarily forgotten about his partner. He stopped near a lamp post and rested his head upon the metal shaft.

'Dead...' he softly answered.

Mike's gaze strayed from the road ahead of him as MacLeod's words sank in.

To his relief, MacLeod spotted the bright lights of Queensway ahead of him. If he could make it to the main road he should be able to flag a taxi or at least commandeer a car. He pushed himself faster towards the main road as another ricochet impacted above his head: his pursuers were closer than he had anticipated.

As he emerged from the end of the alley, he threw himself down a large grassy hill near the main road, tumbling to the bottom uncontrollably. He felt for his scope in his pocket, satisfied it was safe – he ran towards the traffic ahead of him. His pursuer stopped at the top of the hill and watched the agent running into the main road. Smiling, he raised his weapon, aimed out in front of him and squeezed the trigger.

The bullet pushed through MacLeod's left shoulder which jolted him forwards into the verge at the edge of the motorway. He clutched at his shoulder as blood quickly soaked through his jacket. Clenching his teeth he picked himself up from the ground, climbed over the crash barrier and walked into the oncoming traffic. As he raised his right arm, his hand covered in the blood from his shoulder, a second bullet ripped through his chest pushing him into the slow lane. The oncoming cars sounded their horns and swerved to avoid him as he fell forwards onto the tarmac surface. One by one the cars stopped dead and began to collide with one another as they applied their brakes. The sounds of crunching metal, intermittently broken by the sounds of screeching brakes, trailed into the distance as the traffic began to pile up.

MacLeod's pursuer negotiated the side of the steep hill and made his way to the resting place of his victim. As he closed in on the scene- where a large crowd of motorists had accumulated, gabbling in various languages on mobile phones- he saw the large pool of blood running into the gutter. Satisfied with what he had seen, he replaced his weapon and began to casually jog alongside the piled up traffic in the direction of the town centre.

Mike cornered the fast lane of the motorway and immediately applied the brake as he saw the cascade of abandoned vehicles in front of him. Bracing himself, he steered the sliding vehicle towards the vacant spaces of the middle lane before the car came to a gentle rest on the bumper of the vehicle in front of him.

'Shit!' he shouted, punching at the steering wheel.

He pressed MacLeod's quick dial.

The phone rang out to his voicemail.

He got out of the car to see if he could see the cause of the hold up. In the distance he saw the red flashing lights of an ambulance that had picked its way through the contra flow.

Looking in the rear view mirror he saw the cars accumulating behind him.

Resigned to the fact that he was now wedged in a temporary carpark he sat back and pushed his head against the head rest. He wound down the window and casually looked out of the window and spotted a figure jogging towards him on the verge. As he approached Mike leaned out of the window.

'Excuse me, can you tell me what the holdup is?'

The man looked over to him and shrugged his shoulders.

Mike squinted as he looked at the man in the dull, orange glow of the street lights. It was the man from the plane.

Recognising Mike in return he began to quicken his pace.

After the momentary shock, Mike put the car into reverse and pushed his foot onto the accelerator. The car screeched backwards along the warm tarmac. He navigated his way around the parked cars behind him through the back window as the man from the plane ran alongside, unable to escape due to the high mesh fencing separating the motorway from the parkland. Mike's car door swung open as he turned to avoid a parked coach; the door caught the front off-side wing and tore off as if it were a perforated sheet from a note pad.

The car's engine screamed as Mike applied the accelerator with force. With one eye on the man he saw a small vacant area of road. He pulled on the handbrake and threw the car into the space, pulling hard on the steering wheel to bring the front end around. The rear of the car impacted on the crash barrier, tearing off the rear bumper. Mike crunched though the gears and projected the car forwards, sending clouds of thick grey smoke into the still atmosphere. The man was ahead of him now and making his way towards a small suburb. Mike knew he had to intercept him before he found his way into the rabbit warren of streets. He pushed the car faster through the movement of the on-coming traffic. Lights dazzled him as the motorists flashed him out of the way. Around the next corner a large container lorry swerved to avoid him and Mike lost control as the back end slid out to the right. He tried to compensate by spinning the wheel anticlockwise but inertia slid the car to the contrary; the front burying itself into the lorry's grill.

Mike's eyes blinked; he was dazed and shaken, his neck felt like someone had pushed a knife into the back of it and he was aware of a sharp pain from his nose. He opened his eyes to see a sea of white and jolted his head backwards. The airbag had deployed and broken his nose. As his eyes began to clear, he looked out of the passenger window and made out a crowd of people moving towards him and only a few hundred yards further; the man he was pursuing. Unbuckling the safety harness, he kicked the warped passenger door open and pushed himself from the wreckage. Despite the pain from his neck, he began to give chase – his rage providing the necessary adrenalin fuel.

As he closed in on him, the exhausted man turned around, produced his weapon and fired two shots. Mike ducked as a round impacted into the rear window of a passing car. The flow of traffic sounded their horns as the two men chased their way through the steady stream. Mike pulled out his gun and pulled back the chamber. He couldn't fire it towards the traffic; he didn't want to fire it at all and had no idea of what to do if and when he caught up with the man - he had no restraints or back up and he wasn't sure how many rounds were in the magazine. Another round impacted on the rear of another passing vehicle, exploding reflector into the air. Cursing, Mike sped up. Only a few metres in front of him now, the man stopped to fire another round. A car, swerving to avoid him, clipped him with the rear quarter causing him to spin pirouette, drop his weapon and fall to the ground. Mike continued his pace towards him as the man slowly picked himself from the road. An oncoming coach, swerving to avoid the car that clipped him, hit the man and propelled him into the air and finally to rest on the bonnet of a stationary car.

Mike ran towards the vehicle, his weapon out stretched.

'Stay where you are, stay in your vehicles'.

As he reached the man, he saw his limp body lying awkwardly on the dented metal bonnet; his eyes wide open. Mike didn't see the blue flashing lights of an approaching police car as he looked at the dead man's face. Where did he know this man from?

Simon walked up to the entrance of the geometric, red bricked Royal Police Headquarters and stubbed his cigarette out on the ashtray next to the main doors. The air conditioning was soothing from the heat outside as he approached the reception desk where a young lady sat typing.

'Hi, I am Simon Jenkins; I am here to see Mike Williams'.

With an unimpressed expression she pushed a visitor book towards him and continued to type.

Simon's smile faded and he signed the book, pushing it back towards her.

She pressed a button beneath the desk and pointed to the door that had buzzed open to her left.

An officer greeted him as he entered.

'Good morning sir, you must be Mr Jenkins. Mr Fredrico is expecting you just down the hallway, sir'.

Simon nodded in acceptance but was prevented from entering by a solid hand in his chest.

'Ah, would you mind removing your weapon please sir, thank you'.

Simon pulled his automatic from his hip holster and placed it into the tray the officer was holding in front of him.

He walked the length of the bright white corridor until he reached another officer in front of a large barred gate that was slid open for him as he approached. Fredrico and Mike were leaving a cell further down. Mike had been bandaged but was still bleeding profusely from his nose and his movements illustrated fractured ribs.

'Mike!' Simon shouted.

Mike waved in recognition of his partner with a weak arm.

'Thanks Fred, I will see you in a few hours', Mike grumbled whilst clutching at his midriff.

'Go back to your hotel, eat, rest and for God's sake take a shower!' Fredrico smiled.

'I'm sorry to hear about Robinson and MacLeod', Simon offered by way of consolation.

Mike nodded.

'I wrote the car off Si', he joked.

'How come you were here? Were you here all night?'

'No, a brief stint at the hospital first. I have been answering questions since. Fred figured that I'd be safer here for the night, to protect the project and also to evade the press. He has managed to cover it as a carjacking gone wrong. Somehow he swung it'.

'How is my boy?' Fredrico asked as he hung his immaculate Fedora on the hook on the back of Mike's hotel room door. Simon followed him inside where a battered Mike sat on the edge of his bed in a towel.

Mike gave a sarcastic smile and pointed to a large purple bruise on his rib cage.

'Too bad Michael, we have work to do. I have spoken to my brother-in-law and he has agreed to loan us his yacht. I have a contact in Portsmouth Harbour who will register the yacht and the harbour master will automatically enter it into the logbook upon its arrival. She is sailing right now in fact and will be there in about two hours. So within three, she will be a registered and logged vessel. Not bad for a mornings work eh?'

Mike made no sound as he continued to look out of the full length window towards the harbour outside.

'Is something wrong Michael?' Fredrico asked, taken aback by his lack of enthusiasm.

'Wrong? You know that Nelson now know we are here? Two agents are dead - it's bloody hard to keep that a secret'.

'But it is contained at Nelson. It won't affect tonights meeting Mike,' Simon tried.

'If we are right in connecting someone on the inside of Nelson with the pirates then they will have informed De LaCruz, if he actually is part of it, that we are here. De LaCruz will have either fled or he will be packing his sodding suitcases right now!'

Mike pushed his head into his hands.

'But, he doesn't know Michael,' Fredrico's soft Italian voice cut the atmosphere.

'How the hell do you know that?' Mike spat.

'Because… I have tapped his phone lines'.

Mike turned slowly towards the Police Chief who was beaming.

Simon began to laugh 'No way? You did what?'

'Are you serious?' Mike asked, his mood beginning to dissipate.

'Of course, I didn't do it personally, but I had a few of my most trusted men tap Mr De LaCruz's phone lines. I am not stupid Michael. I am pre-empting tonights meeting with… a little precaution shall we say?'

Mike sat up; a smile began to break through the dark blue bruising of his cheek.

'You see, I am directly involved now anyway. This man is potentially connected to the man who not only is involved in bringing illicit items into my territory but is also lying dead on a morgue table after tearing up my highway! So, I am officially aiding in your investigations Michael'.

Mike stood up embrace him.

'Thank you Fred, thank you…'

'Stop that Michael, you are embarrassing me. Now, have you any idea where the tea chests were dropped off? Where were the two agents before they were…'

Mike walked over to his jacket and pulled out a cellophane bag.

'These are MacLeod's possessions; they gave them to me when I identified him earlier'.

He pulled out the dented and dust ridden digiscope.

'This should tell us!'

After twenty minutes of downloading the high resolution data from the digiscope onto his laptop, Fredrico unplugged the equipment and handed it back to Mike.

'Thanks Michael, I will send this to my boys and get a match on your man from the aeroplane. I will find these people don't worry. If they are still on Gibraltar I will find them. I need to make a call'.

He pressed a key combination on his keyboard and stood up to type a number onto his phone.

'Murphy, it's Fredrico… yes and yourself? …good. Have you received the files? Ah good, the wonders of modern technology eh?'

As Fredrico's conversation continued, Simon moved closer to Mike, his eyes locked onto the Police Chief walking into an adjacent room.

'What makes you think you can trust him Mike?' he whispered.

'We have a history'.

'What is this history?'

'Why are you so paranoid Simon?'

'Paranoid? Paranoid? Because it looks like Nelson has turned against us, they know we are lying about our position, four agents are dead, two are still in hospital and you have been beaten, blown up and shot at! Why am I so paranoid?'

'You have every right to be paranoid', Fredrico announced, walking back into the room.

Simon sat back and shut his eyes.

'I didn't mean to…' he began.

'You both have every right not to trust a soul! And, I recommend you exercise that prerogative. You *can* trust me, however. I owe Michael my life'.

'Ah come on Fred…' Mike began.

'Ah, you play it down; I need to justify my trustworthiness to your man here. We were nineteen and working for William Black. We were running rum and tobaccos from Ireland to Cornwall in a small fishing boat. Anyway, we were being pursued by a coast guard at the time and eventually she caught up with us…' he paused to sip from his mug of hotel tea.

'…We took evasive action…' he looked over towards Mike who let out a nasally laugh.

'…We made an about turn, swung into Lemorna Cove, into the fog and waited for an hour or two. Needless to say we drank some of our contraband. Then, when we thought the coast was clear and the engines from the Coastguard vessel had gone – we rowed out into the dense fog - hitting a yacht; the boom swung free and knocked me out of the boat, clean unconscious. I sank like a sack of potatoes. Michael, here…' he patted Mike on the shoulder '…jumped from the sinking boat, dragged my bulk to the shore and resuscitated me. He also went back into the depths of the harbour and managed to rescue some of our goods…'

Mike smiled, 'Happy days eh, Fred?'

Fredrico extended his hand out towards Simon, who looked at him with remorse.

'Friends?'

Simon leapt from the chair enthusiastically and shook his hand.

'I'm sorry, I…'

'Do not apologise. Like I say, you are in a difficult situation, I would be the same'.

As the two men shook hands, Fredrico's phone rang out in his pocket.

'Ah, excuse me gentlemen'.

Mike exhaled as he felt at a new found pain around his jaw, 'This one is the fight I think, not the explosion'.

Simon tried to smile but instead gave an uneasy look. Mike leaned forward towards the laptop.

'I guess we ought to take a look at what's on that digiscope then'.

The folder was open in front of them on the small screen. Mike clicked on the magnification bar and the images resized to barely-visible thumbnails causing him to squint. As he scrolled through them, they began to become more focused and at further magnification.

'Bloody hell, he made use of this thing didn't he?'

The two agents huddled closer to the small compact screen.

'Has Fredrico sent these off already?' Simon asked.

'Yeah'.

'You don't think we should have checked them through beforehand?'

'No, why? These are really high resolution aren't they?'

'We don't know what's on this thing. What if we accidentally implicate one of Fredrico's men?'

'Then he should know about it', Mike dismissed quickly.

As they flicked through the images one of the subject's faces appeared in detail.

'That's him,' Mike stated, 'the man on the plane'.

He scrolled further through the images and then stopped.

'Here's a close-up of one of the chests…'

Mike clicked on to the next thumbnail.

Simon gasped uncontrollably, like a young girl catching a glimpse of a spider on the curtains.

'Oh my God…' Mike sat back and rubbed his mouth; his eyes wide open.

Fredrico marched back into the room.

'Gents, my department has seen one of the…' he paused as he sensed Mike's shock and looked around to see his pale colleague stooping on the floor; his head in his hands.

'I guess you have seen the images then?' Fredrico said softly as he pulled a chair close to the bed where Mike sat motionless.

Mike leaned forwards to look at the image once again.

'They are…' he began, slowly shaking his head.

'The crew of the yachts we can assume', Fredrico interjected.

'But they… they have been…'

'Cut to size – easy transportation. There was a famous case like this in the sixties', Fredrico nodded, 'very brutal'.

Simon shut his eyes, pushed himself from the floor and walked slowly to the hotel room window.

'I think we are most definitely looking at murder now gentlemen. A true pirate, in every sense of the word'.

'Where is that dock Fred?' Mike asked as he reached for his notepad and pen from his jacket that was strewn on the bed.

'That is South from here; looks like Sandy Bay, or nearby. Somewhere east of The Rock', Fredrico said as he stood up from the chair.

'Where were they taking the… bodies?' Simon asked, still staring at the view.

'They will more than likely be burying them inside the many chambers of The Rock. There is a rabbit warren of tunnels and passage ways; a legacy from various wars. Half of them are rarely seen and most of those never visited. It is a smuggler's haven in there. Unfortunately, it seems it has now become a burial chamber'.

Mike began to pull on his trousers underneath his towel and then moved towards his shirt that lay draped over the back of one of the chairs.

'Where are you going Michael?' Fredrico asked looking at his watch, 'you only have a few hours before your meeting with De LaCruz'.

'I'm going to that bay', he stated with determination.

'Wait, just until tomorrow. I will rally a group of my men and we can seal it off. You do not have time now Michael. Patience is a virtue'.

'Time is not on our side Fred! I agree, yes, we will get your men on it tomorrow but for the time being I want to see it with my own eyes'.

Fredrico's Mercedes pulled up in front of the carpark area of Sandy Bay, a small residential cove at the east point of The Rock. A curve of white, stone buildings sat below a dominating steep slope of natural vegetation, proudly looking out towards Spain's Costa Del Sol.

Mike climbed out of the car and looked around him; it was a beautiful afternoon and the warm sea breeze enveloped him like a blanket.

'Up there, is where your men were I think', Fredrico pointed at a small ledge with an adjoining road.

'Which means that the boat must have come in down… here?' Simon pointed at a small wooden jetty.

The three men negotiated the small sandy decline to the precarious jetty sitting amongst the modest swell from the tide. Simon began to comb the area for signs of evidence while Fredrico punched a number onto his phone.

'I will check with the Coastguard to see if anyone was seen here last night'.

Mike walked towards his colleague who had crouched down.

'What have you found Si?'

Simon stood up with his hand clenched into a fist.

'Close your eyes', he toyed, and dropped the object into Mike's hand.

It was a cartridge case.

The small silver casing began an influx of memories of the previous night and his frantic phone conversation with MacLeod.

'When I spoke to MacLeod he said that Robinson had been shot dead, perhaps they shot him from down here?'

'They'd have to be a damn good shot Mike, that's got to be three or four hundred feet up', Simon suggested, looking up towards the small overhang above them.

'Or a marksman', Mike added, 'starting to come together though isn't it? Royal Marines involved in a shooting at The Ship? Silenced pistol shooting with unprecedented accuracy?' Mike spun the cartridge in his fingers, 'and a marksman killing an agent from three hundred feet away'.

'This is rapidly spiralling out of control', Simon added, shaking his head.

Fredrico started the engine and the three-litre Mercedes roared to life.

'I have organised a team to cordon off this area this afternoon; we will take a look this evening and keep you posted'.

The Mercedes traced the narrow streets back to the hotel. Fredrico knew the island roads well, enabling him to make unknown short cuts. His open concern, to get the agents back to the hotel ready for the meeting with De LaCruz, had began to cause anxiety for Simon, who had already began to exhale deep breaths in anticipation.

'Ah, by the way, I have a name for your dead man', Fredrico piped up, 'Derek Prince? Ring any bells?'

'Prince!' Mike shouted, suddenly straightening up from the back seat, 'I knew I recognised him…'

Mike's expression quickly changed from excitement to concern and bashed his fist on the walnut panel of the rear door.

'What is it?' Simon enquired.

'Prince… you know him too…' he sighed.

Simon frowned, desperately trying to recollect both the name and the face.

'Do I?'

'You have emailed him, let's put it that way'.

Simon shook his head; his mind sifting through his mental address book.

'd.prince@nelson.gov.uk?' Mike suggested, inadvertently patronisingly.

Simon's eyes widened and a wave of chill bumps covered his arms.

'You are joking? It must be a different guy. There must be loads of…' Simon paused. It was unlikely there were that many Derek Princes and even less likely more than one in the same building.

'Who is he?' Fredrico asked as he threw the vehicle around the tiny back streets.

'He is a second Lieutenant in the Royal Navy based in Plymouth. He works…' Mike paused, 'he works at Nelson!'

'Are you sure?' Fredrico enquired carefully.

'I saw him a few weeks ago – I passed him in the carpark', Simon confirmed.

'If this is the case and Nelson loses contact with this man Prince; they will want to know why?'

Simon looked at Mike in the sun-visor mirror from the passenger seat. He was right to have been so tentative about their contact with Nelson.

'There is a way you can play this Michael', Fredrico piped up once again as he pulled the giant car into the hotel carpark.

'Oh?' Mike uttered with a demoralised tone.

He unfastened his seat belt and manoeuvred his body in the driver's seat to face him.

'You could play along with them. They hired you for a reason. If they are controlling you then that is also for a reason. Use that to your advantage; to stay in favour with them. Then use that resource to continue your investigations under that cover. I will head up my own investigations with you and keep in contact with you as and when. Put it another way; if they wanted you dead – they would have killed you already. They are steering you'.

'And what about Prince trying to kill me on the highway? He shot at me', Mike asked.

'You are still alive aren't you? He was trying to hinder you, buying time for his escape', Fredrico rationalised. It made perfect sense and furthermore had summarised the numerous questions of doubt that Mike had been asking himself for weeks. His face reflected Fredrico's epiphany and he nodded in wholehearted agreement. Not only did it guarantee their safety but Nelson would also provide the support and resources they wouldn't have been able to achieve if they had gone under the radar.

'Now let's get you both inside ready for tonight', Fredrico said clapping his hands together with a wide smile.

'Oh God', Simon exhaled as he pushed his head into his hands.

Chapter 10

The Lead

The hire car's tyres crunched the gravel at the bottom of the driveway of the Mediterranean villa and stopped just short of two large iron gates.

Mike leaned out of the window towards a metal intercom and pressed a large red plastic button beneath a circular meshed microphone.

'Hola, le puedo ayudar yo?' A gentle female voice crackled through the microphone.

'It's Greene and Steele to see…'

'Ah yes, I saw you arrive, please come in', she invited in a near-perfect English accent.

The huge gates opened with a deafening metallic screech and Mike slowly trickled the car inside towards a gravelled courtyard. In front of them; a vast magnolia and terracotta brick villa of colonial design stood proudly surveying the seascape beyond.

'Someone made it…' Simon concluded as he regarded the splendour of the architecturally impressive building.

Mike pulled the hire car next to a large yellow and black classic Mustang.

'Remember, keep it cool. We will get what we want and come straight out again…' Mike tried to prep-talk his nervous partner. He needed Simon's knowledge and his strength of character but he couldn't afford him to break what they had started to build. He looked at Simon's hands; fidgeting frantically with his cigarette lighter.

'Calm down for God's sake! I will do the talking; just back me up with a nod or two…'

They approached the entrance of the splendid residence and knocked.

Almost instantaneously the door opened and they were greeted by a tall, thirty-something lady wearing a long, red silk dress that clung to every curve of her body and leaving little to the imagination.

'Good evening gentlemen, please come in', her accent was enticing and had appeared to have cured Simon from his anxiety.

The two men entered the highly-polished marble floored foyer. Sculpted statues stood flanking a spiral staircase of flame red carpet and giant palms shimmered in the breeze from the open conservatory ahead of them.

'My name is Sophie, you must be Mr Greene?' she extended her hand towards Mike.

'It's a pleasure to meet you Sophie', he said, trying hard not to sound too flirtatious.

'Making you, Mr Steele?'

Simon took her hand and nodded his head.

Mike rolled his eyes; it was unfolding like a scene from a Brontë novel.

'My husband will be with you shortly, please make yourselves comfortable in the conservatory over there. There are drinks at the bar; please help yourself'.

She swooned from the foyer into an adjoining room, from where a male Spanish voice speaking on a telephone echoed around the stone walls.

They entered the huge conservatory that overlooked the city below and the seascape beyond that.

'My God', Mike shook his head.

'You know you have made it when your living room has a postcard for a view right?' Simon added.

They both moved to a kidney shaped iron-worked bar with glass top where several decanters sat atop silver trays. Simon plucked a bottle of San Miguel from an illuminated refrigerator behind the bar and twisted the top off, 'When in Rome?' he suggested.

Mike smiled and held out his hand to retrieve it.

'What did your last slave die of?' Simon asked under his breath as he relinquished the bottle.

The two men chinked their bottles and stood in silence admiring the breathtaking view.

'Ah gentlemen, so good to see you and right on time'.

De LaCruz marched into the conservatory in a bright white suit, black shirt open at the neck and wearing thick rimmed designer glasses.

'How do you like my view ah?' he asked rhetorically, shaking the men's hands respectively.

'It is a beautiful house Mr De LaCruz', Simon offered to Mike's surprise.

'Dinner is almost ready; perhaps you would follow me into the dining room?'

He walked through the doorway and across the marbled floor of the reception.

'Are you okay?' Mike asked Simon.

'Fine, no problem…' he confirmed.

They followed in the direction of the echoing footsteps and entered an arched doorway that led to the external terrace of the property, where a barbeque smoked away in the corner next to another bar. Sophie stood at the ornate table pouring champagne into four flutes.

'Please sit down', De LaCruz offered as he made his way back to tend to the barbeque.

'It won't be long. I trust you are hungry?'

The two men nodded as they sat down in front of a theatrical backdrop of The Rock, the sea and the horizon. It was a perfect night; although as Mike had spotted, there was a large folded canopy which would extend above them should the weather have turned. Two huge industrial bar heaters warmed the terrace from the side wall of the villa, providing a tropical heat in the coolness of the night.

Their host wandered over to the table where Sophie had just sat down, and placed a large serving tray of Langoustine, Lobster, Crab, Cray Fish, King Prawns and what looked to Mike to be a whole Swordfish underneath.

'I hope you like seafood', De LaCruz laughed. Another rhetoric inspired to evoke the humour of his guests.

The two agents laughed on cue. Mike watched him as he began to serve the kingly feast onto large white china plates. He was an incredibly confident, charismatic and extremely laid back man, coupled with being in the comfort of his own surroundings; he was going to be a tough one to crack.

After the meal, Mike sat back with an enormous cigar that Sophie had lit for him, and exhaled a large plume of thick blue smoke that hung in the warm atmosphere like a single cloud in a blue summer sky.

'Sophie, would you mind – business', De LaCruz gestured towards his wife.

Sophie smiled, picked up her glass of wine and walked across the terrace and in to the house.

De LaCruz placed his elbows on the table in a businessman manner.

'So, you didn't just come here to clean me out of seafood and champagne right?'

Mike sat up. It was time for them to get into character. It was also the first time they were about to talk shop. The meal had taken place amongst stories of Gibraltar, the history of the Spanish Armada, discussions regarding the Euro and sports cars. Not once was the taboo subject of smuggling mentioned despite it being the main topic of both his books and his show.

'I will cut to the point Mr De LaCruz…' Mike spoke through a mouthful of smoke.

'Please, call me Leon, you are in my house now, call me Leon'.

Mike smiled. Simon lit a cigarette, deciding against offering them out.

'Leon, I have a proposition for you…'

'I know. That is why you are here, no? I am listening'.

Simon sat back and watched the two men, readying himself to make an input where required.

'There is a yacht moored in Portsmouth called the…'

'The Golden Raj, I know – you told me that yesterday. What is the proposition?'

De LaCruz's interjection had shocked Mike into a temporary silence; he seemed almost desperate in his inquisition. It also occurred to him that he may yet be talking to the wrong man and that what he was about to ask could be both embarrassing and even worse insulting. Nevertheless they were at a loss for further leads at this point. He looked at his host and inhaled from his cigar, creating a dramatic and purposeful pause in the conversation.

'If you let me finish Leon, you will find out…'

Mike's facade remained as forefront as his cutting remark but inside he was burning with apprehension. He sensed Simon's stare but ignored it.

De LaCruz broke into a smile.

'I like you Greene… now please, continue'.

'The yacht will leave Portsmouth tomorrow morning at about nine, heading for Gijon. It will stop briefly at St Mary's on the Isles of Scilly to collect some passengers, and then make its way down to France'.

Mike stood up and walked towards the bar. An influx of confidence rushed to his legs. He picked up a decanter and began to pour from it into a large crystal tumbler.

'This yacht will, according to my source, be captained by the owner of the exclusive Parisian "Le Bar du Lutetia"'.

Mike inhaled from his cigar and took a sip from the brandy he had poured.

'Nice brandy, what is it?'

De LaCruz frowned and rolled his eyes.

'Brandy? It is a Nineteen Fifty Nine Grosperrin Fins Bois Cognac!'

'Christ!' Mike whispered to himself through pinched lips. He had just poured himself a large tumbler of fifty year old Cognac. Overconfidence would be their downfall and he began to pace himself through the details that Fredrico had worked up for them.

'The yacht will be base to a party of celebrities all heading towards Paris and marks the celebration of ruby wedding anniversary for the owner and his wife. The boat however…' Mike smiled as he sat down, '…will be absolutely packed with bonds!'

De LaCruz raised his left eyebrow.

'These bonds will be unmarked, untraceable and worth well into the millions'.

De LaCruz contemplated what Mike had relayed and sat in silence, tapping his fingers together.

'Who is your contact?'

Mike twitched uncontrollably.

'You want me to divulge my contact?'

De LaCruz smiled.

'Relax, I don't know you from Adam; I want to assure my own safety you know'.

He stood up and walked towards the bar.

Mike stole a second to look at Simon who appeared terrified. The situation was getting the better of him and he was visibly nervous. Mike glared at him to keep it together for a little longer.

'Bonds eh? Now why would they be carrying bonds Thomas?' De LaCruz asked as he poured from a different decanter.

'How should I know?' Mike snapped.

The facts and the figures were correct. Fredrico had gone over the script for hours previously but he had no answer as to why they would be carrying bonds. Why *would* they be carrying bonds? It actually didn't make any sense.

'I think it's a gift', Simon suddenly piped up.

'Ah, the silence has broken', De LaCruz toyed towards him.

Perfect, Mike thought. A wedding anniversary gift.

'I see - makes sense', De LaCruz scratched his chin as he pondered the scenario.

'So, what about this yacht anyway?'

Mike wrinkled his forehead. Did he want him to spell it out?

'I am saying, Leon, you can take that yacht from the water, the second it leaves St Mary's harbour', Mike affirmed.

De LaCruz laughed out loud.

'Just wanted to hear you say it my man. And, how do you suggest I do that?'

Mike grimaced. He had obviously taken the bait and was playing with them. Time for a different strategy.

'I'm sorry Mr De LaCruz, it appears we have made a terrible mistake'.

Mike stood up and dabbed at his mouth with his serviette. Simon slowly stood, watching Mike's move. Was he serious? Were they really about to leave after getting so close to him?

'Okay, okay… I am just teasing…' De LaCruz walked towards Mike and patted him on the back.

'I need to make a call, I will be back, please help yourselves to… my most expensive Cognac'.

He gave Mike a wink and left the terrace with his phone in his hand.

'Christ Mike, what are you trying to do? Kill me?'

Mike smiled, 'Relax Si, this seems to be working…'

'And if it doesn't?' Simon asked eagerly awaiting plan B.

'Well gentlemen…' De LaCruz marched back out onto the warm, tiled terrace floor.

'I have spoken to my contact… and your story checks out'.

'How, is another question…' Mike began to fish for the evidence they were there to ascertain, 'taking that yacht is one thing but getting away with it? That is the real trick. That is why I came to you Leon. Those waters are heavily patrolled and getting in and out will be a problem'.

'Not necessarily. I have a vessel'.

Mike ground his teeth in anticipation of a confession.

'I bought her from the Royal Navy, believe it or not…'

Bingo!

'She is a Nineteen Thirty Nine German U-Boat. You see, the beauty in her is that she…'

There was a pause as De LaCruz waited for the next line.

'Submerges?' Simon offered, nervously.

'Exactly! She submerges. I have used her now and again for things like this. I have a crew in place aboard her and it only takes me a few hours to get to her'.

Now and again? Mike thought. This was exactly what they needed although a location would be useful.

'Where is she?' Mike asked.

De LaCruz frowned.

'You are asking a lot of questions Mr Greene, is there any reason why you want to know where she is right now?'

A bead of sweat ran the length of Simon's forehead.

Breaking the silence, De LaCruz's phone rang. He stood up and marched out to answer it.

'Shit Mike, we have got to get out of here!' Simon whispered nervously.

Mike's phone vibrated in his pocket. He plucked it out and opened it, walking to the far corner of the terrace out of audible range.

'Williams', he whispered. It was Fredrico.

'Michael, get out of there now, he has just received a call from Nelson, get out! NOW!'

Mike's jaw dropped as he closed the phone.

'We've got to go!'

Simon stood up.

'What's going on Mike?'

'It was Fred; they're still monitoring his calls…'

Mike looked over the edge of the terrace. It was a long drop through trees, there was no way they could jump over the wall.

He darted from one corner to the next desperate for an escape route.

'Are you leaving gentlemen?' De LaCruz asked sarcastically as he stomped back onto the terrace accompanied by Sophie.

'I have just had a rather interesting phone call. You wouldn't know of a couple of Revenue agents by the name of… Williams and Jenkins would you at all?'

Mike chewed his cheek, numbed by fear.

Sophie passed a silver Dessert Eagle to her husband from her handbag.

'Thank you dear. Always amazing what ladies pack into their handbags these days… now, which one of you is Mike Williams?' he held the gun out towards Mike.

'Excuse me?' Mike tried, with as neutral an expression as he could muster.

'Don't… just don't. Which one are you? Mike or Simon?'

He pulled back the chamber and released it with a metallic click; loading the weapon.

'If I could offer you a piece of advice it would be this: don't fuck with me, Revenue man! I am well connected here. I could shoot the two of you in the head right here, right now, throw your bodies into the street and still be back here in time for breakfast – a free man! So, no skin off my nose what you decide…'

Mike looked at Simon for a response, his eyes wide with fear.

'Mr De LaCruz, we are…'

De LaCruz fired a round between the two men, the bullet passing clean through the stone wall of the terrace and the blast echoed around the walls and across the city.

'The next one won't miss!' he snarled, 'you were saying?'

'FREEZE De LaCruz!'

Fredrico burst through the terrace doors along with a handful of armed policemen who took up strategic points around them.

'What the hell do you think you are doing!' De LaCruz turned to Fredrico.

'What the hell do I think *I* am doing? You are a fraud, Leon!'

De LaCruz continued to target the two agents.

'Drop the weapon Leon, let's not make this any worse…' Fredrico tried.

De LaCruz reluctantly lowered the weapon and then quickly swung it around towards Fredrico, firing a round towards him. Sophie let out a loud squeal as the round exploded onto the wall next to Fredrico's shoulder, throwing him forwards. The first policeman fired a round at De LaCruz's arm, forcing the gun from his hand and the remaining men wrestled him to the ground.

'You are a dead man', De LaCruz shouted towards Fredrico as an officer pushed his face into the terrace tiles to handcuff him.

Mike and Simon sat patiently inside the police headquarters.

'Simon, I think it's only fair to tell you…' Mike started.

'Tell me what?'

Mike paused. His suspicions had been confirmed.

'The person who called De LaCruz… they were from Nelson'.

Simon nodded, the news confirming his own suspicions.

'What do we do now?'

'Play it as Fred suggested, like nothing has happened. As far as Nelson are concerned we are still investigating our case, how would they know that we knew it was them who contacted De LaCruz? No one except us knew that Fred had tapped his phone lines. We've just got to play it by the book now and launch our own investigation into Nelson…somehow'.

Fredrico entered the office and sat down, placing his Fedora on the side of a computer monitor.

'He isn't budging Michael, he won't say a God damn word'.

'Is he really protected? Will he walk? If he does we can kiss goodbye to this project'.

'He won't walk Michael, he will be done for attempted murder and ownership of an illegal weapon in any case… that will be enough to hold him here for the time being'.

Mike rubbed his face with both of his hands.

'On the other hand Michael, you haven't done anything wrong… you are still in favour with Nelson'.

'But who sold us out? How did De LaCruz know who we were?'

'It was most probably an email he received. The man from Nelson on the telephone simply warned him. I think he came to his own conclusions'.

Mike removed his hands slowly as he began to ingest what Fredrico was telling him.

'So as far as Nelson is concerned we are just doing what they commissioned us to do. They don't know that we suspect them of double crossing us', Simon stated, trying to keep his voice down from the busy police corridor.

'Exactly. If you continue your lines of enquiries, continue the updates and keep your heads down – you can continue your investigations against Nelson from inside Nelson! You could blow this thing open from the inside!'

'So long as De LaCruz doesn't walk', Mike added.

'It appears to me Mike, that whoever is conspiring against you is not trying to stop you but control you', Fredrico said as he replaced his Fedora to his head.

'Get back home Michael, your work here is complete. Get back in favour with Nelson and play it from there. I will continue to be your eyes and ears here'.

'Thank you Fred, I appreciate your help', Mike whispered to him.

'You never know, when De LaCruz eventually plays ball, he may yet implicate your culprit. But, be safe in the knowledge that your trip here was a success in the way that you have confirmed your suspicions and you have directly linked Nelson with De LaCruz, the smuggling operation and the bodies… wherever they came from. I would say that was three days well spent, wouldn't you?'

Mike stood up and shook Fredrico's hand.

'What about the drop off? The bodies and the loot?'

'I will find those crates Mike, leave it to me. I will let you know whenever I find anything out'.

'You are a good man and a good friend Fredrico', Mike smiled.

The two agents exited the police station amongst the influx of drunken arrestees being brought in from the night.

The air stewardess finished clearing the plates from underneath a large scale map, clipped to the rear of the seat in front and folded up and around the window.

'You know', Mike started, chewing the end of a savaged Biro, 'what bugs me is how the vessels were actually attacked. The pirates must have known what to expect and where to expect them'.

Simon looked up from his notes, tracing a circled area with his pen.

'If it were Nelson that…'

'It *is* Nelson, we have established that', Mike cut in.

'Okay, but what I am saying is; if the pirates knew where to be and at what time, it means they have been able to intercept the vessels, knowing the exact positioning, right?'

'Right?' Mike said slowly following Simon's chain of thought.

'So… how do you find out this information? How would you find out where a vessel is headed, what the statistics of the vessel are and who is on board?'

'I guess I would contact the… harbour master?'

'Exactly!'

'But, how would the harbour master find out all the details?' Mike asked, desperate for a resolution. The thought process was heading in the right direction but there was a lack of conclusion.

'The harbour master will see the yacht right? He could search his own database to look for ownership of the yacht from its identification number'.

Mike nodded.

'Once he hits upon a ripe one, one that is rich for the pickings, so to speak… he would verbally speak to the owner, find out where they are going… I don't know, issue them a weather report, as part of his remit then contact…'

'The… Coastguard?' Mike tried, hoping for a wrong answer - implicating a coast guard would be like implicating his own family.

'Or….' Simon waited.

'The Naval Patrols?'

'The Navy!'

'Plymouth?' Mike asked.

'More than likely, Mike. If there is someone in the Navy Command Headquarters that is in on this, drawing routes to feed directly, or indirectly to the pirates they have a perfect scam!'

Simon looked excited by his conclusion and sat back in his seat with an unavoidable smug expression. Mike's mind worked double time to comprehend what Simon had illustrated.

'So, in effect', Simon added, 'Say, the harbour master spots a luxury liner and cross references it with his database. If it's a good one, he'll ask its Captain where he is headed, crossing it from his list of weather issues. He will call it into Navy Command Headquarters who will draw out the route and determine the speed, ETA etc, working out a perfect strike point on the map; somewhere far out to sea, away from prying eyes and where they couldn't be detected. The boat is hit; the pirates take the loot and the crew and leave the vessel to drift. They box up the loot, box up the bodies, send them out on a dinghy. The dinghy makes the drop, the smuggler, such as Coates, picks up the loot, stores it until it can be dispersed and Bob's your Uncle'.

Simon sat back once again, and grinned back at Mike, who looked through him, digesting the gravity of what he was explaining. There was no doubt that it added up and what is more, it felt right.

'And, who would turn down a slice of the kind of cash that this would bring in?'

'That is a point, Mike… makes me wonder just how many people are on the payroll! If we blow this thing open, how many people will be sent down for it? And… how deep will it run?'

'Not our concern!' Mike snapped, 'we are talking about murder now. This isn't just about smuggling contraband anymore…'

Fredrico walked into the holding cell where De LaCruz sat on a plastic chair, his hands cuffed behind his back. Two armed guards stood either side of him.

Fredrico gestured to them and they left, closing the heavy metal door behind them.

De LaCruz looked up at him with curiosity.

'How long are you going to keep me here Fredrico?' he asked with an air of confidence.

Fredrico pulled a chair from the corner of the room and placed it in front of him, sitting himself down and crossing his legs. He took off his hat and moulded it over his knee and began to dab at his brow with a handkerchief.

'As long as I am assured my safety Leon'.

'We both know it is only a matter of hours Fredrico, just a few hours and I will be out of here'.

Fredrico lit a cigar and blew the smoke into De LaCruz's face.

De LaCruz smiled.

'What will he say when he finds out you helped out two Revenue Agents?'

Fredrico looked slightly unsettled by his comment; a look that De LaCruz picked up on.

'I threw in the towel three years ago Leon, he knows it and you know it'.

'Yes, and you agreed to keep your nose out of our affairs. I thought we had an agreement?'

Fredrico leaned closer to the cuffed De LaCruz, 'That is before we got involved in murder!'

He leant back and drew on his cigar.

De LaCruz squinted his eyes.

'What did you think happened to the crews of these boats? Do you think they jumped over board? Disappeared without a trace? You chose to ignore that in favour of the money so don't start that holier than thou shit!'

The two men looked at each other for a few uncomfortable silent moments.

'You are a dead man, Fredrico, a dead man!' De LaCruz spoke softly and confidently.

Fredrico stood up, knocking his chair over, and stormed out of the holding room, signalling the two guards back inside.

Mike and Simon walked into the carpark adjacent to the Lands End aerodrome. Mike held out his key fob ready to unlock the Land Rover.

'When Fred finds the chests, it is going to put a serious strain on our inside investigation you know', Simon suggested to Mike.

'True, but they are expecting us to continue our investigations right? Perhaps we will see a change in mood and maybe that will be our tell-tale sign that we need to identify the main man?'

Fredrico left the Police Station by the back entrance. He looked at his watch; eleven thirty in the evening. He pulled up the collar of his coat and walked across the paved carpark to his silver Mercedes. He stopped as he approached the car and looked at it with contempt. He bought the car with proceeds from the various scams, from the loot recovered from the attacks… from the victims of the pirates. Feeling a sickness in his throat, he opened the door and climbed inside. He pushed the key into the ignition and hesitated. What if…?

He closed his eyes, held his breath and turned the key. The engine turned over and kicked in. Shaking his head he fastened the seatbelt and drove out of the carpark.

Mike sat back from his laptop at his desk and surveyed the empty office of Nelson's second floor. Simon continued to tap away furiously on his keyboard, filling out the bogus reports for the investigation. He could feel Mike's gaze burrowing into his forehead.

'What?' he asked, frustrated that his concentration and workflow had been broken.

Mike leaned forward.

'Don't you feel awkward? Do you get the impression that everyone is against us? That we are sitting in a lion's den, so to speak?' he whispered.

'Not really… how do we know that everyone is against us? I think we need to be cautious yes, but also not let ourselves to be swept away with paranoia'.

Mike sat back and sucked on his pen.

'I know who we can trust in here', Mike whispered.

He stood up and walked out of the office. As the sound from his rapid footsteps echoed around the marble walls, Simon shook his head and returned to the laptop screen.

Fredrico's phone rang in his pocket. He indicated through the traffic of Winston Churchill and pulled into a lay-by.

'Yes?' he answered.

'That was a mistake to arrest Leon, Fredrico', the voice crackled from the ear piece.

His face turned to pale grey stone.

'I… I had to, for integrity…'

'Don't give me that Fredrico, we made an agreement when you severed your connections with us and you have contravened that agreement by becoming involved again'.

'What do you want?'

'Release De LaCruz immediately! He is no good to me where he is at the moment'.

Fredrico closed his eyes.

'And if I… can't?'

'You will… I am paying you a generous sum of money every month for your silence, in case you had forgotten. You have broken that silence, and you have broken the agreement. If you value your life Fredrico, you will find a way'.

'You can't threaten me, I am too well connected', Fredrico tried with a tremor to his voice.

'Yes, Fredrico, I can. You seem to forget how many people in your precinct alone are on my books. Do you feel safe there? How complacent you have become'.

The phone went dead.

Fredrico threw the phone onto the dashboard and bit his fist.

After a few moments he reached for the phone and pressed a quick dial number.

'Garrison', a voice answered.

'This is Chief Fredrico; I want you to release Leon De LaCruz tonight'.

'Sir?'

'Release De LaCruz, immediately!' he shouted.

'Yes… sir… can I ask who is sanctioning this release?'

'I am sanctioning it you idiot!'

'Yes sir, I will have him released within the hour'.

Fredrico threw the phone back onto the dashboard and wiped the sweat from his forehead. He swung the car back into the line of traffic with speed, leaving a trail of smoke from his tyres lingering in the warm air.

Mike jogged down the stairs into the basement offices of the building, the emergency lights being the only illumination. He walked the length of the corridor, flicking his head to each of the identical doors, looking for the name plates. At the end of the corridor the night janitor mopped at the vinyl floor.

Mike stopped at the door with the brass name plate: "Dr D J Faraday MSc, BSc".

He knocked on the thick door; the sounds of which echoed along the empty corridor.

There was no reply. He tried the door and it pushed open. He looked around and entered the dark office.

'Doctor Faraday?' he spoke softly into the darkness.

After closing the door, he groped around for the light switch. Perhaps Faraday was asleep. It was common knowledge that he worked late and was often found asleep at his desk.

'Don?' he repeated.

His hand finally found the light switch.

The room was completely empty with the exception of a few antiquated cupboards and filing cabinets. His desk remained but his chair was gone.

Mike looked around; all of the books had gone, the folders, specimens, everything had been removed.

'He's not here…' a soft Cornish voice from behind him muttered.

Mike spun around in surprise.

'Who are you?'

'I'm the caretaker of the building. Franklin, John Franklin'.

'Where is he? Have they finally moved him above ground?' Mike joked.

Franklin looked at the floor and sighed.

'You a friend of his?'

'Yes, an old friend'.

The caretaker looked back up and cleared his throat.

'He died the day before yesterday; I am terribly sorry Mr…?'

Mike's eyes burned as his tear ducts began to well up.

'What? What do you mean? I am looking for Don Faraday!'

Franklin scratched his head.

'I think they said it was a massive coronary. Died right there in his chair', he pointed to a bare area of the vacant room.

'You been on holiday or something? I'm surprised you weren't told'.

Mike's rage began to overwhelm him and he felt a pain in his stomach. He pushed past the caretaker and out into the corridor, his left foot slipping on the wet vinyl. He began to run down the darkened passageway and punched out at the wall.

Fredrico's mind raced as to his next move. Perhaps he *should* flee? Maybe he could pull the plug on the whole project and expose the principal. He smiled as he thought about the coup that would evolve. Maybe he should inform Mike and martyr himself for the good of the project. Ahead, the traffic lights changed to red and he slowed the Mercedes down to a stop and applied the handbrake.

As he waited, he looked at his phone. Maybe the right thing to do would be to tell Mike. Even though it would mean confessing that all along, during their friendship, he was involved in what was possibly the world's largest smuggling scam - at least it would be a confession leading to the conviction of the leader and all of the connected parties. Perhaps that would outweigh the fact that he was not the valiant chief of police figure that Mike respected so much and for so long?

Nodding in agreement of his thoughts, he picked the phone from his dashboard and tapped it on his chin as he considered his options.

A convertible Lexus drew alongside the Mercedes at the traffic lights. Fredrico glanced across, acknowledging the affluent vehicle. He tapped at his steering wheel with his other hand, and starred up at the red lights, willing them to change to green.

'Hey Fredrico!'

Had he misheard? The noise from the traffic was quite loud and he was feeling susceptible and paranoid.

He decided to dial Mike's number and navigated through his phonebook to the correct entry.

'Hey! Fredrico!'

It was unmistakable - someone was shouting him. He looked around at the source – the man in the Lexus next to him.

Fredrico looked at him and squinted to make him out in the darkness. He certainly didn't recognise him instantly.

'Leon said thanks for the release!' the figure said as he pulled up a silenced automatic from his lap.

'Oh no!' Fredrico said to himself, the realisation that his life was in danger hit him and stunned him into a paralysis.

The weapon made no sound as the bullet shattered the driver's window, passed through Fredrico's temple, and out of the passenger window. Fredrico's body slumped, hanging from the seat belt.

The traffic lights turned green and the Lexus pulled slowly away, leaving the Mercedes standing at the junction.

Mike arrived back at his desk- red with anger, his eyes damp and irritated.

Simon looked up at him.

'Christ, Mike, what's the matter?'

'He's dead'.

'Who?'

'Don, Faraday, he's… he's dead!'

Simon stood up and walked around the desks to his stunned partner.

'My God, Mike, I'm sorry'.

'Everyone's dying'.

'What did he…?'

'Heart attack… A heart attack… Don Faraday? A heart attack?'

Simon looked confused.

'But, Don was…'

'Yeah, fit, I know, he used to run the Marathon for God's sake'.

Mike dropped onto his chair, his limbs lifeless with emotional exhaustion.

Simon ran to the vending machine in the corner of the office and returned with a plastic cup of coffee.

The phone on the highly polished walnut grain table buzzed to life. Vice Admiral Wilkinson stretched to retrieve it.

'Yes', he answered.

'Sir, Fredrico's out of the picture', a man's voice shouted from the noise of busy traffic.

Wilkinson smiled.

'Good work. Any witnesses?'

'No sir'.

'Well done. Get out of Gibraltar tonight!'

'Yes sir'.

Wilkinson closed his phone and sat back in his leather chair.

After a few minutes, Mike's emotions had begun to settle. His eyes were reddened and his mouth down turned but he knew that he had to remain focused. This had become a race against time. If, as they suspected, the deaths were linked to the project then they needed to cut out the core before anyone else was killed. The death toll was inconceivable, yet somehow they were being treated as separate incidents. It was difficult to disassociate paranoia with reality. Coincidence was out of the question. Mike had gone to see Don Faraday who planted the seed about the EMP and the possibility of a Navy vessel being involved. Now, he was dead; removed from the game in order to prevent further leaks of information.

'Si, how many men do we have at the moment, available to us?'

'Give me a second…' he said clicking his mouse and opening a variety of windows on the small laptop screen.

'Forty two, including us, Mrs Jacobs, the quartermasters and the guards. That also includes the admin people. I think we have thirty two agents, including us'.

Mike stood up and took off his glasses to survey the rows of empty desks in the office.

'Thirty agents?'

'Yeah, they culled our resources due to an over resourcing issue in Plymouth, they clawed back about thirty agents into naval duty to ship out to Afghanistan', Simon read from his emails.

'But we still have forty men… and look at them…' he pointed out at the empty desks.

'Forty, weapons trained agents, on loan from the Royal Navy… all working in a… call centre!'

It was true. They were assigned to attend to the overwhelming demand from phone calls and emails from concerned relatives of missing persons, the press and local and national police.

It was both a relief and a pleasure to Simon to see Mike becoming involved again. He had feared for Mike's mentality and his devotion to the project over the past few weeks considering what had happened both to him and to the people involved.

'I want every agent prepared and armed. If there is a spare capacity then I am going to use it! I am going to line the cliffs with these guys, spaced at strategic locations and we are going to catch this bastard!'

Simon shook his head as if to clear his ears.

'You are going to what?'

Chapter 11
<u>The Plan</u>

The sea rolled gently in the moonlight and the swell from the stern of the luxury vessel *Arabian Dream* created a layer of foam on the surface of the water.

Captain Fowler, a seaman of thirty years, looked out of the opulent bridge onto the clear sea ahead of him. Below him; the consistent beat of the music from the party and the occasional drunken female guffaw. He had been Captain on countless charter vessels, which created a welcomed relief from the monotony of the tankers he sailed in his past and the pay was far greater. He casually pushed open the side door of the bridge cabin and wandered into the bitter cold air outside, igniting a cigarette. On the main deck in front of him, a man in a grey striped suit staggered around clutching a bottle of champagne. A lady in a red ball gown followed him, stopping for a few seconds to remove her heels.

Fowler leaned over the railings to try and hear their conversation but to no avail. He relaxed his position and extinguished his cigarette and returning to the warmth of the bridge. He kept an eye on the couple below him partly for safety reasons; charters having a fair fatality rate for inebriated passengers falling overboard, but mainly in case anything developed between the two; again, not unheard of.

The business man drank from the bottle and handed it to the red dressed lady, who was clutching at the railings, partly out of flirtation towards the man but mainly to stablise herself in her drunken state.

'Go on, ask me?' he slurred.

'Not here… I can't, you know Mark is just inside. If he even saw me out here with you he would kill us both!'

'Chicken!' he said, followed by a muted belch, causing the lady to laugh hysterically.

'You know it is only a matter of time Angelique!'

The lady raised her eyebrows and looked into the night sky.

'I love your neck', he tried.

'Stop it James, I am a married woman!' she half smiled at him.

As the couple chatted outside, Fowler looked on from the bridge, smiling at the man's relentless attempts at winning over his lady friend. He reached over for his cup and saucer and noticed that the vessel was rolling slightly. He checked the control panel; the pitch was showing movement. He moved over to the weather station but it didn't seem to be showing any warnings.

The couple outside, holding on to the railings for stability, looked over at the sudden movement in the waves. Fowler squinted to see what they were looking at.

Suddenly the lights went out and the engines began to drone down. The guests below began to make sounds of panic. Fowler checked the fuse cabinet behind him. He pulled out his torch from his pocket and turned it on; Nothing.

'Damn, that's bloody strange…' he muttered to himself.

The cabin door opened and a very drunken man entered.

'Whatsss goin on Fowler?' he slurred incomprehensibly.

'I don't know sir; we appear to have lost power!'

The lady outside on the deck screamed. Fowler ran over to the bridge viewing window as a huge wave thrashed at the side of the vessel. The drunken man fell over next to her on the wet decking. As he watched, a large metallic object jettisoned out of the water next to them. Instinctively Fowler thumped the alarm on the control panel in front of him; nothing happened.

'For the love of God!' he shouted in frustration.

Out on the deck, the lady, sat quivering in fear as the man next to her held the railings, looking out in disbelief at the sobering sight of a submarine that had surfaced adjacent to them.

'What the hell…' he began.

The submarine top hatch opened along with one on the fore deck. The man struggled to see in the darkness and amongst the stinging, salty spray in the atmosphere. He squinted and made out an array of dark figures moving around on the deck.

One of the figures jumped across in front of him, knocking him on to the floor.

The lady shrieked as he fell next to her, blood oozing from a gash to his throat.

Fowler watched as the figures began to swarm around the foredeck. Nervously he fumbled with his phone, it was dead.

'Damn it!' he cursed.

He stormed out of the bridge and down the stairs to the foyer at the stern of the vessel to warn the passengers. As he arrived there was pandemonium as the frightened guests ran chaotically from one position to another to find refuge in the darkness.

A middle aged lady spotted Fowler at the foot of the stairs in the moonlight and ran towards him.

'My God, who are those men outside?'

Fowler looked through the cabin windows. Out of both the left and the right sides he could see the dark figures moving about above them. He turned to the stern entrance and held his breath, trying not to show his fear to the petrified lady clinging to his right arm. The stern doors flung open and the dark figures poured inside like an army of ants. The first man inside ran towards the lady next to Fowler and snatched her away from him, her screams fading to the noise of the crashing waves. One by one the guests, helpless with fear and inebriation, were taken outside. Within a matter of moments the only person left in the cabin was Captain Fowler. Frozen with terror, he clung to the brass stair pole and stared blankly at the stern doors. There was a deadly silence. Suddenly a loud thump came from the deck outside and one of the figures appeared at the stern doorway and made his way towards him.

'Ahoy Captain', he spoke with an educated English, accentless voice.

The man was about six feet tall and was dressed entirely in black with a black balaclava.

Fowler stepped backwards a few feet until he hit a supporting column. Unable to move he watched the figure approach him, unsheathing a large knife from his belt.

The sounds from the hysterical guests had been extinguished, the only noise coming from the footsteps of the figure in front of him combined with the rolling waves, lapping at the vessel's hull. As the figure stopped a few yards from him, Fowler squinted to try and make out his expression. He looked into Fowler's eyes.

'We're taking the ship Captain, I hope you don't mind'.

He lashed out with the blade and slashed Fowler's throat. Fowler clutched his neck and gasped for breath as he dropped to the floor; his blood beginning to soak into the deep pile carpet.

Another dark suited man in a balaclava entered behind him.

'What the hell do you think you are doing? Why have you done that you fool?'

The first figure turned to him.

'What? You expect me to let him go? Push him into the sea?'

'No! I'd have expected you would take him outside and do him out there where it can be cleaned! You any idea how long this is going to take to clean?'

The first figure raised his blade to the second's throat.

'Don't ever tell me what to do, and don't ever call me a fool again!'

He left the second figure in the cabin and marched outside. A third man entered the cabin holding a large bag.

'Oh no', he said as he saw the body of Fowler, draining blood onto the carpet.

'Here's a map', Mike stated enthusiastically as he thrust a large scale map onto Simon's desk, covering his laptop and his coffee mug.

'On it, I have marked strategic locations where we can position emplacements', he pointed with his pen to a line of circles dotted along the coastal pathway.

'It spans from St Agnes up here… to Mullion down here. Every station has two men allocated, armed and equipped with communications and transport - I suggest quad bike'.

182

Simon looked at his proud partner and bit on his lip.

'It is great Mike but… what about sign-off?'

Mike stood up to his full height, confidently tonguing his cheek.

'We are following our instincts, producing a plan of action. If it doesn't get signed off then…' he lowered his voice and leaned closer to Simons ear '…it will rouse too much suspicion on them. They will have to sign it off. I am using this situation to our advantage, as Fredrico suggested'.

Simon smiled with genuine impression.

'I will take it to Jennings then', he agreed.

'Jennings will get it signed off by Wilkinson anyway – he will enjoy the prospect of our being proactive'.

'By the way…' Simon started as he took the map and began to fold it up, 'have you heard from Fredrico lately?'

Mike shook his head as he tapped away on his computer.

'No, I haven't. I am surprised he hasn't given us an update on the chests yet to be honest. I will give him a call later'.

The second dark figure scrubbed at the carpet as three others cleaned the cabin room, intricately picking up particles of streamer, cigarette butt and pieces of food from the deep carpets.

The leader sat on the steps to the bridge, watching the men work, idly playing with the blade between his hands.

One of the men stormed inside the cabin.

'There's a boat approaching Captain, we have about a minute to get out of here'.

The leader stood up and replaced his blade into its sheath. He looked at the blood stain on the carpet.

'Leave it!' he demanded.

'But sir, it's… still visible'.

'It doesn't matter, there's a boat approaching, cover it with that rug over there and let's leave!'

The men began to collect their belongings into large rucksacks. As the leader left the cabin another man drew a large Persian rug over the dark stain, picked up his rucksack and left the cabin, closing the doors behind him.

Outside, they ran across the decking towards the submergible vessel, tethered to it.

As the leader stepped on board the U-boat he looked back at the man who had confronted him about Fowler's death.

'Cast off', he ordered to the figure waiting with the guide rope.

'Excuse me sir?'

'Cast us off now!' he demanded.

'But sir, what about…'

The leader pulled the man close to him by his collar.

'Cast us off now or I will leave you here with him!' he pointed to the man still aboard the yacht.

Reluctantly the man drew the rope from around the mooring ring and pushed them off. The U-boat engines began to rumble beneath the water and a cloud of smoke bellowed into the night. The figure left aboard *the Asian Dream* ran towards the bow.

'Hey, wait! Wait for me!' he shouted.

The leader watched him as he waved his arms to attract their attention. He opened the main hatch and dropped inside, closing it tight behind him. The U-boat propelled into the distance and finally submerged beneath the water leaving a small swell on the otherwise undisturbed surface.

The man took off his balaclava and threw it onto the deck.

'Bastard!' he shouted, his voice trailing into the darkness.

As Simon waited for the elevator he gazed out of the tall window and across the rooftops of the town. It was a beautifully bright, sunny morning and his sleep deprivation had slipped to the back of his mind. He held the map with the strategic positions close to him. If, as they were sure, anyone in Nelson were working against them, they would undoubtedly kill for this map. The elevator arrived and Simon walked inside and pressed the fifth floor button. As the elevator whirred its way up to his destination he reflected on the past few months and how their lives had changed so dramatically. His concerns about Mike had been relatively unprecedented. He had gone through so much; it was amazing that he was as strong as he was. The elevator stopped and the doors opened.

He headed for the office of Lieutenant Jennings; Wilkinson's spokesperson and ambassador in Cornwall. His secretary greeted him and showed him straight in.

'Mr Jennings, Mr Jenkins is here to see you sir', she said in a soft Somerset accent.

Jennings stood up from his chair.

'Ah, Jenkins, good to see you. Just give me a minute to finish typing this will you? Please sit down', he pointed to a leather chair opposite to his desk.

'Good to see you too sir, thank you', Simon replied as he drew the heavy antiquated chair from under the desk. He sat down and waited for the Lieutenant to finish typing an email.

Jennings was a middle aged man who had seen plenty of action in both the Gulf war and Iraq. His uniform was vibrantly decorated and the only reason he was stationed at Nelson was due to a requirement from the Admiralty for a senior position to overlook manoeuvres in the South West. He sported a small scar below his left eye which caused him to twitch every now and again. He clicked a few times, rotated his chair to face Simon and gave an enormous grin.

'Right, what can I do for you Simon?'

Simon hesitated. How would he ask for such a large assignment of resources?

'I need a requisition order sir'.

'For what?'

'We are hatching an operation to guard the shore line sir, and we require a large resource of agents and a weapons warrant for them… sir'.

Jennings frowned and looked into Simon's nervous eyes.

'You are planning to barricade our coast with armed Preventive Agents?'

It sounded as absurd as it was.

'Yes sir. We need to take action fast. The situation is difficult and we need…'

'If this is what you want Simon, who am I to protest?'

That was unsettlingly easy, Simon thought. Where was the need for an explanation?

He handed over Mike's map to the Lieutenant who opened it out and began to make private mumbling noises as he calculated the annotations that Mike had scrawled.

'Right, so you need forty men, armed, split into twenty locations, each group of the twenty requiring a quad bike transport?'

It sounded ridiculous. Simon shuffled uneasily in his seat.

'Yes sir'.

'Right, okay, I will get this signed off by the VA. Hang on a moment will you'.

He picked up the phone and dialled.

'Give me a moment or two will you?' he whispered, thumbing towards the door.

'Oh, sorry sir', Simon answered as he hurried to wait outside.

After the door shut, Jennings pressed the phone to his ear and waited.

He fingered at the map, ingesting the strategic locations that Mike had pin-pointed.

'Wilkinson', the phone crackled to life.

'It's Jennings. Simon Jenkins has just been in here, he has requisitioned forty men to line the cliff lines sir. Armed men!'

'I wondered when they were actually going to use the men we gave to them!'

'He also wants to declare the beaches a no-go zone after eleven o'clock… what do you want me to do sir?'

'Allow it of course. We can't refuse, it will raise too many questions… do you have a copy of the locations?'

'Yes sir, I have a map in front of me'.

'Fax it to me'.

'It's bigger than that sir, it's huge!'

'Photocopy it, scale it down and fax it to me for goodness sake!'

'Yes sir'.

'Don't lose your cool, Jennings, we can use this to pin-point where the strongest locations are… and avoid them. Think of it as a "where not to go" map'.

Jennings smiled.

'Thank you sir'.

He replaced the phone and took the map to the photocopier in his office.

Simon sat outside, looking out onto Penzance Harbour and the fishing vessels bobbing in the tidal current. Half of him wished that he had the responsibilities of a fisherman; get up early, go out onto the seas, haul in a net of fish, return, go to the pub and go home, ready for the next day. He looked at his watch. He had been sitting outside for ten minutes, maybe longer – what was taking so long?

Jennings pressed the fax button and the down-scaled map fed through the machine.

'Come in Jenkins', Jennings shouted from inside the office.

Simon stood up and marched into the ornate office.

'Right', he began, handing Simon the folded up map, 'you have your sign off'.

Simon's mouth dropped in disbelief.

'In fact the VA thought it was a good move, very proactive and he commended you'.

'Thank you sir'.

'I have to go to a meeting of department now, I will see you out'.

He extended his hand to Simon who shook it as the two men left the office.

As he reached the elevator, Jennings continued around the corner and into another office.

Simon suddenly realised that he had left the map in the office. Cursing to himself he turned around and walked back along the corridor.

'I'm sorry, I have left my map in Mr Jennings' office, do you mind if I…?' he asked the secretary who was speaking into her phone.

The secretary nodded her head and held her hand out towards the door, implying him to help himself.

Simon smiled and entered the room. He reached across the wide desk for the map and accidentally knocked a stack of papers from the top of the fax machine with his sleeve.

Cursing once again, he crouched down to the floor and began to gather the scatter of papers. As he sifted through them he noticed a series of down sampled reproductions of the map.

'Oh my God! He faxed it…' he uttered to himself.

He examined them and saw fresh annotations in red marker; Jennings had circled vacant areas, nestled within Mike's strategic points marked on the coast, with notes such as "Possible safe area" and "Enclosed Cove".

'Son of a bitch!'

He took the paper to the photocopier and made himself another copy. Replacing the original on top of the fax machine, he folded up the copy and slipped it inside his pocket with Mike's map.

He left the office, mouthing, "Thank you" to Jennings' secretary on his way to the elevator.

Mike's phone vibrated across his desk.

He slapped his hand on it and answered it, transfixed on his laptop screen.

'Mike Williams?'

He paused as he listened to the earpiece.

'You are kidding me?' he grappled for a pen from a pot on his desk and turned over a scrap of paper.

'*Asian Dream*... Where is she now? Coming to the harbour? Let me know when it's there! Oh, and don't let the press anywhere near it. Thanks Nathan…'

He looked at his notepad and scanned his notes: *Asian Dream*, found by Coastguard crew on routine training. 0030 hours. No crew. Mooring @ PZ.

Mike sat back in his chair and stretched out his legs.

'It's still happening!' he said to himself.

His phone rang again.

'Mike Willi…'

'Mike, it's Simon, meet me outside in five minutes…'

Mike walked out of the grand entrance of Nelson and over to the pavement where his companion stood smoking a cigarette.

'Simon, what's going on?'

'I found this in Jennings' office Mike!' he said, handing over the photocopy of the map.

Mike looked at it, his face beginning to screw up with anger.

'Double crossing bastard! When did he do this?'

'He got me to wait outside his office while he signed off our plan with Wilkinson'.

Mike read the circled notes.

Suddenly and to Simon's surprise, Mike's expression turned into a suspicious grin.

'I think we can work this to our advantage yet again Si!' he said waving the map in Simon's face.

'How?'

'If they now know where our strategic locations are…' he waited for Simon to conclude.

'…then we move our strategic locations to their safe zones?' Simon answered confidently.

'Bingo!' Mike exclaimed.

'We have also just gained authorisation for an armed presence, so in a way… they have literally just shot themselves in the foot!'

Although relieved and celebratory, severity still clouded them. This was getting as deep as Black had originally suggested. Perhaps he was trying to warn them of the situation they were getting themselves into?

Mike looked at the concrete floor in mourning.

'Another drifter's been found'.

'Oh no… where, when?' Simon asked.

'I don't know the specifics Si… it's being towed into Penzance this evening. the *Anglian Princess* picked it up whilst on a training exercise. Did you get the team availability?'

Simon fished in his pocket for his notebook.

'In here; agents available plus the sign-off form from Jennings'.

'Good. Contact Mrs Jacobs, get her to email the team and get them to rally in the meeting room. And get the QM to prepare and issue the weapons'.

Mike pulled out his keys and unlocked the Land Rover parked nearby on the pavement.

'Where are you going?'

'I'm going to check over the Asian Dream when she arrives… keep me updated', he shouted as he closed the door and started the engine.

As he drove towards the harbour, a thought occurred to him; their plan to coincide their new locations on the map to the locations that Jennings had inadvertently supplied to them would aid them in catching, or at the least deter the smugglers but, how do they catch the pirates vessel? How do you catch a submarine? They couldn't very well litter the sea bed with mines, nor could they take pot shots into the sea. Mike contemplated the predicament for a few moments until he arrived at the harbour. He was early. The harbour was quiet with the odd fisherman and dock worker mulling about their business. The *Asian Dream* had not arrived and there was no sign of the Coastguard vessel.

He sat back in the driver's seat and watched the harbour life while he contemplated the situation. The *Scillonian III* had just begun to reverse from the harbour mouth on its way to the Isles of Scilly, which explained the reason the *Arabian Dream* was late in arriving. A trawler had moored nearby and the crew were struggling with a huge net of fish. It was an impressive catch and every crew member rallied their efforts to help its safe unloading. As they pulled the net over the stern deck, the net opened and tons of fish emptied onto the scrub area. The fish lay powerless as the fishermen sifted through them, distributing them into different containers. Then it came to him. The best way to catch it would be to cut its power, to force it to the surface. How better to cut its power than to beat it at its own game?

'EMP!' he shouted, accidentally attracting the attention of the fishing crew.

If he could deploy the power of an electro-magnetic pulse into the direction of the vessel it would render it powerless and drive it to the surface. If only Faraday were alive, he thought. But, technically his knowledge still remained. The EMP technology was well documented, he had practically stated that himself. The technology existed and so it must be accessible by someone, somewhere and outside of Nelson's control.

In the distance, he could see the *Anglian Princess* with a large white yacht in tow. As he gathered his equipment for his analysis of the *Dream*, he began to develop upon his thoughts. If he could access Faraday's work he would undoubtedly be nearer to a solution.

After the usual pleasantries with the Coastguard crew, he boarded the *Asian Dream*; his mind focused on the bigger picture. He stepped over the guide rail and walked around the decking towards the stern. Although only a few months since he boarded the first of these recent finds, he had in mind what he was to expect: nothing out of the ordinary.

'Mike', Nathan called as he waved from the *Anglian Princess*.

Mike replied with a wave, acknowledging his friend, mouthing, "Thank you" over the noise of the boat's engines as it began to back out of the harbour.

Mike opened the stern doors and flashed his torch inside. As he had expected it was immaculate. As he ventured further inside, he noticed on the beige shag carpet, a large rectangular patch where the sun, from the enormous viewing window at the front end of the cabin, had bleached the carpet. It was a relatively old boat, of perhaps twenty years or so and the glazing back then didn't have the protective UV properties as they do in modern vessels. He looked around for a rug or mat that matched the area. As he walked towards the stairwell to the bridge he noticed a rug. It was awkwardly placed at the bottom of the steps. With all aspects being as geometric as one would expect from such a layout, this did not sit right. He leaned down and pulled at the heavy rug which slid away from its location revealing a large brown stain. He crouched down to inspect it; it was still relatively damp to the touch. He walked over to the galley and pulled at a roll of kitchen roll from a dispenser mounted on one of the overhanging units and dabbed at the stain, transferring it to the paper towel. It was unmistakably blood.

He wrapped up the towel, placing it carefully into his jacket pocket and began to take photographs of the scene.

Simon's phone rang in his pocket as he signed the documentation for the weapons that Corporal Smith was preparing for their team.

'Jenkins', he answered.

'It's Mike, I have just been over the *Dream*… they are getting sloppy Si. I think something's got to them. I've just found a large blood stain, covered up with a rug. It's fresh. I've called it in to forensics and they are going to have it analysed'.

'Bloody hell… well, I have got the team briefing ready. The weapons are being prepared and the team has been notified of the operation'.

'Good, get them to rally in the briefing room at half past eight … I have to go somewhere first'.

'Where?'

'I may have just come up with a plan of how to catch these bastards!'

'You were sloppy with the *Asian Dream*. They have found it and they have ordered Forensics to investigate…' the phone crackled in the ear of the boiler-suited crew member who stood facing a heavily corroded wall.

'This isn't how it was meant to be! I didn't sign up to take orders from you! I didn't expect it and I'm not standing for it!'

'Are you threatening me Leon?' the aggressive voice began.

'I'm spelling it out to you that things had better change! If they take me down, you know I will drag you and your department down with me…'

'Don't push me Leon, I can stop this as easily as I started it fifteen years ago!'

'You introduced the Preventive Service into this! Don't blame us for the pressures we are under. It's okay for you to bark orders from your desk back there, behind the lines, but it is us that are taking all the risks! I nearly got it back in Gibraltar when your agents came into my house!'

'Steady Leon… let us take stock here. If we need to pull the plug we can do… now, I have work to do… I will provide you with the safety zones later today. Just be ready! And, no more mistakes!'

The phone went dead.

De LaCruz looked at the phone and screwed it into his fist, slamming it against one of the antiquated pipes that ran the length of the vessel. He stepped over the maze of cables and wires, from one compartment into another within the tight space of the U-boat. He approached a large containment door marked "G-7" and turned the iron wheel in the centre of it. The door creaked open to reveal a dark chamber full of stacked tea chests. De LaCruz stared at them. The hull of the vessel knocked and echoed with the sounds of the ocean enveloping it. He wiped a bead of sweat from his brow.

'No more mistakes...' he retorted.

Faraday's house was a beautifully restored, modest country house dating to the early nineteenth century, located in a small village on the outskirts of Penzance, overlooking St Michael's Mount. The community of which mainly consisted of ex-service men of stature that the cenotaphs, dotted sporadically around the village grounds, illustrated.

Mike pulled into the small gravelled driveway in front of the house, which alerted Faraday's widow who rushed to the bay window of the living room.

He rang the doorbell of the large oak door which she answered almost immediately. The years of being a headmistress and later an influential member of the Devon and Cornwall Council had taken their toll but the recent death of her husband had virtually finished her. As soon as she saw Mike's uniform, she broke down in tears.

After consoling her, she had made Mike a cup of fine Earl Grey tea. Mike was a self-confessed tea hater but Mrs Faraday's tea was an elixir. He hadn't had the pleasure of meeting her prior to this moment but even in her weak mental state, he could tell that she had a hidden inner strength.

'Mrs Faraday…'

'Joan, please…' she interrupted him, dabbing her eyes with a handkerchief.

'Joan', Mike smiled, 'I am here because I need access to… your husband's studies. His work is very important to a project that I am involved with and in order to complete it… I am going to need to access his computer? Is that okay?' he asked in as soft and as friendly manner as he could muster considering the urgency.

She looked at the floor and back up to him.

'I don't think there is a problem. Do you know what you are looking for? Can I help?' she asked.

'You can make me another cup of tea Mrs Faraday', he smiled, handing over the empty china cup and saucer.

She beamed, 'Do you know where the study is? It is just through there on your left Mr Williams'.

Mike nodded and smiled. As she entered the kitchen he paced towards the study.

The door was ajar and exposed a glimpse of a well-stocked library of books and folders and a rack of wooden shelves held an unprecedented collection of rolled up drawings.

There was a small antique table in the far corner, facing a bay window overlooking a well-kept garden and the coastline beyond. On the table stood a wide, flat-screen monitor. A computer sat on the floor beneath it. Mike stooped down and saw the light pulsing, illustrating the machine being in hibernation. He shook the mouse and the screen came to life presenting him with the familiar Windows log-on screen.

'Password!' he said to himself with disgust.

"earl grey"

"Password Incorrect please try again"

Mike screwed up his mouth. How was anyone going to be able to work this one out? He was sure that his wife wouldn't know. Maybe she did?

"Joan"

"Password Incorrect please try again"

He scratched his head. He was sure that there was a rule where the computer would lock up if a password was entered incorrectly more than three times.

Mrs Faraday entered the room, pushing the door with her foot, holding two very full cups of tea, the saucers of which were littered with biscuits.

'Mrs Farra… Joan', he corrected, 'I don't suppose you…' he pointed towards the log-in screen.

'Oh yes', she said, surprisingly, 'it's the name of our cat, Earl!'

He held his breath and typed "Earl"; his finger touched the "Enter" key.

'No wait!' she shouted, 'he changed it recently. He was worried about security, he said. Now what did he… oh yes, "Earl49"… the year we got married', she announced.

Mike adjusted the characters and pressed enter.

The screen opened to display an AutoCAD drawing of a ship's hull.

'Oh, that's our Vitruvian', she said with a sadness in her voice, 'he was going to build our boat when he retired next year. Please excuse me…' she left the room, evidently overwhelmed with emotion.

Now alone, he closed down the windows and began to open folders, searching for related documents.

His phone rang in his pocket.

'Williams'.

'Mike Williams? It's Peter Allan from Forensics. We have found a finger print on the... *Asian Dream*. There were only two in the whole cabin. Someone went to a lot of trouble to clean it...'

'Yeah', Mike answered as he furiously opened and closed folders on the computer.

'We have made a match!'

Mike spat out his tea onto his shirt.

'You are kidding me?'

'No, Mr Williams, we have a name for you'.

Mike wiped at his shirt and picked a pencil from a pot of pens on the desk.

'Go on...'

'Just getting it now... a Mr Leon De LaCruz, you heard of him?'

Mike's jaw dropped open.

'Mr Williams, are you there?'

'Yes, yes I am here. Are you sure it is De LaCruz?'

'Yes sir. It is a new file created in Gibraltar only a few days ago. He was arrested for an illegal weapons charge but was promptly released. I guess he came straight back here then?'

Mike struggled to take the information on board. A large piece of the puzzle had fallen into place.

'It seems that this man, De LaCruz, had been sitting or leaning on the bridge access steps. His print was found on the stainless steel stair pole, right next to the blood stain'.

'Thank you Mr Allan, thank you!'

He closed the phone and rubbed at his eyes. This was an astounding find. It confirmed that De LaCruz was the pirate that he had suspected him to be.

Jennings sat at his desk, his secretary in front of him, scribbling notes on a pad.

'I think that about sums it up, Jane, can you forward that to...'

He was interrupted by an alert noise from his laptop at the other end of the desk.

Diverting his attention, he watched the screen with suspense as the alert pop-up box scrolled onto the screen.

'...to the secretary of defence please. Now if you don't mind?' He nodded towards the door.

The well-dressed lady stood up, collected her notes and made her way to the door.

Jennings slid his chair to the end of the desk in front of his laptop and moved the mouse over the alert box to reveal the description:

"SECURITY COMPROMISE: F101 ACCESSED"

Without hesitation, Jennings grabbed for his telephone and pressed a short dial number.

'It's Jennings, someone has accessed Faraday's home computer!'

Simon stood at the front of the briefing room, facing a large white board covered in annotated diagrams under a projection of a map of the coastline.

'One last thing, gentlemen, you have all signed an Official Secrets Act document!'

He turned to face the agents dressed in black combat fatigues. They were an impressive sight.

'This means that you are to adhere to our protocol. You must not, no matter how unorthodox, contravene what I am about to ask you. Do you understand?'

'Yes sir!' the unanimous reply shouted back to him.

There was no problem with their allegiance. They were acting as phone operatives a few hours prior to this. They were ready and visibly excited by the project and the plan that Simon had unfolded in front of them.

'You must not under any circumstances relay by any means, your positioning on the coastal points to anyone other than your commanding officer; Sergeant Bridges, myself or Mike Williams. This project is highly sensitive and as such will require your total respect to that sensitivity at all times… do you understand?'

'Yes sir!'

Wilkinson sat at his desk, looking out over the Naval Base. He tapped his pen on his cigar case as his brain processed the conundrum that was his situation. It was imperative he eliminated De LaCruz from the scene. Mike and Simon were well on their way to doing this but he needed to get rid of him prior to them completing the project. Perhaps he could offer them a helping hand without compromising his position? If he offered them information that would lead to his capture the questions of his connection to De LaCruz would surface and that would jeopardise his safety and anonymity with regards to the project. For a few moments he wished he hadn't taken any part in the instigation of the project. It had way become a way of life by now. Fifteen years down the line had made him, and his counterparts very rich and the greed had become addictive. The more they made - the more they wanted.

It was time to cleanse himself of that addiction. The link to this was Jennings, who was as heavily involved with the coordination of attacks as he was but

Jennings was sworn to it. He was talking matters into his own hands, perhaps being too cautious. He had a team of Royal Marines at his disposal; something that Wilkinson had granted him for security reasons a few years ago. It was he who had sanctioned the killing of Black at the Ship. Granted, it was a justified action and one that he had commended him for; Black would have given them all up to save his own neck.

By removing Jennings, he would be removing the restraints and create a weak spot in the link between De LaCruz and himself. By removing Jennings and exposing his exploitation of the Royal Navy to Mike and Simon, he would both be offering a helping hand and providing the necessary structural damage to the project that would lead to a rupture of their integrity.

He reclined in the large, leather chair and smiled at the prospect of releasing himself from the stress from the project. He knew that De LaCruz wouldn't risk capture and the impending trial of mass piracy and murder. De LaCruz would sooner die than go down for the rest of his life thus not being able to implicate him as the conspirator and mastermind of the project. The only stick in the mud would be Jennings. He would certainly give up Wilkinson in order to trim years from his sentence. He needed eliminating.

Mike rifled through a folder structure whilst sipping another cup of the fine Earl Grey tea provided by his obliging hostess. The screen reflected in his glasses as he opened and closed folders and moved them from one location to a memory stick on his key ring.

The hallway phone rang and Mrs Faraday excused herself to answer it.

'Joan Faraday', she answered.

'Mrs Faraday, this is Nelson House. I am responsible for security and the integrity of our Secrecy Act. Is there someone accessing your husband's computer at all?'

Mrs Faraday looked perplexed and moved her gaze to Mike frantically copying files in the adjoining room.

'Erm, yes there is… but he…'

'Keep him there please if you can Mrs Faraday, we are sending a security team around now to arrest him. He is using your husband's computer for his own financial gain and he must not be trusted! Please keep him there until we arrive, do you understand?'

Mrs Faraday began to tremble.

'Y-yes, is he… am I in danger?'

'No madam, but it is vital we catch this man. We will be there in about five minutes'.

The phone went dead.

The elderly lady replaced the receiver and sat back in the telephone desk chair. It was true, she didn't know Mike but he seemed genuine enough and Don had mentioned his name more than once in the past.

'Got it!' Mike's voice echoed through the hallway from the study.

Mrs Faraday stood up. She knew she had to keep him occupied for at least five minutes, but how? She wandered into the study, slowly, desperately concerned at what she had been charged to do.

Mike dragged an assortment of documents from a folder into the USB pen drive window.

Mrs Faraday walked in to the study and paused as she saw the agent copying her husband's files. She began to nervously pick at her fingernails.

Mike spun round, sensing her enter.

'Mrs Farra…, Joan, I have found it! Your husband was a genius!'

She moved closer to him and watched as a window displayed a "copying" animation as the files transferred to the pen drive.

'You know, Joan, your husband was one of the only men I trusted at Nelson. He was a good ma…'

Mike paused and watched her fingers.

'Joan, what's the matter? You look… are you okay?' he asked, holding her hand.

She trembled as she looked at him.

'Who was the phone call from Joan? Have you had more bad news or something?'

She looked into his eyes, hers reddening.

'Joan… what is it?' he persisted.

With a long exhale, she made her decision.

'It was the man on the phone… he, he… he told me…'

'Hey, Joan, what is it?' Mike moved closer to her and held her other hand.

'He told me you were just stealing my husband's designs… for your own… financial gain?'

She hesitated as his friendly smile turn downwards.

'What else did they say?' he asked as softly as he could, despite the anger building inside him.

'They said a security team, was it? Was going to be turning up here, in five minutes to arrest you? I trust you Mr Williams, really I do, but I… I just don't know what to do…'

'When did they say this? How long ago?'

'About five minutes ago'.

Mike turned back to the computer and continued to select the relevant files to copy.

'They weren't security, Joan, they want to obstruct me, stop what I am about to find out... I can't tell you everything Joan, believe me, but we are both in danger'.

Mrs Faraday began to whimper.

'Don't worry, Joan, it will be okay. Is there somewhere you can stay for a few days?'

She sat on a small stool next to the desk and thought for a few moments as Mike continued at speed.

'My sister's house'.

'Where is that?'

'Bristol'.

Mike glanced at her.

'I will drop you at the station, Joan'.

A loud alert sounded through the speakers mounted above the desk on the wall and a message appeared on the screen:

"INSUFFICIENT SPACE ON VOLUME: ANOTHER 250MB REQUIRED!"

'Shit!' Mike shouted.

The pen drive was full.

'Joan, do you know if your husband had another one of...' he pulled the full drive from the socket in the monitor.

'...These!' he held it up in front of her. She looked blankly at it.

'What is it?' she asked.

Mike began to search the top drawers.

'He had a thing called an external... now what was it?'

Mike continued rifling through the cluttered desk.

'...hard drive? Is that what you call them?'

'What did you say?' Mike asked.

'An external hard drive, yes that's it, I bought it for him for...'

'Where is it Joan?'

'In the bottom drawer', she replied with conviction.

Mike slid the bottom drawer out, revealing a silver external hard drive with coiled leads on top of it.

'Brilliant!' he exclaimed as he connected it to the computer.

A black Ford Mondeo pulled onto the gravel and parked adjacent to Mike's Land Rover, followed by a black transit van that parked in front of the house, partially blocking the driveway. The rear doors of the van opened and three men dressed in dark blue combat fatigues exited carrying riot batons. The driver's door of the Mondeo opened and a tale male wearing a naval officer's uniform emerged and adjusted his tie before joining the group. As they approached the property, they began to split up, filtering around the side passage and towards the front door.

Mike worked hard; his forehead glistened with beads of sweat as he furiously searched through the folder structures of Faraday's computer.

The inevitable sound of the doorbell, followed by an impatient knock came from the entrance hall.

'It's them!' Mrs Faraday's broken voice shouted.

Mike kept his concentration focused on the remaining information, continuing to copy any file that appeared relevant.

The knocking became louder and more frequent.

'Mrs Faraday!' a voice shouted from outside.

'What do I do?' she asked.

'Slowly walk towards the door and shout that you are on your way, and then quickly get back here. Where's the nearest exit?'

'Out in the hallway', she pointed.

'Right, stand by the doorway and shout back at them that you are on your way. I am nearly done here'.

Mrs Faraday walked slowly towards the entrance to the study. The blue status bar of the "Copying" window slowly moved to the right as the data copied onto the external hard drive.

'Come on, come on…' Mike chanted.

The knocking began to rattle the door furniture.

'Mrs Faraday!' the voice demanded.

'I'm coming, won't be a second', she shouted back, as loud as she could muster.

The status bar paused, two blocks from the end.

The knocks turned into kicks.

'Hurry!' Mrs Faraday shouted back to Mike.

The status bar reached one block to the end.

'Come on!' Mike shouted at the computer screen.

The door vibrated as one of the men shoulder barged it, buckling the top slide lock.

'Done!' Mike shouted as the "Copying" screen disappeared.

Mike ripped the connecting lead from the computer, pushed the external hard drive into his jacket pocket and jumped up from the chair towards the frail widow who was watching in terror as her front door began to disintegrate. He grabbed her hand and pulled her towards the kitchen. The front door crashed open and four of the men barged inside.

'Check the rooms, he's here somewhere', the first man commanded.

The men spread out, two ascending the staircase, the other two making their way into adjoining rooms.

Mike and his elderly fugitive ran through the kitchen. He tried the rear door; it was locked.

'The key? Where's the key?' Mike whispered frantically as their pursuers began to close in on them.

'Oh, here', she said, pulling the key from a nearby hook.

Mike unlocked the door and the pair dashed outside. One of the men, armed with a large riot baton appeared from the side passage in front of them. There was a momentary pause as they made eye contact and then Mike swiped for him, connecting with his jaw and knocking him to the ground.

'Come on!' he shouted to the panic stricken old lady.

The two ran for the side passage leading to the front of the house as the man on the ground began to pick himself up. As they turned the corner into the driveway, Mike pulled out his keys, remotely opened the Land Rover and manhandled Mrs Faraday into the passenger seat. He drew his automatic and stepped back towards the corner of the wall. As he moved around to the driver's side, he heard the unmistakable footsteps on the gravel from the side passage. He drew his automatic and aimed towards the opening. The figure emerged and froze at the sight of Mike's weapon outstretched towards him. Mike slowly manoeuvred into the vehicle with his weapon trained on the man and started the engine. Without closing his door, he crunched the gears into reverse and looked behind him seeing the black van partially blocking the driveway. He looked back towards the passageway; the figure had disappeared. Cursing, he released the handbrake and slammed the door shut.

'Hang on Joan and fasten your seatbelt'.

Mike pushed hard on the accelerator and the Land Rover jolted backwards into the side of the van with a deafening smash, forcing it out of the driveway and onto the road. Once clear, he engaged first gear and threw them forwards as the men arrived on the pavement behind them. One of the men dashed out in front of them and threw out his baton, which shattered the passenger window covering the old lady with tiny cubes of glass.

'Are you okay Joan?' Mike asked as the Land Rover tore down the narrow town road.

The pale lady looked back at him and nodded, stunned by what had unfolded.

'Who are they?' she asked weakly.

'They are…' Mike paused. He couldn't tell her the truth. The less she knew - the better.

As he navigated the hairpins of the ancient road system of the town, he looked into the rear view mirror and spotted the Mondeo in pursuit. He put his foot down and changed down a gear, propelling the vehicle faster and pushing Mrs Faraday back in her seat.

He turned another corner and onto the main road into Penzance; his knowledge of the back streets of the town providing a small relief. Feeling more confident he began to relax and ease off the accelerator. He turned to check on his co-pilot who looked back at him with a half-smile.

'Look out!' she shouted at him.

Mike looked back to the road and the static traffic jam that lay ahead.

He pushed hard at the brakes and the vehicle slid along the tarmac, eventually resting a few feet away from the vehicle in front.

'Damn it!' he cursed under his breath. He looked in the rear view mirror through the hole in the rear window; the black Mondeo gaining on them in the distance.

Mike frantically looked around for options. They were surrounded by orange cones and temporary bollards and in the distance an array of traffic lights. He looked at the mounds of rubble from the excavations to the left of them in front of the strip of Victorian hotels. With another glance in his rear mirror at the ever nearing Mondeo he pulled the second gear lever into the four-by-four position and spun the steering wheel hard left. The Land Rover roared into life and mounted the earthy mound. Within seconds they were six feet above the traffic; Mike navigating the sliding mud and debris, carefully counterbalancing as they progressed.

The Mondeo slid to a halt behind the traffic- and the onlookers that had left their vehicles to witness the sight.

'What the hell?' the driver exclaimed as he stepped out of the vehicle.

'Follow him! We can't lose him!' the officer in the back seat ordered.

The driver got back into the car and accelerated towards the rubble; mounting the curb and plunging into the soft muddy mound, covering the front end of the car.

Mike bumped the Land Rover down onto the pavement again and switched to two wheel drive, casually pulling out into the empty road adjacent to the Victorian baths.

'I used to swim there as a child', the old lady regaled, blocking the past few moments from her mind.

Chapter 12

The Preventive Service

Mike turned the shower off and reached around the corner for his towel.

'So where did she go?' Simon asked.

'Bristol; to her sister's house. Can you throw me the towel?'

Simon unhooked the towel and threw it over the top of the cubicle.

'You completely destroyed our Land Rover you know'.

Mike acknowledged the wit but was too exhausted to think of an appropriate retaliation. He walked to his locker and began to retrieve his clothes.

'So, did you find anything?' Simon asked him, perplexed by the lack of dialogue.

Mike glanced at him and gave him a confident smile as he pulled out the hard drive from his jacket pocket and passed it to him.

'What's this?'

'This is Faraday's work… his drawings, notes, schematics… I was kind of hoping you could plug it in, take a look…?'

There was a pause while Simon waited for an elaboration.

'That thing contains everything I could find on the EMP generator. Remember I told you about it before…'

Simon looked at the box.

'You are serious? This PME thing actually exists?'

'EMP!' Mike corrected, 'I was right. I need you to check this stuff out. After we have placed the men in their locations we need to look at how to get hold of one of these things...'

The men stood proudly in front of the two agents and their commanding officer. They were an impressive sight of dark navy combat fatigues with florescent orange shoulder and leg flashes. Each of them armed with MP5 automatic rifles.

Simon turned to face them.

'One more thing gentlemen; we aren't looking for heroics. You are going to be very vulnerable out there on those cliff tops. We are not the most respected of Her Majesties services and we want you to bear that in mind. Does anyone have any questions?'

Simon watched the eager faces of the men as they stood to attention and blinked as the realisation of the situation landed on him.

'It's a far cry from Dover I can tell you', he mumbled, to a response of jovial murmurs from the men.

'You got anything to add, Mike?'

Mike shook his head.

'Dismissed', the commanding officer shouted.

The men filed out of the door, one by one and into the corridor.

Mike and Simon watched through the office window as the men loaded themselves on board the three large trucks outside the building.

'Can you believe this is happening Mike?'

Mike shook his head and felt at his still bruised ribs.

Wilkinson watched the sunset from his office bay window. Although Jennings had been a loyal servant, he was endangering the successful closure and final stages of the project and most importantly Wilkinson's life. He was beginning to take matters into his own hands and was arousing suspicion. He lit a large cigar that he had been holding and exhaled the smoke into the room causing beams of light to push through the dense cloud. He had a plethora of pirates at his disposal. Perhaps he could muster an accident? Happy with his conclusion, Wilkinson retreated to his desk and pulled the telephone close to him.

Mike steered the Land Rover around the corner of the last location on his map and pulled up in the lay-by near to one of the remaining wartime pillboxes that stood defiantly looking out to sea.

'Okay, let's get the last of the men dug in'.

As the last two men walked towards the emplacement, Mike inhaled the fresh night air and soaked in the ambient sounds of the waves as they lapped the coast below him. It was the first time that he had felt a sense of normality amongst the recent and overwhelming experiences. His thoughts lay in fear of what would happen when it was all over. How would they settle back into a normal way of life again?

He wandered over to Simon who was standing at the edge of the concrete bunker. The two allocated agents carried a wealth of ammunition crates and food supplies from the truck to their new temporary abode. Simon filled out and signed the relevant paper work and handed it to one of the men.

'That's about it gents. If you need anything or see anything call us immediately and sound the alarm', he said tapping his pen on the industrial air horn that he had finished attaching to the concrete wall.

As the two agents climbed back into the beaten Land Rover, Mike turned towards his colleague.

'We need to concentrate on getting to the bottom of this Nelson issue'.

Simon nodded, 'I agree but where do we start? We can't very well talk to Wilkinson can we?'

Mike rubbed his fresh bristles on the end of his chin.

'We go to the next man down the pecking order'.

'Jennings?'

Mike nodded and took a swig from a bottle of spring water.

'Are we going to just barge in his office and...'

'We'll visit him at home', Mike interrupted.

'His home?'

'Why not? It is where he will most vulnerable'.

'We are in the breaking and entering game then now are we?' Simon asked as he pulled the last cigarette from his packet.

'Not in here', Mike pointed at the cigarette in Simon's mouth, 'find his address on your Blackberry'.

'How?' Simon asked sincerely.

'All our home addresses are listed under Contacts. I saw it recently. I think it is something the Navy put into place in case of contacting personnel in an emergency. It must be a legacy of their system setup.'

Simon navigated his way to the contacts screen on his Blackberry and found Jennings' entry.

'Yeah it is here but I don't like barging in unannounced like this'.

'We won't be barging in; we will simply go to his house and ask him a few questions... what time is it?'

"NEW DROP, TEXT DETAILS 4 TIME AND PREF LOCATION"

Wilkinson read the message and smiled. Everything was going to plan. Soon he would be severed from any connections to the pirates, the press would be happy, the Royal Navy would commend him and he would be receiving the last of the loot before Mike could catch up with them. The irony being that the loot would land right in between the locations marked on Mike's map. He took a generous sip from a large crystal glass of brandy and replaced it on the annotated map in front of him and leaned closer. His finger traced the areas where Mike had circled as emplacements and then to a cove.

He pressed the "Reply" button on his phone:

"LOCATION 3. 0200 TONIGHT"

"Send"

As the Land Rover coasted over the brows of the hilly roads back towards the town, Simon busied himself scouring Faraday's hard drive for information on his laptop.

'Bloody hell Mike, you took everything!'

Mike glanced towards the bright screen.

'I took whatever I could find; I didn't have much time so I copied the lot…'

Simon opened and began to read a large Word document.

'This is it, Mike, I think you are right…'

'What is it?' Mike glanced over at the screen.

'I think…' Simon traced a finger over the lines of text in front of him, 'Blah blah blah, Electro Magnetic Pulse, this is it! EMP generator… concept model. It's some kind of presentation material. The drawings are all here. It says that there were two built; one as a concept model and one development of that model. The concept model was… transported away for safety, part of some security protocol'.

'And the other?'

'Sold by…' Simon looked towards him, 'sold by persons unknown and to an unknown recipient. There is an encrypted folder here, I can't open it but I think we could guess who it was sold to and who could afford it…?'

Mike shifted his focus on the road ahead of him.

'The document is watermarked with an Official Secrets Act stamp and it states that the sale was of a private nature to raise capital for the project'.

'De LaCruz!' Mike sneered.

'Makes sense', Simon agreed.

'It also contains a shipment docket… yes! It's for the concept model. It was taken to… Calais!'

'Calais, France?' Mike asked.

'Yeah, a warehouse called Leon Vincent. There is an aisle number, zone and crate number here too'.

'I think we need to pay a visit', Mike suggested.

'You really think that is the best way to catch these bastards? By zapping them with a ray gun?'

Un-amused, Mike continued to stare forward as they entered the town.

'Yes', he answered solemnly.

Mike looked at the map on the tiny Blackberry screen and eventually pulled the Land Rover into a Cul-de-Sac and trickled it along at a slow pace to look for the house numbers.

'Twenty Six, this is it', Mike pointed at an illuminated house with a silver Audi parked outside.

They walked up the pathway of the modest property and arrived at the door. The street was silent with the exception of a dog barking in the distance.

'Play it cool Mike', Simon pleaded.

Mike knocked at the door.

After a few moments it was answered by a lady in a dressing gown.

She stared at the two men with apprehension.

'Can I help you?' she asked in a well-educated voice.

Mike held out his identification card.

'We are from Her Majesties Preventive Service, Madam'.

She looked at the identity card and then to their uniforms.

'The department my husband works for. How can I help you?' she asked.

'I need to speak to your husband if I may?'

'Join the queue', she laughed, 'he hardly ever goes out at night nowadays yet earlier on he told me he had been invited out for drinks by some of his colleagues and was going there straight from the office. He called when he left which was about...' she looked at her elegant watch, 'twenty minutes ago I reckon, he should be there by now'.

'Where?' Mike asked.

'Logan's Rock'.

Simon looked at his watch, 'But it is nearly ten o'clock'.

'I know, he was a bit unsure to go or not but I told him, go on, I said, have a drink, let your hair down'.

Mike frowned and then stepped back from the door.

'Thank you madam, maybe we'll catch him there then'.

'He's not in any trouble is he?' Mrs Jennings asked with concern.

'No, no trouble, thanks again Mrs Jennings'.

The two agents walked away from the house and got back into the Land Rover.

'Logan's Rock, it is then'. Mike stated as he started the engine.

Jennings closed the door of his Honda and armed the alarm. He walked up the steep bank from the carpark towards the stone pub. As he neared the entrance a smell of beer and hot food filled his nostrils and caused him to lick his lips.

As he entered he looked around the lounge amongst the cliental gathered at the bar and the people seated at the tables finishing their meals and then clocked two of his colleagues stood at the far end of the room drinking. He made his way through the precarious obstacle course of waitresses, bar stools and dogs sitting at the foot of some of the tables and extended his hand towards them.

'Ah Lieutenant, glad you came', one of the men stammered, suffering the effects of the beer he was consuming.

'Sorry I am late but you know… work work work', he laughed, 'good to see you out of the office Luke. And Jim, since when did your wife let you out at this time of night?'

'Let me get you a drink', Luke offered.

'I haven't been to the Rock for years', Simon stated as the Land Rover coasted down the long narrow roads.

'Hopefully we will recognise his friends and perhaps join them for now. Then we will steal the chance and him outside in private'.

'What if he doesn't?' Simon asked.

'We can start to drop hints about the project, you know, unsettle him'.

Mike pulled the Land Rover to the right and began to ascend a steep hill.

'We ideally need to get him back to Nelson'.

'How do we do that?'

'We could get him drunk and kidnap him?' Mike smiled.

'Ttime forrr another drink I think David my old lad', Jim slurred as he began to extract his wallet from his back pocket.

Jennings shook his head and looked at his watch.

'Oh shit no, I gotta get home', he exclaimed as he fought to keep his balance.

'You aint driving are you Dave?' Luke asked which a smile.

'Shit yes', Jennings replied with a sudden realisation that he was drunk and thus well over the legal limit to drive.

The two men burst into laughter. The barman produced a line of double whiskeys and Luke turned to pay for them. He moved close to the glasses and subtly tipped the contents of two of them into one glass and then passed it to Jennings. He pretended to drink the empty glass as did his colleague, leaving Jennings staring at an exceptionally large whiskey.

'Come on Dave, this place will shut before you have drank that'.

'How the hell am I going to get home now?' he slurred.

'Already in motion my friend', Jim suggested, 'I have a taxi booked – should be here any minute. We will wait outside – I need a cigarette anyway'.

The two men began to gather their coats from the bar stools enticing Jennings to drink the tumbler of whiskey. He exhaled, defeated, resigning to the fact that he would have to leave the car and get into the taxi and put the glass to his lips. Taking a deep breath he drank the glass dry before accidentally dropping it onto the floor.

The two men cheered and led the way through the few remaining die hard locals in the otherwise empty lounge.

As soon as he left the building, the fresh air hit him like a metal wrench.

'I think I am going to be…' Jennings said as he clutched his mouth.

He vomited across the road and then dropped to his knees.

The two men looked at each other and nodded.

'Get him to the carpark', Luke whispered, 'I will get the car'.

'Quickly, there's a car coming, give me a hand'.

The two men grappled Jennings' limp body and began to drag him down the slope away from the pub.

As they reached a blue Renault, Luke opened the passenger side door and stooped to open the glove compartment.

He stood up producing a large blade that caught the moonlight.

'Hurry up for God's sakes!' Jim spat.

Jennings blinked as he went in and out of consciousness.

'What are you doing?' he slurred as he caught sight of the blade.

'Hold him still!'

Mike pulled the Land Rover towards the carpark as a blue Renault Megane tore around the corner almost clipping them as it careered down the slope. Mike stamped on the brakes.

'Jesus!' Mike shouted, 'never a policeman around when you want one'.

Shaking his head he released the brake and continued. As they turned into a space in the centre of the carpark the headlights picked out a dark object in the far corner.

'Is that a person?' Simon asked, squinting at the shape.

The two agents walked towards the body. Mike fished out his torch and switched it on.

'I reckon he has definitely had enough, don't you?' he toyed.

Simon quickened his pace.

'Shit, it's Jennings!' he shouted.

The two agents crouched down and Simon began to turn him over. He paused and looked at his feet.

'Shine your torch down here'.

Mike pointed the beam to the floor and highlighted the deep red blood running from Jennings' body.

'Call an ambulance Simon', Mike shouted as he took off his jacket. He laid it across the body and tucked it around his neck.

'He's still breathing, get that ambulance here now!'

The sea rolled aggressively into the isolated cove with the fierce wind that whipped up and around the cliff edges, pushing sea mist with it at a tremendous speed.

It was nearly pitch black; all but for the tiny glimmer of moonlight penetrating the clouds and the intermittent lighthouse blink in the distance.

Inside the seventy year old concrete pillbox, the two Preventive men stationed at Morvah Point drank from their thermos' in front of a small portable bar heater.

'I'm going outside for a smoke', Matthews announced as he stood up and stretched out his arms.

Simmons, his partner, nodded as he looked through his digiscope at the horizon.

Matthews opened the small wooden door, ducked and stepped out onto the brittle grasses, pushing it firmly closed behind him. He pulled up his jacket and lit a cigarette in a vain effort to protect the flame from the whipping wind from the cove.

As he successfully lit the cigarette, he straightened himself out and triumphantly exhaled a plume of smoke then began to walk towards the cliff edge. As he idly looked at the darkness of the sea, he noticed a small break in the surface of the water, the waves highlighted by what moonlight there was. He squinted to try and make out the dark shape in the centre that appeared to be getting closer to the shoreline. Unable to make it out he walked back to the bunker and opened the door.

'Hey, don't bring that filthy thing in here!' Simmons shouted.

'Shut up and hand me that scope!'

Frowning, Simmons handed over the scope to his partner who disappeared outside again.

Matthews held the scope up to his right eye, his finger finding the night vision toggle mounted on the side. Simmons left the warmth of the bunker and ventured to the cliff edge where his partner was stood statue like staring down at the shoreline.

'That's a boat down there!'

'Are you sure?' Simmons asked, trying to squint through the stinging sea mist.

'It's definitely a boat, I can see it clearly now'.

Simmons looked deeper through the mist and made out the dark shape drawing in with the tide.

'My God, I think you are right', he shouted excitedly.

Simmons ran back to the bunker and returned with an armful of portable equipment. Matthews struggled with the awkward structure of the floodlight in the blustery wind but managed to mount it successfully in its housing. Simmons looked through the scope.

'There are two… no three of them and they… they have boxes on board. Five boxes by the looks of it'.

Simmons loaded his weapon and took aim, using the night sight.

'Wait for them to come into range', Simmons suggested.

Matthews tapped a number on his phone's keypad.

'There's no time', Simmons whispered.

Agreeing, Matthews returned the phone to his pocket. The neighbouring units would be alerted by the floodlights and the air horn.

Simmons watched through his scope as the small boat got closer to the beach.

Eventually the men jumped from it into the sea and began to drag the boat ashore.

'Any minute now…' Simmons whispered.

Matthews' finger hovered over the floodlight switch.

The first man out of the boat began to haul one of the chests onto the beach.

'Now!' Simmons shouted.

Matthews slapped his hand hard on the switch and the cove illuminated.

Startled, the men from the boat looked up towards the light as Matthews hit the air horn.

'You are totally surrounded, stand back from the boat and put your hands above your heads!' Matthews shouted through a loudspeaker, the sound of which reverberated around the cliff face.

'Jesus! That's Simmons' alarm!' one of the agents from the adjacent watch shouted. The two men gathered their weapons and ran along the cliff top towards the floodlit cove.

The five men on the beach complied, looking up at the lights and around at the cliff edges, each one scanning the ridgeline for life. The first two men out of the boat moved closer to each other.

'I thought you said this was the right beach?'

'It was, chief, it was… It is exactly the point on the map…'

Simmons began to make his way down the coastal path towards the men, his MP5 loaded and outstretched. By the time he had neared the rocky base of the cliff; four more agents had assembled on the cliff line.

Matthews returned to his weapon and took strategic aim from his vantage point inside the pillbox.

Panic had begun to set in with boatmen who shifted around the illuminated beach nervously.

'My God, we are surrounded…'

'What do we do?'

'I aint getting caught, that's for damned sure!'

The leader of the boat crew stepped backwards slowly in a hope to be concealed by the rest of his crew. Matthews spotted him moving through his night scope.

'Stop!' he shouted.

The man jumped towards the boat and pulled a Kalashnikov rifle from inside. The other men dispersed out of fear, pulling hand guns from their belts and began to find cover amongst the small rocks on the beach.

The leading crew member held the Kalashnikov up towards the floodlight and fired.

The deafening noise echoed around the cove, disturbing roosting seagulls in the imperfections of the cliff walls.

The bullets pinged around the pillbox causing ancient concrete to crumble around Matthews' head.

Simmons took aim from the base of the path and returned fire, followed by the other four agents that had set up strategic positions on the cliff line. The boatmen cowered as a hail of sporadic gun fire rained upon the shale, throwing a mix of sand and shell into the air. The leader sprayed rounds indiscriminately amongst the coastal path in an attempt to catch Simmons- who had ducked for cover near the bottom. When the firing had stopped, he stood up and took aim on the man, firing a few rounds. A quick return of fire caught his left shoulder, throwing him backwards into the sea grass.

Matthews emerged from the concrete debris and returned fire on the boatman, squeezing three rounds towards him, the third of which impacted on his chest. The other crew members fired their pistols and automatics from the cover of the rocks, out of sight of Matthews' vantage point.

One of the agents from the cliff line caught two of the crew members in another hail of fire, dropping them to the ground.

Frustrated and out of ammunition; Matthews picked up his mobile phone and dialled Mike's number.

'Yes, he is gone, sir', the voice sounded in the earpiece of the phone.

Wilkinson smiled.

'We left him as you suggested sir, as if he had been mugged'.

'Excellent, thank you Mr Edwards'.

He thumbed the "end call" button and then proceeded to enter a number on the keypad.

Mike sat in the back of the ambulance with the medics as they strapped the unconscious Jennings down for the journey. His phone rang in his pocket.

'Mike Williams', he answered.

'It's Wilkinson'.

Mike looked towards Simon who was stood at the rear of the ambulance smoking a cigarette.

'Yes sir', Mike answered, mouthing "Wilkinson" to his colleague.

'I'm afraid I have some bad news. Jennings has been attacked tonight outside a pub'.

Mike pressed the "hands free" button, stepped out of the ambulance and into the carpark.

'How did he know that?' Simon whispered.

Mike pushed a finger to his lips silencing him.

'Is he alright?' Mike stammered in shock.

'No, I am afraid he is dead. They don't know who did it yet. Some kids after his wallet I expect'.

The two agents looked back at Jennings inside the ambulance, evidently breathing albeit through a machine.

'I am sorry to hear that sir', Mike offered with as much conviction as he could summon.

Getting the "Busy" tone, Matthews retuned the phone to his pocket. The odd, infrequent shot sounded from around the cove. He crouched down and moved, crab-like along the pathway. Above the sound of the waves lashing at the shore, he could hear shouts from the agents as they communicated with each other to close in on the beach.

He froze as he heard a rustle in the grasses ahead of him. Following the noises, a short, fat figure began to make his way towards him. Matthews raised his weapon, pushed the safety catch off and waited. The man stopped a few metres in front of him, looking back towards the beach. Matthews stood up slowly. The man turned to continue his escape.

'Freeze!' Matthews shouted as he held his weapon towards the man.

The man instinctively fired a round at Matthews; the bullet whirred past his left ear. He returned a shot which hit the man in the chest, instantly killing him and pushing him backwards onto the sandy bank. He lowered his weapon and walked towards his victim.

His phone rang.

'It's Williams, I had a missed call from you, is everything okay?'

An ambulance left the lay-by at Morvah Point, its blue lights flashing without siren.

Mike and Simon watched as it passed them by.

Two men from the boat, in restraints were being led to a police van by Matthews and another agent.

Mike walked towards a wounded Simmons sporting a sling.

'You guys had a bit of fun up here then?'

Matthews acknowledged Mike's consolation with a smile.

'Well done Robert, this is exactly what we expected to happen. It is getting close to the end now...'

'The last of the tea chests have been loaded'.

'Thanks. Get them to Nelson for processing'.

Mike turned around and looked at Simon meaningfully.

'It's difficult to take all this in Simon', he said with a slight wobble to his voice.

'And to think that three months ago, I had just busted a man from Jamaica for a kilo of Cannabis... that was my highlight of the year!'

Although he was smiling, Simon noticed Mike's eyes beginning to well up. It was obvious that it was taking its toll on him.

'We need to make sure that Jennings is guarded at all times. We should get someone over to his house, to tell his wife. God knows what Wilkinson told her! And we need to keep this under the radar'.

'I agree', Simon responded, treading on a cigarette butt, 'I guess we can assume that Wilkinson was behind Jennings' attack then'.

'Yeah, he is tying up his loose ends by the looks of it'.

As they headed up the hill towards the lay-by, Mike noticed Matthews and Simmons, standing nearby.

'Hey, have you got a moment?' he asked the two agents.

They picked up their weapons and walked wearily towards him.

'Yes sir?' Matthews replied.

'I want you guys to accompany us on a little trip...'

The two men looked at each other.

'Where to, sir?'

'France!'

Chapter 13

<u>The bust</u>

The vast twenty four hour port of Calais cast a magnificent glow in the darkness of the night like a huge, orange umbrella. Clearly visible from the south-east coast of England, the vast concrete jungle of warehouses and industrial buildings that dominate the west side of the docks compete for height with the giant yellow arms that swing from dock to ship twenty four hours a day like giant spiders weaving a web.

The black Ford transit van approached the main entrance and slowly took the turning towards the warehouse district.

Simon looked at his watch; three thirty exactly.

The complex was eerily quiet with the exception of the odd forklift truck beetling towards the docks.

The four men sat inside the van as Mike slowed to a stop to review the map.

'It should be somewhere…' he looked and traced the entrance route with his finger, 'here!'

He looked out of the window and saw the sign "Leon Vincent" on the signpost and continued towards the giant amber lit buildings. Nervously, they coasted across the desolate concrete plaza as the noises- from the hectic non-stop life of the shipping port grinding through the early hours of the morning- became more defined. The seagulls broke the monotony of the bleak orange sky as they swarmed around the fish stores as the French trawlers deposited their nightly catch.

'Are you sure this is going to work Simon?' Mike asked as a small guard post came into view, rendering the other two agents uncomfortably nervous.

'What do you mean? You are the one who suggested this in the first place!' Simon pleaded for assurance.

The van trickled towards the security hut; a small metal building with three guards standing nearby, one of them armed. The long red and white striped barrier remained horizontal with one of the guards leaning on it smoking a cigarette, facing the oncoming vehicle.

Mike wound down the driver's side window in anticipation.

'I hope they speak English, my French is appalling', he turned around in his seat, 'can anyone speak French?'

The smoking guard waved the van down and walked around to the driver's side.

'Bonjour', Mike offered in a flat tone.

The guard rolled his eyes.

'You can do better than that Monsieur', he replied.

'Ah, you speak English'.

'Can I help you Monsieur?'

'Yes, we are here to collect something for Doctor Faraday'.

Mike handed the guard a copy of the storage docket he had recovered from Faraday's computer.

The guard looked at it and walked inside the hut to confer with his colleagues.

'This isn't going to work!' Simon whispered.

'What do we do if it doesn't?' Matthews asked from the rear of the van.

'Shut up!' Mike snapped, 'it will work!'

The guards intermittently looked up from the paperwork at the van in turn.

Mike bit his fingernails as he watched them discussing what he assumed was the legitimacy of the docket.

After what seemed an eternity the first guard returned to the van.

'Monsieur, who are you with? What company do you represent?'

'We are with Her Majesties Preventive Service… an arm of the Revenue and Customs'.

The guard continued to look through the paperwork. He didn't pay much attention to it but seemed more interested in delaying the proceedings.

'I see, and this… Doctor Faraday - he asked you to collect what exactly?'

Mike paused as he revised his delivery.

'It is secretive, you may notice on page… five I think it is; it is marked with OSA? Official Secrets Act. We don't even know ourselves…'

The guard smirked and returned to the hut.

'Shit, what's the problem with this guy?' Mike growled under his breath.

He returned after a few more agonising minutes.

'This Mr Faraday, he's a friend of yours?'

'An associate'.

'He asked you himself?'

Mike paused. Faraday was dead, and had been for weeks.

'Yes, he did. We are performing an experiment and we require this… unit, for purposes that are also contained within the OSA'.

The guard chewed at his cheek as he flicked through the paperwork once again.

'Your passport please', he demanded, holding out his hand.

Mike fished his passport from his inside pocket and handed it to the guard.

'How did you arrive here Monsieur?'

'The tunnel', Mike replied.

'And you are returning by…?'

'The tunnel again'.

'Do you have export papers?'

'Export papers? No'.

Mike's anger began to build. Perhaps this is what was needed. The guards looked bored and this was obviously an unusual time for activity in this area. They were making a meal out of the situation for the sake of relieving their monotonous night shift.

'Look, we are on a tight schedule!' Mike started.

'Sil vous plait!' the guard raised his hand at Mike's outburst.

Simon watched intently, nervously fidgeting with his cigarette lighter.

'You may pass Monsieur, but you may collect your passport on your departure, oui?'

Mike gave him a look of disgust.

'Oui!'

He revved the van as the guard slowly raised the barrier, then pushed the accelerator, jolting the van forward past the guard post and into the main plaza.

The men remained silent as the situation had left them all with a shock of reality and that it wasn't going to be as easy as they had originally perceived.

Mike pulled the van outside the large red stone entrance of the Leon Vincent warehouse.

He backed up into the cavernous loading bay and turned off the engine.

'We are looking for zone six, row sixty four, crate twenty three', Mike read from the docket.

As they approached the large entrance, Mike noticed a doorbell with a note in English above it:

"FOR OUT OF HOURS ACCESS RING BELL"

Mike pressed it and a cheap buzzer sounded from inside the building.

After a few seconds, the large wooden doors creaked opened, revealing a semi-awake and over-weight guard.

'Oui?'

As Mike moved closer to speak to him, the overwhelming fumes of strong liquor engulfed him.

'Parlez vous Anglais?' he asked.

'Yes', the man slurred.

The three guards at the guard hut saluted as the Chief of Security made his nightly check-in.

'Everything okay?' he asked.

'Oui, everything's fine', the smoking guard replied, offering him a cigarette.

'Merci, voulez-vous du café?'

'Of course'.

The guard hurried in to the hut and returned promptly with a Styrofoam cup of hot, black coffee.

'Merci Beaucoup', the chief replied, receiving the cup with both hands.

'There was one thing actually, sir', the guard started.

'Oh?'

'Oui, a group of men in a van passed through about ten minutes ago… they were heading for Leon Vincent to retrieve a crate. It's probably nothing, sir, but they claimed that they were with Revenue and Customs. I wondered if you were aware of them?'

The chief shook his head as he sipped the coffee.

'Nothing on my agenda for UK Customs, non. What were they collecting?'

'They wouldn't say sir; they stated it was under the umbrella of their Official Secrets Act'.

A frown rippled across the chief's forehead.

'I wasn't notified of this, why wasn't I notified?'

'I have his passport here sir', the guard announced, handing him Mike's passport.

The chief flicked through the pages and looked at the photograph.

'Michael Williams… never heard of him. Certainly not on my list for today'.

The guard looked perplexed.

'He said he was collecting for a Doctor Faraday'.

'Have you checked up on this man, Williams?'

The guard nodded and pointed to a screen inside the hut showing a database with Mike's photograph and some notes.

'Oui, he checks out, with an arm of Revenue and Customs called…' he moved closer to the screen to read the smaller print, '… HMPS'.

'Have you checked out Faraday?'

'Non, I will do a check now sir'.

Mike's flashlight illuminated the darker areas of the vast warehouse, shadowed by the huge towers of wooden crates that lined each aisle. Although the location for the crate was clear, the layout of the warehouse was not. Over the years of deep storage, the organisation had become lost and the structure had become chaotic as was the case with most long term storage depots.

Mike looked at his notes again.

'Zone six, row sixty four, crate twenty three… six, six four, two three…'

It was referred to in five digit numerals which didn't help matters.

'Got it!' a shout came from behind one of the teetering towers.

Mike ran towards the shout to find Matthews and Simon staring and pointing their torch beams at a large crate bearing the numbers "6-64-23", at the bottom of a stack of six other creates of various sizes.

'How the hell do we get it out?'

'Sir', the guard alerted the chief who was putting his cigarette out in the empty Styrofoam cup.

'What is it?'

'Monsieur Faraday… I did a check on him sir, and he is…. deceased!'

'What? When?'

'He died several weeks ago sir…'

The chief walked into the hut and starred at the small screen.

'Merde!'

Simon drove the forklift truck towards the stack of crates.

'If you can remove the front of the crate, we can try and drag the unit out', Mike suggested.

Simon continued to drive the forklift slowly into the front panel of the crate, splitting the wooden slats on impact.

'Go on', Mike encouraged.

The sharp, splitting sound echoed throughout the warehouse as the prongs pushed deeper.

'Carry on!' Mike shouted above the noise.

The side of the crate came away from the edges and shattered as it folded in on itself.

'Excellent, now drag it out'.

Simon reversed the forklift away from the damaged crate.

Inside, illuminated by the beams, sat a large metallic object covered in thick insulation and covered with a mass of coloured wires.

'I guess that's it!' Mike said, anticlimactically.

Suddenly the warehouse filled with the piercing shrill from the alarm.

'Shit! They've rumbled us. We've got to get this thing out of here and into the van… Matthews, you go back to the van and get it started and call Simmons and see if he is at the pickup point yet!'

Matthews nodded and sprinted towards the metal shutters.

'Come on Si, let's get this thing out of here'.

Simon pulled the forklift closer to the crate once again.

'How do you…?' he started.

It suddenly occurred to them both that neither of them had ever properly used a forklift truck prior to this moment. Mike ran to the cab and began to search the controls that were inevitably in French.

'Try this one', he said, pulling a lever which extended the forks horizontally.

Simon slowly manoeuvred the truck towards the crate again, slipping the forks underneath the metal unit inside. Mike leaned against the crates as he watched the forks slide under palette and sensed an unsettling vibration. He stood back and thought for a few seconds, concluding that by removing the side panel from the bottom crate, they had compromised the structural integrity of the tower and as a result, the other three sides of the crate were beginning to buckle under the weight.

'Simon, we need to work quickly!' he shouted above the noise of the alarm.

Simon found the lifting mechanism, by process of elimination and engaged it, lifting the unit a few inches clear of the ground.

'Is it clear yet?'

Mike bent down and shone his torch into the crate.

'Yeah, pull it out!'

Simon reversed the forklift out of the crate dragging the palette along the concrete floor.

The sides of the crate began to split and dust started to fall from where it had settled over the years of storage above them.

The distant voices of the Commissariat officers and guards, as they entered the warren of towers, were just audible above the alarm.

'Come on, we've seriously got to get going!'

Simon concentrated on the unit balanced precariously on the two metal prongs as it began to emerge from the crate.

'Nearly there…' he said as his tongue ran tentatively along his upper lip.

The sides of the crate split further and began to bow as splinters exploded outwards into the air. 'Simon!' Mike shouted.

Simon looked up at the top crate as it began to shake violently. He put his foot against the accelerator and reversed. The unit scraped from the crate housing gouging a shallow trench in the concrete floor. He then pushed the forklift forwards clear of the crate stack as Mike jumped aboard, clinging to the driver's cage like a monkey in an enclosure. As they turned the corner of the aisle, a violent rumble vibrated the floor as the crate buckled, causing the tower to topple over like a child's building blocks.

The Commissariat officers arrived into the debris strewn aisle as the dust began to settle.

The Chief Officer stopped and grimaced at the mass of twisted machinery amongst the shards of pinewood and packing straw.

'They must be on their way out! Get to the loading bay', he ordered his officers.

Simon wrestled with the overloaded forklift around the narrow corners of the warren towards the loading bay. As they approached, Matthews opened the rear doors of the van.

Simon drove the forklift at speed towards the van, raising the forks to an approximate level of the van interior.

'Hurry!' Mike chanted as he clung to the caging.

Matthews darted out of the way at the last second as the prongs impacted with the rear of the van - piercing the body work and throwing the unit from the palette into the interior.

Shaken, Simon put the truck into reverse and applied the accelerator. The wheels spun on the concrete surface as the prongs were buried deep into the twisted metal of the van's bodywork.

'Come on, there's no time!' Mike shouted.

The two men left the truck and entered the back of the van, sliding past the bulk of the unit as Matthews started the engine. The officers flooded the loading bay as the van's wheels spun; trying to clear the entanglement of the forklift truck. Matthews put his foot fully down on the accelerator and the bay flooded with thick smoke from the wheels as they squealed to try and move.

The officers began to spread out around them, covering their mouths and coughing.

'It's not moving!' Matthews shouted.

'It is, it is! Keep accelerating!' Simon shouted back.

The officers moved into range and drew their weapons.

'Shut off the engine or we will shoot!' one officer shouted over the overwhelming noise of the van's tyres battling with the warehouse alarm.

'Come on!' Matthews shouted to the van as it inched forwards.

'It's the weight of this thing!' Simon exclaimed.

The van vibrated with a crackle of gun fire as the rounds impacted around the left side and rear doors. Simon stooped down behind the generator for cover as rounds ripped through the thin, metal bodywork and pinged off the generator.

Suddenly and with a loud crack, the van broke free and propelled at speed out of the loading bay, leaving the rear bumper and tail lights hanging from the prongs.

The officers moved outside into the plaza and followed the van for a few metres on foot, releasing the occasional shot as the van approached the security hut.

Matthews aimed for the barrier.

'Do you think we'll make it through?' he asked with genuine concern.

Mike didn't answer and braced himself against the dashboard.

The van sliced through the barrier producing a fountain of sparks.

The security guard in the hut, cowering for cover, shouted into his radio.

Matthews guided the vehicle around the narrow entrance roads of the port and out onto the highway.

'Well done', Mike said, with a sigh of relief.

Mike turned to Simon who was attempting to close what was left of the rear doors. As he tugged at the bullet hole ridden left door, he spotted a police car screaming around the corner in the distance.

'Oh shit!' he shouted, 'police on our tail!'

Simon squeezed into the cab and produced a map from the glove compartment.

'You want to look for a sign to… Sangatte, along the Rue Nationale… is Simmons there?'

'Yeah, he's there, he's got the boat', Matthews confirmed.

Mike spotted the police car through the cracked wing mirror.

'We're going to have to lose them. Stay off the main roads!'

The van roared along the tarmac road leaving a lightshow of sparks from the trailing debris behind them.

'They are gaining on us!' Matthews shouted as he nervously looked in the mirror.

Mike looked over at Simon's map and looked back at the road.

'Turn right… Turn right…'

'Where?'

'Here!'

Mike grabbed the steering wheel and pushed it to the right. The van swerved, the tyres pushing against the wheel arches as they traversed the highway and careered through the crash barrier into a small copse.

'Jesus Mike!' Matthews shouted.

The van scrambled over the mounds of earth and stumps, toppling saplings and tearing branches from the trees.

The police cars slid to a stop at the broken barrier.

'Follow them!' the chief shouted to the driver.

The reluctant driver turned the Peugeot towards the twisted barrier and bumped up the curb, across the verge and into the copse.

The van bounded through the wooded area towards the haze of village lights in the distance.

'There!' Mike pointed, 'head for those lights and stay off the roads!'

The Peugeot followed the remaining brake light of the van intermittently visible in the distance along the freshly beaten track.

'I think it is left anytime now', Simon suggested as he looked at the map, struggling to navigate with the rollercoaster ride.

Matthews hauled the van to the left, through a barbed wire fence and into a field.

'Switch the lights off', Mike ordered.

The van careered across the uneven field and into the darkness; the rear doors flapping lethargically.

The Peugeot, struggling to pursue, slid to a stop at the broken fence.

'What are you stopping for?' the chief barked, 'follow them!'

The reluctant driver reversed the damaged patrol car and turned to cross the fence debris. As the tyres ran over the barbs they blew out, throwing the car uncontrollably into the field, eventually coming to a halt on an old tree stump.

The chief pushed open the door and watched the van haring into the distance, illuminated by the burnt umber from the sunrise.

'Give me the radio!' he ordered the driver.

'They are heading for Sangatte! Head them off!' he shouted into the mouthpiece.

Matthews engaged neutral, allowing the van to roll freely across the rest of the muddy field then engaged third gear as they approached the farm entrance, propelling them through a wooden gate and out onto the street.

Out of the side window Simon spotted the blue flashing lights heading towards the town.

'The jetty is about… two hundred metres down here… apparently'.

The van's suspension had long since given way causing Matthews to wrestle with the steering as they entered the tiny cobbled streets of the Flemish village.

'Slow it down a bit now', Mike advised.

'I can't, the brakes aren't responding!' Matthews replied, frantically pushing his foot on the defiant foot pedal.

Mike lifted the handbrake slightly and the rear wheels locked, screeching the tyres over the cobbles.

'Subtle entrance!' Simon said sarcastically as he held onto each headrest.

Gradually, the residents filed out onto the streets to witness the commotion.

Mike slowed the van using the handbrake as they approached the wooden jetty and heaved it upwards to a halt.

'Where is Simmons?' Matthews asked.

Mike opened the battered door and jogged to the ancient planks. With the subtle village street lights he could just make out the familiar orange of the Coastguard vessel bobbing at the end of the jetty. Sensing the approaching residents he made his way back to the van.

'Matthews; call Simmons, get him to activate the crane'.

Matthews made the call and Mike released the handbrake, coasting them onto the uneven planks. As they neared the boat Mike spotted the mini crane-arm swing out. He turned the steering wheel as soon as the van had gained enough momentum, swinging them around and then applied acceleration. He crunched into reverse and backed the van towards the boat.

He pulled at the handbrake and the van stopped dead.

'You two get out and get ready to attach that crane to the palette', Mike ordered.

The orange vessel puttered towards the edge of the jetty and stopped within stepping distance.

Simon fastened the four crane hooks around the palette and then signalled back.

The officers arrived at the foot of the jetty and had begun to talk to the locals who had gathered there, unaware of the van and the boat in the darkness below them.

Satisfied that the crane ties were secure the three men stepped aboard the boat.

'Do you think this is going to work?' Simon whispered to Mike.

'Not really', he answered vainly.

One of the police officers looked into the darkness and made out the rear of the van. He shouted to the group of Commissariats and began to run towards them, his weapon drawn.

'Go go go!!!' Mike shouted.

The vessel's twin engines roared to life, throwing a fountain of water into the air as it began to pull the generator from the back of the van. Simmons, monitoring the load, increased the power. The boat began to list as it pulled at the heavy instrument.

'Come on you bastard!' Mike shouted at the precious cargo, wedged between the van walls.

The officers closed in on the van and began to surround it as it began to slide away from them along the wet planks.

The boat spouted huge jets of water towards the officers as the van picked up momentum. A deafening crack signified the rear quarter of the van giving way and buckling under the force from the twin Honda engines of the boat. As the van hit the oak beam at the edge of the jetty, the front end lifted. With a final burst of power, the generator came free from the van walls, tearing the rear quarter from the chassis and causing the front of the van to crash down in front of the officers, instantly dispersing them.

The boat tore across the channel inlet towards the open sea, the generator swinging awkwardly from the crane like a salmon hooked on a fishing line.

The vessel drifted slowly into Penzance Harbour through the clusters of moored boats and slowed to a stop as it reached the road bridge. Mike called the harbour master and after a few minutes the traffic stopped and the bridge opened, allowing them through to the dry dock yard. From the cabin, Mike pointed out the hull section of a Royal Navy vessel that a small team were welding in front of them.

'Type 32, Manchester Class Destroyer', he shouted above drone from the twin engines. He navigated the small vessel into a vacant area of the dry dock adjacent to the giant steel hulk and moored next to a small office unit attached to the main hangar.

A young man of about twenty five jumped down onto the floating jetty, ready to catch the mooring rope.

'Is that him?' Simon asked suspiciously.

'No, that's his son… Martin. Tim will be up on that steel shell somewhere'.

'Do you think he can actually make this thing work?'

'He was doing a Masters in Electrical Engineering', Mike replied confidently as he threw the mooring rope to the young man.

'Do you think they cover EMP in that curriculum?' Simon asked sarcastically.

'You are gonna get me in trouble Williams!' a voice shouted from above them.

A man in orange overalls sat suspended in a harness on the rear of a giant propeller shaft protruding the hull section.

The three men gathered around the generator.

'This is it?' Tim asked, with a disappointed tone.

Tim was a tall, stubbly gentleman, educated in Oxford. He left the university in order to look after the family dockyard after his father was killed in the early nineties, devoting all of his time in the running and directing of the family business with his son.

'This is it, yes', Mike answered proudly.

'I kind of expected a… ray gun or something… this looks more like an oversized washing machine!'

'I need to know if you can make it work, Tim. I can't tell you how important this could be'.

Tim scratched his head and rubbed at his stubble. He walked around the mishmash of tubes, dials and copper coils and poked at the protruding wires like a discerning car buyer.

'Hmm, I've worked on worse', he joked, 'come back in a few hours and we'll crack on with it. Does it come with any instructions?'

'Here!' Simon pulled out the hard drive from his jacket pocket and handed it to him.

'Nice', Tim replied, tapping on the front of one of the many dials, 'quite looking forward to this!'

Mrs Jacobs filed her meticulous nails whilst ingesting the latest fashion news from her monthly magazine, behind the reception desk in the polished floored hallway of Nelson Building. It was a particularly quiet period with most of the agents posted on coastal watches. This time of the morning tended to be quiet; yet made even more so with the lack of constant phone rings, laughter and footsteps around her. The phones had all been diverted to an answer machine computer. She looked at her clock: 7:01am, then back to her article.

The entrance doors burst open as Wilkinson marched through them with a young lady in Navy uniform.

Mrs Jacobs jumped, dropped the magazine and looked up, her eyes transfixed on the unannounced and unexpected visitor.

'Mr Wilkinson, sir, it's…'

'…A surprise?' he finished, 'I am here to replace Jennings with Miss Denford here. She will be responsible for all HMPS communications indefinitely'.

'I am terribly sorry to have heard about Mr Jennings, Mr Wilkinson', Mrs Jacobs said with remorse.

Wilkinson nodded and solemnly looked down to the floor. Mrs Jacobs smiled at the young girl, who returned the pleasantry. Then an uncomfortable silence ensued for a few seconds. Mrs Jacobs, confused by the sudden arrival of the Vice Admiral, froze. It was highly irregular for the VA to arrive out of the blue and without accompanying officers, not to mention the arrival of a new member of staff without prior contact with her.

'Mrs Jacobs?' Wilkinson's deep voice boomed.

'Yes sir... I will contact our admin team and get her set up'.

'Thank you Mrs Jacobs'.

Satisfied with the response he set off towards the elevator with his eager new officer in tow. Mrs Jacobs watched the pair stand in silence as they waited for the elevator to arrive. Eventually the doors slid open and they entered. As they slid closed, she picked up her telephone and dialled.

Mike retrieved his vibrating phone from his pocket and walked towards the other end of the dock, away from the deafening noise of a circular cutter that was slowly eating its way through the metal casing of the generator.

'Mike Williams', he shouted with his left hand clamped firmly over his ear.

'It's Maureen Jacobs... I need to have a word'.

'What is it Mrs Jacobs?'

'It's the Vice Admiral'.

'What about him?'

'He just arrived a few minutes ago... with a lady... a Miss Denford, I think her name was; she is here to replace Jennings!'

Mike bit his lip.

'Who authorised that?'

'Mr Wilkinson. I knew nothing about it. It doesn't follow any of the...'

'Are they there now?'

'Yes, well no, they are heading up to Jennings' office. She is going to take over Comms. It just seemed a bit odd to me that I wasn't informed, so I thought you ought to know'.

'Thank you Mrs Jacobs. Let me know if anything else out of the ordinary happens'.

'Of course Mike'.

Mike shut the phone and closed his fist around it. What was Wilkinson doing? He was obviously placing another puppet onto his stage. How do you recruit someone to choreograph illegitimate operations? He placed himself on the edge of a nearby steel girder as his thoughts preoccupied him. Wilkinson was obviously clutching at straws. Or was he somehow covering his tracks? As he walked back towards the generator and the enormous fountain of sparks, it suddenly occurred to him that if Wilkinson had hired this new position in Comms, he would be using her to their advantage; to send out false signals. She would be undoubtedly being manipulated, whether she knew it or not, to bridge Wilkinson's smuggling activities and she would have contact with the pirates directly.

'We could use her to send false signals to them, to lore them into an ambush', Mike said aloud to himself. This was perfect, although she was under Wilkinson's wing and susceptible to his orders. Getting her on their side would be a challenge.

'Got ya!' Tim shouted as the circular saw began to spin down.

He pulled at the side of the casing and revealed a mass of brightly coloured wires and delicately mounted circuit boards surrounding a giant copper coil. A small, metal dish sat precariously on the edge of the internal framework next to an array of dials.

'Hmm, this is interesting…' Tim said as he pushed his head inside the chaotic apparatus.

Mike and Simon looked at each other blankly as the engineer darted between the generator and a laptop connected to Faraday's hard drive.

'What is?' Mike asked anticipating an elaboration.

'This thing... It's got a variable resistor on it… this thing actually looks like it is going to work!'

'It's got a what?' Mike asked.

Tim poked his head out of the top of the frame.

'A variable resistor. Like a dimmer switch for your house lights. But this seems like it controls range, according to this guy's schematics', he said pointing to a technical drawing on the laptop screen, 'we have got to test this mother out!'

'Basically, that is it' Wilkinson summarised, perched on the side of Jennings' desk. 'You have had prior training on Comms I take it, my dear?' he asked the young trainee.

'Yes of course sir', Denford replied, looking up at him with young, eager eyes.

Wilkinson smiled.

'I need your upmost trust, Miss Denford, I need to entrust you with a project that is subject to the Official Secrets Act. Do you feel comfortable with that?'

Denford nodded with an unavoidable look of apprehension.

Wilkinson chuckled.

'Don't worry my dear, it is quite safe, it is just that you must not under any circumstances discuss any information to anyone but myself about what I am about to tell you'.

She smiled and nodded, pulling her blonde hair from the side of her face. To her, a trainee, to be trusted with a project categorised under the OSA was an unprecedented career progression. How could she refuse? Wilkinson opened a file and placed it in front of her.

She scanned the table of numbers and locations and turned the page revealing Mike's map with the safety zone locations circled.

'We are in the middle of a very important operation, Miss Denford, which involves the dropping off of equipment from an off-shore vessel. These are highly secretive and sensitive materials. You will, as the first part of your duties, be responsible for relaying information between myself and this vessel, regarding drop times and locations. Do you think you can handle that okay?'

Denford looked confused but nodded.

'Very good', Wilkinson squeezed her shoulder.

'Okay… you may want to get out of the boat now!' Tim shouted from behind the generator. Simon waved back at him from inside a small fishing boat in the dry dock harbour. He waved in acknowledgement and reached inside the compact cabin, switching on the lights, the radio and the engine. He jumped across to the small harbour wall and jogged back towards Mike and the excited engineer.

'Oh shit, hold on a minute…' he shouted as he felt at his pockets.

'Three', Tim started the countdown as the generator began to drone to life.

'My phone, I left it on the…'

'Two'.

Simon pointed towards the boat. Mike bit his finger in an attempt to contain his laughter.

'One'.

The three men braced themselves as Tim released a large switch.

The generator spun up and began to vibrate then emanated a small electrical buzz and spun back down.

The three men looked at the device and then to each other.

'Is that it?' Mike asked.

Tim smiled and pointed towards the fishing boat, fifty metres in front of them in the small bay.

'No radio, no lights, no engine… no power!'

The fishing boat drifted silently in the dark harbour.

'Oh my God', Mike exclaimed, 'it actually works!'

'Of course it works!' Tim shouted as he ran along the wall towards the boat.

'This could actually do it; we could actually use this thing against them!' Mike said to his unimpressed colleague.

'What's wrong with you?'

Tim bellowed with laughter as he held up a small black object from the roof of the fishing boat.

'What's that?' Mike enquired.

Simon gave a long drawn out sigh, 'My phone!'

"WE NEED TO DROP THE NEXT SHIPMENT ASAP!"

Wilkinson read the text message and hit reply. This was the test. He stood behind Miss Denford as she read through the folder of instructions that he had given to her.

He looked at her; brand new, full of life, clean from the mess that he had created. Could he actually poison her with this? It was too late, she knew about the coordinates, the contact numbers and the map. There was no turning back for either of them.

'Okay, I have received a message that a new shipment is expected. My crew want to drop it off as soon as possible. I need you to liaise with them and choose one of these points. Try and organise it for tonight. Here is the number…'

He handed her a note with a mobile phone number written across it in large red numbers.

'We will work out now what would be best and then I want you to organise the rest… okay?'

Denford turned to him nervously. He looked at her in a fatherly manner.

'What is the matter?'

She looked back at the folder in a hope that it would make more sense to her, desperate for something to click into place and suddenly become clear.

She looked back at the Vice Admiral, his bulk towering over her.

'N-nothing sir', she trembled.

None perplexed and shrouded by the thought of the last drop, Wilkinson smiled and walked towards the office door.

'I'll make us a coffee', he said jovially.

'It's completely dead!' Simon said, pressing the keypad on his phone.

'It will be', Tim clarified, 'it's just had the same treatment as these boats you've been finding'.

Mike nodded as he furiously typed an email on the laptop.

Simon moved closer to him.

'How many people have you told Mike?'

'No one. I asked for Tim's help, I couldn't very rightly ask him to fix this thing up for us without telling him what it was about could I? And besides I trust him as much as I trust you! We go way back…'

'So did you and Black!'

Mike returned a look of distaste.

'Right…' he began, sliding his laptop across the metal work bench, 'how do we get to this Comms girl!'

Chapter 14

<u>The solution</u>

Simon casually walked into Nelson reception foyer, waved at Mrs Jacobs and ran up the winding stair case, two at a time.

As he approached Jennings' former office, he slowed down and paused to listen at the door. Jennings' name plate had been replaced with "Communications".

He pressed his ear flat against the wooden door to hear the tapping of a keyboard and clicking of a mouse along with the intermittent answers of 'Yes' and 'No'; obviously she was on the telephone. With any luck, Wilkinson wouldn't be in there. He was going to have to think of a damn good excuse as to why he was here if he was. He held his breath, knocked on the door and marched into the room.

Miss Denford sat, alone, tapping at her keyboard, the telephone wedged between her cheek and her shoulder.

'Yes, I have done that sir', she spoke.

She acknowledged Simon's entrance with an 'I won't be a second…' expression.

He waved his hand at her, gesturing 'I will wait'.

He took the time, as she continued, to look around the office. It was imperative that he found a way of getting through to her. How was he going to get her to give him the information he required? She was obviously recruited for the sole reason of relaying movements in connection to the pirates, but how should he approach the subject and what had Wilkinson fabricated to get her to do so? Momentarily he regretted not conceiving a proper plan – as Mike had suggested. Although he and Mike had agreed that an initial reconnaissance was the best way forward, he found himself totally unprepared.

As he looked over her shoulder at her desk, he gasped. Heading for the door he pulled out his phone and gestured that he would come back later.

He ran through the corridor and to the fire escape and pressed Mike's quick dial.

'Mike Williams'.

'Mike, it's me'.

'Have you found a way of…'

'That doesn't matter… she is a trainee, right?'

'Right?'

'She writes everything down! There is an A4 notepad in front of her… it is all there Mike, phone numbers, diagrams… and your map!'

There was a pause.

'Jesus! We have got to get her out of there! Can you distract her?'

'No, she is on the phone… I will get back to you…'

Simon shut the phone and thought pensively for a few moments and then made his way down the stairs towards the ground floor.

He entered the foyer from the fire escape and ran towards the staff register.

'Just checking on something Mrs Jacobs…' he excused himself.

Mrs Jacobs looked at him with a confused expression, 'Can I help you Mr Jenkins?'

'No, just checking the register… as you do', he chuckled awkwardly and continued to trace his finger down the list of names.

'Thanks', he said and dashed out of the entrance doors.

'Mike', he spoke into his phone, 'she took her lunch yesterday at one, I am assuming that she will today too!'

'Well done, I will be ready. I have an idea'.

The Royal Navy truck backed out of the dry dock, slowly along the narrow passage. Tim watched out of the rear, his arm draped over the generator unit, as Mike directed the truck backwards toward the main road. As he cleared the narrow entrance, he made his way to the carpark adjacent to the dock where his Land Rover was parked. The truck roared, belching thick black smoke out of its twin exhausts as it made its way across the hinged bridge and into the town.

Simon sat in his Land Rover outside Nelson. He lit another cigarette as he waited and looked into his packet to see how many he had left.

He looked at his watch, five past one, then back to the entrance. She hadn't appeared yet.

Suddenly she exited the building, running down the steps with her car keys at the ready.

Simon fumbled for his phone and pressed a quick dial.

'She's on the move'.

Mike closed his phone and made his way through the fire escape at the far end of the building and along the corridor towards the foyer.

Miss Denford got inside her blue Mitsubishi Colt and started the engine. Simon watched her and started his. As she pulled onto the street, he waited for a car to come between them and then followed so not to arouse suspicion.

Mike ran over to the reception desk.

'Mike!' Mrs Jacobs greeted him.

'I need you to do me a favour'.

'What is it?' she asked pensively.

'I am investigating a member of staff and it is absolutely imperative that you do as I say. Also, you mustn't tell anyone you have seen me. I am not going to sign in the register today. The fire alarm will sound in about ten minutes. You, as always, will go to the rally point, take the register but I won't be on it. I want you to ensure that the staff wait until the fire service arrive and give the all clear okay? As far as you are aware, this will be a real fire, treat it as such… do you understand?'

She blinked as she ingested the order and nodded, 'Whatever you say Mike… what is all this about?'

'I promise I will tell you when it is all over, but for now please trust me…'

He made his way quickly to the spiral staircase, leaving a perplexed Mrs Jacobs at the reception desk.

Simon kept the Mitsubishi in his sight at all times and a close eye on his watch. She pulled in towards a street deli bar and parked. Simon pulled in and bumped the Land Rover up the kerb a few cars behind her.

Mike ran towards the Communications office and walked casually past the open door. As he passed, he very briefly peered inside; Wilkinson was sitting at Denford's computer, reading a book. He jogged past and into the adjacent gents' toilet.

Once inside, he fidgeted in his pocket for Simon's lighter. He pulled it out and flicked it open. As he raised it up towards the sprinkler system, he paused; if this didn't work, the chances are they would run out of time and they couldn't afford for anything to go wrong. Tim was en-route to placing the EMP, the coastal patrol agents were settling into their positions and Simon was trying to delay Miss Denford. It was all reliant on everything going according to the plan they had formulated at the dry dock.

He took a deep breath and pushed the lighter until the flame touched the heat sensor.

In a split second the glass bubble burst and the sprinkler system activated, spraying water in every direction. The alarm sounded shortly afterwards from outside and he could hear the motion and mumblings of disgruntled staff walking through the damp carpet of the corridor. He eased the door open slightly and caught Wilkinson leaving the Communications office clutching his briefcase.

As the staff made their way out, he ran from the gents, across the corridor and into the office, shutting the door firmly behind him.

The giant truck arrived above the picturesque harbour town of Porthlevan. As it pulled up, blocking the narrow street in front of a row of white washed cottages, a flurry of agents began to unload the heavy generator unit. Tim climbed out of the cab and looked across at the granite church.

'Reckon this will make the news', he said to one of the agents, removing the nylon restraining chords from around the generator.

Miss Denford returned to her car with a paper bag and pulled out into the busy town-centre traffic.

Simon followed, closely.

As she pulled around the street corners amongst the lunchtime crowds, he knew that time was running out. He could hear the sirens in the distance and knew that it was in response to Mike's actions. He had to stop her and now. Ahead of them the traffic lights turned red and the traffic began to slow down. Simon took a deep breath and pushed his foot hard on the accelerator. Miss Denford hummed along to the car radio as she picked a crisp from a packet inside the paper bag. She glanced casually in her rear view mirror and saw the Land Rover coming towards her at speed.

As he approached the vehicle, Simon pulled hard on the hand brake.

The Land Rover slid along the road and then impacted with the Mitsubishi, pushing the rear quarter inside the boot and swinging the back end around onto the kerb. Glass and plastic reflector showered the road, the pavement and the pedestrians.

Mike sifted through the paperwork on the damp desk. Time was of the essence for both the fluidity of the project and the integrity of the ink on the paper that was being washed away by the sprinkler system. As he carefully but quickly picked out the sheets, peeling them from one another he found a notepad full of dictation; phone numbers, contacts and diagrams. Typical notes from a trainee thrown into the deep end and desperate to impress. It was their good fortune that Wilkinson had chosen a young trainee for her naivety and ambition. As he looked closely, she had even drawn a crude submarine doodle with a phone number written inside it. The alarm stopped and Mike looked up at the last few drips from the sprinkler system. He could now clearly hear the sound of the firemen in the corridor.

Simon opened the door of the Mitsubishi to reveal a dazed Miss Denford sitting amongst the remnants of a deflating airbag.

'Are you okay?' he enquired.

'Y-yes I am… okay, I think…' she muttered as she began to climb out of the twisted car.

Simon held her and walked her towards the pavement where a passer-by began to comfort her.

Simon dialled on his phone.

'Mike Willi…'

'It's me. I have had an accident sweetheart…'

Mike looked at the phone with confusion. The sounds of the firemen became more prominent as they moved from office to office.

'What?'

'No, no, I am fine - there are plenty of people around to help!'

Mike frowned and then it dawned on him that the accident had happened and Denford had been delayed.

'Ah, got you! Is she out of the picture for now?' Mike enquired.

'Yes, the car is pretty damaged but she is fine…'

'Simon, I know you can't talk but listen, I don't have much time…'

'Yes my love?'

'I have the contact number here now, I have the code and the locations… but we have got to get the ship to go to Porthlevan!'

'Yes my love, I understand, I will contact our insurance'.

'But, you are going to have to use *her* phone! It isn't here but it specifies that *she* has to make the call, from *her* phone! You are going to have to find it'.

Simon looked awkwardly at Miss Denford's car and then at Denford herself, sitting with a blanket around her as people began gathering bits of debris from the road side.

'Okay, can you just hang on a moment for that?'

Simon walked towards the shaking girl.

'Are you okay?'

She looked up at him and nodded.

'I am terribly sorry, I just didn't see you, I wasn't paying attention, but don't worry I will sort it all out, don't you worry – it was entirely my fault'.

He looked at her car.

'I will just get your keys from the ignition and check if it can be moved…'

Simon walked towards the car and climbed into driver's seat.

He looked around the passenger seat and then saw a phone in the passenger side foot well.

'Got it!' he spoke into his phone quietly.

'Good, what is the number?'

'How should I know?'

'All issued phones have the phone number printed on the back cover'

Simon looked at the back cover - there was no sign of a number.

'Not on this one', he said.

'Is it a Blackberry?'

'No, it's a Nokia!'

'You are looking for a Blackberry, standard issue is a Blackberry! Check her handbag'.

Simon rolled his eyes and returned her phone to the floor well.

Her bag was upside down in the floor well along with a mixture of crisps and sandwich filling.

He bent down and picked it up; lying next to it was a Blackberry.

'Got it, the number is… 07978 867 453', he read from the label.

'Good, got it. I am going to text you a message in compliance with this protocol detailed here and you must forward it to this number, do you have a pen?'

Simon searched her handbag.

'Got one'.

'81122'.

'Is that it?' Simon asked after writing it on the back of his wrist.

'Yes, it is a PO BOX equivalent for a phone…'

Right… when do I send it?'

'As soon as you get the text from me!'

Simon left the car, sliding the Blackberry into his pocket and pulling the keys from the ignition.

'Right, thanks for your help, I will sort it out with her insurance now, thank you'.

He shut the phone and bent down to Miss Denford who had significantly calmed down.

'How are you feeling now?'

'You idiot! How fast were you going? Look at my car! You stupid idiot! How dare you….'

He began to back away, gesturing his apologies towards the hysterical young girl. Evidently she was fine and he had to leave her to send the message; it was critical that they completed this stage of the plan on time.

'I can't believe you are just like, walking away from me! You arrogant…'

The Blackberry had received the message and he pressed the "Forward" button, entering the number he scrawled onto the back of his hand.

Mike replaced the papers back into their positions on the desk and began to leave the office just as the firemen walked into the corridor. He stepped back inside the office and looked around for another exit. He ran towards the window and looked down - there was a terraced roof below. It was possible he could make it, then a simple jump down onto the pavement. The fire crew entered the office. Mike stooped below the shelves near the window and shuffled backwards on the damp carpet into the corner as the firemen looked around.

'Nah, nothing in here, I think it's a false alarm again, sir', the lead fireman spoke through his respirator.

Mike exhaled in relief as the last of the firemen left the room. Returning to the window he pulled it open and climbed out onto the sandstone ledge. He jumped towards the terraced roof and then prized himself down onto the pavement. As his feet hit the ground he closed his eyes; how he had managed to achieve what he had in the past twenty minutes was completely beyond him. All he could think about as he took a welcomed few seconds break, before his run to the Land Rover, was sleeping and eating - it had been a relentless journey over the past few months and he was aching for a rest.

Simon slowly reversed the Land Rover from the back of the Mitsubishi. Miss Denford cringed as the rear bumper snapped from the bent chassis of her car and rocked on the road amongst the glittering fragments of plastic from the rear lights. He smiled and waved at her as he pulled away. She looked at him with contempt and returned with a hand signal. As he drove away from the scene, he felt saddened by what he had done; if he had injured her he wouldn't have known what to do. He would have certainly had to stay with her and take her to the hospital attracting unwanted attention from the police who they suspected the senior officers to be on Wilkinson's payroll.

The blackberry sounded an alert. He pulled it from his pocket.

"MESSAGE RECEIVED"

"View"

"NEW LOCATION.ADVISE WILKINSON WILL B THERE 4 0100"

Simon's arms flooded with goose pimples.

As Mike pulled into a cordoned area next to the church, he spotted the truck parked on a hill on the opposite side of the harbour and smiled.

As he left the Land Rover he looked at the swarms of agents around the harbour, setting up strategic positions on the harbour walls, on the elevated front gardens of the harbour front hotels and making their way to the endless rows of houses.

Matthews ran over to him.

'Mike, good to see you'.

'You too, are the troops in place?'

'Not just yet sir, they are positioned up here, sprinkled around the harbour down there and across a few of the rocks. They'll be well out of sight sir'.

Simon's Land Rover pulled up next to them.

'Sorry I am late; I had to talk to the insurance company…'

Mike looked at the front of the Land Rover and the remains of blue Mitsubishi still evident in the grill and bumper.

'What time is it?' Mike asked.

Simon looked at his watch, 'three thirty'.

'Right, that leaves us… nine hours to get the town evacuated and our men set up. I also want that EMP tested - we can't leave anything to chance'.

A dark gloved hand knocked on the old wooden door of the public house overlooking the harbour mouth. A middle aged lady opened the door.

'Excuse me madam, sorry for the intrusion', the female agent produced her identity card, 'we are with Her Majesties Preventive Service and we carrying out an operation in this area tonight…'

The agents gradually made their way along the extensive rows of hotels and houses along each side of the harbour, informing the residents.

'What do we do?' an elderly man asked.

'We have booked you into a hotel and a fleet of taxis will be here at about six o' clock to pick you up'.

The gentleman looked puzzled.

'But I don't want to go to a hotel… why can't I stay here? What is going on?'

The agent smiled, 'Sir, the people we are trying to apprehend are potentially dangerous'.

'Can't I just stay inside, lock the doors and shut the curtains?'

'I'm afraid not sir, it is possible they will be armed'.

'I know how to defend myself you know I was…'

'Sir! They are, in many ways classable as terrorists. There is a possibility that gunfire could be exchanged and we cannot guarantee the safety of the inhabitants in this locality'.

The mention of terrorism was something that Mike suggested as a last cause for the stubborn individuals.

The old man's eyes widened.

'I see, what time was that taxi?'

De LaCruz stared at a metal instrument panel as he leaned against the periscope housing as the helmsman began to run through his procedure in the dimly lit red ambience.

'You'd think after all these years we would have translated some of these into English…' he whispered as he scratched his head, searching for a translation to a labelled circuit diagram.

De LaCruz wiped the sweat that was forming on his brow with the back of his sleeve.

One of the crewmen appeared from a narrow doorway and stood next to him.

'Sir, we are running on full power, we will be at Porthlevan in about three hours'.

De LaCruz continued to stare at the instrument panel.

'Sir?'

'Leon!' he shouted.

De LaCruz turned to face him.

'What is it?'

'What is wrong with you?'

De LaCruz frowned.

'Something doesn't feel right about this Charlie… the location is new, the text message was in a different manner… I don't like it'.

Charlie looked around at the other men, looking for any sign of agreement. There was none.

'Sir, we have been down here for a very long time; four days now, there is no problem. You said yourself that Jennings had been dismissed and Wilkinson had brought in some new trainee… that explains the difference in format, I guess…'

The explanation soothed De LaCruz's apprehension and he released his gaze from the instruments.

'Continue on full speed and let me know when we get within shallow waters'.

He left the bridge and moved into a separate cabin, shutting the small wooden door behind him. He sat down on a metal swivel chair, pulled out his mobile phone and dialled a number.

Wilkinson stood above his trainee as she typed up legitimate strategies for the navy, as part of her training.

His phone rang.

'Wilkinson', he answered, as he moved to the back of the office.

'It's Leon, are we still on for tonight? For one o'clock?'

Wilkinson tilted his head upwards. It was unusual for De LaCruz to be calling him on the night of a drop. He loosened his collar. It was no secret that there was distaste between them and that their relationship had dwindled over the years but this seemed like the development of distrust. He had been careful to cover his tracks; there shouldn't be any reason for this sudden requirement of confirmation.

'Of course, Leon'.

'You'd better not be setting me up James!'

Wilkinson unfastened the top button of his shirt.

'Relax Leon; the drop zone is on Williams' map! I want this thing done as smoothly as you do'.

De LaCruz relaxed his stiffened posture and took a few breaths.

'We will be there for half past one! Just make sure your man is there to meet us!'

'He will be there, just don't lose your cool and detonate the loot this time'.

'Don't push me James'.

Wilkinson swallowed as the phone went dead. He put it back inside his pocket and returned to his trainee.

'You should go home, Miss Denford, it is getting late'.

'I don't mind sir, honestly I don't.'

'No, you have been through a lot today, with the accident and everything, just go home, I will see you tomorrow'.

The young trainee reluctantly began to gather her things together as Wilkinson stared out of the window.

'Okay, sir, the town and the harbour have been evacuated and cordoned off. The men are now in their positions and the EMP is working', Matthews proudly informed.

Mike looked up from the harbour wall where both he and Simon were sitting.

'Thanks… We'll keep in contact via phone. See you later'.

As Matthews walked away with a small group of agents, Simon turned to Mike, offering him a chewing gum.

'Do you think, seriously think, this is going to work?' he asked.

Mike watched the sunset dancing in the ripples of the water around the harbour wall below them.

'What do you want out of this Si?' he asked, selecting a stick of gum from the packet.

'What do you mean?'

'I mean, we aren't going to be famous, we aren't going to be paid extra for this and we are going to suffer a barrage of hatred for months to come, having severed the secondary income for most of Cornwall. What do we have to look forward to? Going back to work?'

Simon frowned at him.

'What's on your mind Mike?'

'I haven't been able to think about anything else other than this moment for four years. I have taken the mystery and romanticism away from the dark ship I wrote about and took pictures of all those years ago and I feel like it is all coming to an end'.

The sudden negativity began to unnerve him.

'Mike, we are going to break the biggest act of piracy, possibly in maritime history. I think we will be recognised for that!'

'It's not about the recognition, it's about how we will feel; how I will feel. We are about to destroy the lives of countless people. Can't you see that?'

'Destroy the lives?' Simon shouted, 'destroy the lives of countless murderers! It doesn't matter, Mike, they are all part of the same game! You can't disassociate De LaCruz from Coates can you? Coates was simply storing the loot in his locker but he knew where it came from! The people who buy the loot for cash, they all know where it comes from Mike… have you ever bought a stolen television?'

Mike looked at him with confusion.

'No?'

'Why not?'

'What do you mean?'

'Why wouldn't you buy a stolen television?'

'Because it is stolen… ah… I see what you are getting at'. A smile began to cross his face.

'We are stopping the trading of stolen goods, by preventing the smuggling which ultimately and above all comes from the stopping of a mass murderer! If that doesn't make you feel better – nothing will!'

Mike nodded in agreement and blew a bubble of gum.

'So, do you seriously think this is going to work?' Simon tried again.

'Of course it is!' he laughed, 'if this doesn't, nothing will and you know what they say… if you can't beat 'em, join 'em!'

'I've heard there's a lot of money in it', Simon laughed.

'We are approaching the West coast now sir', the helmsman informed.

De LaCruz sucked his teeth, 'If I can't count on that fat bastard's loyalty, at least I can count on yours. Slow to half speed'.

'Slow to half speed sir', the helmsman confirmed.

The prop shaft slowed and the propellers began to drone down until the submarine glided through the dark, murky water.

Wilkinson paced the Communications office, lit solely by the blue haze from the moon in the deep petrol sky. Perhaps he had been greedy. Perhaps he should have severed the connection after the last drop. After all, the last drop was seized by Mike and the drop after that was destroyed by De LaCruz himself. It signified the end was drawing near, which was a calculated risk when the project was conceptualised. In order for him to sever his connections and close the project, it was inevitable he would have to suffer a loss.

As he gazed out of the large window onto the town below he caught sight of a young couple standing under a streetlight. For one rare moment his heart sank; he had become so entangled with the lust for wealth that he had forgotten how to live. His wife had left him years prior to the project, and he had been alone ever since with only his thoughts for company.

But, this was the last of it. He was getting out. He had booked an open air-ticket months ago in anticipation. He quietly thought about the millions of pounds worth of loot sitting below him in the base of the building; a potential goldmine to buyers all over the world, but it was too risky trying to disperse it now. It would be too easy for him to arrange a robbery or a fire in the building; it was empty all but for the janitor and the night shift reception. The loot could be out of there in a matter of minutes, but it was one more thing to go wrong. At that moment, as far as he was concerned, he was safe. He could disappear as soon as he wanted to. But, as he stood, considering his future, the pull was too much. The loot downstairs in the warehouse he *could* forget about, but the remains on-board the submarine; that was something else. There was the remains of a heist over two years ago; a diamond necklace, easily worth a million pounds, or so the Sotheby's valuation stated. He couldn't let that go. As soon as the drop was received; he would disappear. By the time he was identified as a major suspect, if that time arose, he would be in South America, living out a new identity.

'What time is it?' Mike asked

Simon looked at him with disbelief.

'Where is your watch Mike? You have been asking me the time for months now… Is it broken?'

Mike looked back towards the harbour mouth.

'It doesn't matter'.

'What doesn't?'

'Don't push it'.

'Push what? You always ask the time. Why don't you wear a watch?'

'It isn't important'.

'But you always ask'.

Mike engaged with Simon's inquisitive eyes and sighed.

'I'm…' he paused, shaking his head.

'You're what?'

'I'm… Chronophobic!'

Simon looked blank.

'It's a… fear of clocks… I can't look at a clock…'

Simon bellowed a laugh that echoed across the harbour.

'Thank you for your sensitivity', Mike said with a sarcastic tone.

Simon's face straightened.

'You are serious!'

Mike nodded.

'Oh my God! You have a fear of time? Of clocks?'

'Mine is a fear of looking at the time. I kind of work around time, it is a… anyway, what's wrong with having a phobia?'

'Nothing', Simon said looking at his watch, 'it is twelve forty two, by the way'.

'Quarter of an hour then…' Mike said as his mind began to simulate all possible outcomes of the operation.

Wilkinson's peace was disturbed by his phone ringing on the desk. He walked over to it and picked it up: "Withheld" caller.

'James Wilkinson', he answered apprehensively.

'It's DCI Raymond'.

Wilkinson gritted his teeth.

'Do you know what time it is? What do you want?'

'I thought you should know, Preventive Service Agents have cordoned off and evacuated most of Porthlevan, without our knowledge. What's going on James?'

Wilkinson's eyes widened and his jaw dropped.

'Porthlevan? Evacuated? How do you know?'

'One of the residents rang his brother-in-law, a copper on my force, to find out what was going on with the harbour and he didn't know. One call led to another and then it came to me. I want to know what they are doing'.

'I have no idea!'

'Is it a drop point? Are you expecting another drop tonight James? Because two things occur to me; firstly, why didn't I know about it? Or were you cutting me out of this one? Secondly; if it is a drop then I think the HMPS know about it…'

Wilkinson swallowed. Surely it was a mistake. Maybe the Preventive Service had made a mistake? But, in the back of his mind he knew it was a possibility. With episodes such as the false fire alarm and Miss Denford's crash, things were beginning to add up.

'Are you there James?'

Wilkinson shut the phone and looked at his watch, five to one.

'God help me'.

The U-Boat slowly and silently manoeuvred through the array of jagged rock formations and ledges in the dark murky channel at the foot of Porthlevan; an area that had claimed so many vessels in the past.

'We are here sir, just entering the harbour mouth now'.

De LaCruz licked his dry lips as he looked at the antiquated radar.

'Watch the rocks. Lord only knows why he wanted a drop here!'

De LaCruz looked at his watch, two minutes to one.

'Full stop', he shouted.

'Full stop sir'.

As he stood poised next to the periscope, his phone rang in his pocket. Looking back at the time he ignored it in favour of devoting his concentration on the drop. It was the first time they had put the vessel into port in over five years and so it was important that this went according to the plan that he and Wilkinson had hatched.

Simon counted down on his watch.

'Thirty seconds Mike!'

Mike's heart began to beat hard inside his chest, reverberating through his hands and fingers.

'Thirty seconds until she arrives', he whispered to himself in anticipation.

'She?' Simon whispered back.

'The Dark Ship', Mike responded, 'I can't believe I am going to meet her after all these years'.

Simon acknowledged his remark with a faint smile.

'Here goes', Mike whispered as he flashed his flashlight towards the agents positioned on the opposite side of the harbour.

Matthews, seeing the tiny flash, looked at his watch and hand signalled to the flanking teams.

A crackling sound echoed the harbour walls; they armed their weapons as he reached for the remote control for the EMP generator, a few yards down the street and pointing out towards the harbour mouth.

'Three, two, one', Matthews counted and plunged the red button on the remote.

The EMP generator began to drone and after a few seconds emitted a quiet electrical buzz, before spinning down.

The U-Boat's internal lights faded plunging the crew into darkness. The engines grinded to a halt and the propeller shafts droned to a stop.

'We've lost all power sir!' the helmsman shouted as the crew shuffled around in the darkness for something to hold on to.

'What? What's going on? Has the EMP misfired? Has anyone touched it?'

'No sir, it hasn't been powered up'.

There was a terrifying silence as the submarine began to drift off course.

'Do something!' De LaCruz ordered.

Mike and Simon peered into the dark water. Had it worked? Was the U-Boat actually there in front of them? An unsettling silence ensued.

The vessel began to drift inwards with the tide, the large grey bulk of the hull washing around in the swell. Suddenly and inevitably they collided with one of the many ridges, breaking a large section of rock from its housing and creating a horizontal tear in the port side of the hull.

'Look!' one of the agents pointed to a flurry of bubbles rising to the service.

The dull, distant rumbles of the vessel impacting upon the rocky ridges came to the surface with the bubbles.

'It's working!' Mike exclaimed excitedly, 'it's actually working!'

De LaCruz clung onto the periscope shaft as the vessel began to bounce from the rock faces beneath the surface. The panic stricken crew rushed around the dark confined space; the inertia throwing them to the floor and into the sharp corners of the instrument panels.

'We're taking on water sir!' one of the crew members shouted in panic as he emerged from a compartment.

De LaCruz stood fast, gripping the large metallic shaft.

'We've been sold out boys, ambushed', he shouted, to the horror of his crew.

Suddenly the vessel shunted again and began to list heavily to starboard.

'Surface!' De LaCruz shouted amongst the chaos, 'surface now!'

'We can't sir, the power's gone!'

'Surface! Do it manually!'

The men ran the lengths of the listing vessel's pitch black corridors, ducking under the trailing pipe work. Two of the men felt in the dark for the manual override controls and heaved on the huge wheels, causing a deafening noise as the tanks blew outwards.

The bubbles began to rise more rapidly and soon developed into a large swell in the mouth of the harbour.

'This is it everyone, get ready!' Mike shouted as he drew his automatic.

The agents behind him, standing at the foot of the church loaded their weapons and took aim.

The U-boat began to rise as the tanks filled with air and then at speed; the swell becoming more aggressive until Mike could just make out the metallic bow rising towards them.

'This is it!' he shouted.

Within a few seconds the U-Boat surfaced at tremendous velocity; propelling the bow out of the water and into the air like a missile, then down onto the surface on top of a moored fishing boat nearby -causing an explosion of wooden shards and metal debris from the winch. A huge wave reared up towards the agents and washed over them, covering the harbour wall and the base of the church. Wooden debris from the wrecked fishing boat rained down with the sea spray as the scuppered U-Boat finally settled on the surface.

Mike looked with awe at the vessel that had caused him so many obsessions over the years. It was a mighty boat, impressive in structure and prominently painted with tiger shark charcoal and grey striping. He smiled as he looked at the large stylised skull and crossbones, daubed with white paint on the side of the bridge.

'Hello my beauty', he whispered.

De LaCruz stood in the dim light, loading his hand guns and pushing them into his belt.

He looked on at his demoralised crew.

'Men, we have been led into an ambush that we will not escape'.

The men looked nervously at their captain. Even though he had worked with them for over twenty years, even before they had used the anonymity of the U-Boat, he hadn't once had to march them into battle.

'We are wanted for nearly every maritime crime there is… there is no way out! But, we can still be what we are and have been for twenty odd years! Pirates! I am descended from a pirate, I have lived as a pirate and I will die as a pirate!'

The men began to cheer; there was no disputing their loyalty.

'So, we must now take our weapons and fight as pirates!'

De LaCruz roared, a long drawn out battle cry, enticing his men follow. Within seconds the crippled U-boat was filled with a terrifying roar from the crew.

Mike chewed his lip. The dark ship rested in the harbour mouth in front of them, mocking him with silence.

'Do you think they are on board?' Simon asked.

'They are there… call Matthews and get him to keep an eye out. These things are full of hatches. My guess is they will use them as turrets'.

Simon pulled out his phone.

'It's dead Mike, the EMP must have wiped it out'.

'Shit! I never thought of that'.

As they looked at Simon's phone, a corroded metallic creak came from one of the stern hatches as it began to twist open.

'Get down, get ready!' Mike whispered.

The aft main hatch began to slowly open and a thick tattooed arm pushed it vertically clear. A head slowly followed. As the man began to emerge, he pulled out a Kalashnikov assault rifle from beneath him.

'They're armed, stay put', Mike whispered at the agents behind him.

The figure walked out onto the aft decking, holding his weapon out stretched, squinting to see into the dark harbour.

'The lights, Simmons, the lights!' Mike whispered through gritted teeth.

Upon the cliff top, the agents looked down on the surreal sight of the impressive wartime exhibit.

'Can you see anything yet?' Simmons asked an agent, looking through a digiscope at the vessel.

'Nothing yet sir'.

As the figure walked from behind the bridge section, the agent spotted him.

'Got him, there's a man on the aft deck sir, he's armed!'

Simmons plunged the large lever on the remote unit, switching on a series of floodlights, simultaneously illuminating the cove with blinding white light.

The figure staggered back in shock, shielding his eyes.

Mike held a loudspeaker to his mouth and switched it on.

'This is Her Majesties Prev…'

The megaphone had been destroyed by the EMP.

Hearing Mike's voice in the darkness, the figure turned and fired indiscriminately. Bullets peppered around the church walls as the agents ducked for cover. The agents on the opposite side took aim and one by one began to fire toward the figure.

The figure fell from the deck, over the metal railings and into the sea.

Mike stood up again and signalled the men behind him to move in on the vessel.

Suddenly, several of the hatches around the boat opened simultaneously and weapons of all descriptions came into view, firing from all directions of the vessel.

Simmons watched as two agents fell to the ground nearby as the bullets hailed towards them. Two of the floodlights exploded into a shower of sparks and glass, as the pirates began to target them in an effort to put them back into darkness.

Mike and Simon moved closer, stooping for cover behind seafront benches and railings as they made their way forward.

Wilkinson looked out of the window once again, his face a mixture of anger and panic. He was relieved at the thought of Mike potentially catching up with De LaCruz and that part of the project was working according to his plan but he felt uncontrollably saddened by the fact that it was almost at the end. He shook his head, clear of the negativity and concentrated on getting all of the evidence removed; anything that could link him to this. He had to completely remove himself from any records, to delete his having anything to do with De LaCruz, Raymond, Jennings… the list was long. He logged on to Miss Denford's computer and began to delete any relevant files.

The sound of gun fire filled the once peaceful and idyllic tourist haven and shots rang out from the makeshift battlements of the hatches on board the U-boat. As the pirates gained the advantage of the partial retreat of the Preventive Service agents they began to make their way out onto the decking with another colossal roar.

The agents on the harbour wall near to one of the two ornate cannons were alerted by the cry and stood up, picking the approaching pirates off one by one, their bodies falling onto the concrete harbour side and into the sea.

One of the crewmen charged towards an agent near to the long stone jetty, desperately trying to reload his automatic and sliced him across his chest. Mike fired two shots into his back and he dropped to the ground like a bag of potatoes.

The crewmen from the U-Boat began to hurl themselves selflessly towards the waiting agents and fell in succession in a hail of sporadic fire. After a few bloody minutes of exchange, the agents ceased fire and began to move quickly toward the wounded.

Mike reloaded his automatic and moved closer to the U-boat.

Seeing the numbers of pirates bodies, Matthews signalled the remaining agents to move across the harbour gates towards the vessel.

Mike stepped onboard the U-boat with Matthews and another agent backing them up from behind. Matthews pulled the pin from a smoke grenade and began to climb the rusty ladder on the side of the bridge. He dropped the grenade into the hatch and ducked down. There was a dull thud as it detonated- followed by thick, grey smoke that poured from the hatch and vents.

Mike lowered his weapon.

The agent returned to the aft deck.

'No one on board there sir, they'd be choking if they were stupid enough to stay down there'.

The agents regrouped on the harbour wall as the last of the ambulances had taken the wounded away. Matthews ran over to where Mike and Simon were standing, talking to the local coast guard.

'Mike', Matthews shouted.

'Matthews, well done'.

'Thanks. There is no sign of De LaCruz; we have matched his photo up to the bodies we dragged in from the sea and we have searched the harbour walls and I have had a team scour the U-boat; nothing!'

Mike scratched his head and then wiped his brow with the back of his sleeve.

'Where the hell is he?'

He paused and inhaled a deep breath.

'What is it Mike?' Simon asked.

'Shit!' he shouted as he started to run along the harbour wall and back towards the carpark.

'I know where he is!'

'Mike, wait!' Simon shouted after him.

Wilkinson closed his brief case and watched the progress bar of the deletion window reach "100%". It had taken an hour for all of the files and folders to be erased. He took one last look around the office for anything he may have missed; fifteen years was a long time and a large accumulation of paperwork.

As he walked towards the door, he noticed his diary on the desk. Cursing, he walked back to retrieve it.

'Are you leaving the sinking ship, James?'

Wilkinson jumped and spun around to see De LaCruz standing at the doorway with a sawn off shotgun outstretched. He was bleeding from a wound to his shoulder and was soaking wet.

Paralysed by fear Wilkinson remained in the same posture, like a Michelangelo sculpture, as the figure stood in his path.

'I think the words you are looking for, are… Shit, Leon, what are you doing here?'

'Leon…' Wilkinson uttered.

De LaCruz stepped forwards, causing Wilkinson to step backwards.

'I have seen and done things in my time that made me believe I was insusceptible to surprise, James, but what you have done tonight has really, really knocked me back. I must congratulate you; you certainly took me for a ride'.

Wilkinson stepped further backwards until he hit the desk, preventing his escape.

'Leon, I genuinely had nothing to do with it…'

'To do with what? How would you know what I am talking about if you had nothing to do with it?'

'Leon, stop, I…'

'Stop your blagging James, it doesn't suit you. You know you have sold me out, I had inkling, but I didn't think you had it in you!'

'Leon, I swear…'

De LaCruz raised the shot gun, level to his head.

'Enough!' he shouted, 'it's over James. I think I owe you this and you most definitely deserve it'.

Wilkinson's hand searched his open briefcase on the desk behind him.

Mike ran along the corridor and slowed as he saw the droplets of blood and footprints on the floor leading to the office. He crept toward the door; his weapon drawn.

'You know James, how long has it been since we first met?'

Wilkinson's hand located a small pistol under a stack of folders inside the case and carefully removed it.

'About twenty five years?' he answered.

'Twenty five years! And in all that time, we have had a relationship based on trust. More than that, one of confinement'.

Mike desperately needed Wilkinson alive and at this rate De LaCruz will have finished him.

'You sold me out! I was the one who did all the dirty work! I have committed over two hundred murders for you, robbed ships of millions of pounds… for relatively nothing! Did I ever complain? No!'

Wilkinson's face dropped.

'How dare you! Who the hell do you think you are? Barging into my office like this, holding me to gun point! Yes, I was going to sell you out, why wouldn't I? You became sloppy; you were leaving too many traces. You are an amateur Leon. This was going to be my last drop! After this one, I was out of here. I planned this months ago. I even created the HMPS in order to keep the press quiet, to stop people asking questions…'

Mike frowned. Was he serious?

'…and I employed someone like Williams to catch you! But, the beauty is - I knew you wouldn't be caught and would go down in a fight so wouldn't have the chance to rat me out! Mike, on the other hand, well, he was getting too close to the truth; I knew that would be a risk, so I blocked most of his avenues, steering him in one direction – towards you! I was in a win-win situation, don't you see? I either ridded the world of you, kept the loot and disappeared or… you would have gotten to his team first, the HMPS dissolves and I buy more time…'

De LaCruz began to clap the back of his hand, the shotgun still outstretched.

'Bravo, James, bravo. You are quite the hero. Well, old friend, it's time to put an end to this! Give my regards to Fredrico you son of a bitch'.

As De LaCruz raised his gun, Mike took a deep breath and stepped around the door frame.

'Put the gun down Leon!' he shouted.

Shocked, De LaCruz spun around and fired both barrels towards Mike; the shots peppered the door frame and Mike's chest, throwing him backwards into the hallway. Wilkinson simultaneously drew the small hand gun from his desk and fired it at De LaCruz, catching him in his back, pushing him forwards into a glass display cabinet. His body smashed through the doors and landed awkwardly crumpled on the floor.

Wilkinson stepped over towards the gurgling De LaCruz as he tried to push himself from the mass of glass and wood. He fired a second shot through his back.

He walked over to the desk, shut his case and then made his way towards Mike, who was lying on his back amongst the splinters from the door frame.

'Michael… I didn't foresee you saving my life and for that I thank you'.

Mike blinked; he was losing blood and had gone into shock. He felt his breath shorten as Wilkinson towered over him.

'I am sorry it had to end like this Michael, you did an excellent job. You played brilliantly. But, now, the bad guy has to run away, coward like… but a hell of a lot richer. It is surprising how money can sooth a painful conscience, you of all people must know about a painful conscience…'

He aimed the gun at Mike's head. Mike closed his eyes.

'Goodbye Michael… I won't forget you…'

As his finger moved towards the trigger, a shot hit his shoulder pushing him backwards into the office. Simon ran over to the doorway where his colleague's pale body lay in a pool of blood amongst the debris.

'Mike, are you alright?' Simon shouted.

'Wilkinson', Mike gasped as he attempted to move his arm from underneath him.

'Stay still Mike', Simon demanded as he stood up to enter the office.

He stretched out his weapon and aimed it inside. A blood stain illustrated where Wilkinson had been but there was no sign of him. He reached for the phone and dialled.

'Ambulance!' he shouted into the mouthpiece.

He turned to look at his colleague in the corridor and caught sight of De LaCruz's body slumped inside the remains of a display cabinet.

Chapter 15
<u>The End</u>

The sun shone brightly, illuminating the white stone buildings around the harbour and providing the tourists with a light show on the sea - a few of them braving to swim.

DCI Raymond exited the police station and looked into the air. He took a large breath and sighed as he walked down the stone steps flanked by two officers-each with a hand on his shoulders. They lead him to a waiting car and pushed the cuffed DCI's head into the back.

Simon stood above his bandaged colleague, behind the one-way glass of the Interview room at Nelson, watching Jennings relay his knowledge to a group of investigating officers. The death of De LaCruz coupled with Wilkinson's disappearance had terrified Jennings to a point that Mike had begun to feel a sense of remorse. It was difficult to imagine that the terrified man, sitting not a few feet away from them, was the co-mastermind behind what reporters were claiming was the largest act of piracy and mass murder this side of the Second World War.

Simon squeezed Mike's shoulder as he fought against his emotions. They had been through a lot, seen their colleagues killed, been double crossed, lost faith and been victimised by the public. The latter of which had begun to subside as the press had hailed them as an "Heroic Force protecting the countries coastlines from the disdain of terrorists", a headline which had been cut out and pinned to the inside of the booth.

The two agents watched from a distant car as a wave of officers raided the police headquarters and escorted dozens of men and women into awaiting vehicles for questioning. The scale of the project incalculable, so was the amount of lives ruined, which, as Simon well knew, was where Mike's empathy really lay. So many of the village folk of both Cornwall and the Isles of Scilly had depended on a slice of the smuggling as an alternative income. It took Mike days to persuade the courts to leave them out of the picture; the Income Tax department had been ready to pounce.

Jennings had broken down in court as he saw his wife weeping in the stalls. He confessed to everything and to everyone he knew of. He even confessed to what happened to the bodies that were taken to Gibraltar. To Mike's astonishment, they were disposed of in the military incinerator; leading to ten or so more arrests there alongside a full military investigation.

Mike approached his cottage, weary and battered. Since the shooting, he had not slept well, nor had he been back home. He pushed his front door open to a mountain of letters. He stepped over them and slammed the door with his foot, pushing part of the pile outside.

As he walked into his living room, the stench of stale food engulfed him. He walked over to his computer and stared at the wall above and the cut outs he had collected of the ship sightings, intermixed with his own photography. A sense of nostalgia washed over him. There was no disputing that it had been an adventure but at what cost. The personal cost was that he had no interest in going back to the Coastguard department whatsoever. It had occurred to him that the only thing fuelling his love for the ocean, over all of his years at sea was the thrill of being an apprentice smuggler under the notorious Captain Black, then as he matured – a coast guard desperate to catch the offenders of the oceans.

He walked to his window and threw the curtains open with his left hand, his right being bandaged in a sling. The sunlight streamed into his living room, illuminating the dust particles in the atmosphere. As he looked at the glistening ocean over the cliff top in front of him, his thoughts turned to those whom he had lost within the last few months and whose lives had been disrupted and changed through the discoveries the project had led to.

It was time for a change.

The Land Rover pulled up towards Mike's cottage and stopped at the gate. A galvanised chain strapped the gate firmly to the post, secured by a large steel padlock.

In the wind, a large wooden "For Sale" sign swung to and fro, creating a rhythmical high pitched creak. The cottage that once had lustre and life, now remained depressed and overrun with ivy and other climbing weeds. The wind swept through the empty courtyard sweeping the leaves and branches from the gravel.

The Land Rover window wound up and it slowly moved away.

Epilogue

Mike sat behind his desk, staring out of the seventeenth floor window at the forest of glass and steel, shimmering in the sunlight in front of him. His eyes flicked back to his monitor and then to a sheet of paper daubed in red ink. Around him, people went about their business inside their segregated cubicles, answering phones, furiously tapping on keyboards and continuously clicking mice. He felt at his ribs and inadvertently winced as his fingers found the fracture. The fight at the Benbow seemed like years ago. A bulky man of about fifty years, wearing a retrospective brown suit and a short tie, appeared at Mike's cubicle clutching stack of papers bound with string.

'Williams', he shouted in a stern East London accent. His voice tarnished, as were his teeth, by years of cigar intake.

Mike blinked out of his computer trance and sat back in his chair to face his visitor.

'Yes, sir'.

He could have been Black, give him a few more years of alcohol abuse coupled with a tangled mass of black hair on his face. Of course, he would have to lose the accent. He inadvertently smiled.

'This is your story, your report', he threw the paper stack onto Mike's keyboard, causing an eternal line of commas to fill the screen, 'it is alright, but not great, I want something great, something outstanding, not mediocre. Don't get me wrong, I admire your style but this… this is not what we run here…'

There was a standoff between their gazes as Mike expected an elaboration and his boss expected an apology.

Mike broke first.

'I will go through it sir, refine it'.

'We hired Mike Williams, the heroic author of his biography "Dark Ship" six weeks ago, not Mike Williams who sits before me, tired, dishevelled and altogether not what I had been led to believe'.

'I will make the alterations', Mike offered while trying to fight back a yawn.

'It will take more than that Mike… I want you to start again, from scratch, from a different perspective'.

Mike's jaw dropped.

'It is a newspaper we run here- not a tabloid. We write columns- not gossip. Why can't you relight that passion in your autobiography? I want the real Mike Williams back today, not Mike Williams who sits staring out of the window'.

Mike grimaced and straightened himself up at his desk. He hadn't intended this to happen. After the news story broke, nearly six months ago he was offered an incentive to write a lengthy report for a small publishing company who were third party to a national newspaper. Before he knew it the editor had called and offered him a job. He suspected at the time that it was a marketing ploy "Buy our newspaper, we have Mike Williams with us now" as they usually do with of-the-moment celebrities.

'I'm a prostitute', he inadvertently mumbled.

'What did you say?' the editor asked irately.

'Yes, okay, sir… give me a week to finish this…'

'Ha! You have three days! This goes to print in three days!'

The editor stormed off back towards his office, leaving Mike in mid-sentence.

He turned to his computer and deleted the row of commas that the printed document had created.

Mouthing a curse under his breath, he began to look at his amendments and shook his head.

'Three days? Maybe seventy two hours straight', he mumbled to himself as his fingers traced over red circles. Suddenly, images of the location map flashed in his mind diverting his attention. Had he really given it all up? It was easy for him to be desperate for a normal nine to five job when he was in the thick of the project but now the momentum had gone, he found himself aching to be back.

An office junior, complete with earphones and tinny beat, arrived at his desk with the daily post. He double checked the labels and dropped a jiffy bag and two letters onto Mike's keyboard.

Mike rolled his eyes and shook his head, 'Why the bloody keyboard?' he mumbled as the teenager moved on. As he took a sip from his coffee he looked at the letters, disregarding them in favour of the exciting jiffy bag. He placed his mug on top of the two letters and tore the strip from the end of the manila pouch. Emptying the contents onto his desk he was surprised to find two black and white photographs. He looked in the pouch for any supporting documents but it was empty. He held up the first photograph and sighed. It was a dark and grainy blurred picture of the sea and horizon. After a few moments studying he moved on to the second. It was an enlargement of the first and, although blurred and pixelated, it was the unmistakeable shape of a tall mast ship. He frowned and shook his head slowly. Was this some sort of joke? Or a report he had to write? He turned the photograph over to reveal some handwriting. His mouth dropped open as a flurry of goose bumps ran the length of his spine.

"It is not over

This is not a joke

We need you back now!

SJ"

With special thanks to

Mum, Dad and Grandma for their constant encouragement; Jeef for designing the cover; Phil Heeks for the music; my editor Rachael Hewison; Butts for the good luck; Chris Hewison for the website; Stuart Reeves for his superior photoshop knowledge; Andy Otter for helping with the video; my friends for their support; and Jen… for believing in me!

www.darkship.co.uk

www.facebook.com/darkship.book

Printed in Great Britain
by Amazon